They *turned away from the monsters* and sped through the trees. As she raced toward the sandy clearing where she had trained with the other apprentices, Squirrelpaw wondered grimly how the Clan could have survived with the Twolegs and monsters so close. The sun was high in the sky, and the training hollow was crisscrossed with shafts of cold sunlight. She dug her paws into the soft ground and pushed on ahead of Brambleclaw and Stormfur, her chest tightening with fear as she tore along the trail that led to the gorse tunnel. Without hesitating, she ducked her head and raced into the thorns.

"Firestar!" she yowled as she exploded into the clearing.

It was completely empty. The whole camp was silent. No cat stirred, and the scent of the Clan was stale.

WARRIORS

THE PROPHECIES BEGIN

THE NEW PROPHECY

POWER OF THREE

OMEN OF THE STARS

DAWN OF THE CLANS

EXPLORE THE
WARRIORS
WORLD

MANGA

NOVELLAS

Also by Erin Hunter

SEEKERS

THE NEW PROPHECY

WARRIORS

DAWN

ERIN
HUNTER

HARPER

An Imprint of HarperCollinsPublishers

Dawn

Copyright © 2006 by Working Partners Limited

Series created by Working Partners Limited

Map art © 2015 by Dave Stevenson

Interior art © 2015 by Owen Richardson

Library of Congress Cataloging-in-Publication Data

Hunter, Erin.

Dawn / Erin Hunter—1st ed.

p.   cm — (Warriors, the new prophecy ; #3)

Summary: The questing cats return to a forest devastated by the Twolegs, where they must find a way to convince their Clans to leave in search
of a new home, even though they have no idea where they are going.

ISBN 978-0-06-236704-4 (pbk.)

[1. Cats—Fiction. 2. Fantasy.] I. Title. II. Series.

PZ7.H916625Daw 2005   2005009175

[Fic]—dc22   CIP

                                                                AC

Typography by Ellice M. Lee

19   20   21   BR/CG   20   19   18

❖

Revised paperback edition, 2015

Special thanks to Kate Cary

ALLEGIANCES

THUNDERCLAN

LEADER

FIRESTAR—ginger tom with a flame-colored pelt

DEPUTY

GRAYSTRIPE—long-haired gray tom

MEDICINE CAT

CINDERPELT—dark gray she-cat
APPRENTICE, LEAFPAW

WARRIORS

(toms and she-cats without kits)

MOUSEFUR—small, dusky brown she-cat
APPRENTICE, SPIDERPAW

DUSTPELT—dark brown tabby tom
APPRENTICE, SQUIRRELPAW

SANDSTORM—pale ginger she-cat

CLOUDTAIL—long-haired white tom

BRACKENFUR—golden brown tabby tom
APPRENTICE, WHITEPAW

THORNCLAW—golden brown tabby tom
APPRENTICE, SHREWPAW

BRIGHTHEART—white she-cat with ginger patches

BRAMBLECLAW—dark brown tabby tom with amber eyes

ASHFUR—pale gray (with darker flecks) tom, dark blue eyes

RAINWHISKER—dark gray tom with blue eyes

SOOTFUR—lighter gray tom with amber eyes

SORRELTAIL—tortoiseshell and white she-cat with amber eyes

APPRENTICES (more than six moons old, in training to become warriors)

SQUIRRELPAW—dark ginger she-cat with green eyes

LEAFPAW—light brown tabby she-cat with amber eyes

SPIDERPAW—long-limbed black tom with brown underbelly and amber eyes

SHREWPAW—small, dark brown tom with amber eyes

WHITEPAW—white she-cat with green eyes

QUEENS (she-cats expecting or nursing kits)

GOLDENFLOWER—pale ginger coat, the oldest nursery queen

FERNCLOUD—pale gray (with darker flecks) she-cat, green eyes, mother of Dustpelt's kits

ELDERS (former warriors and queens, now retired)

FROSTFUR—beautiful white she-cat with blue eyes

SPECKLETAIL—pale tabby she-cat

LONGTAIL—pale tabby tom with dark black stripes, retired early due to failing sight

SHADOWCLAN

LEADER **BLACKSTAR**—large white tom with huge jet-black paws

DEPUTY **RUSSETFUR**—dark ginger she-cat

MEDICINE CAT **LITTLECLOUD**—very small tabby tom

WARRIORS　　OAKFUR—small brown tom
APPRENTICE, SMOKEPAW

CEDARHEART—dark gray tom

ROWANCLAW—ginger tom
APPRENTICE, TALONPAW

NIGHTWING—black she-cat

TAWNYPELT—tortoiseshell she-cat with green eyes

QUEENS　　TALLPOPPY—long-legged light brown tabby she-cat

ELDERS　　RUNNINGNOSE—small gray and white tom, formerly the medicine cat

BOULDER—skinny gray tom

WINDCLAN

LEADER　　TALLSTAR—elderly black and white tom with a very long tail

DEPUTY　　MUDCLAW—mottled dark brown tom
APPRENTICE, CROWPAW—dark smoky gray, almost black tom

MEDICINE CAT　　BARKFACE—short-tailed brown tom

WARRIORS　　TORNEAR—tabby tom

WEBFOOT—dark gray tabby tom
APPRENTICE, WEASELPAW

ONEWHISKER—brown tabby tom

ROBINWING—light brown she-cat with blue eyes
APPRENTICE, THISTLEPAW

QUEENS
ASHFOOT—gray queen

WHITETAIL—small white she-cat

ELDERS
MORNINGFLOWER—tortoiseshell she-cat

OATWHISKER—creamy brown tabby tom

RIVERCLAN

LEADER
LEOPARDSTAR—unusually spotted golden tabby she-cat

DEPUTY
MISTYFOOT—gray she-cat with blue eyes

MEDICINE CAT
MUDFUR—long-haired light brown tom
APPRENTICE, MOTHWING—dappled golden she-cat

WARRIORS
BLACKCLAW—smoky black tom
APPRENTICE, VOLEPAW

HEAVYSTEP—thickset tabby tom
APPRENTICE, STONEPAW

STORMFUR—dark gray tom with amber eyes

HAWKFROST—dark brown tom with a white underbelly and ice blue eyes

SWALLOWTAIL—dark brown tabby she-cat with green eyes
APPRENTICE, SPLASHPAW

QUEENS
MOSSPELT—tortoiseshell she-cat

DAWNFLOWER—pale gray she-cat

ELDERS
SHADEPELT—very dark gray she-cat

LOUDBELLY—dark brown tom

THE TRIBE OF RUSHING WATER

TRIBE HEALER   **TELLER OF THE POINTED STONES (STONETELLER)**—brown tabby tom with amber eyes

PREY-HUNTERS (toms and she-cats responsible for providing food)

GRAY SKY BEFORE DAWN (GRAY)—pale gray tabby tom

BROOK WHERE SMALL FISH SWIM (BROOK)—brown tabby she-cat

CAVE-GUARDS (toms and she-cats responsible for guarding the cave)

TALON OF SWOOPING EAGLE (TALON)—dark brown tabby tom (formerly leader of the outcasts)

JAGGED ROCK WHERE HERON SITS (JAG)—dark gray tom (former outcast)

ROCK BENEATH STILL WATER (ROCK)—brown tom (former outcast)

BIRD THAT SINGS AT DUSK (BIRD)—gray tabby she-cat (former outcast)

CRAG WHERE EAGLES NEST (CRAG)—dark gray tom

SHEER PATH BESIDE WATERFALL (SHEER)—dark brown tabby tom

NIGHT OF NO STARS (NIGHT)—black she-cat

KIT·MOTHERS (she-cats expecting or nursing kits)

WING SHADOW OVER WATER (WING)—gray and white she-cat

FLIGHT OF STARTLED HERON (FLIGHT)—brown tabby she-cat

CATS OUTSIDE CLANS

BARLEY—black and white tom who lives on a farm close to the forest

RAVENPAW—sleek black cat who lives on the farm with Barley

CODY—a tabby kittypet with blue eyes

SASHA—a tawny-colored rogue she-cat

OTHER ANIMALS

MIDNIGHT—a stargazing badger who lives by the sea

HIGHSTONES

BARLEY'S FARM

FOURTREES

WINDCLAN CAMP

FALLS

CAT VIEW

SUNNINGROCKS

RIVER

RIVERCLAN CAMP

TREECUTPLACE

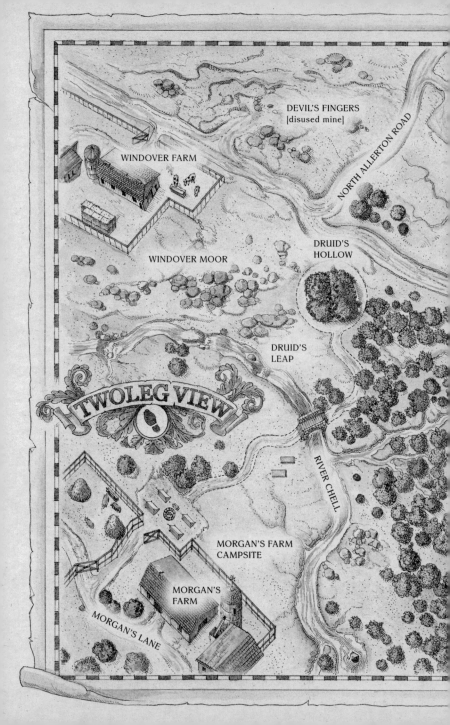

DEVIL'S FINGERS
[disused mine]

WINDOVER FARM

NORTH ALLERTON ROAD

DRUID'S
HOLLOW

WINDOVER MOOR

DRUID'S
LEAP

TWOLEG VIEW

RIVER CHELL

MORGAN'S FARM
CAMPSITE

MORGAN'S
FARM

MORGAN'S LANE

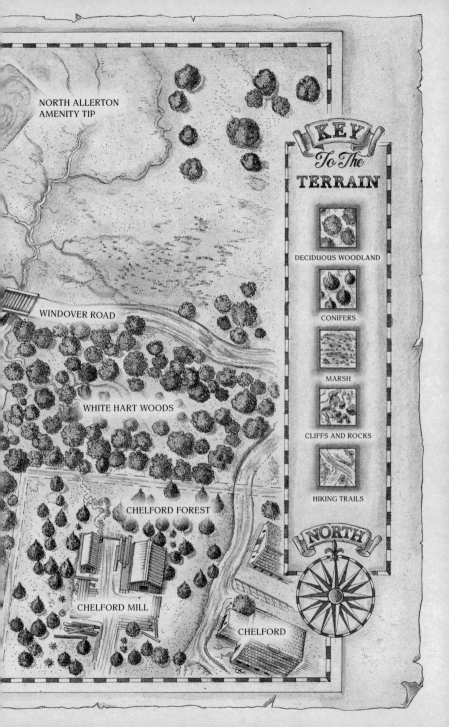

PROLOGUE
❧

Stars glittered coldly on a forest stripped bare by a bitter leaf-fall. Shadows moved through the undergrowth—thin shapes, fur flattened by the chilly evening dew, slipping between the stems like water through reeds. The cats' pelts did not ripple with muscle as they once had; instead, their fur clung to the bones beneath their thin frames.

The flame-colored tom leading the silent procession lifted his head and tasted the air. Even though nightfall had silenced the Twoleg monsters, their stench clung to every dying leaf and branch.

The cat took comfort from the scent of his mate beside him; her familiar scent mingled with the hateful Twoleg odor and softened its cruel tang. She matched his pace stubbornly, even though her faltering stride betrayed her long-empty belly and wakeful nights.

"Firestar," she panted as they padded onward. "Do you think our daughters will find us when they come home?"

The flame-colored cat flinched as though he had trodden on a thorn. "We can only pray that they will, Sandstorm," he said softly.

"But how will they know where to look?" Sandstorm glanced back at a broad-shouldered gray tom. "Graystripe, do you think they'll know where we've gone?"

"Oh, they'll find us," Graystripe promised.

"How can you be so sure?" growled Firestar. "We should have sent another patrol to search for Leafpaw."

"And risk losing more cats?" Graystripe meowed.

Firestar's eyes clouded with pain and he hurried ahead along the shadowy path.

Sandstorm twitched her tail. "This was the hardest decision he's ever had to make," she whispered to Graystripe.

"He *had* to put the Clan first," Graystripe hissed back.

Sandstorm closed her eyes for a moment. "We have lost so many cats this past moon," she mewed.

The wind must have carried her voice, because Firestar turned his head, his gaze hardening. "Then perhaps, at this Gathering, the other Clans will finally agree that we must join together to face this threat," he growled.

"Join together?" A defiant mew sounded from a tabby tom. "Have you forgotten how the Clans reacted last time you said that? WindClan was half-starved, but you might as well have suggested they eat their kits. They are too proud to admit they need help from any cat."

"Things are even worse now, Dustpelt," Sandstorm argued. "How can any Clan stay strong when its kits are dying?" Her voice trailed away as she realized what she had said. "Dustpelt, I'm sorry," she murmured.

"Larchkit may be dead," snarled Dustpelt. "But that doesn't

mean I will let ThunderClan be ordered around by another Clan!"

"No Clan is going to give us orders," Firestar insisted. "But I still believe we can help each other. Leaf-bare is almost here. The Twolegs and their monsters have driven most of our prey farther and farther away, and they have poisoned what remains so that it's not safe to eat. We cannot fight alone."

Suddenly the whispering of the wind through the branches grew to a roar, and Firestar slowed his step, pricking his ears.

"What is it?" Sandstorm whispered, her eyes stretched wide.

"Something's happening at Fourtrees!" Graystripe yowled.

He broke into a run, and Firestar rushed after him, closely followed by their Clanmates. All the cats skidded to a halt at the top of a slope, looking down into a steep-sided hollow.

Bright, unnatural lights, sharper than moonshine, blazed against the trunks of the four giant oaks that had guarded this sacred place since the time of the Great Clans. More lights shone from the eyes of huge monsters squatting at the edge of the clearing. The Great Rock—the vast, smooth gray stone where Clan leaders stood to address the Gathering each full moon—looked small and exposed, like a kit crouched on a Thunderpath.

Twolegs scurried around the hollow, shouting at one another. A new sound sliced through the air, a screech-ing, high-pitched whine, and one Twoleg raised a massive shiny forepaw that flashed in the brilliant lights. The Two-leg pressed it against the trunk of the nearest oak, and dust flew out from the tree like blood spraying from a wound. The shiny forepaw howled as it bit viciously into the ancient bark, pushing deeper into the tree's heart until the Twoleg cried out a warning and the hollow rang with a crack so loud that it drowned the rumbling monsters. The great oak began to lean over, slowly at first, then faster, faster, until it fell crashing to the ground. Its leafless branches clattered as they struck the cold earth, then stilled into deathly silence.

"StarClan, stop them!" mewed Sandstorm.

There was no sign that their warrior ancestors had seen what was happening at Fourtrees. The stars glittered coldly in the indigo sky as the Twoleg moved on to the next oak, his forepaw screaming for another kill.

The cats watched in horror as the Twoleg worked its way around the clearing until the last oak had been felled. Fourtrees, the place where the four Clans had met for many, many generations, was no more. The four giant oaks lay sprawled on the ground, their branches quivering into stillness. Twoleg monsters snarled at the edge of the clearing, ready to move in to carve up the fresh-kill, but the cats stayed frozen at the top of the slope, unable to move.

"The forest is dead," murmured Sandstorm. "There is no hope left for any of us."

"Have courage." Firestar's eyes glittered as he turned to face his Clan. "We still have our Clan. There is always hope."

CHAPTER 1

♣

It was Crowpaw who scented the moorland first as the morning sun spread creamy light over the dew-soaked grass. Although he made no sound, Squirrelpaw saw his ears prick up and sensed him shake off a little of the weariness he had struggled against since Feathertail's death. The dark gray WindClan cat quickened his pace, hurrying up the slope, where mist still clung to the long grass. Squirrelpaw opened her mouth and drew in a deep breath until she too could taste the familiar scent of gorse and heather on the cold morning air. Then she dashed after him with Brambleclaw, Stormfur, and Tawnypelt following fast behind. They could all smell the moorland scents now; they all knew they were close to the end of their long, exhausting journey.

Without saying anything, the five cats stopped in a line at the edge of WindClan territory. Squirrelpaw glanced at her Clanmate, Brambleclaw, and then at Tawnypelt, the Shadow-Clan she-cat. Beside her, Stormfur, the gray RiverClan warrior, narrowed his eyes against the cold wind; but it was Crowpaw who stared most intensely at the rough grassland where he had been born.

"We would not have come this far without Feathertail," he murmured.

"She died to save us all," Stormfur agreed.

Squirrelpaw winced at the raw sorrow in the RiverClan warrior's voice. Feathertail was Stormfur's sister. She had died saving them from a ferocious predator after they had met an unfamiliar group of cats in the mountains. The Tribe of Rushing Water lived behind a waterfall and listened to their own set of ancestors—not StarClan, but the Tribe of Endless Hunting. A mountain cat had been preying on the Tribe for many moons, picking them off one by one. When it had invaded the Tribe's cavern yet again, Feathertail had managed to dislodge a pointed spur of stone from the roof and send it crashing down to kill the beast. But she had been fatally wounded in the fall, and now she lay beneath rocks in the Tribe's territory, close by the waterfall with the sound of rushing water to guide her to StarClan.

"It was her destiny," Tawnypelt commented gently.

"Her destiny was to complete the quest with us," Crowpaw growled. "StarClan chose her to travel to the sun-drown-place and hear what Midnight had to tell us. She shouldn't have died for another Clan's prophecy."

Stormfur padded to Crowpaw's side and nudged the WindClan apprentice with his muzzle. "Bravery and sacrifice are part of the warrior code," he reminded him. "Would you have wanted her to make any other choice?"

Crowpaw stared across the wind-ruffled gorse without replying. His ears twitched as if he were straining to hear

Feathertail's voice on the breeze.

"Come on!" Squirrelpaw bounded forward over the stunted grass, suddenly eager to finish the journey. She had argued with her father, Firestar, before she left, and her paws pricked with nervousness as she wondered how he would react to her return. When she and Brambleclaw had left the forest, they had not told any of the Clan where they were going, nor why. Only Leafpaw, Squirrelpaw's sister, knew that StarClan had spoken to one cat from each Clan, telling them in dreams to go to the sun-drown-place to hear Midnight's prophecy. None of them had guessed that Midnight would turn out to be a wise old badger; nor could they have imagined what momentous news she had to share with them.

Crowpaw raced past her to take the lead, knowing the territory better than any of them. He headed toward a swath of gorse and disappeared along a rabbit track with Tawnypelt close behind. Squirrelpaw ducked her head to avoid catching her ears on the prickers as she followed them along the narrow tunnel. Brambleclaw and Stormfur were hot on her heels; she could feel the thud of their paws through the soil.

As the gorse closed around her, memories beat dark wings inside her head, reminding her of the dreams that had been disturbing her sleep—dreams of darkness and of a small space filled with panic and fear-scent. Squirrelpaw was sure these terrifying dreams were somehow connected to her sister. She told herself that now that she was home, she would be able to find out exactly where Leafpaw was—but feeling a fresh wave of alarm, she raced toward the light.

She slowed down when she emerged into an open grassy space. Brambleclaw and Stormfur burst out after her, their fur raked by the sharp gorse spines.

"I didn't know you were scared of the dark," teased Brambleclaw, falling in beside her.

"I'm not," Squirrelpaw objected.

"I've never seen you run so fast," he purred, his whiskers twitching.

"I just want to get home," Squirrelpaw replied stubbornly. She ignored the glance Brambleclaw and Stormfur exchanged as they padded along beside her. The three cats were trailing behind Tawnypelt and Crowpaw, who had disappeared into a bank of heather.

"What do you think Firestar will say when we tell him about Midnight?" Squirrelpaw wondered out loud.

Brambleclaw's ears twitched. "Who knows?"

"We're only the messengers," meowed Stormfur. "All we can do is tell our Clans what StarClan wanted us to know."

"Do you think they'll believe us?" Squirrelpaw asked.

"If Midnight was right, I don't think we'll have much trouble convincing them," Stormfur pointed out grimly.

Squirrelpaw realized that she had thought of nothing except returning home to her Clan. She had pushed from her mind all thoughts of the threat that faced the forest. But her heart twisted with fear at Stormfur's words, and Midnight's terrifying warning echoed in her mind: *Twolegs build new Thunderpath. Soon they come with monsters. Trees will they uproot, rocks break, the earth itself tear apart. No place left for cats. You stay, monsters tear you too, or you starve with no prey.*

Her stomach tightened with dread. What if they were too late? Would there even be a home to return to?

She tried to calm herself by recalling the rest of Midnight's prophecy: *But you will not be without a guide. When return, stand on Great Rock when Silverpelt shines above. A dying warrior the way will show.* Squirrelpaw breathed deeply. There was still hope. But they had to get home.

"I smell WindClan warriors!"

Brambleclaw's yowl jerked Squirrelpaw back to the moorland. "We must catch up with Crowpaw and Tawnypelt!" she gasped. The impulse to face danger side by side with her traveling companions had become so instinctive that she had forgotten Crowpaw was actually WindClan and would not be in any danger from his Clanmates.

She burst out of the heather into a clearing and nearly collided with a scrawny WindClan apprentice. She stopped dead and stared at him in surprise.

The apprentice was a very young tabby, barely old enough to leave the nursery, from the look of him. He was crouching in the center of the clearing with his back arched and his pelt bristling even though he was outnumbered and outsized by Crowpaw and Tawnypelt. He flinched as Squirrelpaw hurtled out of the heather, but bravely stayed where he was.

"I knew I smelled intruders!" he hissed.

Squirrelpaw narrowed her eyes. Did a pathetic scrap like this really expect to take on three full-grown cats? Crowpaw and Tawnypelt looked calmly at the WindClan apprentice.

"Owlkit!" Crowpaw meowed. "Don't you recognize me?"

The apprentice tipped his head to one side and opened his mouth to scent the air.

"I'm Crowpaw! What are you doing out here, Owlkit? Shouldn't you be in the nursery?"

The young apprentice flicked his ears. "I'm Owl*paw* now," he snapped.

"But you can't be an apprentice!" Crowpaw exclaimed. "You're not six moons old yet."

"And you can't be Crowpaw," growled the tabby. "Crowpaw ran away." But he loosened his battle-ready muscles and padded over to the WindClan cat, who stood calmly while the apprentice sniffed his flank.

"You smell strange," Owlpaw declared.

"We've traveled a long way," explained Crowpaw. "But we're back now, and I need to speak with Tallstar."

"Who must speak with Tallstar?" A belligerent meow made Squirrelpaw jump, and she turned to see a WindClan warrior pick his way out from the heather, lifting his paws high to avoid the thorns. Two more warriors followed him. Squirrelpaw stared at them in alarm. They were so thin she could see the ribs beneath their fur. Hadn't these cats been catching any fresh-kill recently?

"It's me! Crowpaw!" meowed the WindClan apprentice, the tip of his tail twitching. "Webfoot, don't *you* recognize me?"

"Of course I do," meowed the warrior in a flat tone. He sounded so indifferent that Squirrelpaw felt a jab of pity for her friend. This was no sort of homecoming—and Crowpaw hadn't even given his Clanmates the bad news yet.

"We thought you were dead," Webfoot meowed.

"Well, I'm not." Crowpaw blinked. "Is the Clan okay?"

Webfoot's eyes narrowed. "What are these cats doing here?" he demanded.

"They traveled with me," Crowpaw replied. "I can't explain now, but I will tell Tallstar everything," he added.

Webfoot seemed uninterested in Crowpaw's words, and Squirrelpaw felt the scrawny warrior's gaze rake over her as he hissed, "Get them off our territory! They should not be here!"

Squirrelpaw couldn't help thinking Webfoot was in no state to drive them out if they refused to go, but Brambleclaw stepped forward and dipped his head to the WindClan warrior. "Of course we'll leave," he meowed.

"We have to return to our own Clans anyway," Squirrelpaw added pointedly. Brambleclaw shot her a warning glance.

"Then hurry up," snapped Webfoot. He looked at Crowpaw. "Come on," he growled. "I'll take you to Tallstar." He turned and began to head for the far side of the clearing.

Crowpaw twitched his tail. "Surely the camp is that way?" he meowed, signaling toward the other direction.

"We live in the old rabbit warrens now," Webfoot told him.

Squirrelpaw saw confusion and anxiety flash in Crowpaw's eyes. "The Clan has moved?"

"For now," Webfoot answered.

Crowpaw nodded, though his gaze was still filled with

questions. "Can I say good-bye to my friends?"

"Friends?" One of the other warriors spoke, a pale brown tom. "Do your loyalties lie with cats from other Clans now?"

"Of course not!" Crowpaw insisted. "But we have traveled together for more than a moon."

The WindClan warriors glanced uncertainly at each other but said nothing as Crowpaw walked over to Tawnypelt and touched her mottled flank with his nose. He brushed affectionately past Brambleclaw and Stormfur; as he stretched his head to touch his muzzle against hers, Squirrelpaw was surprised by the warmth of his farewell. Crowpaw had found it hardest out of all of them to fit into the group, but after all they had been through together, even he felt the bond of friendship that connected all five cats.

"We must meet again soon," Brambleclaw murmured, his voice low. "At the Great Rock, just as Midnight told us. We need to see the dying warrior so that we know what to do next." He flicked his tail. "It might not be easy to convince our Clans that Midnight is telling the truth. The leaders aren't going to want to hear that they must leave the forest. But if we've seen the dying warrior . . ."

"Why don't we just bring our leaders with us?" Squirrelpaw mewed. "If they see the dying warrior too, they'll have to believe Midnight is right."

"I can't imagine Leopardstar agreeing to come," Stormfur warned.

"Nor Blackstar," Tawnypelt agreed. "It's not full moon, so

there's no truce among the four Clans."

"But it's so important," Squirrelpaw persisted. "They *must* come!"

"We can try," Brambleclaw decided. "Squirrelpaw's right. This might be the best way to share the news."

"Okay," Crowpaw meowed. "We'll meet at Fourtrees tomorrow night, with or without our leaders."

"Fourtrees!" Webfoot's growl made Squirrelpaw jump. The WindClan warrior had obviously overheard their conversation. She felt a stab of guilt, although she knew there was no disloyalty to their Clans in what they were planning—quite the opposite, in fact. But Webfoot seemed to have other fears on his mind.

"You can't meet at Fourtrees. There's nothing left of it!" he spat.

Squirrelpaw felt her blood chill.

"What do you mean?" Tawnypelt demanded.

"All the Clans watched the Twolegs destroy it two moon-rises ago, when we arrived for the Gathering. The Twolegs and their monsters cut down every one of the oaks."

"They cut down the oaks?" Squirrelpaw echoed.

"That's what I said," growled Webfoot. "If you're mouse-brained enough to go there, you'll see for yourself."

Squirrelpaw's fierce desire to return home, to see her Clan and father and mother and sister, washed over her again like a wave, and her paws twitched with the urge to run back to the forest. The others seemed to share her feeling; Brambleclaw's gaze hardened, and Stormfur kneaded the ground impatiently with his paws.

Crowpaw glanced at his Clanmates and then back at his friends. "Good luck," he meowed quietly. "I still think we should meet there tomorrow night, even if the oaks have gone." When Brambleclaw and Stormfur nodded, he turned and followed Webfoot into the heather.

As the WindClan cats disappeared from sight, Brambleclaw scented the air. "Let's go," he ordered. "We're heading over the old badger set toward the river, Tawnypelt, but I think you should stay with us till we reach the WindClan border."

"But it would be quicker if I head straight toward the Thunderpath," Tawnypelt argued.

"It will be safer if we keep together till we're off the moorland," Stormfur meowed. "You don't want to be caught alone on WindClan territory."

"I'm not scared of WindClan," Tawnypelt hissed. "Judging by those warriors, they're hardly battle-fit."

"We mustn't do anything to provoke them," Brambleclaw warned. "No cat knows yet where we've been, or what we have to tell them."

"And we don't know what the Twolegs have done here," Stormfur added. "If we run into any of their monsters, we'll be better off together."

Tawnypelt gazed intently at her companions for a moment, then nodded.

Squirrelpaw blinked with relief. She did not want to say

good-bye to another friend just yet.

Brambleclaw charged away over the moor, and the three other cats followed close behind. As they raced across the grass, the weak leaf-fall sunshine scarcely warmed the fur on Squirrelpaw's back. They ran in silence, and she felt their mood darken as though a cloud had covered the sky. Ever since leaving the mountains, they had concentrated on nothing but reaching the forest, all equally desperate to return home. Squirrelpaw was beginning to think it might have been easier to keep traveling, to journey forever through unfamiliar territory, rather than face the responsibility of having to tell the Clans that they would have to leave their homes or else face a terrible death. But there was still the sign of the dying warrior to come—they had to see this through.

The reek of Twoleg monsters stung her nostrils as they approached the border. There was no sign of any prey: no birds in the sky and no scent of rabbits among the gorse. WindClan had never been an easy territory to hunt in, but there had always been traces of prey on the breeze or in the sandy soil. Even the buzzards, which often hovered over the wide stretch of moorland, were gone.

The four cats reached the crest of a rise, and Squirrelpaw swallowed hard, fighting the urge to retch as the tang of monsters grew stronger. Taking a deep breath, she forced herself to look down the slope. A whole slice of land had been carved out of the moorland, brown and gray and broken instead of the smooth green expanse that had been there when the cats began their journey. In the distance, Twoleg monsters growled across the ground, chewing the earth with their heavy paws to leave a trail of useless mud.

Trembling, Squirrelpaw whispered, "No wonder Wind-Clan moved to the rabbit warrens! The Twolegs must have destroyed their camp."

"They've destroyed everything," Brambleclaw breathed.

"Let's get out of here," Tawnypelt hissed. Squirrelpaw heard anger in her voice, and saw her long, hooked claws sink into the grass.

Brambleclaw continued to stare at the ravaged landscape. "I can't believe how much they've destroyed."

Squirrelpaw's throat tightened. Seeing Brambleclaw's misery was almost as bad as looking at the ruined moor. "Come on," she urged. "We have to get home and find out what has happened to our Clans."

He nodded. Squirrelpaw saw him brace his shoulders as if he were literally carrying the weight of the message they had to take to their Clan. Without saying anything else, he headed down the slope, keeping well away from the Twoleg monsters, and together the cats picked their way across the swath of churned-up ground. Squirrelpaw was grateful for the cold night that had set the mud hard; if it rained, this would turn into a clogging brown river, enough to swallow kits and suck at the bellies of the longest-legged warriors.

When they reached the WindClan border where the land swept down to the forest, Tawnypelt paused. "I'll leave you here," she meowed. Her voice was calm but her eyes betrayed her sadness. "We'll meet at Fourtrees tomorrow, whatever the

Twolegs have done," she promised.

"Good luck with Blackstar," Brambleclaw meowed, rubbing his muzzle along his sister's cheek.

"I don't need luck," she replied grimly. "I will do whatever it takes to persuade Blackstar to come with me. Our quest isn't over yet. We have to keep going for the sake of our Clans."

Squirrelpaw felt a renewed burst of energy as the tortoiseshell warrior pelted away toward the ShadowClan border. "And we'll persuade Firestar!" she called after her.

The grass grew softer under their paws as Brambleclaw, Squirrelpaw, and Stormfur approached the RiverClan border; soon Squirrelpaw could scent the markers and hear the distant thundering of water in the gorge. RiverClan territory lay on the other side, and just beyond the gorge there was a Twoleg bridge that would take Stormfur across the river to his camp.

Brambleclaw paused as if he expected Stormfur to leave them there, but Stormfur just looked into his eyes. "I'm coming with you to the ThunderClan camp," he meowed quietly.

"Coming with us? Why?" Squirrelpaw exclaimed.

"I want to tell my father about Feathertail," he replied.

"But we can tell him," she offered, wanting to spare Stormfur the pain of telling Graystripe, the ThunderClan deputy, about his daughter's death. Graystripe had fallen in love with a RiverClan she-cat, Silverstream, many moons ago. She had died bearing his kits, and though Stormfur and Feathertail had grown up in RiverClan, they had always known their ThunderClan father.

Stormfur shook his head. "He has already lost our mother," he reminded her. "I want to be the one to tell him about Feathertail."

Brambleclaw nodded. "Then come with us," he mewed gently.

In single file the three cats followed the path away from the gorge and down into the trees. Squirrelpaw's fur prickled with anticipation as she breathed the musty smell of fallen leaves. They were nearly home. She quickened her pace until her paws were flying across the soft forest floor. She felt Brambleclaw's pelt brush against hers as he sped up to join her.

But Squirrelpaw wasn't running from excitement or joy at being back in the forest. Something was calling her home— something even more desperate than the threat of the Twolegs and their monsters. The sinister dreams that had disturbed her sleep flooded her mind again and echoed in her heart like the warning cry of a hawk. Something was terribly wrong.

CHAPTER 2

❧

"Spottedleaf!" Leafpaw called desperately into the forest. There was no reply. The wise medicine cat had guided her many times before in dreams; if ever Leafpaw had needed Spottedleaf's help, it was now.

"Spottedleaf, where are you?" she called again.

The trees did not even tremble in the breeze. No prey-sound whispered in the shadows. The silence tore at Leafpaw's heart like a claw.

Suddenly an unfamiliar yowl echoed in her ears, forcing its way into her dream. Leafpaw opened her eyes with a jolt. For a moment she couldn't think where she was. Her fur was ruffled by a cold draft, and instead of a soft, mossy nest there was a strange, cold, shiny web beneath her paws. She stood up in panic, and more shiny web grazed her ears. Wherever she was, it was a very small space, hardly taller than she was. Taking a deep breath, Leafpaw forced herself to look around, and everything came rushing back to her.

She was trapped in a tiny den, with walls, floor, and roof made entirely from cold, hard web. There was just enough space to stand and stretch, but no more. It was packed among other dens lining every wall of a small wooden Twoleg nest.

Leafpaw longed to see the stars, to breathe in the comforting presence of StarClan and know they were watching her, but when she looked up she saw nothing but the nest's steeply pitched roof. The only light came from a shaft of moonlight that streamed through a small hole in the wall at one end of the nest. Her den was on top of others; the one directly below was empty, but beneath that she could just make out a bundle of dark fur. Another cat? Not a forest cat, since its scent was unfamiliar. The shape was so still, it must have been sleeping. If it was alive at all, Leafpaw thought grimly.

She listened again for the yowl, but the cat that had cried out was silent now, and Leafpaw could hear only the soft mewling and shuffling of cats trapped in the other dens. She sniffed the air but recognized no scents. An acrid Twoleg stench filled the nest, tinged with fear. Leafpaw unsheathed her claws, feeling them catch on the shiny web.

StarClan, where are you? The thought fleetingly crossed her mind that she was already dead, but she thrust it away with a shudder that made her claws scrape against the floor of the den.

"You're awake at last," whispered a voice.

Leafpaw jumped and craned her neck to look over her shoulder. A heap of tabby fur stirred in the den beside hers, and she smelled the unmistakable Twoleg-tainted scent of a kittypet. There had been kindness in the she-cat's voice, but Leafpaw felt too wretched to reply. Her mind flooded with bitter memories of how the Twolegs had trapped her while she was hunting with Sorreltail and brought her to this awful place. She had been separated from her Clan and locked in darkness. Overwhelmed by despair, she buried her nose in her paws and closed her eyes.

Another voice sounded from a den farther along. It was too quiet to make out the words, but there was something familiar about it. Leafpaw lifted her muzzle to taste the air, but all she could smell was a sour tang that reminded her of the herbs Cinderpelt used for cleaning wounds. The voice spoke again, and Leafpaw strained her ears to listen.

"We must get out of here," the cat was mewing.

Another cat answered from the far side of the nest. "How? There's no way out."

"We can't just sit here waiting to die!" the first voice insisted. "There have been other cats here—I can smell them, and their fear-scent. I don't know what happened to them, but whatever it was must have scared their fur off. We've got to get out before *we* become nothing but stale fear-scent!"

"There's no way out, you mouse-brain," came a rough mew. "Shut up and let us sleep."

The words made Leafpaw feel sick with fear and sadness. She didn't want to die here! She flattened her ears and closed her eyes, clawing for the safety of sleep.

"Wake up!" A voice hissed in Leafpaw's ear, jolting her out of troubled dreams.

She lifted her head and looked around. Watery sunlight filtered in through the hole in the wall, though it did nothing to lift the chill from her fur. In the weak dawn light she could see the tabby she-cat in the den next to her more clearly. The stranger was soft and well groomed, and Leafpaw was conscious of her own matted pelt as she stared at her. She was definitely a kittypet, plump and soft-muscled beneath her tabby pelt.

"Are you all right?" asked the kittypet, her eyes wide with worry. "You sounded as if you were in pain."

"I was dreaming," Leafpaw replied hoarsely. Her voice felt strange, as if she hadn't spoken for several days, and as she spoke memories of her nightmare came flooding back: images of water-swollen rivers scarlet with blood—and great birds swooping out of the sky with thorn-sharp claws. For a heartbeat, Leafpaw saw Feathertail hidden in darkness and then swathed in starlight, and without understanding why, her paws trembled.

Outside a Twoleg monster roared into wakefulness, bringing her back to the wooden nest and the den that pressed around her.

"You don't look well," the kittypet commented. "Try eating some breakfast. There's some in the corner of your cage."

Cage? Leafpaw wondered at the strange word. "Is that what this den is called?" The kittypet was nodding through the web that separated the two "cages" toward a half-empty holder of stinking pellets.

Leafpaw looked at the Twoleg food in disgust. "I'm not eating that!"

"Then at least sit up and give yourself a wash," the kittypet urged. "You've been hunched up like a wounded mouse since the workfolk brought you here."

Leafpaw twitched her shoulders but didn't move.

"They didn't hurt you when they caught you, did they?" the kittypet asked. There was concern in her voice.

"No," Leafpaw mumbled.

"Then get up and wash yourself," she went on more briskly. "You're no use to yourself or any cat moping around like that."

Leafpaw did not want to get up and wash herself. The web floor scratched against her paws, and blood oozed from beneath one of her claws. Her eyes stung with the filthy air that filtered into the nest, fouled by the monsters outside. And StarClan had sent no comfort to ease the desperate fear that gripped her heart.

"Get up!" repeated the kittypet, more firmly this time.

Leafpaw twisted her head around to glare at her, but the kittypet held her gaze.

"We're going to find some way to escape," she mewed. "Unless you get up, stretch your muscles, and have something to eat and drink, you're going to be left behind. And I'm not leaving any cat here if I can help it!"

Leafpaw blinked. "Do you know a way out of here?"

"Not yet," admitted the kittypet. "But you might be able to help me find one if only you'd stop feeling sorry for yourself."

Leafpaw knew she was right. She wouldn't solve anything by curling up and waiting to die. Besides, she wasn't ready to join StarClan. She was an apprentice medicine cat—her Clan needed her here, in the forest. Whatever was left of it.

Pushing away the misery that had sapped her strength, she pulled herself up onto her paws. Her cramped muscles screamed in protest as she uncurled her tail and flexed her legs.

"That's better," purred the kittypet. "Now turn around. There's more room to stretch if you face the other way."

Leafpaw obediently wriggled around and reached her paws to the corner of the cage, gripping the web to brace herself. As she stretched, pressing her chest down and flexing her shoulders, she felt her stiff muscles soften. Feeling a little better, she began to wash herself, swiping her tongue over her flank.

The kittypet huddled closer to the mesh and watched her with bright blue eyes. "I'm Cody," she meowed. "What are you called?"

"Leafpaw."

"Leafpaw?" echoed Cody. "What an odd name." She shrugged and carried on. "Well, bad luck on getting caught, Leafpaw. Did you lose your collar too? I wouldn't be here if I hadn't pulled mine off—the wretched thing! I thought I was so clever managing to wriggle out of it, but if I'd still been wearing it, the workfolk would have taken me home instead of bringing me here." She tucked in her chin and licked an unkempt clump of fur on her chest. "My housefolk are going to be mad with worry. If I'm not in by midnight they start rushing around the garden shaking the pellet pot and calling for me. It's nice that they care, but I can look after myself."

Leafpaw couldn't help letting out a purr of amusement. "A kittypet, look after itself? If it weren't for the food the Two-legs give you, you'd starve!"

"Twolegs?"

"Sorry." Leafpaw corrected herself for the kittypet's benefit. "Housefolk."

"Well, where do you get your food from?" asked Cody.

"I hunt for it."

"I caught a mouse once . . ." Cody meowed defensively.

"I catch all my food," Leafpaw retorted. For a moment, she forgot she was trapped in a stifling cage, and saw only the green forest rustling with the tiny sounds of prey. "And I catch enough for the elders, too."

Cody narrowed her blue eyes. "Are you one of those woodland cats that Smudge talks about?"

"I'm a Clan cat," Leafpaw told her.

Cody's gaze clouded with confusion. "A *Clan* cat?"

"There are four Clans in the forest," Leafpaw explained. "We each have our own territory and customs, but we all live together under StarClan." She saw Cody's eyes stretch wide, and she went on. "The cats of StarClan are our warrior ancestors. They live in Silverpelt." She flicked her tail toward the roof, indicating the sky. "All Clan cats will join StarClan one day."

"Smudge never mentioned any Clans," murmured Cody.

"Who's Smudge?"

"A cat from another garden. He had a friend a long time ago, a kittypet who went off to join the woodland cats . . . I mean *Clans*."

"My father was born a kittypet," meowed Leafpaw. "He left his Twolegs to join ThunderClan."

Cody pressed herself against the shiny web that separated

them. "What's your father called?"

Leafpaw stared back at her. "Do you think he might be that cat your friend used to know?"

Cody nodded. "Maybe! What is his name?"

"Firestar."

Cody shook her head. "Smudge's friend was called Rusty." She sighed. "Not Firestar."

"But he wasn't always Firestar," Leafpaw mewed. "That's his Clan name. It's a leader's name. He had to earn it, just as he had to earn his warrior name."

Cody glanced at her thoughtfully. "Names are important to the Clans, then?"

"Very. I mean, each kit is given a name that means something, that recognizes the way it is different from all its Clanmates." She paused. "I guess you could say that we are given the name we deserve."

"What did your father do to deserve the name Firestar?"

"His pelt is as orange as flame," Leafpaw told her. "So when he came to ThunderClan, the leader named him Fire—" She broke off. Cody was staring at her in astonishment.

"It *must* be Smudge's friend!" she gasped. "Smudge always said Rusty had the brightest orange pelt he'd ever seen. And now he's the leader of your Clan! Wow, I can't wait to tell Smudge!"

A pang of sorrow gripped Leafpaw's heart as she wondered if Cody would have another chance to speak to Smudge, or if she herself would ever see her father again. *Oh, StarClan, help us!*

Cody glanced down at the floor as if she had followed

Leafpaw's terrified thoughts. "Your ears look like another wash wouldn't do any harm," she mewed, changing the subject.

Leafpaw licked her paw and drew it over one ear as Cody continued. "Your father must be wondering where you've gone. I bet he's as worried about you as my housefolk are about me."

"Yes," Leafpaw agreed, though privately she doubted that Twolegs had the same connection with their cats as she did with her kin. She reminded herself that Cody seemed devoted to her housefolk—she sounded as concerned about them as Leafpaw was about her Clanmates. "We must find a way out of here." Her voice hardened with determination. Firestar was already worried enough about Squirrelpaw without another daughter going missing.

She stared at the hole high up in the nest wall where the sunshine filtered in, and wondered if it was big enough for a cat to squeeze through. She might just manage it, even if she left some fur behind. But how could she escape from her cage? She studied the catch that held the door shut.

"It's no use," Cody mewed, following her gaze. "I've tried reaching my paw through, but I can't get a grip on the catch."

"Do you know why the Twolegs are trapping us like this?" Leafpaw asked, dragging her eyes away from the door.

Cody shrugged. "I suppose they think we get in the way of what they're doing in the forest," she mewed. "They caught me after I chased a squirrel into the woods, farther than I usually go. One of the monsters came roaring through the trees, and I panicked. I was so startled I didn't see the workfolk all around. One of them scooped me up and shoved me in here. Even without my collar, he must have been as stupid as a pup to mistake me for a forest cat!" She bristled indignantly, then let her fur lie flat as she caught Leafpaw's eye. "Sorry, I wasn't thinking. I mean, you're much nicer than I thought you'd be," she finished awkwardly.

Leafpaw shrugged. Forest cat or kittypet, they were equally trapped. "I don't usually come to this part of the woods either," she meowed. "I was looking for Cloudtail and Bright-heart, two of my Clanmates."

Cody tipped her head to one side.

"They went missing not long ago," Leafpaw explained. "Some of the Clan thought they'd just run away, but I know they'd never leave their kit."

"So you decided the Twolegs must have caught them and came looking for them," Cody guessed.

"I didn't even know the Twolegs were trapping cats," Leaf-paw mewed. "I just followed a clue, and I came across the scent of a RiverClan cat who'd gone missing too."

She paused, her fur prickling. If Cloudtail, Brightheart, and Mistyfoot had been trapped by the Twolegs, they could be here now! She stared frantically around the nest, brighter now as the morning light strengthened. Finally she saw a shape she had hoped to find, the ginger-splashed fur familiar even in the gloom.

"Brightheart!" Leafpaw tried to call her Clanmate's name, but a new noise silenced her cry. The nest door opened and light streamed in. Leafpaw quickly scanned the cages for more familiar shapes as a Twoleg marched into the nest.

The Twoleg began opening each cage and tossing something inside. When it reached hers, Leafpaw jumped back. She watched, trembling in fear, as the Twoleg dropped fresh pellets into the pot near the front and slopped stinking water into the holder beside it. But when the Twoleg opened Cody's cage, the kittypet brushed against its giant paw, purring as the Twoleg stroked her soft fur.

The Twoleg shut Cody's door and left the nest. The cages were plunged once more into shadow.

"How could you let it touch you?" Leafpaw hissed.

"The workfolk might be our best way out of here," Cody pointed out. "If I can persuade it that I'm nothing but a poor lost kittypet, it might let me go. You should try it too."

Leafpaw shuddered at the idea of any Twoleg touching her, and she knew her Clanmates would feel the same. She tried to find the cage where she had recognized Brightheart's soft pelt.

"Brightheart!" she called, her tail twitching anxiously.

"Yes," came the wary reply. "Who's that?"

Leafpaw pressed herself against the front of her cage, feeling the web hard and cold through her fur. "It's Leafpaw!"

"Leafpaw!" The voice came from somewhere else in the nest, and Leafpaw let out a muffled purr as she recognized Cloudtail's familiar mew. She searched the cages until she saw his thick white pelt.

"You're both still alive!" Leafpaw exclaimed.

"Are those the cats you were looking for?" Cody asked.

Leafpaw nodded.

"Leafpaw?" Another voice came from the gloom. "It's me, Mistyfoot."

"Mistyfoot!" Leafpaw echoed. "I thought I found your scent before I was trapped! What were you doing so far from the RiverClan border?"

"I wouldn't have been caught in that fox-hearted Twoleg trap if I hadn't been chasing a thieving WindClan warrior off my territory," growled the she-cat.

A trembling meow sounded from below. "I didn't know it was a trap when I hid in it."

"Who's that?" Leafpaw asked, peering down.

"Gorsetail of WindClan," came the reply.

"Are there any other Clan cats here?" Leafpaw called, only half hoping for a reply. However relieved she was to find that her Clanmates and friends were still alive, she'd far rather no forest cats had been caught at all—herself included. But she heard only the steady crunching of pellets as the other trapped cats ate their food.

"There's about the same amount of rogues here as Clan cats," Mistyfoot hissed.

"What are rogues?" Cody whispered in alarm.

"They're cats who choose not to belong to a Clan," Leafpaw explained. "Or to Twolegs, either."

"They care only about themselves," Mistyfoot added.

"Yeah, well, look where caring about your Clanmates got you," muttered a reproachful voice near the floor of the nest.

Leafpaw strained her eyes and saw a scraggly old tom with

ripped ears crouching in a cage on the floor.

"Ignore him," spat Cody. "He'll be no help."

"Do you know him?" Leafpaw asked in surprise.

"He used to steal from my housefolks' garbage," Cody explained. "He may call himself a rogue, or whatever, but he's no better than a rat, if you ask me."

"Do you live in Twolegplace?" Cloudtail called to Cody. "Do you know a cat called Princess?"

"A tabby with white paws?"

"Yes." Cloudtail's eyes shone in the gloom. "She's my mother! How is she?"

"She's great," Cody answered. "A dog came to live in the next house—a yappy thing—but Princess soon let him know it was her territory. She sat on the fence and hissed at him till he went running for cover!"

"Look," Mistyfoot snapped. "This is all very heartwarming, but can we figure out a way to escape?"

"Does any cat know what the Twolegs are planning to do with us?" Brightheart's voice was hoarse with terror.

"What do you *think* they're going to do with us?" muttered the rogue tom. "They didn't catch us and lock us up in this stinking hut because they're fond of cats."

"At least they're feeding us," Cody mewed quickly. "Even if it's not quite as tasty as I'm used to."

Leafpaw glanced at her. "Let's concentrate on finding a way out of here, like Mistyfoot suggested," she mewed.

"Why don't you all just shut up?" hissed the rogue. "You'll bring the Twoleg back with all your mewling."

As he spoke the noise of heavy footsteps sounded outside, and Leafpaw froze. She pressed herself to the back of her cage as the Twoleg came in with another cage. Leafpaw could tell by the fear-scent that a she-cat crouched inside, but she didn't recognize its smell. With a guilty pang of relief, she knew that the latest victim of the Twoleg traps was definitely not a Clan cat.

Another rogue, she decided as the Twoleg placed the cage on top of Cloudtail's. *And judging by the other rogues in here, she won't be much help with planning a way to get out.*

But as soon as the Twoleg left the nest she heard Mistyfoot exclaim in astonishment, "Sasha!"

CHAPTER 3

Squirrelpaw raced ahead of Brambleclaw and Stormfur toward the ravine where the ThunderClan camp lay. The stench of Twoleg monsters hung in the air, and her heart grew as heavy as a stone when she heard a rumbling roar up ahead.

"They're here already!" she whispered. There was an unfamiliar slash of brightness where a gap had appeared in the trees that bordered the ravine. Before, the forest had crowded right up to the edge of the steep slope that led down into the camp.

Squirrelpaw felt Brambleclaw's pelt brush hers as he crept alongside and peered out from the trees. "Go carefully," he murmured without looking at her.

A broad trail had been gouged through the forest. The ground, once hidden by ferns and smoothed by many moons' pawsteps, was lumpy and muddy, churned up like the moorland. Their way to the ravine was blocked by monsters, roaring and growling as they chewed through more trees. Squirrelpaw shrank back under the bracken, flattening her ears.

"Midnight warned us it would be bad," Brambleclaw reminded her. His voice was oddly calm, and Squirrelpaw pressed herself close to him, seeking comfort from the warmth of his fur. "We can't cross here," he went on. "It's too danger-ous. We'll have to go around and approach the camp from the other side."

"You lead the way," Stormfur suggested. "You know the forest here better than I do." He glanced at Squirrelpaw. "Are you okay?"

Squirrelpaw lifted her chin. "I'm fine. All I want to do is get back to the Clan."

"Come on then," mewed Brambleclaw, and he set off at a fast trot, away from the Twoleg devastation.

They turned away from the monsters and sped through the trees. As she raced toward the sandy clearing where she had trained with the other apprentices, Squirrelpaw wondered grimly how the Clan could have survived with the Twolegs and monsters so close. The sun was high in the sky, and the training hollow was crisscrossed with shafts of cold sunlight. She dug her paws into the soft ground and pushed on ahead of Brambleclaw and Stormfur, her chest tightening with fear as she tore along the trail that led to the gorse tunnel. Without hesitating, she ducked her head and raced into the thorns.

"Firestar!" she yowled as she exploded into the clearing.

It was completely empty. The whole camp was silent. No cat stirred, and the scent of the Clan was stale.

On trembling legs, Squirrelpaw padded to her father's den underneath the tall gray rock where he normally stood to address the Clan. For one wild moment, she thought Firestar might still be there in spite of the danger that roared at the brink of the ravine. But his mossy bedding was damp and musty, unused for several days. Squirrelpaw slipped out of the cleft in the rock and found her way into the nursery. Kits and elders were always the last to leave the camp, and there was nowhere safer than in the heart of the bramble thicket that had protected many generations of ThunderClan cats.

There was nothing inside except the stench of a fox, almost hiding the faint scent of helpless kits and their mothers. Blind panic rose in her chest. There was a rustle of branches, and Brambleclaw appeared at her side.

"F-fox!" she stammered.

"It's okay," Brambleclaw reassured her. "The scent is stale. The fox must have been trying his luck, hoping the Clan had left unguarded kits behind. There's no sign of bl—of a fight," he amended hastily.

"But where has the Clan gone?" Squirrelpaw wailed. She knew Brambleclaw had been about to say *blood*. It seemed impossible that the whole Clan could have vanished without some blood being spilled. *Oh, StarClan, what happened here?*

Brambleclaw's eyes glittered with fear. "I don't know," he admitted. "But we'll find them."

Stormfur joined them. "Are we too late?" he whispered hoarsely.

"We should have come home quicker," Squirrelpaw protested.

Stormfur shook his broad gray head as he looked around

the abandoned nursery. "We should never have left in the first place," he growled. "We should have stayed and helped our Clans!"

"We *had* to go!" Brambleclaw hissed, unsheathing his claws and sinking them into the moss. "It was StarClan's will."

"But where have our Clanmates gone?" Squirrelpaw cried. She pushed past the other cats back into the clearing. She heard them follow more slowly, Stormfur cursing under his breath as a bramble scraped against his flank.

The RiverClan warrior padded over to stand beside Squirrelpaw. He looked around the camp for a long moment, ignoring the scratch on his hind leg. "There's no blood anywhere, no trace of a struggle," he murmured.

Squirrelpaw followed his gaze and realized Stormfur was right. Even out here, the camp showed no signs that the Clan had been attacked. Surely that meant the Clan had been unharmed when they left? "They must have moved somewhere safer," she meowed hopefully.

Brambleclaw nodded.

"We should keep looking for scents," Stormfur suggested. "They might give us a clue to where the Clan has gone."

"I'll check Cinderpelt's den," Squirrelpaw offered. She charged down the fern tunnel that led to the medicine cat's clearing, but the hollow amid the sheltering ferns was as empty and silent as the rest of the camp.

She skirted the edge, poking her nose into the bracken. Cinderpelt sometimes flattened out small nests here for sick cats, but there were no fresh scents now. She turned away and padded toward the split rock that formed one end of the clearing. This was where Cinderpelt made her own nest and kept her supplies of herbs safe and dry.

In the shadows, the pungent smell of roots and herbs was as strong as ever, but there was only the faintest trace of Cinderpelt's scent, as stale as Firestar's had been in his den.

Disappointed, Squirrelpaw backed out of the cleft and stared desperately around the clearing. A sudden, terrible realization clutched at her belly: Cinderpelt's scent was faint, but her sister's scent was even fainter. Wherever Thunder-Clan had gone, Leafpaw had left before them.

A screeching warrior's cry sounded from above, jerking her out of her thoughts. Squirrelpaw glimpsed a flurry of dark fur; then her legs buckled as a cat landed heavily on her back. Fury made her hair stand on end, and her paws scrabbled as she thrashed wildly. The journey to the sun-drown-place had made her strong and lean, and she heard the cat gasp with the effort of clinging onto her pelt. Instinctively, Squirrelpaw rolled onto her side. She felt claws rake her flank as her assailant thudded to the ground.

Hissing with anger, Squirrelpaw spun to face her attacker, her hackles raised and her lips drawn back.

The other cat had scrambled up as well and was glaring at her with her tail fluffed up. "Trying to steal my supplies, were you?" she spat.

"Cinderpelt!" Squirrelpaw gasped.

The medicine cat's eyes stretched wide with surprise. "Squirrelpaw! Y-you've come home!" she stammered. She rushed forward, pushing her muzzle along Squirrelpaw's cheek. "Where have you been? Is Brambleclaw with you?"

"Where is everyone?" Squirrelpaw demanded, too worried about her Clanmates to answer Cinderpelt's flurry of questions.

The sound of paws pounding along the fern tunnel interrupted her, and Brambleclaw and Stormfur burst into the clearing.

"We heard fighting," panted Brambleclaw. He blinked in surprise as he spotted Cinderpelt. "Are you both okay?"

"Brambleclaw! I'm so pleased to see you!" Cinderpelt looked at Stormfur and confusion clouded her gaze for a moment. "What are you doing here?"

"He's with us," Brambleclaw explained shortly. "Who attacked you?" He stared around, his hackles raised. "Did you chase them off?"

"Actually, it was me," Cinderpelt confessed. "I didn't recognize Squirrelpaw from the top of the rock. I thought she was trying to steal my herbs. I'd come back to fetch some supplies—"

"Come *back*?" Brambleclaw echoed. "Where is everyone?"

"We had to leave," Cinderpelt explained, her eyes glistening with distress. "The monsters were getting nearer and nearer. Firestar ordered us to abandon the camp."

"When?" Brambleclaw's eyes were round with astonishment.

"Two moonrises ago."

"Where did you go?" demanded Squirrelpaw.

"Sunningrocks." Cinderpelt looked distractedly around the clearing. "I only came back to get some supplies. Now that I don't have Leafpaw to help me collect fresh herbs, I'm always running low. . . ."

Squirrelpaw's heart lurched. "What happened to her?"

Cinderpelt glanced at her, and the pity in her eyes made Squirrelpaw want to turn tail and flee from what she was about to hear. "The Twolegs have been setting traps for us," she said. "Leafpaw was caught in one the day before we abandoned the camp. Sorreltail saw everything but was powerless to help."

Squirrelpaw's legs seemed to lose their strength altogether, and she swayed. With a sickening flash of horror, she understood all her dreams of fear and darkness and being trapped in a small space.

"Where did the Twolegs take her?" Brambleclaw's voice sounded as if he were a long way away. Squirrelpaw shuddered, trying to fight the shock that dragged at her body like rushing water.

"We don't know."

"Has Firestar sent out a search patrol?"

"He sent a rescue patrol as soon as Sorreltail returned. But the place where the Twolegs had trapped her was overrun with monsters tearing up the trees, and there was no sign of Leafpaw." Cinderpelt stepped forward and pressed her cheek against Squirrelpaw's. "It wasn't safe to look for her after that," she murmured. Squirrelpaw pulled away, but Cinderpelt stared intently into her eyes, and she felt as if the medicine cat were willing her to understand.

"Your father had to think of the whole Clan," she meowed. "He couldn't risk putting more cats in danger to search for Leafpaw." She looked away, and Squirrelpaw heard bitter regret in her voice as she went on. "I wanted to go out looking myself, but I knew I'd be no use." She glanced furiously at her hind leg, weakened by an old injury on the Thunderpath. Cinderpelt knew only too well the damage that Twoleg monsters could do to cats' fragile bodies.

For the first time Squirrelpaw noticed how the medicine cat's pelt seem to hang from her, showing the sharpness of bone beneath.

Brambleclaw must have noticed too. "How is the Clan managing?" he asked.

"Not well," Cinderpelt admitted. "Larchkit died—Ferncloud couldn't make enough milk to feed her. Prey has been so scarce, we've all gone hungry." Grief made her voice tremble. "Dappletail's dead too. She ate a rabbit that Twolegs had poisoned to get rid of WindClan." A look of alarm flashed in her eyes. "You haven't eaten any rabbits, have you?"

"We haven't seen any rabbits," Stormfur replied. "Not even in WindClan territory."

Cinderpelt lashed her tail. "The Twolegs have ruined everything! Brightheart and Cloudtail are missing as well—we think they were captured by Twoleg traps, like Leafpaw was."

Brambleclaw dropped his gaze to the cold, muddy ground. "I didn't think it could be this bad!" he murmured. "Midnight warned us, but . . ." Squirrelpaw wished she could comfort him. But there was nothing she could do or say to make him feel better.

Cinderpelt was staring at Brambleclaw in confusion. "Midnight warned you?" she echoed. "What do you mean?"

"Midnight is a badger," Squirrelpaw explained. "That's who we went to see."

"You went to see a *badger*?" Cinderpelt glanced around as if she expected to see a ferocious black-and-white-striped face appear through the undergrowth behind them.

Squirrelpaw could understand her reaction. Badgers had never been trusted by cats; they were notoriously bad-tempered, unpredictable creatures. Squirrelpaw and her traveling companions had taken a while to get over the shock when they discovered exactly who they had been sent to meet.

"At the sun-drown-place," Squirrelpaw went on.

"I don't understand," murmured Cinderpelt.

"StarClan sent us there," put in Stormfur. "One cat from each Clan."

"They told us to go to the place where the sun falls into the sea at night," Brambleclaw added.

"*StarClan* sent you there?" Cinderpelt gasped. "I . . . we thought they had deserted us." She stared at Brambleclaw. "StarClan spoke to you?"

"In a dream," Brambleclaw admitted quietly.

Stormfur was kneading the ground, his fur ruffled. "Feathertail had the same dream."

"And Crowpaw and Tawnypelt," Squirrelpaw added.

Cinderpelt stared at the three cats, her eyes wide. "You must come and tell Firestar everything. We have heard nothing from StarClan since they sent the message about fire and tiger."

"Fire and tiger?" Squirrelpaw echoed, mystified.

"You'll learn about it soon enough." Cinderpelt didn't meet her gaze. "Come back with me now. The Clan needs to hear your story."

CHAPTER 4

Sunningrocks was the safest place to hide," Cinderpelt told them as she wove through the bracken.

Squirrelpaw was surprised. "But there's so little shelter there!" Sunningrocks was a wide stone slope near the RiverClan border, bare of trees or bushes except for a few scrubby tufts of grass. Aware that Stormfur was only a few pawsteps behind, Squirrelpaw lowered her voice. "And what about RiverClan? They've tried to claim it as their territory before—wasn't Firestar afraid they might attack the Clan?"

"RiverClan has made no threats lately," Cinderpelt replied. "Sunningrocks is as far from the Twolegs and their tree-destroying monsters as we could get within our territory, and close to what little prey is left in the forest."

Despite her limp, she led them quickly through the forest, but Squirrelpaw noticed that the medicine cat's scrawny flanks heaved with the effort. She glanced at Brambleclaw. He was watching Cinderpelt too, his eyes narrowed with concern.

"We're in much better shape than she is," Squirrelpaw whispered to him.

"Our journey has made us stronger," Brambleclaw commented.

Squirrelpaw felt an uncomfortable pang of guilt that their long and difficult journey had kept them safer and better fed than the cats they left behind. The sun was sinking in a clear blue sky, and a chill wind swayed the branches above them, tugging at the last stubborn leaves. She paused, listening. A few birds chirped a muted chorus, but in the distance she heard monsters all the time, humming like angry bees. Their sticky stench hung in the air and clung to her fur, and Squirrelpaw realized that she had returned to a forest that no longer smelled or sounded like home. It had become another place, one where cats could not survive. *No place left for cats. You stay, monsters tear you too, or you starve with no prey.* Midnight's prophecy was already coming true.

The pale gray bulk of Sunningrocks loomed beyond the trees, and Squirrelpaw made out the shapes of cats moving over the stone.

A yowl startled her, and she saw white and ginger fur flashing through the undergrowth. A heartbeat later, Sorreltail and Brackenfur burst out of the bushes in front of them.

"I thought I could smell a familiar scent," Sorreltail meowed breathlessly.

Squirrelpaw stared at the two warriors. They were as disheveled as Cinderpelt, and beside her, Brambleclaw's eyes were wide with shock as his gaze flicked over their gaunt bodies.

"We didn't think you were coming back," Brackenfur meowed.

"Of course we were coming back!" Squirrelpaw protested.

"Where have you been?" Sorreltail demanded.

"A long way away," Stormfur murmured. "Farther than any forest cat has ever been."

Brackenfur glared suspiciously at the RiverClan warrior. "Are you on your way home?"

"I need to talk to Graystripe first."

Brackenfur narrowed his eyes.

"Let him come," Cinderpelt advised. "These cats have a lot to tell us."

Brackenfur's whiskers twitched, but he dipped his head and turned to lead the way through the trees toward the rocks.

"Come on," Sorreltail mewed, padding after Brackenfur. "The others will want to see you."

Squirrelpaw fell into step beside her, trying to ignore the anxiety that gnawed her stomach like hunger pangs. It was starting to look as if their journey had been in vain, and hearing what Midnight had to tell them had come too late to help the Clans. She prayed that the dying warrior's sign would be enough to save them. Glancing sideways at Sorreltail, she saw that the tortoiseshell warrior's tail was drooping and her gaze rested wearily on the ground.

"Cinderpelt told me about Leafpaw," Squirrelpaw murmured.

"I couldn't do anything to save her," Sorreltail answered

dully. "I don't know where they've taken her. I wanted to look, but we moved camp the next day, and there hasn't been a chance." She paused and looked at Squirrelpaw, her eyes flashing with desperate hope. "Did you see her while you were traveling? Do you know where she is?"

Squirrelpaw's heart twisted. "No, we haven't seen her."

The strong, familiar scent of ThunderClan filled the air. Squirrelpaw longed to rush forward to greet her Clanmates, but instinct warned her to approach them warily. She stood still for a moment, hoping that her thudding heart couldn't be heard by every cat on Sunningrocks.

The smooth stone slope, lined with gullies and small hollows, rose ahead of her. Trees bordered one side, and at the far edge, where the slope fell steeply away, Squirrelpaw could see the tips of more trees, following the river as far as Fourtrees—or the place where Fourtrees had been. The cold stone, blasted by the leaf-bare winds, was a chilly resting place for the Clan. Squirrelpaw looked at Sorreltail's paws and saw dried blood staining the white fur around her claws. She remembered how the rocks in the mountains had grazed her own paws while they were staying with the Tribe of Rushing Water.

There was no central clearing here for cats to gather, as there had been in the ravine. Instead, the cats were huddled in small groups; Squirrelpaw spotted the dark pelt of her mentor, Dustpelt, sheltering beneath an overhang, with Mousefur next to him. He seemed much smaller than when she had left, his bony shoulders jutting out from beneath his ungroomed fur. Frostfur and Speckletail, two of the Clan elders, were crouched in the deepest gully. Even in the shadows, Squirrel-paw could see that their pelts were matted and dull, speckled with scraps of moss and dried mud. Farther down, where the gully widened, the pale gray shape of Dustpelt's mate, Fern-cloud, was hunched over her two remaining kits.

"It's more sheltered down there," Cinderpelt explained, following Squirrelpaw's gaze. "But the queens still feel very exposed after being used to a nursery made of brambles. The apprentices make their nests in that hollow over there," she went on, lifting her muzzle to point at a dip in the rocks. Squirrelpaw recognized the brown fur of Shrewpaw, one of Ferncloud's first litter, fluffed up against the cold.

Squirrelpaw glanced at Brambleclaw, who gave her a tiny nod, but there was anxiety behind his eyes, and his shoulders were tense as he began to pad up the slope. Nervously she fol-lowed him. As she passed Ferncloud, the queen looked up at her, and her green eyes darkened with anger.

Squirrelpaw flinched. Did the Clan blame *them* for what had happened?

Some of the other cats had spotted them too. Thornclaw heaved himself out of a gully near the top of the slope, flatten-ing his ears; with a menacing hiss, Rainwhisker padded from a crevice at the edge of the rocks. The dark gray warrior's eyes gleamed, but not with any warmth or welcome for the return-ing cats.

Stormfur was scanning the rocks for Graystripe. Squirrel-paw followed his gaze, but there was no sign of the gray ThunderClan deputy, or of her own father. She fought down the urge to turn tail and flee back to the forest, back to the mountains even. She miserably met Brambleclaw's gaze. "They don't want us here," she whispered.

"They'll understand once we've explained," he promised. Squirrelpaw hoped he was right.

The sound of rapid pawsteps behind them made her spin around, startled. A pale gray warrior, Ashfur, skidded to a halt in front of her. She searched his eyes, afraid to find rage, but there was only surprise.

"You came back!" He held his tail high and reached out his muzzle to touch hers in greeting.

Squirrelpaw felt a rush of relief. At least one cat seemed glad they had returned.

Shrewpaw scrambled out of his hollow and raced across the rock toward them, with Whitepaw close behind.

"Shrewpaw!" Squirrelpaw cried, trying to sound as if she'd been no farther than Highstones, and for no more than a couple of sunrises. "How's the training going?"

"We've been working hard," Shrewpaw answered breathlessly as he reached her.

Whitepaw halted beside him. "We would have seen our first Gathering if the Twolegs hadn't destroyed Four—"

Ashfur shot the white she-cat a warning glance. "They won't have heard about that yet," he hissed.

"It's okay," Brambleclaw put in. "We know about Fourtrees. Webfoot told us."

"Webfoot?" Ashfur narrowed his eyes. "Have you been on WindClan territory?"

"We had to travel back that way," Squirrelpaw explained.

"Back from where?" meowed Shrewpaw, but Squirrelpaw didn't answer. She had seen Dustpelt and Mousefur emerging from their makeshift den. Sootfur crept out from a hollow beside them. All the warriors were moving closer now, like ghosts slipping through the shadows. Squirrelpaw stifled a shiver as they padded down the rock. She backed away, brushing against Brambleclaw's pelt and feeling Stormfur edge closer, equally wary. It reminded her of their first meeting with the cats from the Tribe of Rushing Water. Fear stabbed Squirrelpaw's heart as she realized that it was not just the forest that had changed. Her own Clan was different, too.

"So? Where did you go?" growled a distinctive voice. Frostfur had climbed out of the elders' gully above them. The old she-cat had lost much of the sleekness from her snow-white pelt, but Squirrelpaw still flinched under her icy stare.

"We've been on a long journey," Brambleclaw began.

"You don't look like it!" Ferncloud had left her kits and pushed her way to the front. "You look better fed than us."

Squirrelpaw tried not to feel guilty about the amount of fresh-kill she had caught on the journey. "Ferncloud, I heard about Larchkit, and I'm sorry. . . ."

Ferncloud was in no mood to listen. "How do we know you didn't just desert the Clan because you couldn't face a hungry leaf-bare with the rest of us?" she hissed.

Squirrelpaw heard Mousefur and Thornclaw mew in agreement, but this time anger overcame her fear. "How could you think such a thing?" she spat, her fur bristling.

"Well, your loyalty clearly lies outside the Clan!" growled Mousefur, staring at Stormfur.

"Our loyalty has always been to the Clan," Brambleclaw replied evenly. "That's why we left."

"Then what's a RiverClan warrior doing with you?" Dustpelt demanded.

"He has some news for Graystripe," Brambleclaw meowed. "He'll leave as soon as he's spoken to him."

"He'll leave now," Mousefur hissed, taking one pace forward.

Cinderpelt stepped between Mousefur and Brambleclaw. "Tell them about StarClan's prophecy," she urged.

"A prophecy? StarClan has spoken?" Squirrelpaw's Clanmates stared at her and Brambleclaw like hungry foxes.

"We must tell Firestar first," Squirrelpaw mewed quietly.

"Where's Firestar?" Brambleclaw called out.

"He's away hunting." It was Sandstorm's voice.

Squirrelpaw waited breathlessly, half-joyful and half-anxious, as the ginger she-cat padded toward her daughter and stopped a tail-length away to stare at her.

"We're back." Squirrelpaw searched her mother's expression for some sign of welcome.

"You're back," Sandstorm echoed wonderingly.

"We had to leave. StarClan gave us no choice." Brambleclaw defended Squirrelpaw, and she was grateful for the warmth of his flank as he pressed closer. She wanted to confess to her mother that StarClan had not sent the dreams to her, and that she had insisted on going along with Brambleclaw even though he had been reluctant to take her away from the Clan, but fear made the words stick in her throat.

Then Sandstorm's whiskers quivered and she bounded forward. "One of my kits has returned!" she mewed, rubbing her cheek against Squirrelpaw's with fierce love.

She felt a rush of relief. "I'm sorry I left without telling you, but—"

"You're back," Sandstorm meowed. "That's all I care about." Her warm breath grazed Squirrelpaw's muzzle. "I wondered if I'd ever see you again."

Squirrelpaw heard a soft purr trembling in her mother's throat. It reminded her of when she was a kit, curled in the nursery, her sister at her side. *Oh, Leafpaw! Where are you?*

A deep meow interrupted them. "It seems that I have my apprentice back," Dustpelt commented. He was as gaunt and hunted-looking as the other warriors, but his eyes were filled with warmth as he came over to greet her.

"Wherever you have been, you ate well," he remarked, his eyes widening as he looked at Squirrelpaw's sturdy muscles and glossy coat.

The tip of Brambleclaw's tail twitched. "We were lucky. There was plenty of fresh-kill where we traveled."

"Fresh-kill is what we need more than anything," mewed Dustpelt. "If you have found good hunting, the Clan should know where."

"It's a long way away," Brambleclaw warned.

Dustpelt flicked his ears. "Then it is not for us," he meowed. "We have made our home here. We will not let the Twolegs and their monsters drive us out again." A faint, defiant ripple of agreement sounded from the other cats.

Squirrelpaw stared at them in horror. But they had to leave! Midnight had told them that the Clans would have to find a new home—the dying warrior was going to show them the way—and Squirrelpaw had assumed that the fact that ThunderClan had been driven out of their camp would make the task of persuading them to leave a little easier.

Then she saw a figure on top of the rock, silhouetted against the rosy evening sky. Even though the shadows made it impossible to tell what color the cat's pelt was, there was no mistaking the powerful shoulders and the long tail held aloft in greeting.

"Firestar!" Squirrelpaw called.

"Squirrelpaw!" Firestar bounded down the rock, then halted. His whiskers twitched for a heartbeat before he thrust his head forward and licked Squirrelpaw's ear. She closed her eyes and purred, briefly forgetting the horror that was engulfing the forest. She was home, and that was all that mattered.

Firestar stepped back. "Where have you been?" he demanded.

"We've got so much to tell you," she answered quickly.

"We?" Firestar echoed. "Is Brambleclaw with you?"

"Yes, I'm here." Brambleclaw pushed his way through the cats and stood beside Squirrelpaw, dipping his head in respect. The rest of the Clan waited, their eyes glinting in the half-light, and even the wind dropped, as if the forest were holding its breath.

"Welcome home, Brambleclaw." Squirrelpaw thought she saw a guarded look in her father's eyes, and she felt a chill run through her.

A flurry of gray fur caught her eye, no more than a shadow flitting down the darkening slope. It was Graystripe. He skidded to a halt beside Firestar. "So, fire and tiger have returned!" he purred.

"Fire and tiger?" Squirrelpaw echoed. What did Graystripe mean?

"There's time to tell them about that later," Firestar murmured, his gaze flicking around the watching Clan.

"Oh, of course," Graystripe meowed, dipping his head. Then his eyes brightened once more. "Have you seen my two kits?" He glanced hopefully from Squirrelpaw to Brambleclaw.

Squirrelpaw nodded. "They went with us," she explained. "Stormfur—"

"I'm here." Stormfur pushed his way through the cats.

Graystripe's ears twitched in surprise and pleasure. "Stormfur!" He hurried forward and greeted his son with delighted purrs. "You're safe!" He glanced back at Squirrelpaw and Brambleclaw. "You're all safe. I can't believe it."

Squirrelpaw's heart tightened.

"Where's Feathertail?" Graystripe's gaze flicked past Stormfur as if he expected to see the pale-gray she-cat waiting at the foot of the rocks.

Squirrelpaw stared at her paws. Poor, poor Stormfur. He brought the worst news of all, to RiverClan as well as ThunderClan.

"Where is she?" Graystripe asked, sounding puzzled.

"She's not with us," Stormfur replied. He looked directly into his father's eyes. "She died on the journey."

Graystripe stared at him in disbelief.

Firestar lifted his chin. "Graystripe and Stormfur should be left to grieve in peace," he called to the Clan.

Squirrelpaw felt a ripple of gratitude toward her father. At least they could explain everything to Graystripe away from the scrutiny of the others. As Firestar guided their Clanmates away up the slope, she pressed closer to Brambleclaw.

Graystripe was gazing at the rock beneath his paws as though he held an adder there and dared not release it in case it bit him.

"We couldn't have saved her," Stormfur told him. He gently nudged his father's shoulder with his nose.

Graystripe swung his head toward Brambleclaw. "You should never have taken her away!" His eyes gleamed with anger.

Squirrelpaw flicked her tail. "It's not his fault! It was StarClan who chose Feathertail to go on the journey, not Brambleclaw!"

Graystripe closed his eyes. His shoulders sagged until he looked half his usual size. "I'm sorry," he murmured. "It's just so unfair. She was so much like Silverstream. . . ."

As his voice trailed away, Stormfur laid his muzzle against Graystripe's flank. "Feathertail died a brave and noble death, worthy of the greatest warrior," he told him. "StarClan chose her to go on the journey, and then the Tribe of Endless

Hunting chose her to fulfill a prophecy of their own. You would have been proud of her. She saved us all, not just the Tribe."

"The Tribe?" Graystripe echoed.

Squirrelpaw could hear the other cats milling about farther up the slope. Their murmuring grew louder and more impatient until Firestar silenced them, his voice ringing across the rock. "I know you all want to hear where Brambleclaw and Squirrelpaw have been," he meowed. "Let them tell me first; then I promise I will share everything with you."

"I want to hear why my apprentice left," Dustpelt growled.

"And what about the prophecy they mentioned?" Mousefur demanded. "We have to know what it is!"

Brambleclaw put his muzzle against Squirrelpaw's ear. "It sounds like we'd better join them." He looked at Stormfur. "Are you coming?"

"Thank you, Brambleclaw," Stormfur answered, "but I'd like to go home." He gazed at Graystripe. "They will tell you the whole story, but I wanted you to know you would have been very proud of Feathertail," he said. "She died to save us."

Graystripe blinked and did not reply.

Stormfur turned to Squirrelpaw and Brambleclaw. "I know it's going to be difficult," he murmured, "but we have to keep going with what we know to be right. Remember what Midnight told us. We're doing this for all our Clans."

Brambleclaw solemnly dipped his head. Squirrelpaw leaned forward to press her muzzle against Stormfur's cheek. "See you tomorrow at Fourtrees," she whispered. Her paws trembled with the pain of saying good-bye to one of her closest friends. For more than a moon she hadn't thought of him as RiverClan and herself as ThunderClan—they were merely Clan together, struggling to finish their journey and save all the cats in the forest.

As Stormfur padded down the slope, Squirrelpaw saw Mousefur and Thornclaw staring reproachfully at her from up on the slope. She knew how disloyal her affection for the RiverClan warrior must appear, but she was too sad and too tired to bother explaining what their journey meant for the six cats who had traveled to the sun-drown-place—and the five who had made it home.

"All right," Firestar meowed. "The senior warriors will join us to hear what Squirrelpaw and Brambleclaw have to say. And you, Cinderpelt." He gestured with his nose to the overhang where Squirrelpaw had seen Dustpelt and Mousefur sheltering. "We'll meet up there."

Snorting, Mousefur turned and began to climb the slope toward the overhang. Graystripe and Dustpelt followed her. As Firestar, Cinderpelt, and Sandstorm padded after them, Squirrelpaw stood still for a moment, letting the breeze ripple her fur. She didn't care how cold she got—in a way, the colder she was, the closer she came to sharing her Clanmates' suffering. There wouldn't need to be any strength in the wind for it to slice through their unkempt fur.

Suddenly she heard Thornclaw let out a low growl. She turned, alarmed, and saw Stormfur standing at the foot of the rocky slope with a plump fish in his mouth.

"What's the matter?" snarled Thornclaw. "Doesn't your own Clan want you back?"

The RiverClan warrior dropped the fish by his forepaws. "I have brought a gift from RiverClan."

"We don't need your gifts!" Frostfur spat.

There was a quiet padding of paws behind Squirrelpaw, and Firestar spoke. "It was kindly meant, Frostfur." There was a note of warning in his voice. "Thank you, Stormfur."

Stormfur didn't reply; he just looked up at the Thunder-Clan leader with his eyes full of sadness. His gaze rested briefly on Squirrelpaw; then he dipped his head and disappeared into the reeds that led down to the water, leaving the fish behind.

Squirrelpaw's belly growled with hunger. She had not eaten since they left the Twoleg territory on the far side of the moorland.

"You'll have to wait till later and see if you can track down a mouse or two," Firestar meowed, hearing her belly complain. "We must feed Ferncloud and the elders first. You're going to have to get used to hunger now that you are back with the Clan."

Squirrelpaw nodded, trying to readjust. She had grown used to hunting when she felt hungry, sharing only with her friends.

Firestar called down to Thornclaw, "Divide the fish between Ferncloud and the elders," before turning back toward the overhang.

As Squirrelpaw slipped beneath the jutting rock, she saw

that it reached back farther than she had expected. Smooth rock shielded the sides of the cave, but a chill wind swirled through the opening, stirring the jumbled scents of many cats. Her heart ached for the order and comfort of the old camp, and she closed her eyes, wishing that when she opened them again, she would see the thickly laced branches of the apprentices' den around her instead of cold, hard stone.

"All the warriors share this den," Dustpelt murmured in her ear, as if he had guessed what she was thinking. "There are not as many suitable sleeping places here."

Squirrelpaw opened her eyes and looked around the hollow with rage pulsing through her paws. Twolegs had driven her Clan to this! The least she could do was lead them to a place of safety, where there would be proper sleeping places and enough fresh-kill for all the cats.

"At least there's a little shelter," muttered Sandstorm, although her fluffed-up fur suggested she was chilled to the bone.

Firestar sat near the back of the hollow. Sandstorm and Graystripe settled on either side of him. The ThunderClan deputy was hunched over in his private misery; Cinderpelt sat beside him, concern clouding her eyes.

"Now," Firestar began, curling his tail over his paws. "Tell me everything from the beginning."

Squirrelpaw felt the questioning eyes of her Clanmates burn into her pelt. Brambleclaw swept his tail along her flank before facing Firestar.

"StarClan visited me in a dream and told me to go to the sun-drown-place," he explained. "I-I didn't know if I should believe it at first, but StarClan sent the same dream to a cat from each of the other Clans: Crowpaw of WindClan, Feathertail of RiverClan, and Tawnypelt of ShadowClan."

Firestar tipped his head to one side as Brambleclaw went on. "We were all told to make the journey to hear what Midnight told us."

"What *midnight* told you?" Dustpelt echoed, bemused.

Firestar's green gaze rested on Squirrelpaw, and she forced herself not to duck away. "Did you have this dream too?" he asked.

"No," she confessed. "But I had to . . . I wanted to go. . . ." She searched for the words to explain why she left, but she did not want to tell Firestar that she had been trying to escape their quarrel. She fell silent, hanging her head.

"I'm glad she came with us!" Brambleclaw burst out. "She was equal to any of the warriors!"

After what seemed like nine lifetimes, Firestar nodded. "Carry on, Brambleclaw."

"We headed toward the sun-drown-place, thanks to Ravenpaw's help. He'd heard about the place of endless water from other rogue cats."

"It was such a long way," Squirrelpaw put in. "We thought we were lost so many times."

"Ravenpaw told us which direction to go, but we didn't know exactly how to get there," Brambleclaw explained. "But

StarClan had sent us, so we had to keep going."

"Even though we didn't know *why* they had sent us," Squirrelpaw added.

Brambleclaw flexed his claws, making a tiny scraping sound on the hard floor. "We were only trying to do our duty to the Clan," he murmured.

"A loner helped us through Twolegplace," Squirrelpaw went on, remembering Purdy's rather erratic sense of direction.

"And eventually we came to the sun-drown-place. It was like nothing we'd seen before," Brambleclaw mewed. "High sandy cliffs with caves underneath, and dark blue water for as far as any cat could see, endlessly washing up and down the shore. The crashing water frightened us at first, it was so loud."

"Then Brambleclaw fell in. I rescued him, but we were in a cave, and then we found Midnight." Squirrelpaw's words tumbled out incoherently.

"What do you mean, you 'found midnight'?" Dustpelt demanded.

Brambleclaw shuffled his paws. "Midnight is a badger," he meowed at last. "StarClan wanted us to find her because she could tell us what StarClan wanted us to know."

"And what did she tell you?" Firestar's ears twitched as he spoke.

"That the Twolegs would destroy the whole forest and leave us to starve," Squirrelpaw mewed, her heart suddenly hammering as hard as the first time she had heard Midnight's warning.

"She told us to lead you away from the forest and find a new home," Brambleclaw added.

"New home?" Sandstorm stared at him in disbelief.

"So we should leave the forest just because a badger we've never heard of thinks it would be a good idea?" Dustpelt meowed.

Squirrelpaw closed her eyes. Was ThunderClan going to ignore Midnight's warning? Had their journey and Feathertail's death been for nothing?

"And did she say how we should find this place?" Graystripe sat up and leaned closer, the tip of his tail twitching.

Midnight's words echoed in Squirrelpaw's mind once more and she found herself repeating them out loud. "'You will not be without a guide'—that's what she said. 'When return, stand on Great Rock when Silverpelt shines above. A dying warrior the way will show.'"

"Have you been to the Great Rock yet to look for this sign?" Firestar asked.

Brambleclaw shook his head. "We were going to meet there tomorrow with Tawnypelt, Stormfur, and Crowpaw. We were going to bring our leaders, if we could persuade them to come. . . ."

"Are you going to go?" Mousefur flattened her ears.

"Nothing would keep me away," Firestar replied.

Dustpelt stared wide-eyed at his leader. "You're not actually thinking of taking the Clan out of the forest, are you?"

"Right now, I don't know what I'm going to do," Firestar admitted. "But I'm not sure the Clan can survive leaf-bare."

He met Dustpelt's stare, and for a moment Squirrelpaw saw his eyes flash. "I cannot let my Clan suffer if there's anything I can do to prevent it. We cannot ignore this message, however it came to us. It may be our only hope of survival. If there is a sign, I want to see it for myself."

He straightened and looked at Brambleclaw. "Tomorrow, I will go with you to Fourtrees."

CHAPTER 5

"Sasha!" Mistyfoot called again. "Is that you?"

There was no reply.

Leafpaw pressed her muzzle against the web and peered out. She had heard of Sasha many times, and was curious to see the rogue she-cat who had taken Tigerstar as her mate and given birth to Mothwing and Hawkfrost while staying with RiverClan. But in the half-light of the wooden nest, she could only just make out Sasha's tawny pelt huddled at the back of the cage the Twoleg had just brought in.

"Sasha, are you okay?" Mistyfoot called more urgently.

"Give her time to recover," Cody advised. "The new ones are always quiet."

"I don't need time to recover," came a furious hiss. "How dare they put me in here? If I could get out, I'd rip that Twoleg to shreds!"

"What were you doing in the forest?" Mistyfoot asked.

"I wanted to see my kits," Sasha replied. "I had heard about the Twolegs destroying the forest, and I wanted to make sure they were safe."

"I saw Mothwing not long ago!" Leafpaw mewed. "She was

fine. She's going to be a medicine cat."

"Who's that speaking?" Sasha called.

"I'm Leafpaw, ThunderClan's apprentice medicine cat," Leafpaw told her. "I'm friends with Mothwing."

"Do you know Hawkfrost too?" Sasha demanded. "Is he safe?"

Leafpaw did not answer. Her paws prickled as she pictured Sasha's other kit. He had an icy-blue gaze like the sky in leaf-bare, and his shoulders were as broad and powerful as those of a warrior of twice his age and experience. Last time Leafpaw had met him, he had threatened to drag Sorreltail back to the RiverClan camp because she had strayed across the border by mistake. Luckily, Mothwing had persuaded him to let Sorreltail go.

Mistyfoot called from her cage, "Hawkfrost was fine when I saw him last."

"Thank goodness," Sasha breathed.

The relief in her voice surprised Leafpaw. "She sounds as worried as a Clan queen would be!" she whispered to Cody through the web that separated them.

"Of course." Cody had been listening quietly to the exchange. "She's talking about her kits—she's a she-cat just like any other, after all."

"But she gave them away to be raised in RiverClan!" Leafpaw exclaimed, almost forgetting to keep her voice low.

"Why didn't she let her own Clan raise them?" Cody sounded puzzled.

"Sasha's not a Clan cat," Leafpaw explained. "She's a rogue."

"That's right, call me names just because I choose not to live among the rest of you," Sasha growled, overhearing. "Not that I care, as long as my kits are safe."

"I'm sorry," Cody apologized. "This is such a small nest it's hard not to get involved." She glanced sideways at the cage next to hers where a tattered black rogue crouched without giving any sign that he had heard their conversation. "With some cats, at least," she added pointedly. Leafpaw knew that Cody had been trying to befriend the black tom but had not managed to get any answer from him except his name—Coal.

"You're a kittypet, aren't you?" Sasha asked Cody bluntly. "You sound too polite for a rogue, and you look too fat to be a Clan cat."

Leafpaw saw Cody bristle. "Cody's a friend!" she mewed, leaping to her defense.

"I didn't say she wasn't," Sasha meowed. "I'm just trying to work out who's who in this place."

Mistyfoot explained: "They're mostly rogues, but there are a few other forest cats here." Gorsetail, Brightheart, and Cloudtail meowed greetings as Mistyfoot went on, "Cody's the only kittypet, as far as we know."

"Have any of you worked out a way to escape from this foxhole?" Sasha asked.

"Not yet," Mistyfoot admitted.

"Even StarClan hasn't given us a clue," Leafpaw added.

"StarClan!" In the shadows, she saw Sasha curl her lip. "Do you Clan cats still believe in that nonsense after what's happened to the forest?"

"Of course we do!" Leafpaw hissed.

"Well, say a prayer for me, little one," Sasha sighed unexpectedly. "I think we're all going to need as much help as we can get."

Sunhigh passed, and the tepid warmth of the afternoon sun began to fade.

"Here comes the Twoleg again," Cody called to the other cats.

Over the distant grumbling of the Twoleg monsters, Leafpaw heard footsteps outside and instinctively crouched at the back of her cage. The nest door opened and the Twoleg came in carrying the food pellets.

"There's no way you'll persuade that Twoleg to let us out of here by purring at it," Leafpaw whispered to Cody as the Twoleg began opening the cages and putting in more food.

"I guess not," Cody shrugged. "But it won't hurt to make him trust me."

As she spoke a hiss exploded from the cage next to her. The Twoleg leaped backward from Coal's open door. Blood trickled down its forepaw as it stamped around the nest, spitting in rage. Leafpaw strained to see Coal through Cody's cage. She could just make out his shadowy outline as he flattened himself against the floor. The blood pulsed in her ears as she glanced over her shoulder at the Twoleg. It had stopped screeching and was staring menacingly at Coal. Suddenly, with a vicious cry, it thrust its paw back into the cage, and

Leafpaw heard the tom screech in pain. Muttering, the Twoleg slammed the door shut.

Leafpaw shuddered. What had the Twoleg done?

When the Twoleg opened Cody's door and tipped pellets into her pot, the kittypet shied away. She was not purring at it now.

As soon as the Twoleg had gone, Leafpaw yowled, "Are you okay, Coal?"

A muffled groan came from the cage beyond Cody's. "That stinking Twoleg!"

Leafpaw sniffed the air and smelled the warm tang of blood.

"It looks bad," Cody whispered to Leafpaw. "There's blood on the floor of his cage."

"Where are you hurt?" Leafpaw asked Coal.

"I've cut my leg," replied the rogue. "That badger-pawed Twoleg shoved me against something sharp."

Leafpaw thought quickly. What did Cinderpelt use to stop bleeding? "Can any cat reach a cobweb?" she called. "Come on; we have to help him!"

"There's one near me," answered Gorsetail. "I think I can reach it. Hang on."

Peering down, Leafpaw saw Gorsetail's tawny paw reach out from a cage below her. A large cobweb stretched from the floor of the nest to the top of his cage. He reached toward it, squeezing his foreleg through the hole in the side of his cage. Finally he managed to plunge his paw into the thick tangle and drag it down. Twisting his foreleg around, Gorsetail held the cobweb as far up toward Leafpaw as he could.

Leafpaw flattened herself against the cage and pushed her paw through the shiny floor. It scraped against her fur but she clenched her teeth and forced her leg through a little more until she could take the wad of sticky cobweb from Gorsetail. She pulled it quickly into her cage and then began passing it to Cody. "Give him this!" she urged, squeezing the last pieces of cobweb through with her paws.

Cody nodded, unable to talk because she was holding a wad of cobweb in her mouth. As she dragged it into her cage, some of it stuck to the sides of the hole, wasting a few of the precious threads.

"Be careful!" Leafpaw gasped.

The voice of a rogue beneath them called anxiously up. "There's blood dripping through the top of my cage! That cat's badly hurt."

Leafpaw's heart beat faster. "Coal! Are you okay?"

"It won't stop bleeding," Coal replied, his voice trembling.

"Take the cobweb from Cody!" Leafpaw ordered. "Press it against the wound for as long as you can."

She heard Cody breathing hard as the kittypet passed the cobweb through to the next cage, followed by the sound of Coal's paws scrabbling on the blood-soaked floor.

"Don't panic, Coal!" she mewed. "Just press the cobweb onto the wound."

"It's already soaked with blood!" Coal panted.

"That's okay," Leafpaw reassured him. "It'll still stop any more blood coming. Just hold it in place!"

She waited. Silence gripped the nest. Leafpaw's head began to spin, and she forced herself to take slow, deep breaths.

"Is he okay?" Brightheart called after a while.

"The blood's stopped dripping on me!" reported the rogue from underneath Coal's cage.

"Coal?" Leafpaw called. "How is it?"

A ragged sigh came from Coal's cage. "That's better," he murmured. "It didn't even sting."

Leafpaw felt a rush of relief. "Keep the cobweb there for a bit longer," she told him. "Then you can give the cut a gentle lick to clean it. Not too fierce—you don't want it to start bleeding again."

"Well done, Leafpaw," Cody whispered from her cage.

Leafpaw blinked. For the first time since she had been captured, she didn't feel entirely helpless. Closing her eyes, she sent a prayer of thanks to StarClan. She had never helped a rogue before, but she knew her warrior ancestors would approve. Loyalty to one Clan alone was no longer the way to survive.

She realized her belly was growling with hunger. She might as well follow Cody's advice and keep her strength up. Trying not to breathe in the horrible stench, she nibbled at a few of the foul pellets the Twoleg had left. *I suppose I should be grateful for the easy meal*, she thought as she forced herself to crunch the dry morsels.

"These are disgusting," she muttered.

"Not the best I've tasted," agreed Cody. "My housefolk tried to give me something similar once, but I soon let them know what I thought, and they never gave them to me again."

Leafpaw nearly choked with surprise. "You can make your Twolegs do what you want?"

"They're not so hard to train," Cody mewed. She sat up and began washing her paws.

Sasha called across the nest, "Can you train the mongrel that hurt Coal to be gentler?"

"I doubt it," Cody answered. "These workfolk are nothing like my housefolk."

Leafpaw saw Brightheart's face appear behind the mesh of her cage. The ginger patches on her white fur looked almost black in the dim light, and it was impossible to see that one side of her face had been terribly scarred by a dog attack many moons ago. "What do you think they're going to do with us?" she whispered.

"Perhaps they're going to turn us into kittypets?" Leafpaw suggested. Much as she disliked the idea, at least that might give them a chance to escape and return to the Clan.

There was a snort from Sasha's cage. "I don't think so," she rasped. "We're hardly the sort of fluffy, pampered cats that Twolegs go for."

Leafpaw glanced at Cody, hoping she wouldn't take offense, but to her surprise the kittypet was nodding.

"Sasha's right," she agreed. "These folk don't care about

cats—Clan, rogue, or kittypet. Trust me, I know the sort of—what do you call them? Twolegs?—that make good housefolk. These just want to get rid of us."

Leafpaw tried to swallow, but her mouth had suddenly become too dry, and the pellets she had eaten seemed to be lodged halfway down her throat. Trying not to bring them up again, she lapped a few mouthfuls of slimy water. She fought the urge to curl up in the back of her cage and lose herself in dreams. She could not rely on StarClan to get her out of this place. She had faith that her warrior ancestors were watching the destruction of the forest, but her instincts told her they were powerless against Twoleg cruelty; it was her own wits she would have to rely on now. She had to find a way to escape. She couldn't let Cody or her Clanmates down.

She remembered Gorsetail stretching his paw out of his cage to reach the cobweb. "Cody," she mewed. "You told me you tried reaching the catch that keeps the cage locked."

"Yes, but I couldn't get a grip on it," Cody confirmed.

"What about the rest of you?" Leafpaw called out to the other cats. "Can anyone undo his catch?"

"Mine's too stiff," replied Gorsetail.

"My web is ripped," Cloudtail reported. "I can almost get two paws out, but I can't reach the catch."

"You're all wasting your time," Sasha growled. "Face it, there's no way out of here."

Outside, the noise of the Twoleg monsters rumbled on, making the nest shudder. Leafpaw couldn't believe there was no way out of the nest, whatever Sasha thought. If she gave up, there would be no hope left at all. As she listened to the Twolegs calling gruffly to one another in the growing dusk outside, she reached through the web at the front of her cage and began to claw at the catch that held it closed.

CHAPTER 6

The waning moon cast just enough light through the leafless branches
to make the forest glow with eerie silver. Frost traced the outline of the dying ferns as Squirrelpaw padded through the
trees beside Brambleclaw.

"It'll be cold at Fourtrees," she fretted, hoping that her sister was warm, wherever she was.

"But at least it's clear," Brambleclaw answered in a low
voice. "Silverpelt will be shining."

They were following Firestar and Cinderpelt through the
forest. The pace was slower than the two younger cats had
been used to on their long journey, but Cinderpelt was still
struggling to keep up. Cold and hunger had made her limp
worse than usual.

"If there is a sign," Squirrelpaw wondered out loud, "how
long do you think it'll be before we go?" She wanted a chance
to find her sister before the Clans left the forest.

"I don't know," Brambleclaw replied. "You saw what happened last night. Firestar can't force the Clan to leave. He's
bound by the warrior code as much as any cat, and even though
he's our leader, he has to obey the will of the Clan."

Squirrelpaw's belly tightened as she remembered the Clan's reaction. Beneath the stars, huddled against the icy wind that whipped the rock, Firestar had told them the message she and Brambleclaw had brought back from StarClan. A shocked cry had rippled around the gathered cats.

"We can't leave the forest!" Frostfur had wailed. "We'll all die."

"We'll die if we stay!" Sorreltail had pointed out.

"But this is our home." Speckletail's rasping mew had cracked as she'd raised her voice.

At least Shrewpaw had sounded eager. "When are we going?" he'd asked.

But the memory of Hollykit's piteous mew made Squirrel-paw's pelt prickle even now. "We don't have to go, do we?" the kit had cried.

"What if Dustpelt is right?" Squirrelpaw hissed to Bram-bleclaw as they leaped over an abandoned foxhole, a yawning black mouth amid the shadows. "What he said in the den made sense—why should any cat follow the advice of a badger they'd never met?"

"But *StarClan* sent us to see Midnight," Brambleclaw argued. "What Midnight told us must be true."

Squirrelpaw guessed he was trying to convince himself as much as her.

"We just have to hope that we see the sign at Fourtrees tonight," she said. "If StarClan has something to say to the Clan—to *any* of the Clans—it's not up to us to prove it." She trembled to think what Midnight had meant by 'a dying warrior,' but if the sign told them what to do next, they might still be able to save the Clans.

Their journey to Fourtrees took longer than usual, not just because of the slow pace but because they had to skirt the parts of the forest that the Twolegs had ruined, keeping low as they passed swath after swath of mud and felled trees. After a while, Squirrelpaw stopped looking at the empty, ravaged spaces.

"How can any cat think this is still our home?" she murmured.

Brambleclaw just shook his head and padded after Firestar toward the top of the slope that led down into Fourtrees.

For a moment, it felt like the start of every other Gathering Squirrelpaw had attended, and when she closed her eyes she could almost hear the murmur of cats below, sharing tongues as the four Clans met in peace under the full moon. But there was no full moon, and this was not a Gathering. Her eyes snapped open, and she peered over the crest of the rise. As her eyes adjusted to the dark, her breath caught in her throat. Even though Webfoot had warned them that the Twolegs had cut down the four great oak trees, Squirrelpaw hadn't let herself imagine what it would look like. Not in nine lifetimes could she have imagined anything as terrible as what she saw now.

The four giant oaks that had once guarded the Great Rock had completely disappeared; even their stumps had been torn from the ground. Their trunks lay in pieces, neatly sliced by giant claws. Squirrelpaw could smell the bitter sap that seeped like blood from each mutilated piece of wood.

The heart of the forest—and the roots of life for the four Clans—had been ripped out. Nothing would ever be the same again.

Squirrelpaw wondered how their warrior ancestors could bear to look down from Silverpelt at the ruined clearing. "Webfoot told us they had destroyed Fourtrees, but I didn't think . . ." Her voice trailed away as her father looked at her, sympathy in his eyes.

"Come on," he hissed, leading them down the slope.

As she picked her way over the sliced trees, sticky sap clung to Squirrelpaw's fur, and tree dust wafted up to sting her eyes and tickle her throat. Blinking, she scanned the clearing, then stared in disbelief. "The Great Rock is gone!"

Brambleclaw stopped dead and followed her gaze. "How could that happen?" he gasped. He bounded over to peer into the huge hole that gaped where the rock had once stood.

"I-I thought it had roots like a tree," Squirrelpaw murmured dazedly, looking down into the hole. "I thought they reached down so far that nothing could ever move it."

"Over here!" Firestar called from the side of the clearing.

He and Cinderpelt were standing almost belly-deep in the mud beside a vast gray stone. It looked clumsy and awkward, and the shape was unfamiliar—after a few moments, Squirrelpaw realized it was upside down—but it was definitely the Great Rock.

Brambleclaw thrashed his tail. "Twolegs did this!" he spat. "They must have used their monsters to move it."

In the cold, unfeeling moonlight, Squirrelpaw could see gouge marks scarring the rock where the monster's talons had scratched it. This was worse than losing every single tree in the forest; every cat knew that trees were living things that grew old and died just like they did, but the Great Rock had been there for moons upon moons before the cats came, and should have lasted for uncountable moons more.

A harsh voice rang out across the clearing. "There will be no more Gatherings now." Squirrelpaw recognized Blackstar's meow, and shadowy movements on the logs around them told her what the scent of the sap had disguised—that the other cats were here already. Remembering Mousefur's dire warnings of an ambush, she looked closely in the half-light and spotted, with a twinge of relief, Tawnypelt, Crowpaw, and Stormfur among them.

"Tawnypelt!" Brambleclaw ran over to welcome his sister. Squirrelpaw heard a disapproving growl rumble in Firestar's throat, and her paws pricked with frustration. How could he question their loyalty when he knew they were only working together to save the Clans?

Each cat had brought their leader and medicine cat. But Squirrelpaw felt a jolt of surprise when she saw that two other cats had joined them: Mudfur, the elderly RiverClan medicine cat, had brought his apprentice, Mothwing, and Mothwing's brother, Hawkfrost, had come too. Squirrelpaw recognized them from Leafpaw's descriptions. The dark brown tom wasn't looking at the Great Rock but was watching the other cats, his ice-blue eyes expressionless in the moonlight.

"It cannot be true!" Mudfur hissed, staring at the Great Rock. Every hair on his pelt stood on end, and his tail quivered like a near-dead mouse. Mothwing tried to calm him with rapid licks on his shoulder, but he did not stop shaking. Cinderpelt picked her way awkwardly across the logs, her injured leg barely touching the ground, and pressed her body against his.

Squirrelpaw followed her father as he joined the other cats at the bottom of the Great Rock. She glanced at Crowpaw, Stormfur, and Tawnypelt, desperate to know how their Clans had received them, but they stood silently beside their leaders.

"How will we climb it now?" Tallstar asked, his voice trembling as he stared up the sheer rock face towering above them. Even half-hidden in shadow, the black-and-white WindClan leader looked so frail that Squirrelpaw was surprised he had managed the journey here at all.

"These marks will give us a grip," Leopardstar said, stretching her forepaws up the smooth rock to where the monsters' talons had scraped long wounds into the hard stone.

She pushed her hind paws into the mud and scrabbled upward. Blackstar clawed his way after her to the top of the rock. He looked strong and determined, but his dull white pelt hung from his bony frame as he climbed. Tallstar watched them, his thin frame seeming smaller than ever.

"I'll follow you," Firestar offered.

Tallstar nodded and scrambled up toward the lowest gouge mark, clinging to the slippery rock with his claws. Firestar sprang after him, propping the WindClan leader with his shoulder to stop him sliding back down again.

"Shouldn't we climb the Great Rock too, to see Midnight's dying warrior?" Squirrelpaw whispered as the leaders disappeared over the top and the medicine cats went around to the other side.

"I don't think it matters who sees it," Brambleclaw answered, but his eyes were clouded with worry.

"She didn't say it had to be us," Stormfur chipped in. "She just said 'stand on the Great Rock.'"

"At least we have a chance to talk now," Tawnypelt murmured. "Blackstar says he is ready to leave the forest."

Squirrelpaw blinked. "Really? That's great!" She wished her own homecoming had been so straightforward. "Firestar hasn't decided yet."

Tawnypelt flicked her ears. "To be honest, I think Blackstar had already decided to go, even before I came back with Midnight's warning."

"But what did he say when you told him? Did he believe you?" Squirrelpaw demanded.

The tortoiseshell warrior didn't reply.

Brambleclaw pressed closer to his sister. "Did they give you a hard time?"

Tawnypelt shook her head. "They acted like I was a stranger." Sadness glimmered in her eyes. "Tallpoppy's kits were frightened of me."

"It wasn't easy for us either," Squirrelpaw mewed. "It's as if we're not part of the Clan any more."

"Of course we're part of the Clan," Brambleclaw reassured

her. "It'll just take a while for things to get back to normal."

Stormfur snorted. "Nothing's ever going to get back to normal!" he spat. "I've seen what the Twolegs have done to WindClan and ThunderClan territory, and I can imagine it's the same in ShadowClan." He glanced at Tawnypelt, and she nodded grimly. "Even though they haven't reached River-Clan territory yet, everything's changed," Stormfur went on, lashing his tail. "Mistyfoot's gone missing, and Hawkfrost is deputy now."

"Mistyfoot's missing?" Squirrelpaw gasped.

"Was she taken by Twolegs?" asked Brambleclaw.

Stormfur looked puzzled. "Why would Twolegs take her?"

"They took Leafpaw!" Squirrelpaw told him. "We know what happened because Sorreltail was there, although she got away."

"Gorsetail's missing too," Crowpaw mewed, his gaze flicking from one cat to another.

"No ShadowClan cats have been taken, but I'd guess it's only a matter of time," Tawnypelt mewed. "And meanwhile the Twolegs have invaded so much of our territory that we're starving. There's hardly any prey left, and leaf-bare's only just begun."

Brambleclaw sat down carefully on the muddy ground. "Whether it's Midnight's message or starvation that drives the Clans out, I don't see any way we can stay in the forest."

"But the Twolegs haven't touched RiverClan territory," Stormfur reminded him. "And Hawkfrost thinks they never will. He pretty much called me a traitor for being concerned about the other Clans, and he said I should never have gone on the journey." His amber eyes glistened with sadness. "He said Feathertail would still be alive if I hadn't let her get caught up in other Clans' problems."

"It wasn't the journey that killed Feathertail. It was staying with the Tribe so long," hissed Crowpaw.

Stormfur flinched and looked down at his paws.

"We had to help them!" Squirrelpaw stared at Crowpaw, puzzled. She had found him arrogant and impatient at the start of the journey, but he had become much easier to be around as they traveled, and by the end of their adventure she would have considered him one of her closest friends. Now he was as prickly as ever. Did their journey, the importance of the message they all had to take to their Clans, mean nothing to him?

"Crowpaw?" Brambleclaw meowed. "What did WindClan say when you told them?"

"They accepted Midnight's words without question," he muttered. "It's our last hope of survival." His voice was flat and dull, like stone. "I didn't think the Clan could be suffering any more than when I left, but it is. There's nothing left to eat on the moors at all. A bird if we're lucky. Sometimes a mouse, just one to feed the whole Clan. WindClan kits have *never* gone hungry like this before."

"So Tallstar wants to leave?"

Crowpaw lifted his eyes and met Brambleclaw's gaze. "Oh, yes," he agreed. "He wants the Clan to go as soon as we can. His greatest fear"—he broke off and swallowed—"his greatest fear is that we're not strong enough to make it."

"Oh, Crowpaw!" Squirrelpaw exclaimed, immediately for-giving his harsh words to Stormfur. "I'm so sorry."

"We don't need your pity," growled the WindClan appren-tice. "I will fight with all the strength I have to make sure my Clan survives." He glared at her, his eyes cold.

Squirrelpaw felt a surge of anger rise in her belly. "What are you talking about? You're acting as if you're the only one who can save your Clan! Don't you remember that we're in this together? Or have you forgotten there were six of us on that journey?"

"Squirrelpaw!" Brambleclaw stopped her with a flick of his tail. "We mustn't fight now."

Squirrelpaw grumpily fell silent. Crowpaw looked away, but he flexed his claws, tearing at the cold earth.

Tawnypelt gazed up at the rock. There was no sign of their leaders. They were hidden behind the brow of the rock's tow-ering summit. "Everything would be easier if we knew where we were meant to be going," she mewed. "Do you think the sign will come?"

"Perhaps we're too late," murmured Stormfur. "We were a long time in the mountains." He glanced at Crowpaw. "Believe me, I wish we hadn't stayed."

"We *all* agreed at the time," Brambleclaw reminded him.

Crowpaw stared at his paws without saying anything.

There was a yowl from above them, and Firestar's call rang around the hollow. "We should wait awhile longer!"

"Why? What's the point?" growled Blackstar. His bony

frame appeared, silhouetted against the stars, on the edge of the rock. "We have wasted our time coming here. There will be no sign tonight. And do we really need one to tell us that the forest is being destroyed? Just look around you!"

Squirrelpaw and the others backed away as the Shadow-Clan leader bounded down the rock and landed in the mud beside them. Leopardstar followed him.

"But it's not even moonhigh!" Firestar protested, peering down from the top of the rock.

Leopardstar looked up at him. "Even if StarClan does send a sign about leaving the forest, it's no concern of RiverClan's," she meowed.

However frustrated she was by Leopardstar's selfishness, Squirrelpaw could understand why she wasn't as troubled as the other leaders. Her glossy coat proved that she and her Clanmates were as well fed as ever, and their sleep wasn't disturbed by fear of monsters snarling and munching their way into the camp.

"Hunger will soon make her change her mind," Crowpaw hissed.

"But surely you want to see what StarClan thinks we should do?" Firestar argued.

"It's too cold to wait any longer," meowed Blackstar. "My fur is thinner than I'd like these days—and that's not a sign from StarClan. It's the fault of those fox-hearted Twolegs stealing my Clan's prey."

"You can't leave yet!" Firestar yowled as the ShadowClan leader clambered away over the logs.

"There'll be no sign here tonight," Blackstar called over his shoulder. "Look at this place! It's ruined."

"StarClan will not desert us!" Firestar leaped down from the rock and scrambled awkwardly over the logs to the Shadow-Clan leader.

Blackstar faced him, his pelt bristling. "I did not say StarClan had deserted us! But my Clan would rather rely on their leader's judgment than on the muddled rumors of some inexperienced warriors and a *badger.*"

"But StarClan is going to show us the way!" Tallstar slithered over the edge of the Great Rock, half scrambling, half falling down its side. Crowpaw leaped forward, reaching up with his forepaws to soften his landing. Tallstar hit the mud clumsily but staggered to his paws, shaking Crowpaw off. "They will know where we can find new territories, far away from these dangers," he insisted.

"We are perfectly capable of finding a new home for ourselves." There was a chilling certainty in Blackstar's words.

"You have somewhere in mind already, don't you?" Cinderpelt looked up from where she crouched beside Mudfur.

"We are going to live in Twolegplace where BloodClan used to rule," he announced. "I still have one of their former warriors among my elders. He will show us the best places to find food and shelter. Now Scourge is dead, we'll be the strongest cats there."

"You can't do that!" Firestar protested. "That will leave only three Clans in the forest!"

"Soon there won't *be* a forest," Blackstar pointed out grimly.

"Only the bodies of dead cats. This is one battle in which I cannot see how it would help us to join with other Clans. It's not a matter of fighting an enemy, but of finding enough prey to feed the mouths we already have. I'm sorry, but we go alone."

He turned to leave, but Firestar stood in his way. Blackstar curled his lip to reveal sharp teeth.

"We can't let them fight!" Squirrelpaw hissed to Brambleclaw.

"I know," he agreed. He leaped over the logs to Firestar's side. "Firestar, you have to persuade ShadowClan to come with us! That's what StarClan wants. If there isn't a sign, like Midnight said, then we should go back to the sun-drown-place and ask her if she knows where we should go."

"You want us to go to a strange place just because you think StarClan sent *you* there?" Leopardstar snarled. "Since when do you make decisions for all the Clans?" Her gaze swept over Squirrelpaw, Tawnypelt, and Stormfur. "In fact, why should we trust any of you? You are all part ThunderClan!"

Tawnypelt unsheathed her claws. "Are you questioning my loyalty to my Clan?"

"My sister died on the journey to fetch this message!" Stormfur hissed.

Squirrelpaw wondered if StarClan was watching them and thinking that these quarrelsome Clans didn't *deserve* to be saved.

"Stop!" rasped a feeble voice, and Tallstar padded unevenly over. "If we fight, the sign will never come!"

"How many times do I have to tell you? We don't need a sign," growled Blackstar. "ShadowClan is going to leave the forest, and we already know where to go."

Firestar didn't argue with him. Instead, he turned to Leopardstar. "What do you plan to do?"

"RiverClan has no need to travel to some distant place on the word of a few dreaming warriors," Leopardstar replied. "The river is still full of fish. It would be stupid for us to leave. The other Clans' troubles are not ours to worry about."

"But if our troubles are not yours as well, why was Feathertail sent by StarClan with the other cats?" Cinderpelt challenged quietly.

"Only Feathertail can answer that, and she is dead," Leopardstar retorted.

Hawkfrost climbed up beside his leader. "If you can't survive in the forest anymore, then I agree that you should leave," he meowed, his gaze flicking around the cats to include Tallstar. "After all, what sort of leader would let his Clan starve?"

Squirrelpaw was rather taken aback by the bold way he addressed the other Clan leaders. After all, he wasn't much older than her.

Brambleclaw glared at Hawkfrost. "You just want us to leave so you can steal our territory!"

"If you aren't here, then you won't need it anymore."

Brambleclaw bristled. "You might feel differently if you were truly Clanborn."

"Show some respect, Brambleclaw!" Firestar snapped. "Hawkfrost is not responsible for his birth."

Brambleclaw opened his mouth, ready to argue, then seemed to think better of it and looked down at his paws. Squirrelpaw thought she saw Hawkfrost's whiskers twitch with satisfaction and felt a surge of anger on Brambleclaw's behalf. How dared he gloat?

"This is getting us nowhere," Tallstar meowed fretfully.

"The four Clans must remain together," Firestar insisted. "We have lived beneath Silverpelt for as long as any cat remembers. We share the same ancestors. How could StarClan watch over us if we are separated?" But Blackstar had jumped down from the tree trunk and was padding away, signaling to Littlecloud, the ShadowClan medicine cat, to join him.

Tawnypelt looked uneasily at her friends. "I have to go," she whispered to Squirrelpaw.

"What about the sign?" Squirrelpaw reminded her. She shivered, and not just from the cold. Where was the sign that was supposed to save them?

Doubt flickered in the ShadowClan warrior's gaze. "I'm sorry; I can't wait." She hurried after Blackstar and Littlecloud. The hollow felt even emptier and more exposed without the three ShadowClan cats.

"Good luck, Firestar," Leopardstar meowed. She looked over to where Mothwing was crouched beside Mudfur. "Is he well enough to travel?"

"Of course I am!" Mudfur rasped, struggling to his paws. "I made it here, didn't I?"

"Then come," Leopardstar ordered, and, turning away, she led her cats from the clearing.

Stormfur brushed against Squirrelpaw's pelt as he passed. "I'll try to speak to you and Brambleclaw soon," he whispered.

"What can we do without the sign?" Squirrelpaw hissed frantically.

Stormfur flashed her a look of despair. "I don't know," he said. He gazed back at the Great Rock, dragged from its ancient seat. "Perhaps StarClan has no power here anymore."

Squirrelpaw stared at him in horror. Could that be true?

Firestar watched the RiverClan cats leave. "I cannot persuade them." He sighed.

"Then we two must go alone," Tallstar wheezed. He sat down to catch his breath. "Firestar," he croaked, "I must find new territory for my Clan before the next full moon. We are starving." Squirrelpaw felt her heart twist with pity as he went on. "But we are too weak to make the journey alone. Travel with us, Firestar. Help us like you did when you brought WindClan back from exile, after Brokenstar drove us out."

Firestar miserably twitched his ears. "We can't leave without the other two Clans. There have always been four Clans in the forest, and wherever we end up, four Clans must be there as well. How else can we be sure the fifth Clan will come with us?"

The fifth Clan? Squirrelpaw wondered what her father meant. She glanced at Brambleclaw, but he looked as puzzled as she felt.

"StarClan will be with us always," Tallstar argued, and Squirrelpaw understood: StarClan was the fifth Clan.

She saw a glimmer of anger enter the WindClan leader's

tired eyes. "You are too proud, Firestar," he warned. "I can tell ThunderClan is on the brink of starvation just like Wind-Clan. If you insist on staying in the forest while you wait for the other two to make up their minds, your Clanmates will die."

Firestar looked away. "I'm sorry, Tallstar," he meowed. "I want to help you, but my heart tells me that ThunderClan cannot leave until all the other Clans agree to leave as well. We will have to keep trying to persuade them."

Tallstar thrashed his tail. "Very well," he hissed. "We cannot travel without you, and so we will wait. I don't blame you for the hunger we suffer, but I'm disappointed you will not help us now." He padded away with Barkface close beside him, ready to support him if the WindClan leader stumbled on paws that hardly seemed strong enough to carry him to the edge of the clearing, let alone all the way back to the moor.

Squirrelpaw turned to Brambleclaw. "Why wasn't there a sign?" she protested.

Brambleclaw gazed at her. "Do you think Midnight was wrong?" His wide eyes reflected the moon. "After all, did she really tell us anything we can't see from what is happening around us?" He gestured with his tail to the ravaged clearing, to the swaths of fallen trees around them. "Every cat *knows* the forest is being destroyed by Twolegs. Perhaps Blackstar is right, and each Clan should just try to save itself, without waiting for any more signs."

Squirrelpaw fought to control the panic that fluttered in her chest. "You can't mean that! We have to believe that

Midnight was right!" she argued. "StarClan sent us to speak with her, and that must mean StarClan wants us to save the Clans."

"But what if we can't?" Brambleclaw murmured.

Squirrelpaw stared at him in dismay, her mind suddenly filled with an image of falling trees, roaring monsters, and blood spilling down Sunningrocks into the river. "Don't give up, Brambleclaw!" she whispered. "We didn't make that journey and lose Feathertail for nothing. We *have* to save the Clans!"

CHAPTER 7

❦

Squirrelpaw curled up beside Shrewpaw and tried not to think about the warm, moss-lined den where the apprentices had slept before. At least the small gully they were lying in gave some shelter from the chilly night breeze. It felt strange to be sleeping apart from Brambleclaw after their long journey together, but at least Shrewpaw seemed happy to have her back. Her paws ached with tiredness, and she closed her eyes, folding her tail over her muzzle for comfort. At first she couldn't stop thinking about the disastrous meeting at Fourtrees, but gradually dreams wove into her waking thoughts and drew her into sleep.

She was alone among the trees, and she could smell prey-scent. A cold wind breathed through the forest. Squirrelpaw lifted her nose and tasted the air. A fat mouse was snuffling among the leaves. It was the plumpest piece of prey she had found since returning to the forest, and she swiped her tongue hungrily over her lips. Brambleclaw would be pleased to have a share of this fresh-kill.

Crouching, Squirrelpaw crept silently toward the unsuspecting creature. It had its head half-buried under an oak leaf and hadn't noticed her. This was going to be an easy catch. Suddenly, rapid pawsteps sounded behind her. Terrified, the mouse darted out from under the oak leaf and scuttled away beneath the roots of a tree. Squirrelpaw spun around, bristling with fury.

A tortoiseshell cat with gentle amber eyes was standing behind her. "Hello, Squirrelpaw," she mewed. "I have something to show you."

"You've just ruined the best catch I'm likely to get all day!" Squirrelpaw snapped back. She had never seen this cat before, though she carried the scent of ThunderClan. She stopped and put her head to one side. "Who are you, anyway?"

"I'm Spottedleaf."

Squirrelpaw blinked. She had heard all about the long-dead ThunderClan medicine cat. Why would Spottedleaf come to her?

She stepped forward to touch the she-cat's nose in greeting, but as she went closer, the image faded.

Bewildered, Squirrelpaw stared into the trees. She pricked her ears, listening for movement, but heard nothing and turned to resume her hunt. The scent of prey that hung in the air was too tempting. Perhaps Spottedleaf had wanted only to greet her, nothing more.

Squirrelpaw prowled deeper into the woods, following a path that led toward Snakerocks. But as she crept through the undergrowth, the forest seemed to change, and she didn't recognize the trees around her. Surely she should have reached Snakerocks by now. Had she taken the wrong path? She quickened her pace until she was racing through trees she had never seen before.

A tiny voice in her mind reminded her that it was just a dream, and she wasn't really lost. She blinked, trying to wake up. But when she opened her eyes, she was still trapped in the strange woods, and her alarm grew until her heart pounded like a woodpecker's beak on bark. She ran on, hoping to find a landmark she recognized, but the forest grew darker and more silent, as if the trees themselves were watching her. There didn't seem to be anything else alive in these woods—no sound of prey, no scent of her Clanmates or any other Clan.

"Spottedleaf!" she called. "Help me!"

There was no reply.

The trees grew more thickly here, and the shadows between the trunks swallowed her until she could hardly see where she was putting her paws.

"Don't be frightened."

The soft voice seemed to echo from every direction at once, and Squirrelpaw spun around, trying to find where it came from. There was a faint scent of ThunderClan, and then she saw Spottedleaf's pale pelt glowing among the trees like the distant moon in a mottled sky.

"I'm lost, Spottedleaf!" she called.

"No, you're not," Spottedleaf reassured her gently. "Follow me."

Panting with relief, Squirrelpaw wound her way through the tree trunks. As she approached, the shadows seemed to draw away and the forest grew lighter, although there wasn't any moon that she could see.

"Follow me," Spottedleaf murmured. She turned and headed into the trees, running as confidently as if she were following an invisible path. Squirrelpaw pelted after her.

Spottedleaf ran like the wind, but Squirrelpaw raced over the ground until she felt as though she were swooping through the trees like a bird. Exhilaration flooded her so that she hardly noticed the forest become familiar once more. Then she recognized the Great Sycamore, reaching high into the sky. And here were the Snakerocks, a tumbled heap of round, sandy boulders where snakes basked in greenleaf, but which offered good prey in colder weather. Spottedleaf leaped up to the top of the rocks, then down the other side and on through the forest. Squirrelpaw scrambled after her quickly.

On they went until Squirrelpaw detected the tang of the Thunderpath. Suddenly, without warning, Spottedleaf stopped. Squirrelpaw skidded to a halt, nearly bumping into her, and followed the medicine cat's gaze. Ahead of them, every single tree had been stripped away, and the forest floor was churned into mud right to the edge of the Thunderpath. Wooden Twoleg nests ringed the clearing, and monsters sat hunched and silent nearby.

"This way," Spottedleaf mewed. She led Squirrelpaw across the slippery, rutted earth toward the nests.

"It's so quiet," Squirrelpaw whispered. Oddly, she felt soothed by the eerie quiet, and she followed Spottedleaf over the open ground without fear.

Spottedleaf stopped beside one of the wooden nests, and

Squirrelpaw looked up at it in surprise. "What is this place?" she mewed. "Why have you brought me here?"

Spottedleaf twitched her gold-and-brown-striped tail. "Look through the hole," she urged. "Look at the cages."

Cages? The word sounded strange to Squirrelpaw's ears. She noticed a small gap in the wall, about a fox-length up. She stretched her forepaws up the side of the nest, her belly brushing the scratchy wood, and peered in.

Rows of dens made of cold-looking shiny web were stacked along the walls. Those must be the "cages." Squirrelpaw could see a dark, soft-edged shape huddled in each cage. *Cats!* Her heart raced as scents flooded her nose—RiverClan, WindClan, rogue. She stared breathlessly through the hole, and then she smelled the warm scent of ThunderClan. With a jolt of recognition she saw her sister curled up in one of the cages near the roof of the wooden nest.

"Leafpaw!" She gasped. She clawed herself upward, thrusting with her hind legs, trying to clamber through the hole.

"You can't get in, Squirrelpaw." Spottedleaf stood on her hind legs to reach up beside her. "This is only a dream," she murmured. "But when you wake, Leafpaw will still be here."

"Will I be able to rescue her?"

"I hope so," Spottedleaf answered softly.

"But how?" Squirrelpaw yowled, jumping down to the ground.

"Stop fidgeting, for StarClan's sake!" Shrewpaw muttered.

Squirrelpaw's eyes shot open. She was lying in the narrow cleft in Sunningrocks. The hollow was dark, and she could only just make out the soft shapes of sleeping cats around her. She sat up and stared over the lip of the gully. Outside, frost glittered on the smooth stone, and beyond that she saw the outlines of leafless trees, black and spiky against the sky.

"What's the matter?" Shrewpaw asked sleepily.

"I know where Leafpaw is!" Squirrelpaw whispered. "I have to go and rescue her."

Shrewpaw's eyes blinked open. "How do you know?"

"Spottedleaf told me in a dream!"

"Are you sure?"

"Of course I'm sure!" Squirrelpaw snapped.

Shrewpaw twitched his ears. "You can't just disappear without telling any cat where you're going," he warned. He didn't add, *Again*, but Squirrelpaw guessed that was what he was thinking.

"I could wake Firestar up," she mewed. "Now I know where Leafpaw is, he could send out a rescue party."

"Not in the middle of the night," Shrewpaw pointed out. "It's too cold. Besides, it was just a dream."

"It was more than a dream," Squirrelpaw insisted.

"But you're not a medicine cat," Shrewpaw argued. "No cat's going to go on a rescue mission in the middle of the night because you had a dream." His amber eyes were gentle. "They might listen to you in the morning, though. Settle down and go back to sleep."

Squirrelpaw sighed, but she knew he was right. She slumped back down again, still seeing the wooden nest filled with cages. Shrewpaw lay down beside her and rested his tail comfortingly on her flank. "We'll find her in the morning," he promised, closing his eyes.

His breathing slowed as he drifted into sleep, but Squirrelpaw stayed awake, gazing up at the narrow strip of Silverpelt she could see through the mouth of the gully. A cat from StarClan had visited her to tell her where Leafpaw was! She knew Spottedleaf had had a special bond with her father when he first came to the forest. Could it be that she wanted to help Firestar's daughters because she still loved him?

Squirrelpaw opened her eyes and sat up with a start. Bright light streamed into the gully, though the air was cold, colder still because all the other apprentices had left. Quickly, she stretched and scrambled out of the crevice. Her dream was still clear in her mind. She had to tell her father so he could organize a rescue party.

Shrewpaw was washing on the stone slope in front of the den.

"Where's Firestar?" Squirrelpaw demanded.

"He's out patrolling with Graystripe," Shrewpaw replied, rubbing at his cheek with his paw.

She twitched her tail in frustration. "Why didn't you wake me?"

"You didn't sleep well, remember?" meowed Shrewpaw. "I thought you could get some extra rest and join me on a later patrol. Firestar agreed."

"Didn't you tell him about my dream?" Squirrelpaw pricked her ears. "What did he say? When is he sending out a patrol?"

"I-I didn't mention the dream," Shrewpaw stammered. "I thought you would have forgotten it. It was only a dream, after all."

Squirrelpaw glared at Shrewpaw. "It was a message from StarClan!"

"I'm really sorry." He shuffled his paws and stared at the ground.

Squirrelpaw let her fur lie flat again. "No, *I'm* sorry." she sighed. "It's not your fault I overslept."

"It's okay." Shrewpaw shrugged. "Did you really see Leafpaw in your dream?"

Squirrelpaw nodded. "And the other cats that are missing from the forest. Or at least, I definitely smelled WindClan and RiverClan scents."

"That's amazing!" He glanced past her and twitched his whiskers. "Looks like there's been some successful hunting already today. That should put Firestar in a good mood, at least."

Squirrelpaw turned to see Brambleclaw padding up the slope with a vole in his jaws. He carried it over to where Ferncloud lay in the sunshine watching her kits play. She accepted Brambleclaw's offering with only a blink of her leaf-colored eyes, as if she didn't have the strength to thank him. Squirrelpaw noticed with a prick of unease how small Ferncloud's kits were. They looked hardly old enough to leave the nursery, let alone journey all the way to the sun-drown-place. By leaf-bare, kits were usually strong and healthy, ready to face the cruelest season. If Squirrelpaw and Brambleclaw succeeded in persuading the Clan to leave the forest, how many cats would never see their new home?

She shook her head. Right now, she didn't want to go anywhere without rescuing Leafpaw.

"Brambleclaw!" She bounded down the slope toward him. "I know where Leafpaw is! StarClan came to me in a dream! The Twolegs have trapped her in a little nest, past Snakerocks. We have to go and rescue her."

Brambleclaw pricked his ears. "Really?" He scanned Sunningrocks. "Have you told Firestar? Is he organizing a rescue party?"

Squirrelpaw shook her head. "He's on patrol. But if you came with me, we could rescue her together."

Brambleclaw blinked. "Are you mad? Rescue her from a Twoleg nest? We wouldn't stand a chance on our own."

Squirrelpaw's paws pricked with frustration. "But StarClan must want us to rescue her *now*!" she argued. "Why else hasn't Spottedleaf come before? Leafpaw must be in more danger than ever."

"Let's wait till Firestar gets back. He'll know what to do."

Squirrelpaw couldn't believe her ears. "Does that mean you won't help me?"

"It means I won't let you go on such a dangerous mission!" Brambleclaw snapped.

Squirrelpaw wanted to rake his ears in frustration. "You're afraid!"

Brambleclaw bristled. "What if we tried to rescue Leafpaw and got caught ourselves?" he pointed out. "Who else knows the way through the mountains? Who would lead Thunder-Clan to their new home?"

"You weren't like this when we were traveling! You agreed to go back and rescue Stormfur!"

Frustration flashed in his eyes. "Yes, and look what happened to Feathertail when we did!"

"But this is my sister!" Squirrelpaw thrashed her tail. "Why won't you understand?"

Brambleclaw blinked. "I'm only asking you to wait till Firestar gets back—"

"But you won't help me now!" Squirrelpaw couldn't keep the desperation out of her voice.

Brambleclaw's gaze softened. "Let's wait till Firestar returns. He'll send out a patrol. We'd need more warriors. . . ."

Squirrelpaw couldn't bear to listen anymore. "I didn't think that you of all cats would let me down," she spat, stalking away into the trees.

As she reached the undergrowth, the sound of rushing pawsteps made her stop and look around. She hoped it was Brambleclaw coming after her to tell her he had changed his mind, but it was Sorreltail.

"I heard what you were saying!" she panted. "If StarClan has told you where Leafpaw is, they must want us to rescue her as soon as possible!"

"That's what I thought," Squirrelpaw growled. "But Brambleclaw won't help me."

"I will," Sorreltail offered. Grief shadowed her face. "I couldn't stop the Twolegs from taking Leafpaw, but I'd do anything to help her now."

"Do you mean it?" Squirrelpaw tried to ignore the twinge of jealousy that pricked her belly—why shouldn't Leafpaw have made friends with another cat while she was away?

"Of course!"

"Come on, then!" she yowled. "Let's go!"

She pelted into the forest, wanting to get away before any of the senior warriors spotted her and ordered her to join a hunting patrol, or even worse, overheard them and told Firestar what she was planning. She heard Sorreltail pounding after her. The two cats raced past the ravine without even looking down into the abandoned camp, and headed for the Great Sycamore. The monsters were still there, chewing up more and more of the forest. If they weren't careful, they'd tumble right into the ravine and smash themselves to bits on Highstones, Squirrelpaw thought hopefully.

"Keep low," she warned as the roaring grew louder, but Sorreltail was already ducking down to follow her through the dying bracken.

"Thank Silverpelt they've left us some trees to hide in!" she hissed.

They scrambled over Snakerocks. Squirrelpaw was determined to follow the exact trail Spottedleaf had shown her in her dream, but she hoped that the weak sun hadn't tempted any snakes out to bask. Safely over the rocks, they headed back into the trees toward the Thunderpath.

The hateful stench of the Twoleg monsters stung her nose a heartbeat before she heard them roaring up ahead. By the time she reached the edge of the muddy clearing she was breathing hard, her paws trembling. Fear gripped her from ear-tips to tail.

Sorreltail skidded to a halt beside her and peered out from under a thick bramble bush. "What are we going to do now?"

"I'm not sure," Squirrelpaw admitted. The clearing was busy with Twolegs shouting and monsters churning up the ground as they prowled back and forth. It looked nothing like her dream, even though she was sure they had come to the right place. There was no trace of the stillness and the silence she had padded confidently through with Spottedleaf. But the noise and activity made her paws prick with determination. StarClan had brought her here knowing full well how dangerous it would be. They must have faith in her.

"Leafpaw's over there." She gestured with her tail to the wooden nest Spottedleaf had led her to. There was a monster crouched outside the door, grumbling quietly to itself. It was much smaller than the tree-munching monsters, and its round black paws seemed half-sunk in the mud.

"Look," Squirrelpaw hissed suddenly. "They've left the door open!"

She froze as a Twoleg emerged from the nest, carrying a cage. Inside crouched a mangy tabby, its eyes wide with terror. The Twoleg pushed it into the belly of the waiting monster, then went back inside the wooden nest and came out with another cage.

Squirrelpaw stared in horror at the bundle of fur hunched

inside the cage. "Leafpaw!" Without stopping to think, she dashed out of the trees.

Leafpaw must have spotted her, because as the Twoleg pushed her cage into the monster's belly, she yowled, "Squirrelpaw, get away from here!"

Her shriek startled the Twoleg, and it turned around sharply, spotting Squirrelpaw at once. With eyes sparkling in triumph, it put down Leafpaw's cage and ran toward her. Squirrelpaw scrabbled to a halt, her paws slipping as she tried to bolt back to the safety of the trees. The Twoleg chased her with its forepaws outstretched, its long legs gaining on her as she fought to get a clawhold on the slimy mud. *StarClan! Help me!*

Just when her heart was about to burst with fear, Sorreltail exploded from the bushes with a vicious snarl. She rushed at the Twoleg, raking her claws across its grasping paw until it howled in pain. Then she grasped Squirrelpaw's scruff in her teeth and hauled her toward the trees. Squirrelpaw found her footing with a gasp, and Sorreltail released her. Together the two cats sped into the woods. When they reached the safety of the brambles, Squirrelpaw skidded to a standstill.

"Keep running!" Sorreltail hissed. "They won't give up that easily." She nudged Squirrelpaw hard, pushing her further into the clump of brambles.

Squirrelpaw stumbled as the thorns scraped her fur. "What about Leafpaw?"

"Do you want to join her?" Sorreltail spat. "Keep running!"

Too terrified to think straight, Squirrelpaw obeyed and raced after the warrior into the trees.

Only when they had run all the way to Snakerocks did Sorreltail slow down, her flanks heaving. Squirrelpaw stood beside her, too shocked to speak.

"What in StarClan's name is going on?" Graystripe's deep meow echoed off the rocks as he emerged from the bracken with Thornclaw and Rainwhisker close behind him. The ThunderClan deputy stared at the two trembling cats. "What's wrong with you? You look like you've just seen Tigerstar's ghost!"

"It's Leafpaw!" Squirrelpaw cried. "We found her, but the Twolegs are putting her inside a monster's belly. They're going to take her away; I know they are!"

Graystripe narrowed his eyes and opened his mouth to speak, then stopped and glanced at the bushes behind him. "Brambleclaw?" he called. "Is that you?"

"Yes." The branches quivered and Brambleclaw stepped out. "I'm looking for Squirrelpaw." He blinked when he spotted her standing beside Sorreltail. "Are you okay?"

"I found Leafpaw!" Squirrelpaw hissed. "The Twolegs are going to take her away! We have to rescue her *now*, or I'll never find her again."

Graystripe glanced at Brambleclaw, then at Rainwhisker and Thornclaw. The ThunderClan warriors stood with their chins raised high and flexed their powerful shoulders.

"We can't let the Twolegs take our cats if there is anything we can do to stop them," growled Rainwhisker.

"We should not give up without a fight," Thornclaw agreed. Their meaning was clear. This was still their forest. They may not have been able to protect it against all the Twolegs and their monsters, but this was one battle they could take on.

Graystripe narrowed his amber eyes at Squirrelpaw. "Very well," he meowed. "Show us where she is."

"This way," she panted. She leaped back over Snakerocks, Sorreltail close behind. Graystripe, Thornclaw, Rainwhisker, and Brambleclaw followed. Hearing their pawsteps, Squirrelpaw felt a surge of confidence. With five ThunderClan warriors at her side, she must be able to rescue her sister!

When they reached the bramble thicket at the edge of the trees, Graystripe hissed for the cats to stop. "Stay low!" he commanded.

To Squirrelpaw's relief, the small monster was still waiting outside the wooden nest, and the Twoleg was carrying out more cages to stow in its belly. "Leafpaw's already inside," she whispered.

"Right," muttered Graystripe. "Thornclaw, you and I will attack the Twoleg. We've got to keep him distracted while Sorreltail, Brambleclaw, and Rainwhisker let the other cats out."

"What about me?" Squirrelpaw asked.

"You stay here as lookout," Graystripe ordered curtly. "Tell us if more Twolegs come."

Squirrelpaw stared at him in shock. "But—" she began, but Graystripe ignored her.

"Most of them must be in the monster by now," he went on.

"Brambleclaw and Sorreltail, I want you to climb inside and start getting the cats out. Rainwhisker, you go into the nest and help any that are left."

Squirrelpaw glared at Graystripe. "I'm getting my sister out of that monster!"

The gray deputy stared back at her for a long moment, and Squirrelpaw felt as if she'd forgotten how to breathe. "Very well," Graystripe agreed at last. "But if anything goes wrong, get back to the trees as fast as you can."

Squirrelpaw nodded. When she glanced at Brambleclaw, his eyes were shadowed with worry. *I faced greater danger than this on the journey to the sun-drown-place!* she wanted to tell him. *Stop treating me like a kit!*

"Right," Graystripe meowed, turning back to watch the monster. "The Twoleg is going to fetch another. We'll be ready to take it by surprise when it comes out."

He dashed from the trees, keeping low as he raced over the mud. Thornclaw, Sorreltail, Rainwhisker, and Brambleclaw ducked out from under the brambles and ran across the churned earth behind him. Squirrelpaw scrambled after them, feeling the mud suck at her paws and cling to the fur on her belly.

A few tail-lengths from the open door, Graystripe hissed, "Wait!" and the cats halted in the sticky mud.

The Twoleg stepped out of the wooden nest. It was carrying another cage and did not see the six cats waiting in ambush.

"Now!" Graystripe screeched, and he leaped at the Twoleg. When he sank his claws into its hind leg, the Twoleg dropped the cage. The cage cracked open with a sound like a splintering branch. Squirrelpaw stared in astonishment as she recognized the gray pelt inside. It was Mistyfoot! The River-Clan warrior leaped out and hurled herself at the Twoleg's other leg, hissing in rage. Thornclaw joined the attack, gripping the Twoleg as though he were clawing his way up a tree. The Twoleg bellowed in agony and hopped around with a cat clinging to each leg.

"Come on, Squirrelpaw!" Brambleclaw yowled. He jumped into the open belly of the monster, Sorreltail close behind him. Squirrelpaw heard the blood roaring in her ears as she watched Rainwhisker slip into the nest. She hoped there wasn't another Twoleg waiting inside. Taking a deep breath, she hauled herself up into the monster with Brambleclaw and Sorreltail.

Rows of cages were lined up in the gloom. The fear-scent was overpowering, and for a moment Squirrelpaw froze. How in StarClan's name were they going to rescue all these cats? Then she saw Leafpaw, pressed against the mesh of her cage.

"Squirrelpaw! Over here!" she wailed.

"I'm coming!" Squirrelpaw streaked over to her and used her teeth to tug at the catch on the front of the cage. "It's loosening!" she hissed as the catch began to tear away like the wing of a pigeon. She pulled as hard as she could until the cage sprang open and sent Squirrelpaw toppling onto the floor of the monster's belly.

Leafpaw leaped down and quickly rubbed her muzzle against her sister's. "It's really you!" she breathed.

"Spottedleaf told me where you were!" Squirrelpaw gasped, scrambling to her paws.

Leafpaw blinked, then shook herself. "Tell me everything later. Come on; we've got to get all these cats out!" She raced to the nearest cage and began pulling at the catch.

Squirrelpaw turned to another and struggled until she thought she'd be spitting out broken teeth, but the catch eventually came free, and a matted rogue tom leaped out. Without a word he fled from the monster and sprinted toward the woods.

"You're welcome," Squirrelpaw muttered before starting on the next cage.

Unfamiliar cats leaped around her as Brambleclaw, Sorreltail, and Leafpaw worked on the cages one after another. The cages mostly contained rogues who were gone as soon as their doors were open. Then Squirrelpaw felt a cat push her aside, heading deeper into the monster's belly, and saw Mistyfoot barging past. The RiverClan warrior made straight for the cage at the end.

"Sasha!" Mistyfoot yowled, and she began scraping at the catch with her claws.

"This way works better," Squirrelpaw told her, nudging her out of the way to use her teeth. Instantly the catch opened and Sasha sprang out.

"Get out of here!" Mistyfoot urged.

Sasha hesitated, looking at the cages that were still closed.

"We'll deal with these!" Mistyfoot promised.

Sasha's fur was standing on end, and her blue eyes were

huge with fear. She was shaking so much that she wouldn't be able to open the cages even if she tried. At last she nodded and leaped from the monster.

Only a few cages still held cats. Leafpaw scanned the inside of the monster and called to Squirrelpaw, "Cloudtail and Brightheart are still in the hut! Go and help free them; I've got to let Cody out."

"Who's Cody?" Squirrelpaw asked.

"I'll tell you later! Quick! Get Brightheart and Cloudtail!"

Squirrelpaw leaped out of the monster's belly and raced toward the wooden nest. Her heart lurched when she saw that another Twoleg had arrived to help. Thornclaw finally lost his grip on the first Twoleg. The ThunderClan warrior landed heavily in the mud, but he scrambled to his paws and raced back to rejoin Graystripe in the attack.

As Squirrelpaw dashed into the nest, she was almost knocked flying by a brown tabby rogue running out. She swerved quickly out of the way as the scraggy tom hurtled past her; then she scanned the nest, searching for Cloudtail and Brightheart.

Cloudtail was already free. He was helping Rainwhisker scrape at Brightheart's catch. "We can't open it!" Cloudtail yowled, his voice rising in panic.

"Try your teeth," called Squirrelpaw.

Cloudtail bit down hard, and Squirrelpaw saw him tremble with effort as he pulled, but still it would not open. More Twoleg voices sounded outside, and Graystripe raced into the nest.

"There are too many Twolegs!" he yowled. "We have to get out of here!" He pushed Squirrelpaw toward the doorway. "Get back to the trees!"

"But Brightheart is still trapped!"

"I'll take care of her!" Graystripe promised, pushing Squirrelpaw with his nose. "Just get out of here!"

He leaped over to where Rainwhisker and Cloudtail were still tugging at Brightheart's catch and shoved them out of the way. "Get to the trees!" he spat. "Now!"

Cloudtail didn't move, but stood stiff-legged, staring in horror at Brightheart's cage. Her panic-stricken face was pressed against the mesh.

"Come on!" Rainwhisker hissed at him and bundled the white warrior toward the door. Squirrelpaw glanced over her shoulder at Graystripe as he grabbed the stiff catch in his powerful jaws, then followed the others out of the nest.

As she emerged a Twoleg lunged for her, but she spun around and bolted along the side of the nest. There were Twolegs everywhere, howling in rage. She spotted Cloudtail and Rainwhisker making for the trees and pelted after them, thrusting her way into the tangle of brambles. Rainwhisker kept running into the forest, but Cloudtail skidded to a halt and turned back to watch what was happening outside the nest. Squirrelpaw crouched beside him and peered across the clearing. Leafpaw and a tabby she didn't recognize were running toward them.

"Hurry!" she screeched. A Twoleg was gaining on them, his huge paws taking giant strides across the mud. As Squirrelpaw watched, willing the cats to outrun the Twoleg, the white-and-ginger pelt of Brightheart caught her eye in the doorway of the nest. Graystripe had opened her cage!

The ThunderClan she-cat hurtled toward the trees, the scars on her face half-hidden by splatters of mud. She brushed past the Twoleg that was chasing Leafpaw, unbalancing him in the slippery mud so that he fell over with a roar.

Leafpaw and the tabby reached the safety of the bushes and scrambled in among the thorns.

"I can't believe you saved us!" panted the tabby.

Squirrelpaw was already rubbing her nose along Leafpaw's cheek, breathing in her familiar scent. "I'm sorry we were nearly too late," she whispered.

"I thought I'd never see you again!" Leafpaw was panting hard. "Where's Brambleclaw?"

Squirrelpaw felt a jolt of alarm and scented the air. She smelled the fresh fear scent of Thornclaw and Sorreltail. Then she recognized a clump of dark tabby fur snagged on a bramble thorn, the blood still wet where it had been torn from his pelt. She trembled with relief. If Brambleclaw had gotten this far, he must have escaped.

"He's okay," she mewed. "Did Mistyfoot get out?"

"Once the last cat was free she started heading for the trees," Leafpaw told her.

"Then everyone escaped!" Squirrelpaw breathed in relief.

As she spoke, Brightheart crashed into the brambles, her eyes huge with terror. "Graystripe!" she gasped.

"Where is he?" Squirrelpaw demanded.

Cloudtail nearly bowled Brightheart over as he leaped toward her. "I shouldn't have left you!" he cried, licking her all over her ravaged face.

"Where's Graystripe?" Squirrelpaw repeated.

"Twolegs!" panted Brightheart, pulling away from Cloudtail.

Squirrelpaw's heart jumped into her throat. "What do you mean?"

"One of them grabbed him!"

Squirrelpaw peered out from the undergrowth. A Twoleg was closing the belly of the monster. Hissing and spitting at the other Twolegs, who were staring wildly around the clearing, it climbed into the front. The monster roared into life and, spraying mud from beneath each of its fat black paws, began to pull away. Then Squirrelpaw saw something that made her stomach flip over. A lone face peered from inside the monster, a face she had known since she was a kit. It gazed desperately at the trees as the monster picked up speed and raced away.

"Graystripe!" Squirrelpaw gasped.

CHAPTER 8

❧

Leafpaw watched the monster pull away and opened her mouth to howl, but no sound came out. The forest spun around her and she blinked, fighting the urge to lie down and never get up again.

Twolegs began to run toward the trees, shouting and waving their paws.

They were not safe yet.

Brambleclaw exploded from the undergrowth behind them. "Quick! Run!" He raced to Squirrelpaw's side and gave her a shove.

Squirrelpaw dragged her horrified gaze from the clearing and stared at Brambleclaw. "What about Graystripe?"

"There's nothing we can do for him right now," he hissed. "Hurry! We have to get out of here!"

"Which way?" Cody yowled, staring into the trees.

"Follow me," Brambleclaw ordered.

Leafpaw hadn't seen Brambleclaw since he left the forest with Squirrelpaw. This was a very different cat that had returned—an experienced, confident warrior, calmly issuing commands in spite of the huge danger they were all in. This wasn't the time to find out exactly where they had been for the last moon. Pulling her paws free from the mud, she scrabbled through the undergrowth behind Squirrelpaw and Cody. Cloudtail passed her, with Brightheart so close to him that their fur touched.

Relief flooded through Leafpaw when she saw the familiar pelts of Sorreltail and Rainwhisker flash through the trees up ahead. Mistyfoot was with them. All the trapped cats had been freed—but they had lost Graystripe.

She heard the Twolegs crashing through the forest behind them. Glancing over her shoulder, she watched them blunder through the bushes, swerving clumsily around the trees and stumbling over trailing brambles. Leafpaw knew they would not catch her now. This was her domain; she could race through it as fast as any creature, her lithe body perfectly suited to slipping through the undergrowth like the wind.

The cats scrambled down Snakerocks. The Twolegs were far behind now, and Leafpaw slowed her pace. Cody fell in beside her as they padded breathlessly into the leaf-strewn glade beside the Great Sycamore. The other cats were sprawled on the ground, exhausted. Cloudtail was licking Brightheart's ears as if he would never get them clean. Mistyfoot watched them, her pale gray flanks heaving.

Cody looked nervously around the clearing. "Is it safe here?"

"The Twolegs won't catch us now," Leafpaw assured her.

"But what about foxes and badgers?" Cody's eyes were huge.

"Aren't the woods full of all kinds of dreadful things?"

"Like wildcats?" Leafpaw joked weakly. She collapsed onto the soft leaves next to the other ThunderClan cats.

Rainwhisker struggled to sit up. His dark gray fur stood on end, and there was blood oozing between the claws on one of his front paws. "Are you sure they got Graystripe?"

Squirrelpaw flattened her ears. "The monster carried him away. I saw him!"

"But he was fighting like a TigerClan cat!" Thornclaw protested. "They couldn't have caught him!"

"There were too many Twolegs," Squirrelpaw explained.

Mistyfoot dipped her head toward Squirrelpaw. "I owe him my life," she murmured. "I thought we would never escape." She stared intently at her. "You saved us."

Squirrelpaw sat up. "It wasn't just me," she insisted. "We all risked our lives. Graystripe led the way."

Leafpaw narrowed her eyes and studied her sister. That was the reply of a warrior, not an apprentice. She noticed how much leaner and stronger Squirrelpaw had become—much fitter than the scrawny ThunderClan warriors. Leafpaw bent her head to lick her own patchy, unkempt fur. For the first time, she felt awkward around her sister, unsure what to say when so much had happened since they had last seen each other.

"What will the Twolegs do to him?" Sorreltail wailed, grief-stricken.

Leafpaw wished she could offer comfort, but she didn't

know what to say. If it hadn't been for her brave Clanmates, she would be making that journey instead of Graystripe.

"May StarClan help him," murmured Thornclaw.

"StarClan is helpless against the Twolegs," Squirrelpaw spat.

"StarClan was with us today," Leafpaw reminded her. "They gave you the strength to face the Twolegs. They will look after Graystripe."

Sorreltail hauled herself to her paws and touched Leafpaw's muzzle with hers. "Thank StarClan the Twolegs didn't take you as well," she murmured. "Squirrelpaw saw you in a dream, trapped in that place. She insisted we rescue you."

"It wasn't just me you saved," Leafpaw meowed, looking gratefully at her Clanmates.

"You saved all of us," Cody agreed, padding over to Leafpaw's side.

Sorreltail pulled away from Leafpaw and looked sharply at the kittypet. "Who are you?" she demanded. "You're not a forest cat, but you don't look like a rogue, either."

"This is Cody," Leafpaw meowed. "She stopped me from feeling sorry for myself, and made me believe we might be able to escape."

Sorreltail sniffed. "You're a kittypet?"

Rainwhisker sat up and stared at the tabby she-cat. Thornclaw flattened his ears.

"Yes, I'm a kittypet," Cody confirmed.

Brambleclaw got to his paws and padded over to Cody.

Leafpaw saw her friend try not to flinch away from the broad-shouldered warrior, whose coat was streaked with mud and blood. "Do you want us to show you the way back to Twoleg-place?" he offered.

"It's not safe enough to go that way yet," Leafpaw warned. "The Twolegs might be searching the woods."

Brightheart sat up and stared nervously around the glade.

"It's okay," Cloudtail reassured her. "We can outrun them from here."

"We'll be even safer back at the camp," mewed Squirrel-paw. "Why doesn't Cody come with us for now?"

The kittypet stared uncertainly at the cats. For all her courage when they were trapped, she was obviously feeling daunted by being around so many of the wildcats she had heard about in bloodthirsty stories.

"You'll be made welcome," Leafpaw meowed. She looked at Brambleclaw and Rainwhisker, hoping she was right.

"Firestar won't turn away a cat who's in trouble," Bramble-claw agreed.

"Won't your Twolegs be missing you?" Sorreltail asked pointedly, and Leafpaw glanced at her in surprise.

"Yes, of course." Cody kneaded the ground with her paws. Some of the fire returned to her blue eyes. "But it sounds as if it wouldn't be safe for me to travel through that part of the forest alone, and I don't want to put any more of you in danger."

"We'll get you home as soon as it's safe," Leafpaw promised.

"I suppose we should be going then." Sorreltail sighed. She looked at Brambleclaw. "What are we going to tell Firestar about Graystripe?"

Leafpaw swallowed. Graystripe was the ThunderClan deputy, one of the bravest and most experienced warriors, and Firestar's best friend. How would the Clan cope without him?

The cats fell into a miserable silence as they trekked though the forest. Leafpaw noticed that Thornclaw seemed to be leading them toward Sunningrocks rather than the ravine. Why weren't they going to the camp? She glanced at Squirrel-paw, puzzled.

"The Clan had to abandon the old camp," her sister explained. "The Twolegs were getting too close."

Leafpaw gulped. "Has it gotten that bad?"

"I'm afraid so," Thornclaw answered grimly.

"Surely there's not enough shelter for all of us at Sunning-rocks?" Cloudtail meowed.

"How are the kits?" Brightheart asked anxiously.

"Not as well fed as they should be," Squirrelpaw admitted.

"We should leave before they get any weaker," Brambleclaw muttered.

Leafpaw wondered what he meant, and felt even more confused when Thornclaw flashed him a sharp glance. Brambleclaw and Squirrelpaw had only just returned to the forest—why were they talking about leaving already?

"Are we nearly there?" Cody called from behind.

Leafpaw could hear the murmuring of the river through the leafless trees. They were nearing the RiverClan border, and Sunningrocks was not far ahead. "Yes, it's not far now," she called back.

Thornclaw padded onward, and Leafpaw followed with the others through a swath of bracken. They emerged at the top of the slope that led down to the RiverClan border. Leafpaw could see water rippling at the bottom. It was unexpectedly comforting to find that the river was still there in spite of everything the Twolegs had done to the rest of the forest.

Mistyfoot padded down to the river. At the water's edge she stopped and called back to the ThunderClan cats, "I honor the warriors of ThunderClan for rescuing me. And I mourn the loss of Graystripe with you." Her blue eyes clouded for a moment; then she turned and pushed through the swirling water with powerfully churning paws till she reached the other side.

The ThunderClan cats headed for Sunningrocks. Leafpaw quickened her pace, impatient to be back with her Clan and anxious to know what had happened to their old home in the ravine. Cody matched her step for step, sticking close to her side; Leafpaw could tell by the flicking of her ears that the kittypet was both excited and nervous about meeting the Clan.

"Are you sure they won't mind my coming back with you?" she whispered.

Leafpaw hardly heard her. She had just spotted Firestar sitting near the top of the broad gray slope. The sun lit up his fiery pelt, picking out his bony frame. He looked thin and tired, and his eyes were half-closed. How could she tell him that Graystripe had been lost in rescuing her? The thought pierced Leafpaw's heart like a thorn.

The breeze must have carried her scent, for Firestar suddenly turned and stared down the rock. He jumped to his paws and raced down to them with his tail held high. "Leafpaw," he panted, sliding to a halt. "You're safe!" He licked her ears, and a purr throbbed in his throat.

"I missed you so much," Leafpaw mewed, pushing her face into the familiar warmth of his pelt.

"Thank StarClan I have both of you back." Firestar's mew was thick with emotion.

Brambleclaw and Squirrelpaw waited at the bottom of the slope with the other ThunderClan warriors, while Cody hung back among the trees.

Cloudtail and Brightheart shot past them onto Sunningrocks, calling for their kit. "Whitepaw!" Cloudtail called. "We're back!"

The snowy-pelted apprentice was dozing in a sheltered dip in the rock. At the sound of voices, she raised her head and leaped to her paws. "You escaped!" she cried, hurtling down the slope to greet her mother and father. She skidded into them, purring with delight. Cloudtail wrapped his tail around her, while Brightheart licked her so fiercely that Whitepaw ducked out of the way with a muffled squeak.

Sandstorm came racing out from an overhang at the side of Sunningrocks. She bounded down the slope and nudged Firestar out of the way. "Leafpaw! Did they hurt you?"

"No," Leafpaw answered as Sandstorm enthusiastically began to lick away the stench of the Twoleg nest from her daughter's pelt. "I'm fine, honestly."

"How did you escape?" Firestar demanded.

"Squirrelpaw rescued us." Leafpaw delightedly fought to keep her balance against her mother's eager grooming.

"I had a dream last night." Squirrelpaw stepped forward. "Spottedleaf told me where Leafpaw was trapped."

"Why didn't you tell me?" Firestar stared in amazement at his daughter.

"You were away on patrol," Squirrelpaw explained. "It couldn't wait. So Sorreltail and I found Leafpaw by ourselves—"

"And there wasn't time to come all the way back to camp for help," Sorreltail broke in. "The Twolegs were already starting to take all the cats they'd caught away from the forest."

"We couldn't rescue them by ourselves," Squirrelpaw chipped in. "But we found Graystripe and Brambleclaw near Snakerocks."

"And Thornclaw and Rainwhisker," added Brambleclaw. "But it was Graystripe who led the rescue. He assessed the danger and decided it was worth trying to save all the cats the Twolegs had trapped."

"Graystripe," Firestar murmured. "I might have known he'd try something foolish." He looked around for his old friend. "Where is he?"

Leafpaw felt the rock sway under her paws. Sandstorm

stopped washing her, as though she sensed something was wrong.

Firestar looked at her with his head to one side. "Why didn't he come back with you?"

Leafpaw saw him read her expression. His face suddenly seemed to be cast in shadow. "The Twolegs caught him," she forced herself to say, the words dropping like stones in the cold air.

"They trapped him inside a monster and took him away," Squirrelpaw explained hoarsely.

"Graystripe's gone?" Firestar whispered. He sat down, drawing his tail around him. Leafpaw's legs trembled. Her father had never seemed so far away, so far beyond her reach to comfort him.

"W-we should have gotten a bigger patrol together before we attacked," Brambleclaw stammered, staring grief-stricken at his leader. "I should have stopped him. I'm sorry."

Firestar stared at the dark brown tom in front of him. A fire seemed to burn in his eyes, and, for a moment, Leafpaw was afraid that her father was going to take out his pain on the young warrior. Beside her, Squirrelpaw unsheathed her claws—would she really defend Brambleclaw against their father? Leafpaw wondered—but Brambleclaw met his leader's gaze without flinching.

"You have brought back my daughter, and Cloudtail and Brightheart." Firestar almost seemed to be persuading himself that he could not blame Brambleclaw for what had happened.

"Graystripe will find his way back to us."

"But they trapped him in a monster," Rainwhisker murmured.

Firestar stared at the gray warrior, hollow-eyed. "He will return," he repeated. "I have to believe that or everything will be lost."

Sandstorm moved closer to Firestar and pressed her cheek against his shoulder. But Firestar just turned away and walked slowly toward the shadowy overhang. Suddenly he looked old beyond his years.

Sandstorm padded after him. "We have both our daughters back." Her voice drifted over the rock. "That is a miracle we never thought would happen."

Firestar gazed at her. "Graystripe would have sacrificed himself for them in an instant," he admitted.

"That is why he will always be a good friend," Sandstorm murmured. She sat beside Firestar and curled her tail around him.

"Leafpaw!" Cody hissed from the shadow of the trees. "Is everything okay?"

Leafpaw could not answer. She was still staring at her father with a pang of sorrow so great she could hardly breathe. She felt her sister's tail sweep gently down her flank.

"Don't worry," Squirrelpaw murmured. "Firestar will be all right, so long as he believes Graystripe will return."

"But they trapped him in a monster," Rainwhisker repeated, as if he would never get the image out of his head.

Mousefur looked grim. "Firestar will have to choose another deputy before moonhigh," she meowed.

Squirrelpaw's eyes flashed with rage, and she rounded on Mousefur, making Leafpaw jump. "You're acting like Graystripe is dead!" she cried. "He's not dead! You heard what Firestar said. He *will* come back. We must not give up hope."

CHAPTER 9

❧

A *mournful yowl echoed around the* rocky cleft, jolting Leafpaw awake. For a moment she thought she was back in the cage, and that her terrifying escape had been nothing but a dream. Then she smelled the scent of the forest and the river on the icy breeze, and remembered she was at Sunningrocks, in the new ThunderClan camp. She blinked open her eyes and looked over the edge of the hollow, her breath billowing like smoke in the freezing air.

"What is it?" Cody whispered. The kittypet had slept beside her in the apprentices' gully last night. Leafpaw felt her soft fur bristling against her flank.

"It sounded like Ferncloud," she mewed. "But I can only see Dustpelt from here."

The striped warrior stood on the frost-covered slope, silhouetted by the early morning light. A kit dangled limply from his jaws.

As Dustpelt carried the kit away, Ferncloud cried out again from the hollow that formed the camp's makeshift nursery.

Leafpaw scrambled out, struggling to get a grip on the icy stone, and raced to Ferncloud's side. "What's happened?"

"Hollykit is dead!" Ferncloud whispered. "Dustpelt's gone to bury her." She tucked her remaining kit close to her belly. "I woke and she was cold. So cold!" Her voice cracked with grief. "I licked her and licked her but she would not wake up."

Leafpaw felt sorrow grip her heart. What kind of medicine cat was she if she hadn't even noticed Hollykit was so close to death?

"Oh, Ferncloud," she breathed. "I'm so sorry."

One by one, the Clan gathered above the nursery in grim silence. Cody stood among them, her eyes round with sympathy. To Leafpaw's relief, her Clanmates took no notice of the kittypet. They shared a common enemy now—the Twolegs who were trapping cats and tearing up the forest.

Cinderpelt scrambled down into the hollow. "Fetch some poppy seeds," she ordered. "Ferncloud must not waste what little energy she has left on grieving."

Leafpaw hurried to the crack in the rock where Cinderpelt stored her tiny heap of remedies and reached in to pull out a leaf-wrapped hoard of poppy seeds. She wished with all her heart they were still in the ravine, where the medicine cats had kept their den in the rock well stocked. Looking at the shriveled leaf beneath her paw, she guessed there were only two or three doses of poppy seeds left, and there was no hope of finding more with leaf-bare nearly upon them.

Firestar's call startled her. "Leafpaw!" She turned to see her father bounding up the slope with Brambleclaw and Mouse-fur. "How is Ferncloud?" he asked.

"Cinderpelt told me to get some poppy seeds to calm her," Leafpaw told him.

"I didn't think it would get this bad so soon!" Firestar growled. "Oh, StarClan! What can I do to help these cats?" He raised his eyes to Silverpelt, fading quickly in the dawn light.

"Last night was so cold," Mousefur remarked. "The poor little mite didn't have enough flesh on her bones to make it through."

"Birchkit survived," Leafpaw reminded them. "We must do everything we can to make sure Ferncloud can feed him properly."

"But the nights are only going to get colder, and once the snow comes . . ." Firestar trailed off and stared into the treetops beyond Sunningrocks.

Brambleclaw glanced uneasily at Leafpaw. "If we are to leave the forest we should go soon," he meowed. "Before snowfall makes the mountains too difficult to cross."

Leafpaw narrowed her eyes. She had been torn by doubts since her sister had told her about Midnight's warning. She could tell that many of her Clanmates couldn't believe that StarClan really intended them to go, but she trusted that her sister and Brambleclaw had a role to play in their Clan's destiny. She did not want to leave her forest home, and she feared the Clan were not strong enough for such a journey, but how could she ignore the will of StarClan?

"You already know how I feel. We cannot go without the

other Clans," Firestar pointed out. Leafpaw silently agreed with him. However much hardship one Clan was in, they had to remain together for StarClan's sake.

"I must take these to Ferncloud," she murmured, picking up the bundle of seeds.

As she reached the crevice, Sorreltail was padding away, her eyes dull with sorrow. She didn't even look up as she went past. Leafpaw noticed that she trod carefully on the freezing stone as if it hurt her paws. She scrambled into the hollow and dropped the poppy seeds at Cinderpelt's paws. Ferncloud was lying with her eyes wide, staring at nothing. Birchkit was huddled beside her, too shocked and hungry to mew. To Leafpaw's surprise, Cody was there too.

"Thank you," Cinderpelt whispered, taking the leaf bundle and carefully unwrapping it with her teeth.

"Shouldn't you be outside?" Leafpaw gently prompted Cody.

"I thought I might be able to help," came the reply. "I lost a litter once."

"A whole litter? That's so sad!"

"They didn't die," Cody explained quickly. "My housefolk sent them away to new homes. But I felt the loss as badly."

"And these are the Twolegs you want to go back to?" Leafpaw mewed in disbelief. "How could you possibly forgive them?"

"It is normal for kittypets not to raise their kits. We don't expect anything else." Cody blinked. "My housefolk are gentle and kind. They chose good homes for each kit. They wouldn't have known that I miss them."

Cinderpelt silenced them with a warning stare. Ferncloud had grown fretful again, writhing on the cold stone and letting out tiny moaning sounds. "Hollykit is with StarClan now," Cinderpelt whispered to her. "She will never know cold or hunger again."

"I tried my best," Ferncloud wailed. "Why couldn't I have died instead of her?"

Firestar's deep mew sounded from the rim of the hollow. "Because then there would be no cat left to look after Birchkit. You must have courage, Ferncloud."

Leafpaw looked up. Cody flattened her ears. She had not met the ThunderClan leader yet.

"Ferncloud, I'm so sorry about Hollykit," Firestar went on. "We will make sure Birchkit survives."

Ferncloud stared up at him. "Birchkit *must* survive," she hissed.

Cinderpelt placed a poppy seed on the ground beside her. "Here," she mewed. "Eat this; it will help soothe your pain."

Ferncloud looked uncertainly at the seed.

Cody stretched forward and sniffed the black speck. "Eat it," she advised, pushing it nearer to Ferncloud with her paw. "You need to save all your strength for the kit you have left."

Firestar watched her curiously. "Sandstorm told me Leafpaw had brought a kittypet back with her. Is that you?"

"Yes. I'm Cody. Come, Ferncloud, eat the poppy seed."

"You can see that the Clan cannot offer you much as a place of safety," Firestar apologized. "But it's even more dangerous for you to travel alone. When I have a free warrior, you'll be escorted home. Until then, you can stay with us."

"Thank you," Cody murmured.

Firestar's gazed flicked back to Ferncloud. "Will she be all right?"

"She just needs rest," Cinderpelt told him.

"And Birchkit?"

"He always was the strongest of the three." Cinderpelt bent down to lick the small scrap of fur that had begun to knead his mother's belly in search of milk.

"Do your best." Firestar turned and padded away.

Cody's shoulders drooped. "It's hard to believe your father was ever a kittypet," she muttered to Leafpaw.

"I never really think about it," she admitted. "It's not as if I knew him back then. I was born after he became leader." She looked at Cody. "Will you be all right, staying here?"

"Of course." Cody sounded surprised that Leafpaw should have any doubts. Sweeping her tail gently along Leafpaw's flank, she turned and crouched down beside Ferncloud. "You two go," she meowed to Leafpaw and Cinderpelt. "You have many cats to look after. There is little I can do for the rest of the Clan, but at least I can take care of Ferncloud."

Cinderpelt looked uncertainly at the kittypet, but Cody reassured her. "I'll make sure she eats the seed," she promised. "And while she sleeps I can look after Birchkit. He'll be missing his sister."

"Very well," Cinderpelt agreed. "But call me if Ferncloud becomes more distressed."

Cody nodded, and Leafpaw followed Cinderpelt out of the den, glancing back just once to blink appreciatively at her friend.

The Clan was huddled in small groups on the exposed flank of the rock, their faces grave. Leafpaw suddenly longed to run through the woods on her own. The Clan she had returned to seemed filled with more suffering than she could ease, and she wanted to be away from it, if only for a short while.

She padded down the slope toward the trees. Pushing through the undergrowth she inhaled the earthy odors of the forest, drinking them in gratefully. She detected the familiar smells of Squirrelpaw and Brambleclaw, and when she put her head to one side to listen she heard their voices mewing urgently up ahead. Weaving through the bracken, she found them in a small clearing near the RiverClan border.

"I told Firestar we'd have to leave soon," Brambleclaw was meowing. "We shouldn't try to cross the mountains after the snow comes, and we'll never make it to newleaf if we stay here."

"But how do we know we should go through the mountains?" Squirrelpaw argued. "The sign never appeared when we were at the Great Rock. A warrior was meant to show us the way, but no warrior came!"

"With no sign, how do we know we're meant to go at all?" Brambleclaw muttered. "Perhaps Midnight was wrong."

"How could she be wrong?" Squirrelpaw mewed. "StarClan sent us to her!"

Leafpaw froze, her tail quivering. She closed her eyes, wishing for some sign that StarClan was listening, and then opened them again impatiently. Why was she being so feeble? If StarClan had a sign they would send it. Until then, they would have to figure this out by themselves.

"Squirrelpaw?" she called. "Brambleclaw, it's me." She pushed through the bracken to join her Clanmates. The pair sprang away from each other and faced her warily.

Brambleclaw shifted his paws. "Did you hear what we were talking about?"

"Yes."

"What do you think?" He stared at her. "Could Midnight have been wrong?"

Part of Leafpaw *wanted* Midnight to be wrong. She wanted to stay in the forest where she had been born. This was StarClan's home, too. But why else would they have ordered Brambleclaw and the others to make such a dangerous journey? They would not have risked the cats' lives for nothing. "Is it StarClan you doubt or yourselves?" she murmured.

Brambleclaw wearily shook his head. "The journey was difficult enough. We didn't think things would be even harder once we returned. We were so sure StarClan would show us the way, but they haven't, and we can't afford to wait. Taking the Clan away from their home is such a big responsibility. . . ."

"And we don't know when we should leave or where we should go," Squirrelpaw put in.

"In the end, it has to be Firestar's decision," Leafpaw reminded them. "You can only tell him what you have seen and heard."

Brambleclaw nodded.

"How did you get to be so wise?" Squirrelpaw asked her sister fondly.

"How did you become so brave and noble?" Leafpaw teased, flicking Squirrelpaw's flank with her tail. She felt a surge of happiness at being with her sister again. Then she remembered Ferncloud and Graystripe, and her heart sank.

"If Firestar does decide to leave," she breathed, "what about Graystripe?"

Squirrelpaw looked sad. "Graystripe will find us, wherever we are."

"I hope so," Leafpaw mewed. "But until he does, who'll be deputy?"

"Graystripe is still our deputy," Brambleclaw meowed.

"But he's not here, and the Clan needs strong leadership more now than ever," Leafpaw argued.

"Firestar can't appoint a new deputy as long as he believes Graystripe is still alive," Brambleclaw insisted.

Leafpaw shook her head. She couldn't agree with him, but she admired his loyalty.

"Let's not argue about it," Squirrelpaw pleaded. "There's already too much to worry about." She glanced at Leafpaw. "There's something I wish I'd asked Graystripe to explain before we lost him."

Leafpaw tipped her head on one side. "What?"

"It just seemed strange at the time, and Firestar silenced him before he could explain. . . ."

Brambleclaw pricked his ears as she went on.

"When we first returned, Graystripe welcomed us by

saying, 'Fire and tiger have returned.'" Squirrelpaw blinked. "It just seemed like an odd thing to say."

Leafpaw looked at her paws, unsure what to say. Should she tell Squirrelpaw and Brambleclaw about Cinderpelt's ominous warning? Or would they be better off without that hanging over their heads? After all, they had enough to worry about already.

"You know something, don't you?" Squirrelpaw prompted.

Leafpaw shuffled her paws, feeling a flash of frustration that she could never hide anything from her sister. "Cinderpelt had a message from StarClan."

Brambleclaw leaned forward. "I thought StarClan had been silent?"

"It was just before you left," Leafpaw explained. "StarClan warned her that fire and tiger would destroy the Clan."

"Fire and tiger?" Squirrelpaw echoed. "What's that got to do with us?"

Leafpaw twitched an ear. "You are *Fire*star's kit." She turned to Brambleclaw. "And you are *Tiger*star's."

Squirrelpaw's eyes widened. "So we're fire and tiger?"

Leafpaw nodded.

"But how could anyone believe we would destroy the Clan?" Squirrelpaw protested. "We've risked our lives to help save them!"

"I know." Leafpaw dipped her head. "And no cat really thinks you would—in fact, only Firestar, Cinderpelt, Sandstorm, Graystripe, and I even know about it. . . ." She was desperate to reassure her sister. "We believe you would never do anything to harm us." Leafpaw realized that Brambleclaw had said nothing. But he was staring at her, his eyes dark with worry, and she felt a flash of inexplicable fear. "Brambleclaw?"

"Are you sure we wouldn't destroy the Clan?" he growled.

"W-what do you mean?"

"Of course we wouldn't!" Squirrelpaw rounded on Brambleclaw in anger and confusion.

"Not on purpose," Brambleclaw meowed. "But it's us, isn't it—fire and tiger—who want to lead the Clan away from its home and on a long, dangerous journey when we don't even know where we're meant to be going?"

A cold shiver rippled down Leafpaw's spine. Cinderpelt's prophecy suddenly seemed more frightening than it ever had before. If the Clan left the forest, following Squirrelpaw and Brambleclaw, what terrible fate awaited them?

When the three cats returned to Sunningrocks, the leaf-bare sun was already low in the sky. Each cat carried a piece of fresh-kill: Leafpaw had caught a mouse; Brambleclaw held a starling in his jaws; Squirrelpaw carried a plump thrush.

Leafpaw longed to go to sleep and forget Brambleclaw's worrying warning. But she was a medicine cat, and she could not rest until she knew the Clan was all right. As she followed her sister up the slope, she wondered if Cody had managed to persuade Ferncloud to eat the poppy seed.

Brackenfur met them. "The fresh-kill pile is over there." He gestured with his tail to a meager heap farther up the rock. Ashfur sat guard beside it, scanning the sky for birds of prey.

The days were gone when the fresh-kill pile lay at the edge of the camp, well stocked and unguarded.

As Leafpaw dropped her offering onto the pile she was shocked by how small it was. There would not be enough for a whole piece of prey each. Tonight she would go without, she decided. She felt too tired to eat anyway.

She padded toward Cinderpelt and Mousefur, who were lying underneath a shallow overhang. The medicine cat looked exhausted, as much in need of her healing herbs as any of her Clanmates.

"How's Ferncloud?" Leafpaw asked.

Cinderpelt looked up. "She's resting now. Cody's taking good care of her."

"Not bad for a kittypet, that one," Mousefur added with a twitch of her tail. "She looked so nervous when she arrived I didn't think she'd settle in. But it looks like she'll be okay here—for a while, anyway."

Leafpaw blinked gratefully at the dusky brown cat, then turned to Cinderpelt again. There was something she had to ask, even though she dreaded hearing the answer. "Will Ferncloud lose her other kit?"

"Birchkit is strong enough for now," Cinderpelt reassured her. "And with only one mouth to feed, Ferncloud should be able to give him more milk."

"He won't last the winter if we stay here, though," Mousefur commented. Her eyes betrayed alarm as she saw Dustpelt padding toward her. "I hope he didn't hear that," she whispered. "He's mourned enough today."

"I did hear, Mousefur," Dustpelt meowed wearily. "And I agree. We must leave the forest."

Leafpaw stared at him in shock. Hollykit's death seemed to have crushed the last morsel of strength in him.

Dustpelt raised his voice so that his deep meow rang around the rock. All the other cats stared at him in astonishment.

"We must leave the forest as soon as we can!" he insisted, his eyes blazing. He swung his head around to look at Bramble-claw. "Your message from StarClan is the only sign of hope we've had," he meowed.

Mousefur stood up. "Before we can leave, we'll need a new deputy."

As she spoke, Firestar appeared from the edge of the forest, carrying a scrawny blackbird. He had clearly heard her words. His eyes glittered as he dropped the blackbird onto the fresh-kill pile and strode up the slope. "ThunderClan has a deputy. When Graystripe returns, he won't find another cat in his place." He turned to face Dustpelt. "I'm glad you agree we must leave," he meowed. "But we cannot leave yet, not without the other Clans."

"I have only one kit left," Dustpelt meowed. "He will die if we stay. We will probably all die."

"Then we must try harder to persuade the other Clans to leave," Firestar growled.

"The other Clans can come when they are ready," Dustpelt retorted. "We are ready now."

Firestar returned the warrior's gaze. "We cannot leave yet," he repeated.

"Ferncloud still needs to rest," Cinderpelt put in quietly.

Firestar acknowledged her support with a brief nod.

Brambleclaw faced Dustpelt. "I know you are mourning two kits," he mewed. "And that you fear for the other. But Firestar is right. StarClan would not want us to leave without the other Clans." He turned to the other cats. "StarClan chose a cat from each Clan to carry Midnight's message back. We had to work together to survive, without ever thinking of the differences between our Clans. StarClan wanted us to share the journey, to learn how to help one another. They must want us to travel together now."

Firestar padded across the rock to stand beside the young warrior. "We need to send out more hunting patrols," he meowed. "We are under no threat from the other Clans now. RiverClan has more food than we do. They have no need to attack." He stared around at the gaunt, hungry cats. "We can devote all our patrols to hunting from now on. We will find enough food in the forest until it is time to leave. Yes, Dustpelt, we *will* leave. I will visit RiverClan and ShadowClan and try to persuade them once more."

Relief washed over Leafpaw as the cats began to nod their acceptance. Then her heart lurched again as Mousefur stepped forward.

"But what about Graystripe?" When Firestar flinched, she went on: "Whether he's coming back or not, we need to find another deputy for as long as he's not here, someone to carry out his duties."

"Yes," Dustpelt agreed. "You haven't named anyone yet."

He glanced at Brambleclaw. "You should choose someone young. Some cat StarClan clearly approves of."

Leafpaw looked around. Ashfur, Whitepaw, Frostfur, and Cloudtail were staring at Brambleclaw. Even Thornclaw seemed to be watching the young cat, as though he might be the one to fill Graystripe's pawprints. Only Mousefur and Rainwhisker were looking elsewhere.

"Brackenfur has enough experience," Mousefur suggested. "He is young and strong and has earned his warrior name many times over."

Rainwhisker nodded. "Brackenfur would be a good deputy."

"Why are you talking like this? Graystripe is not dead!" Firestar spat. "He is still our deputy." The bristling fur along his spine warned the other cats not to argue. He shook himself and blinked, calming down. "But you are right. Someone must carry out Graystripe's duties. So until he returns, the senior warriors shall share them." He glanced at Brackenfur. "You shall organize the new hunting patrols. Sandstorm can organize work within the camp. Brambleclaw, you can help me try to convince ShadowClan and RiverClan that we must leave the forest together." He stalked toward the overhang, and as he passed Leafpaw he called to her, "I want to speak to you," he meowed. "Alone."

Leafpaw followed him uneasily to the hollow. She glanced down at Cody, who was still in the makeshift nursery. The kitty-pet was busy washing Birchkit, ignoring the tiny kit's mews of complaint. Ferncloud lay sleeping beside them. Feeling relieved that the cat who needed it most was resting, Leafpaw ducked beneath the overhang into the shadowy cavern.

Firestar looked urgently into her eyes. "Leafpaw," he meowed. "You must tell me if you have had any sign from StarClan."

"No, nothing," she answered, surprised by his intensity. "What about Cinderpelt?"

"She has heard nothing either." Firestar blinked. "I was hoping they might have spoken to you."

Leafpaw shifted her paws awkwardly. Though she was pleased her father had such faith in her, she felt uncomfortable that he thought StarClan might share with her rather than the Clan's medicine cat.

"Why are they so quiet?" Firestar continued angrily, unsheathing his claws against the cold stone floor. "Are they trying to tell us each Clan must look after itself rather than leave the forest together?"

"I felt the same when the Twolegs captured me," Leafpaw admitted. "StarClan did not visit me once in my dreams while I lay in that stinking cage. I felt as if I was utterly alone. But I wasn't." She returned her father's solemn gaze. "My Clanmates came to rescue me."

Firestar opened his eyes wide as she went on. "StarClan won't do anything to keep the Clans together. They don't have to. Being one of four Clans—not two, not three, but four—lies within our hearts, just like the ability to track prey and hide in the forest shadows. No matter what the other Clans say, they cannot turn away from the divisions, the differences, the rivalries that bind us. The line that separates us from Wind-Clan or RiverClan is also the line that connects us. StarClan know this, and it is up to us to have faith in that connection."

Firestar stared at his daughter as though he were seeing her for the first time. "I wish you could have known Spottedleaf," he murmured. "You remind me of her."

Touched beyond words, Leafpaw lowered her gaze. She sensed that this was not the time to tell her father that Spottedleaf had spoken to her in dreams several times. It was enough that Firestar thought her a worthy companion of the former ThunderClan medicine cat, who padded tirelessly through the stars, watching over her Clanmates.

She just hoped with all her heart that Spottedleaf, and their other warrior ancestors, would come with them when the Clans finally abandoned the forest.

CHAPTER 10

Firestar led the patrol upriver, keeping close to the border where tempting prey-scent drifted across the water from River-Clan's territory. Squirrelpaw padded behind him in step with Brambleclaw, while Ashfur brought up the rear. It was the first time in days that she and Brambleclaw had left the camp together. Firestar had taken the tabby warrior with him to RiverClan and ShadowClan, to plead with them once more to leave the forest. He'd done his best, but Leopardstar and Blackstar both still refused to believe that their future lay with the other Clans, far from their forest home.

Clouds had rolled in overnight, and freezing drizzle hung under the trees, refusing to fall as proper rain but still soaking everything it touched. Squirrelpaw's fur clung uncomfortably to her body as the dampness soaked into her pelt. The trees shone wetly in the bleak leaf-bare light and dripped water onto the fallen leaves below, turning the loose, crisp piles into slippery clumps.

Suddenly Firestar stopped and lifted his nose to scent the air. Squirrelpaw took a deep breath, hoping to catch the welcome aroma of mouse or thrush or vole. But there was no prey-scent coming from this side of the river, only something that seemed strange and familiar all at the same time.

"I think I recognize that smell," she whispered to Brambleclaw.

"It smells like a rogue," Brambleclaw growled.

"Hush!" Firestar commanded. He paused, then dashed forward with his hackles raised. The bushes ahead shivered and a tawny cat burst out. As it streaked away Brambleclaw yowled a battle cry, joining the chase.

"Come on!" he called, but Squirrelpaw was already charging after him.

The tawny cat swerved toward the scent-markers at the RiverClan border. Firestar headed after it without slackening the pace. Squirrelpaw felt a jolt of alarm as she neared the warning scents. The ThunderClan cats were gaining on the rogue as she pelted over the border. The moment Firestar's paws crossed the line in pursuit, a furious yowl sounded close by, and a dark brown RiverClan warrior leaped from a swath of bracken, snarling viciously.

Firestar turned, skidding on the wet leaves, and stopped barely over the border. Brambleclaw and Ashfur almost crashed into him, but managed to stop in time.

"Hawkfrost!" Brambleclaw gasped.

Firestar took a step backward over the border. But he continued to stare at Hawkfrost, his eyes stretched wide as though he were staring into the face of a StarClan warrior. Squirrelpaw was surprised that Hawkfrost's ambush had shocked her father so much. It was hardly strange to encounter a warrior patrolling this close to the border, when every cat in River-Clan knew how close their neighbors were to starvation.

"What are you doing on RiverClan territory?" Hawkfrost demanded.

Firestar did not answer at first. Then he seemed to recover himself, letting his fur lie flat and relaxing his shoulders. "I was chasing that rogue out of ThunderClan territory," he replied. He glanced at the tawny she-cat who had halted behind Hawkfrost. "Why challenge me when you have allowed a rogue to cross your borders?"

Hawkfrost exchanged a long look with the rogue before he answered. "My mother will always be welcome in RiverClan," he meowed.

Sasha! Suddenly Squirrelpaw recognized the rogue she had helped escape from the Twoleg nest. She felt the mild triumph of curiosity satisfied. It was common knowledge that Hawk-frost and his sister, Mothwing, had been left in RiverClan by their rogue mother, though she hadn't stayed in the forest long enough to be known by other Clans.

But Firestar seemed to have more unanswered questions, because he stood rigid, staring at mother and son with his ears pricked.

With a small dip of her head, Sasha meowed a greeting. "I have heard much about you, Firestar," she murmured. "It is . . . interesting to meet you at last." Her voice was icy and dignified, and Squirrelpaw felt self-consciously young and awkward by comparison.

"So you are Sasha?" Firestar meowed softly, his eyes glittering.

"You look as if you expected something else," Sasha suggested.

Firestar's gaze swept along her well-groomed pelt. "You don't look like a rogue."

"And you don't look like a kittypet," Sasha countered. Squirrelpaw winced, but her father showed no anger. Instead he met Sasha's proud gaze evenly.

"I have often wondered why a rogue would choose to leave her kits with a Clan."

"Why would a Clan make a kittypet their leader?" Sasha responded. She did not wait for an answer. "Not all cats are true to their birthright, Firestar. Some choose their own path."

Firestar narrowed his eyes. "Are you such a cat?"

"Maybe," Sasha meowed. "Maybe not. But I hope my kits are." She glanced at Hawkfrost, and Squirrelpaw saw a flash of pride in her eyes.

"Will you stay with RiverClan awhile?" Hawkfrost invited her. "We have plenty of prey." He cast a mocking glance at Firestar, but Firestar didn't react. He simply watched, his eyes still narrowed in thought as Sasha gave her answer.

"I won't stay long," she told him. "But I would like to see Mothwing before I leave."

Hawkfrost curled his lip at Firestar. "I shall send a patrol as soon as I get back to the camp to make sure you have not been stealing RiverClan prey," he warned.

"We have no need to steal," Firestar retorted. He looked at his patrol. "Come on."

Though the air still crackled with tension, Squirrelpaw knew that the danger had passed. Hawkfrost and Firestar turned from each other and padded away from the border. She prepared to follow her father, but before they had reached the safety of the trees, Firestar halted and called out to Sasha. His voice was strangely calm.

"Tigerstar was their father, wasn't he?"

Sasha didn't seem surprised by the question. She nodded. "Yes, he was."

The ground lurched beneath Squirrelpaw. No wonder Firestar had looked so surprised when Hawkfrost had leaped out in front of him. He must have thought it was Tigerstar himself, granted a tenth life. He'd seen Hawkfrost before at moonlit gatherings, and at the disastrous meeting at Four-trees the other night, but perhaps this was the first time they had come face-to-face in daylight.

Then she heard a gasp beside her and saw Brambleclaw standing with his eyes wide. "But Tigerstar was my father too!" he croaked. "Does this mean I have kin in *two* other Clans?"

Hawkfrost flicked his gaze to his half kin. "I'm surprised you hadn't guessed," he meowed. Squirrelpaw looked from one cat to the other, finally noticing the similarities in their tabby pelts and powerful shoulders.

"I thought Tawnypelt and I were the only ones . . ." Brambleclaw murmured.

"At least you had a chance to know our father." Hawkfrost

twitched his tail. "I envy you that."

"I learned more from Firestar than I ever did from Tiger-star," Brambleclaw retorted.

"But still, Tigerstar knew you. He never even set eyes on me."

Squirrelpaw felt a twinge of sympathy for him, knowing how much she cherished her relationship with her own father, but she pushed it away. There was something about the River-Clan warrior that she didn't trust.

Hawkfrost's gaze hardened. "Get away from this bor-der," he warned, kneading the ground with his long, hooked claws—claws like those of the black-and-gold tigers that elders described in their stories; claws that had given his father his warrior name. "I will defend my Clan against any cat if I have to."

He turned and led his mother down to the river, and together they waded through the water and disappeared into the bushes on the other side. Squirrelpaw watched them go in silence, knowing he meant his threat.

CHAPTER 11

❧

The rain grew heavier as Firestar led the patrol back to camp.
Squirrelpaw was disappointed with how little prey they had
caught. Brambleclaw had managed to scramble up an oak and
catch a squirrel dozing in the crook of a branch, but the effort
had left him breathless, and Squirrelpaw realized that the
hungry days since they had returned to the Clan were beginning to have an effect on them both.

"I think it's best if we don't tell the others what we learned
about Hawkfrost," Firestar decided as they trekked through
the dripping trees.

"But shouldn't the Clan be prepared in case"—Squirrelpaw
faltered—"in case anything happens?" she finished lamely.

Brambleclaw dropped the squirrel he held in his jaws. Rain-
water streamed from his whiskers. "I think Firestar's right," he
agreed. "It would be better for the Clan if they didn't know."

Squirrelpaw narrowed her eyes. Was it the Clan Brambleclaw was interested in protecting, or himself? Was he afraid of
what the other cats would say? He had struggled long enough
already to prove his loyalty, and yet no cat could forget his
father's efforts to destroy ThunderClan.

"There's no point stirring up unnecessary hostility," Firestar went on.

Ashfur gave a low growl. "But what if Hawkfrost shares his father's ambition to take over the whole forest?" He clearly shared Squirrelpaw's secret fear.

"We mustn't jump to conclusions," Firestar warned. "It's clear that Hawkfrost's first loyalty is to his Clan. He said he would fight to defend them. Does that sound like Tigerstar to you?"

Reluctantly, Ashfur shook his head, and Firestar went on. "Hawkfrost is no threat to us."

"Yet," Ashfur mewed pointedly.

"Until he proves he is, there's no need to worry the rest of the Clan," Firestar continued. "We might need RiverClan's help before this is over."

Ashfur swished his tail in frustration, but did not argue.

"Don't worry, Ashfur," Squirrelpaw reassured him. She hoped she sounded more confident than she felt. "Hawkfrost is just Hawkfrost. Tigerstar has left nothing bad in the forest except memories."

Brambleclaw picked up the squirrel without commenting and padded away toward Sunningrocks. Squirrelpaw cast an anxious glance at her father.

"He'll be okay," he meowed quietly as he brushed past her.

By the time the cats reached Sunningrocks, rain was battering the exposed rock, and water ran down in rivulets, turning the earth around the rocks to mud. But instead of finding shelter, the cats were gathered halfway up the slope, huddled in a circle. Moans of sorrow mingled with the rattling of the rain on the stone.

With a startled mew, Firestar bounded up the rock, and Squirrelpaw followed, pushing through the cats with her heart beating in her throat. A small dark brown shape lay in the center, pelted by rain which turned pale red as it streamed away down the stone. Squirrelpaw stared down at the limp, sodden body, too shocked to speak as she recognized the narrow muzzle. It was Shrewpaw.

Cinderpelt and Leafpaw crouched beside the apprentice.

"His neck is broken," Cinderpelt murmured. "He must have died as soon as the Twoleg monster hit him. He would have felt no pain."

Squirrelpaw closed her eyes. *StarClan, what are you doing?* she yowled silently.

A desolate cry sounded from the nursery hollow, and Ferncloud hurtled down the slope. Shrewpaw had been one of her first litter. The cats parted to let her see her dead kit.

"What have I done to StarClan that they would steal so much from me?" she wailed.

"Don't blame StarClan," Leafpaw mewed gently. "It is the Twolegs that have done this."

"Why didn't StarClan stop them?" Ferncloud sobbed.

"They are powerless against the Twolegs, just like we are," Leafpaw whispered. She gave herself a shake, then straightened up and called, "Cody?"

Squirrelpaw watched the kittypet weave her way through the gathered cats. Her ribs were beginning to show through her flanks, but she hadn't tried to insist that any warriors be spared from hunting patrols to take her home.

"I think Ferncloud should go back to the nursery," Leafpaw meowed.

"It's flooded with rain," Cody told her. "I've put Birchkit in the warriors' den beneath the overhang. I'll take Ferncloud to join him."

"Good idea," Leafpaw mewed. "Do you still have the poppy seeds?"

Cody nodded. She looked at Ferncloud, who was distraught with grief. "Birchkit is hungry and crying for food," she murmured. "But I think he can manage solid food if I chew it up first. Ferncloud isn't going to be able to feed him herself for a while, poor thing."

"Brambleclaw caught a squirrel. He could have that," Squirrelpaw suggested.

"I'll bring it to the den," Ashfur offered.

Cody nudged Ferncloud with her nose, and with Leafpaw's help they managed to lead her away from her dead kit and back to the shelter of the warriors' den.

"How did this happen?" Firestar demanded when they had gone.

"He was with me," began Thornclaw, Shrewpaw's mentor. His fur stood on end, and his eyes were huge with despair. "He was chasing a pheasant."

"Why didn't he see the Twoleg monster?"

"He was chasing a *pheasant*," Thornclaw repeated. "It would have fed half the Clan. He forgot to be careful."

"Didn't you hear or smell the monster and warn him?" Firestar's question was filled more with sorrow than accusation.

Thornclaw miserably shook his head. "With prey so scarce, the hunting is better if we split up. I wasn't close enough to see what was going on."

Firestar dipped his head, understanding.

"I'll sit with him." Whitepaw's young voice sounded over the beating of the rain. Shrewpaw had been her denmate since kithood, and the sorrow of losing him glistened in her green eyes. "I don't care if we've been driven out of our camp. We can still hold a vigil."

"I'll join you," Thornclaw croaked. He leaned down and pressed his nose against Shrewpaw's bloody flank.

The other cats began filing past to bid farewell to their young Clanmate. When it came to her turn, Squirrelpaw stooped low over Shrewpaw's body, her heart aching. "You were an apprentice in ThunderClan, but you'll be a warrior with StarClan," she whispered.

She turned away and padded down the slope toward the shelter of the trees, her sadness feeling like part of the rain and tiredness that seemed to seep right through to her bones. She spotted Brambleclaw sitting beneath a larch tree, watching her.

"I can't believe Shrewpaw is dead." She sighed.

"I know," Brambleclaw murmured, entwining his tail with hers.

Squirrelpaw leaned closer to him. "Ferncloud is heart-broken."

"She will find comfort in having the rest of her Clan around her." Brambleclaw sighed.

Squirrelpaw couldn't help feeling that he was talking about more than Ferncloud's grief.

"After all, the Clan means more to a cat than real kin," he went on.

"Even Tawnypelt?"

"She is with ShadowClan now. My loyalty to her comes second to ThunderClan, and she understands that."

"And what about Hawkfrost and Mothwing? Do you feel anything for them, now that you know you share the same father?"

"Knowing we share the same father doesn't change anything," Brambleclaw went on. "I am nothing like Hawkfrost." The tip of his tail twitched anxiously. "Am I?"

"Of course not," Squirrelpaw replied hotly. "No cat would think you are."

"Even when they find out what we have in common?"

"ThunderClan will always think of you as a brave warrior, loyal to his Clan," Squirrelpaw reassured him.

"Thank you." He gave her a quick lick on the cheek before getting to his paws and moving away toward the river.

Squirrelpaw followed, keeping pace with him until he sat down and stared across the border into RiverClan territory.

Squirrelpaw followed his gaze. The river carved its way

though the small glade, its surface shattered by the pouring rain. She peered closer and blinked. "Look, Brambleclaw!" she mewed in surprise. "Look at the river!"

"What about it?"

"Do you remember when Hawkfrost and Sasha waded across it earlier?"

"Yes." Brambleclaw twitched his ear. "So?"

"Well, they *waded* across it," Squirrelpaw repeated. "They didn't swim; they *waded*."

Brambleclaw looked baffled.

"Look at the stepping-stones!" Squirrelpaw jumped up and pointed with her tail. "They're sticking right out of the water. After rain like this, in the middle of leaf-bare, they should be nearly covered."

"You're right." Brambleclaw sat up.

"Surely the river shouldn't be this shallow?"

"Well, it's been quite dry lately," Brambleclaw commented.

"Not that dry," she argued. "It's been pouring all day today, but the river's not swollen at all. Something must be wrong."

"Like what?"

Just then a familiar voice called from the bank opposite, "What are you two up to?"

Stormfur appeared and waded across the stream. "Are you finding it as hard as I am, being cooped up in camp after our journey?"

"Yes. Everything is harder. Shrewpaw died," Squirrelpaw told him sadly. "Whitepaw's sitting vigil." Suddenly she wondered if they should be back at camp, mourning their lost Clanmate. She glanced at Brambleclaw, who seemed to understand her anxiety.

"We'll join them soon," he promised.

"Do you want me to catch you a fish to take back?" Stormfur offered.

"The Clan needs all the fresh-kill they can get," Brambleclaw meowed. "But I don't think they'd accept it."

"Are you sure?" Stormfur asked. "They're easy to catch now that the water's dropped."

"So I was right. The level *is* lower than usual," Squirrelpaw mewed, gazing again at the shallow stream. "Is something wrong?"

Stormfur shrugged. "Just a dry spell. This rain will get it flowing again."

Squirrelpaw picked up a trace of Sasha's stale scent on the breeze. She glanced at Stormfur; the mystery of the river seemed suddenly less important than how the rest of River-Clan felt about the rogue she-cat who seemed to come and go as she wished—and whose kits had so much influence in their adopted Clan. "We saw Sasha this morning," she began.

"You know Sasha?" Stormfur looked surprised. "Oh, I forgot. You met her when you rescued Mistyfoot, didn't you? When . . . when my father was taken."

His voice trailed away, and Squirrelpaw pressed her flank against his. "I'm so sorry," she murmured helplessly.

Stormfur nudged her with his nose. "So am I. I wish I could have been there to help," he meowed. "But my father made his own decision to help the trapped cats." He took a deep breath before he went on. "Thanks to him we got Mistyfoot back. The whole of RiverClan was amazed when she showed up."

"Hawkfrost especially, I'm sure," Brambleclaw commented. Squirrelpaw shot him a warning glance. Hawkfrost had been made deputy when Mistyfoot disappeared, which meant he might not have welcomed Mistyfoot back with the same enthusiasm as every other cat, but was Brambleclaw giving away too much interest in Sasha's kit? They couldn't be sure how much Stormfur knew about Hawkfrost's parentage.

"Well, I doubt he wanted to stop being deputy quite so soon," Stormfur agreed. "But he welcomed her return as much as any cat. He's a good warrior. He knows he'll be deputy one day, and he doesn't mind waiting."

"He sounds very confident," Squirrelpaw remarked carefully.

"He's always been like that," Stormfur replied. "What's more important is that he's totally loyal to the Clan, and sticks to the warrior code like a caterpillar to a leaf."

Squirrelpaw blinked. Somehow she didn't think Stormfur had the faintest idea of who Hawkfrost's father was. She looked at Brambleclaw, trying to read his reaction, but Brambleclaw had something else on his mind.

"Do you think there's any chance Leopardstar will change her mind about leaving the forest?"

"Leopardstar says she's not going anywhere as long as there's fish in the river," Stormfur told him.

"Doesn't she care about the Clans staying together?" Squirrelpaw demanded.

"She did ask Mudfur if he'd had any sign from StarClan, just to be sure," Stormfur told her defensively. "But Mudfur hasn't left his nest much recently."

"So he's had no sign either?" Squirrelpaw asked, disappointed.

"Nothing." Stormfur sighed. "It looks like the sign Midnight promised us isn't going to come, now that the Twolegs have destroyed Fourtrees."

"Perhaps we've seen the sign but just not realized what it was," Squirrelpaw wondered out loud.

"Well, we've seen plenty of dying since we got back," Brambleclaw muttered darkly. "Not just warriors, but kits and apprentices, too. But you know what? I'm beginning to think that no cat's going to show us the way. Wherever we're going, we'll have to find our own way there."

CHAPTER 12
♣

Leafpaw raked through the fur at the base of her tail, scraping out the troublesome flea. She cracked its fat body between her teeth, tasting with some satisfaction the blood it had stolen from her. "Got it!"

"Don't tell the others you had an extra piece of fresh-kill," Squirrelpaw joked. "They'll all want one."

Leafpaw's belly growled. The vole she had just shared with her sister had barely touched her hunger. They were lying side by side in a shallow dip in the stone, watching the sun sink behind Sunningrocks. The clouds had cleared, and a perfect half-moon hung in the blue evening sky.

"Has Cinderpelt decided whether you're going to make the journey to the Moonstone tonight?" Squirrelpaw meowed.

"She's speaking with Firestar about it now," Leafpaw replied. The medicine cats of every Clan met each half-moon at Mothermouth to share tongues with StarClan. They didn't need the half-moon to secure a truce—medicine cats lived outside the differences between Clans that sometimes led to quarrels—but it was an important time for sharing concerns and advice about treating their Clanmates.

Leafpaw saw Cinderpelt emerge, and she clambered to her paws, keen to find out if they would be going to Highstones in spite of the dangers that lurked in the forest.

But Cinderpelt shook her head as she came over and stood at the edge of the hollow. "Firestar agrees with me," she reported. "We can't risk the journey with so many Twolegs and monsters about."

"But we need to share with StarClan now more than ever!" Leafpaw protested.

"Firestar says he cannot risk losing us, and he's right. Where would the Clan be without a medicine cat?"

Leafpaw sighed and scraped at the rock with her claw.

"StarClan will share with us if they wish to," Cinderpelt mewed.

Leafpaw shrugged. "Maybe."

"Well, I'm glad you're not going," Squirrelpaw meowed as Cinderpelt padded away. "I nearly lost you to the Twolegs once. I don't think I could bear it again."

Leafpaw gave her sister a quick, fond lick on her head and settled down again. "Do you think the RiverClan cats will go to Highstones?" she wondered out loud. It was strange to think that the other medicine cats might be making the journey without them. Would StarClan think Cinderpelt and Leafpaw were being cowardly?

"I doubt they'll risk it," Squirrelpaw told her. "Last time Brambleclaw and I saw Stormfur, he said Mudfur was pretty sick."

"I was just hoping that, if the medicine cats from all the

Clans traveled to the Moonstone together, it might bring us closer," Leafpaw admitted.

Squirrelpaw nodded. "I know. You'd think trouble like this would unite us, like it did when BloodClan attacked, but instead we seem forests apart."

"Each Clan seems to have its own idea about what to do." Leafpaw sighed. "If only StarClan would give us a sign!"

"Were you hoping that StarClan might share something with you tonight?"

Leafpaw gave a small nod, avoiding her sister's gaze. She didn't want to betray the fear that had made her heart pound all day: the cold dread that they would go all the way to the Moonstone and find StarClan silent even there.

"It's stupid that the Clans should find it so hard to come together." Squirrelpaw's mew interrupted her thoughts. "They have far more in common than they think."

Leafpaw looked thoughtfully at her sister, suddenly wondering what Squirrelpaw was hinting at.

"After all, ShadowClan, RiverClan, and ThunderClan even share kin," Squirrelpaw went on.

"You mean Tawnypelt and Stormfur?"

"Not just them." Squirrelpaw's tail twitched as she spoke. "There are other cats linked to ThunderClan by blood."

With a jolt Leafpaw wondered if her sister had discovered a secret she had known for a moon and kept to herself. "Are you talking about Tigerstar being Hawkfrost and Mothwing's father?"

Squirrelpaw stared at her in astonishment. "Have you been sharing my dreams again?"

Leafpaw shook her head. "I've known for some time," she admitted.

"Why didn't you tell me?" Squirrelpaw demanded.

"I didn't think it mattered. Not right now, when all the Clans are in danger. Why should it make a difference if Tigerstar is Hawkfrost and Mothwing's father?" Leafpaw knew she was trying to convince herself. The last thing the Clans needed was another cat with Tigerstar's hunger for power.

"A warrior like Hawkfrost can't be trusted," Squirrelpaw insisted.

Leafpaw felt an uneasy knot twist in her belly. "But Tigerstar is Brambleclaw's father too," she pointed out. "And Brambleclaw is a loyal warrior."

"Brambleclaw has nothing to do with this," Squirrelpaw snapped.

"Of course not," Leafpaw agreed quickly. "I only meant that having Tigerstar as a father doesn't mean a warrior has to follow in his pawsteps." She prayed this was true.

"Good." Squirrelpaw nodded. "Because Brambleclaw is completely different from Hawkfrost. They have nothing in common. Nothing."

Leafpaw curled into a ball beside her sister and buried her nose under her paws for warmth. Squirrelpaw's words had sounded like an echo—were they Brambleclaw's, perhaps?

"Good night, Squirrelpaw," she whispered, curling up close to Squirrelpaw, their sharp words forgotten. Leafpaw did not need a visit from StarClan to tell her that her sister was falling in love with Brambleclaw. Amid everything else that was going on, and however much Leafpaw missed the connection that once only the two of them shared, this felt right and good for the whole Clan.

She closed her eyes. *I wonder if StarClan will share my dreams,* she thought as sleep tugged at her like a gentle river. It was a half-moon, after all; that had to count for something, even if they weren't at the Moonstone.

Leafpaw felt the insistent nudge of a nose prodding her awake. "Who is it?" she whispered sleepily.

"It's me, Mothwing." The young cat's voice trembled with fear.

Leafpaw blinked open her eyes and saw the RiverClan apprentice outlined in the pale moonlight.

"Come quick; I need you," Mothwing mewed under her breath.

Leafpaw felt her sister stirring beside her. "What's going on?" Squirrelpaw yawned.

"It's Mothwing," Leafpaw told her.

Squirrelpaw was on her paws in an instant. "What are you doing in our camp?" she hissed.

"I need Leafpaw's help," Mothwing explained. "Mudfur is very ill."

"And you thought you'd just creep in here in the middle of the night?"

"Be quiet, Squirrelpaw, before you wake the whole Clan," Leafpaw growled. She wanted to tell her sister to stop seeing Tigerstar's daughter standing in front of them, and see her instead as a medicine cat in trouble, but she didn't want to make Mothwing feel uncomfortable. "Wait here, both of you," she meowed. "I'll go and tell Firestar and Cinderpelt."

"But—" Mothwing began.

Leafpaw silenced her with a glance. "I'll come with you, but I have to tell them where I'm going." Leaving the two cats in uneasy silence, she hurried up the slope to the overhang. She crept into the shadowy cavern and followed her father's scent.

Firestar lifted his head drowsily. "Is that you, Leafpaw?" Beside him, Sandstorm shifted but did not wake.

"Mothwing's come to ask if I can go and help Mudfur. He's really ill."

She saw a shadow moving toward her from the back of the den, and scented Cinderpelt.

"What's she treating him with?" the medicine cat called under her breath.

"I don't know," Leafpaw replied.

"Do you think it's safe to go?" Firestar's eyes gleamed anxiously in the gloom.

"Mothwing wouldn't lie to me," she assured him, guessing he feared an ambush from strong RiverClan cats.

"Then you must go," Firestar murmured. "But if you are

not back by dawn, I'll send a patrol to fetch you."

"We'll be back," Cinderpelt promised. She met Leafpaw's surprised gaze. "I'm coming too. We must do everything we can to help Mudfur." She led Leafpaw out of the den to the crevice where she kept her supplies and pulled out several bundles of leaves.

Leafpaw picked up half the bundles, and they hurried down the rock to where Mothwing waited with her sister.

"I'm coming with you," Squirrelpaw announced.

Leafpaw shook her head. "No need," she muttered through the bundles dangling from her teeth.

"I'll make sure they both return safely," Mothwing meowed.

Squirrelpaw stared distrustfully at the RiverClan cat, and Leafpaw knew her sister was seeing a different cat, broad-shouldered and with gleaming amber eyes. Though they had been born many moons after Tigerstar's death, both sisters had heard him described enough times to be able to picture him as well as any of their Clanmates.

"Remember Brambleclaw," she whispered to her sister. Sharing Tigerstar's blood did not mean a cat shared his dark heart.

"Lead the way, Mothwing." Cinderpelt's order was muffled by the bundles she carried, but Mothwing nodded and bounded silently down the slope.

They waded easily across the river, keeping the herbs above the water. Leafpaw thought back to barely a moon ago, when she had crossed the stepping stones to help a RiverClan apprentice; she had nearly been swept away by the force of the water, and only the spirit of Spottedleaf had stopped her from plunging into the rain-swollen flood. Now the stream trickled quietly around the rocks, hardly covering the pebbles on the riverbed.

Mothwing led the ThunderClan cats into the reed beds; they were no longer marshy, but felt dry underpaw. Leafpaw's heart quickened at the thought of entering another Clan's camp, but Mothwing seemed unconcerned and took them straight into the clearing among the reeds. Unfamiliar eyes gleamed in the shadows, but there was nothing but worry and curiosity in their faces.

"Good, you have come," Leopardstar greeted them. Even in the moonlight Leafpaw could see that the RiverClan leader was not as well fed as she had been lately. Her pelt hung from her body, and her eyes had the dullness of hunger that Leafpaw had begun to accept as normal.

But why should RiverClan cats be starving when the Twolegs were still a long way from their territory?

"Mudfur is in his den," Leopardstar meowed. "Mothwing will take you." She stared into Cinderpelt's eyes. "Do everything you can, but don't let him suffer. He has served this Clan well, and if StarClan needs him more than we do, then we should let him go in peace."

Leafpaw followed Cinderpelt and Mothwing through a narrow reed-lined passage that opened into a smaller clearing. It was so similar to the medicine clearing in the ravine that she felt a pang of longing for her old home.

A low moan came from a shadowy corner.

"It's all right, Mudfur," Mothwing whispered. "I've brought Cinderpelt."

Cinderpelt hurried over to examine the medicine cat, sniffing him and pressing gently along his flanks with her paws. Whatever it was, the sickness had taken hold far inside his frail body. Mudfur was clearly in agony, his words indistinct and filled with pain.

"Cinder . . . pelt . . . let . . . me . . . go . . . peacefully," he begged in a voice that rasped like claws scraping on bark.

"Lie still, my friend." Cinderpelt looked up at Mothwing. "What have you given him so far?"

"Stinging nettle for the swelling, honey and marigold to soothe the infections, feverfew to cool him, and poppy seeds for the pain." Mothwing listed her remedies so quickly that Leafpaw blinked. Last time she had seen Mothwing face a crisis—when the RiverClan apprentice nearly drowned—she had been frozen with panic, and Leafpaw had stepped in to treat the young cat instead.

"Good, that's exactly what I would have given him," Cinderpelt agreed. "Have you tried yarrow yet?"

Mothwing nodded. "But it made him sick."

"It can do that sometimes." Cinderpelt looked down at Mudfur, and her blue eyes clouded with sympathy. "I'm sorry. I don't think there's much more we can do."

"But he's suffering!" Mothwing protested.

"I'll give him more poppy seeds," Cinderpelt meowed. "Do you have any marigold left?"

"Plenty." Mothwing hurried to a gap in the reed wall and drew out a pawful of crushed petals. Taking some dried berries from one of the bundles, Cinderpelt began to knead the petals into them. The berries still had enough softness in them to make a pulp. Cinderpelt sprinkled in more poppy seeds than Leafpaw had seen her use before, then she pushed the mashed herbs to Mudfur.

"This will soothe your pain," she whispered. "Eat as much as you can."

The old medicine cat began to lap at it, his eyes growing soft with gratitude as he recognized what was in the mixture. For a wild moment, Leafpaw wondered if Cinderpelt had given him enough poppy seeds to make him sleep all the way to StarClan, but she knew from the gentleness in her mentor's eyes that she was only trying to ease Mudfur's pain. However silent their warrior ancestors had been lately, Cinderpelt still trusted them to come for Mudfur when they chose to.

"Leave us now," Cinderpelt murmured to Leafpaw and Mothwing. "I'll sit with him till he sleeps."

"Will he die?" Mothwing asked, her voice quavering.

"Not yet," Cinderpelt told her. "But this will ease his suffering until StarClan calls him."

Leafpaw backed away and followed Mothwing through the tunnel to the main clearing.

"How is he?" Leopardstar demanded as soon as they emerged into the silvery pool of moonlight.

"Cinderpelt's doing all she can," Mothwing reported.

Leopardstar nodded, then turned and padded away.

"I've never been here before," Leafpaw mewed, hoping to distract Mothwing. "It's well-sheltered."

The young cat shrugged. "It's a good camp."

"I'm not surprised Leopardstar doesn't want to leave it," Leafpaw went on, being careful to keep her voice non-threatening. She was curious about Leopardstar's sudden thinness—and by the look of the other cats moving around the edge of the clearing, the RiverClan leader was not the only cat going hungry here.

"You're running out of fish now that the river's so low, aren't you?" Leafpaw guessed bravely.

Mothwing looked at her for a long moment. "Yes. We haven't eaten well for a while."

"Does that mean Leopardstar might consider leaving now?"

To her dismay, Mothwing shook her head. "Leopardstar says we will stay as long as there are no Twolegs in our territory. She says that if the river cannot feed us, we will have to learn to hunt new prey."

Leafpaw felt a searing pang of frustration with the stubborn RiverClan leader—there *was* no new prey, she longed to screech—but she did not want to show disrespect for Mothwing's Clan. "You've become a great medicine cat," she mewed, clumsily changing the subject. "Cinderpelt wouldn't have done anything different to help Mudfur."

Leafpaw almost leaped out of her fur when Hawkfrost's voice sounded beside her ear.

"You're right," he agreed. "The Clan will be lucky to have such a good medicine cat when Mudfur goes to hunt with StarClan."

"I think Hawkfrost has more faith in me than I do myself," Mothwing murmured.

"You have no reason to doubt yourself," Hawkfrost insisted. "Our father was a great warrior. Our mother is proud and strong. They shared only one flaw: that their only loyalty was—and still is, in Sasha's case—to themselves above all other cats." He paused and glanced around the clearing. "We're not like that. We understand what it means to be loyal to our Clan. We have the courage to live by the warrior code. And because of that we'll be the most powerful cats in RiverClan one day, and our Clanmates will *have* to respect us then."

Leafpaw felt as if she'd been flung headfirst into the icy river. However much Hawkfrost pledged to live by the warrior code, that sort of ambition could make him dangerous—like his father before him.

Mothwing gave a purr of amusement. "You mustn't take anything my brother says too seriously," she told Leafpaw. "He's the bravest and most loyal cat in RiverClan, but he gets carried away sometimes."

Leafpaw blinked. She hoped with all her heart that

Mothwing was right. But the arrogance that glinted in Hawkfrost's eyes filled her heart with unease. Something told her—some instinct that made her fur crawl—that this was only the beginning.

Hawkfrost could not be trusted.

CHAPTER 13

✤

Squirrelpaw dropped the mouse onto the fresh-kill pile. It did little to bulk up the meager offerings of a sparrow and a vole already brought in by the dawn patrol. Sorreltail had hunted with her, but had caught nothing.

"Take that straight to the elders," Firestar mewed, padding over to them.

"Not Ferncloud?" Squirrelpaw queried.

"Cinderpelt says she won't eat anything yet." Firestar sighed. "But Cody has been sharing food with Birchkit."

"That kittypet should go back to her Twolegs and stop eating our fresh-kill," Sorreltail commented irritably. "She's no good for hunting."

"Cody takes hardly anything for herself," Firestar pointed out. "And while she cares for Birchkit, the other cats have more time for hunting."

Squirrelpaw glanced sympathetically at Sorreltail. She probably resented Cody more for taking up Leafpaw's time than for being a kittypet. She picked up the mouse and carried it to where the elders were making the most of the frail warmth of sunhigh at the top of Sunningrocks.

Frostfur and Speckletail had their eyes closed, dozing. Longtail, the blind tom who was no older than some of the warriors, sat up. "I smell mouse," he mewed.

"It's not very big, I'm afraid," Squirrelpaw apologized.

"It's fine," Longtail assured her. He prodded the mouse with his paw, and the tip of his tail twitched excitedly when the little body shifted, as if the desire to hunt for himself had not dimmed.

Suddenly he lifted his head and opened his mouth to scent the air. "WindClan!" he exclaimed, more in surprise than alarm.

"What, here?" mewed Squirrelpaw, looking around. She didn't think her father was expecting visitors.

At the foot of the rock, Tallstar was leading a small, bedraggled patrol out of the woods. The ThunderClan cats watched them climb slowly up to where Firestar waited. No cat challenged them. Tallstar's step was so faltering, his frame so emaciated, that Squirrelpaw was amazed he had made it all the way here. The two warriors that accompanied him were in no better condition; Onewhisker and Tornear were so thin they looked like they were made of twigs and leaves, and Squirrelpaw half feared the breeze might blow them away.

Crowpaw was at the rear of the patrol, looking thinner than he had on the journey to the sun-drown-place, though he was not quite as scrawny as his companions. Squirrelpaw bounded down the slope to touch noses with him in greeting. When she got closer, she saw that his eyes were as dull as his Clanmates', and his fur was ungroomed.

"Crowpaw!" she exclaimed. "Are you okay?"

"I'm as fit as any of my Clan," Crowpaw growled.

Tornear blinked at her. "Crowpaw has been hunting like a whole patrol on his own, finding prey to feed nearly all the Clan," he reported.

Squirrelpaw pricked her ears.

"He even caught a hawk two sunrises ago," Tornear went on. Even though starvation seemed to have robbed the Wind-Clan warrior of all emotion, Squirrelpaw thought she detected a hint of pride in Tornear's voice.

Crowpaw shrugged. "I used a trick the Tribe taught us."

"Crowpaw!" Brambleclaw came bounding up the rock. Squirrelpaw saw his eyes darken, and she guessed he was as shocked as she had been to find their friend so gaunt and life-less.

Tallstar's voice distracted her. "Firestar, we have come to plead for ThunderClan's help," he rasped. As if the effort of speaking were too much, his legs buckled and he collapsed onto his side. Squirrelpaw started to go over to help him, but Brambleclaw held her back with a touch of his tail.

"The Twolegs have started to destroy the warrens where we have been sheltering," Tallstar panted. "We cannot stay a moment longer on the moor, but we are too weak to travel alone. I don't care that we haven't had another sign. I just know we have to leave. Take us to this sun-drown-place, I beg you."

Firestar looked down at Tallstar, and Squirrelpaw saw sorrow flash in his eyes. "We have been allies many times," he murmured. "And to watch you starve is more than I can bear." He lifted his gaze and stared into the forest, and, as he did so, the brambles under the trees rustled and a pale bracken-colored shape exploded from the bushes.

Tawnypelt! The ShadowClan cat's pelt bristled, and her eyes were wild with fear.

"The Twolegs are attacking our camp!" she yowled, her voice echoing over the rock. "They have surrounded us with their monsters! Please come!"

Firestar bounded down the slope ahead of the others. Even Tallstar hauled himself to his paws and hurried toward the ShadowClan warrior.

"Please help us," Tawnypelt cried to Firestar. "Help us for the sake of the ThunderClan blood that runs in my veins, if nothing else."

Firestar brushed the tip of his tail across her mouth. "We will come for the sake of ShadowClan," he told her gently. "And for the sake of all the Clans in the forest." He looked at his warriors. "Thornclaw, Mousefur, Sandstorm, you will each lead a patrol. We will take all those strong enough to fight." Instantly the three warriors began weaving among the cats, issuing orders.

"What about defending the camp?" Dustpelt called.

"Defend it from what?" Firestar replied. "The only creatures that threaten us now are already attacking ShadowClan."

"What about RiverClan?" Leafpaw's quiet mew sounded from higher up the slope. She fell silent as the ThunderClan warriors turned to stare at her.

Squirrelpaw's heart lurched. Her sister was right. With the camp undefended, Hawkfrost might persuade RiverClan to claim Sunningrocks for themselves.

But the warriors clearly misunderstood Leafpaw's warning. "RiverClan won't help us!" Mousefur spat.

"They might," Cinderpelt argued. "The river's drying up. RiverClan are not as well-fed as they used to be."

Squirrelpaw glanced at Brambleclaw. They weren't the only ones to have noticed the river. If RiverClan were suffering, they were more likely to help ThunderClan than attack them. But her nagging suspicion of Hawkfrost remained.

Firestar's eyes lit up with hope. "Brambleclaw!" he called. "Go to RiverClan and ask Leopardstar for help!"

"Yes, Firestar!"

"Find Mistyfoot first," Squirrelpaw whispered. "And make sure Hawkfrost comes too. He shouldn't be left behind at the camp."

Brambleclaw narrowed his eyes. "You think he would attack here?"

"It's better to be safe."

Brambleclaw snorted. "You're too suspicious," he growled, and pelted away.

Squirrelpaw felt a prickle of guilt. She hoped Brambleclaw didn't think her suspicions included him.

"Squirrelpaw, you'll join my patrol," Sandstorm ordered. "Stay near me or Dustpelt."

Squirrelpaw nodded. Her paws tingled with excitement. It was time to fight back—or time to accept that the forest had been lost, and leave. Even the WindClan warriors seemed to have brightened at the prospect of a battle. Onewhisker thrashed his tail in agitation, while Tornear paced back and forth in front of him.

"We will come with you," Tallstar announced, his croaking voice finding new strength.

Firestar shook his head. "You are not strong enough."

Tallstar fixed Firestar with a stern gaze. "My warriors and I are coming."

Firestar dipped his head. "Very well," he mewed respectfully. He surveyed his Clan. "Mousefur, Sandstorm, Thornclaw, are your patrols ready?"

The three warriors nodded.

"This may be our last battle in the forest," Firestar went on, his voice barely louder than a growl. "We won't be able to stop the Twolegs completely, but we can try to save ShadowClan." He looked at Leafpaw. "We'll need you with us to look after any wounded cats. Cinderpelt will stay behind and take care of the cats here."

Squirrelpaw knew that the medicine cat's old injury meant she would be more valuable to the Clan here at Sunningrocks, ready to tend to any cat who returned from the battle injured. She felt a flash of protectiveness toward her sister, then reminded herself that medicine cats learned fighting skills as well as any warrior.

As Firestar led his Clan down the slope, Squirrelpaw heard Onewhisker whispering to his leader.

"Tallstar, you are on your last life," he was mewing urgently. "Please stay here."

"Whether I'm on my first life or my ninth, my duty is to the forest," Tallstar replied calmly. "I will not miss this battle."

Squirrelpaw saw icy determination in the old cat's eyes, and felt glad for the sake of his dignity when Onewhisker just nodded and walked beside him down the slope to the other cats.

Firestar paused for a moment at the edge of the trees to check that all the patrols were ready before charging into the forest. Squirrelpaw pelted after him with Tawnypelt beside her, their paws thrumming on the hard ground. She glanced back. No cat had fallen behind; even Tallstar was keeping pace. They followed the river until they were safely past the Twoleg clearing nearest the ravine, then swerved around to reach the crest of the slope that led down to Fourtrees. Firestar didn't hesitate, but led them straight over the top of the rise. In the hollow, the slaughtered trees had been neatly stacked in piles. With a sickening jolt Squirrelpaw saw that the Great Rock been utterly crushed, reduced to nothing more than a massive pile of cracked stone.

Crowpaw wove through the running cats and fell in step beside her. "Don't look at it," he warned. "Even if the Great Rock were still here, it wouldn't help ShadowClan."

Suddenly a yowl rang out from behind them, and Firestar swerved to a halt. The cats behind him stopped and spun around.

Mistyfoot, the RiverClan deputy, stood at the top of the

slope. She had her Clan's finest warriors beside her: Storm-fur, Blackclaw, and Mothwing, and beside them the imposing shape of Hawkfrost. Next to him stood Brambleclaw, the outline of his head and shoulders matched with Hawkfrost's against the pale sky.

"Wait!" Mistyfoot called down. "RiverClan will join you!"

Brambleclaw raced over to Squirrelpaw.

"How did you persuade Leopardstar to let them come?" she gasped.

"It wasn't hard," Brambleclaw told her. "They're hungry and growing desperate."

Stormfur pushed his way through the restless cats to join them. "We'll be fighting together."

"It's as it should be," Crowpaw growled from behind.

Looking around, Squirrelpaw realized that all the cats that had returned from the sun-drown-place were beside her—Brambleclaw, Stormfur, Crowpaw, and Tawnypelt. She glanced up at the sky. *Feathertail, are you watching us?* She closed her eyes for a moment, hoping that they hadn't left their friend behind forever with the Tribe of Rushing Water.

"Come on!" Firestar called. With a fierce battle cry, he led them toward ShadowClan territory.

The Thunderpath that had divided ThunderClan from ShadowClan for many moons lay eerily silent.

"They stopped the other monsters from coming here just before they started destroying our part of the forest," Tawny-pelt whispered to Squirrelpaw. "At least it makes it easier to cross," she added dryly.

The hard surface felt icy underpaw as Squirrelpaw raced over it and into the trees. She heard the distant roaring of monsters and smelled their acrid scent. Her paws trembled, but fury urged her on. Crowpaw raced alongside her, his eyes grimly focused on the path. Squirrelpaw was amazed that his bony, ragged body possessed such strength.

She glimpsed a Twoleg monster through the trees. Its great yellow forepaws were lowered, its claws unsheathed as it tore through the undergrowth. Suddenly a violent and unnatural sound filled the forest, and Squirrelpaw scrambled to a standstill. All around, the forest rang with a dreadful creaking and groaning that seemed to split the air.

Flattening her body against the trembling forest floor, she saw a Twoleg monster only tail-lengths away. With massive paws it ripped an oak from the ground, dragging its roots from the earth as if it were a blade of grass. The tree's branches crashed like hail as the monster tipped it over and began to strip the trunk, showering the cats with chips of bark. Something growled behind them, and Squirrelpaw whirled around to find their escape blocked as another monster rolled steadily toward them.

"They're nearly at the camp!" Tawnypelt yowled.

With a sickening feeling of dread, Squirrelpaw saw more monsters ahead, churning their way toward the tangle of brambles that hid the ShadowClan camp.

"We'll have to go that way," Firestar called, gesturing with his tail toward a gap in the trees the monsters had not yet reached.

"No!" spat Crowpaw. "It'll be quicker this way!" He darted forward, heading straight for the camp.

"Stop! You'll be killed!" Squirrelpaw leaped onto Crowpaw's back and dragged him to the ground, digging in her claws.

He collapsed beneath her, hissing with fury. "Get off me!"

Brambleclaw raced over to them. "Don't be such a fool, Crowpaw!"

"He's gone mad!" Squirrelpaw shrieked. "I'm not going to let him kill himself!"

"I'm not frightened of joining StarClan," Crowpaw spat back. "The forest is dying anyway. At least in StarClan, Feathertail will be waiting for me!"

CHAPTER 14

♣

Brambleclaw leaned down and snarled into Crowpaw's face. "You would rather join a dead warrior than fight to save live ones?" Squirrelpaw felt the fight drain from Crowpaw's body, but Brambleclaw went on. "Your Clan needs you more now than ever! Use your head and follow Firestar's orders! Squirrelpaw, you can take your claws off him now."

Gingerly she let go, half expecting Crowpaw to dart off into the trees again, but the WindClan apprentice only stood up and shook himself.

Behind them, the elm-killing monster attacked its victim. Thorn-sharp splinters of wood shot through the air, and Squirrelpaw felt searing pain as a tiny sliver of bark stabbed into her flank.

"Now!" yowled Firestar. The cats leaped forward just as the monster tore a branch from the elm, sending it crashing onto the forest floor where the cats had stood a heartbeat before.

Firestar stopped when they reached the bramble thicket. "Sandstorm, take Leafpaw and the rest of your patrol and get the kits and queens out," he ordered. "Mousefur, take Tornear and Crowpaw with your patrol and find the elders."

Squirrelpaw turned to follow her mother, but Firestar called her back. "Squirrelpaw, I need you here!" he commanded. "Thornclaw, you help the apprentices to get out. RiverClan warriors, go with him, please." Mistyfoot nodded and darted off with the ThunderClan cat. "Dustpelt, wait at the entrance and make sure everyone escapes. Don't let any cat block the way."

"What about me?" Onewhisker demanded as the others charged away.

"I'll get to you soon," Firestar promised. He turned to Tawnypelt, who was tearing at the ground with her long, hooked claws. "You know this part of the forest better than us. We can't go back the way we came. Which way's the quickest out of here?"

"That way!" Tawnypelt answered at once, nodding to a break in the trees. "If we're quick, we'll get to it before the monsters and pick up a trail that will take us to the tunnel under the Thunderpath."

Firestar turned back to Onewhisker and Tallstar. "You two must defend our escape route," he meowed. It was the least dangerous of all the tasks, and Squirrelpaw guessed that her father was trying to preserve the WindClan leader's last life.

Firestar looked at Brambleclaw and Squirrelpaw. "You two, let Tawnypelt take you into the camp. She'll know which den is which. Make sure that no cat remains inside the camp. If you hear me yowl, get out at once. It'll mean the monsters have reached the brambles."

Brambleclaw pressed his muzzle to Squirrelpaw's ear. "Are you okay with this?"

"Of course I am! What do you take me for—a kit who's never left the nursery?" Squirrelpaw jerked indignantly away. He blinked at her, his eyes glittering with concern, and she realized with a jolt that he was just worried about her. "I'm fine," she promised. "It feels like a battle, and I need to fight for the forest—even if we can't win. We can't let Tawnypelt down."

She whirled around and raced for the camp entrance. Tawnypelt was already scrambling through the prickly tunnel that led into the camp. As Squirrelpaw pounded after her into the clearing, the stench of terror nearly stopped her dead in her tracks. Pelts flashed everywhere as the ShadowClan cats bolted in blind panic. Terrified yowls tore through the air as queens called for their kits, and warriors shrieked orders.

Amid the chaos, the newly arrived warriors were somehow managing to stay calm: Squirrelpaw spotted Sorreltail and Tornear flanking a group of confused ShadowClan elders to herd them across the clearing; on the far side, Leafpaw urged Runningnose, the old ShadowClan medicine cat, toward the camp entrance.

Blackstar's white coat stood out among the shadows. A gray apprentice crouched beside him, his fur standing on end. "Don't be afraid!" the ShadowClan leader growled, nudging the apprentice to his paws. "I won't let you die."

He began to push the petrified apprentice toward the tunnel. Suddenly a kit squealed from the far end of the clearing. Blackstar turned to look, and Squirrelpaw followed his gaze. The tiny scrap of dark brown fur had flattened itself on the ground and screwed its eyes tightly shut.

Blackstar glared at Squirrelpaw. "Don't just stand there! Get Smokepaw out while I get that kit!" He shoved the apprentice toward her and headed for the kit.

Smokepaw stared at her, too stunned to speak or move. There was no time for formal introductions. Squirrelpaw grasped the scruff of his neck in her teeth and started to haul him across the ground. She pushed him into the tunnel and scanned the clearing. Blackstar had grabbed the kit and was pelting toward her. Squirrelpaw darted out of the way just in time to let the ShadowClan leader hurtle past.

She rushed over to the nursery thicket and thrust her head into the nest. Peering into the shadows, she scented the air and listened for mewling above the roaring of the monsters. The nest was empty.

"Is everyone out?" Mothwing stood beside her, pelt bristling.

As Squirrelpaw nodded, she heard Hawkfrost call to one of his Clanmates, "We've done enough. Get out now, before the camp is destroyed!"

"We'll stay until every cat is out!" Mistyfoot countermanded instantly, her sharp yowl making Hawkfrost freeze in surprise.

"Stop acting like you're in charge!" Mothwing hissed angrily to her brother.

"Maybe not now," Hawkfrost spat back. "But one day!"

Squirrelpaw felt a shiver chill her fur, but there was no time to think about it. A tortoiseshell ShadowClan queen was struggling to carry her two kits across the clearing. She kept dropping one and dashing back to fetch the other. Squirrelpaw raced over.

"I'll take this one!" she breathed, picking up the tiny bundle in her teeth.

The queen flashed her a grateful look, and together they made for the entrance. Dustpelt was waiting outside. Squirrelpaw thrust the kit at him and ran back down the tunnel.

The camp was emptying quickly, and the roar of the monsters was deafeningly close. *Make sure that no cat remains inside the camp.* Firestar's order rang in her ears. She scoured the shadows of the camp wall for cats, terrified that any moment a monster would crash through, but only Brambleclaw, Tawnypelt, and Mothwing were left in the clearing.

"Mothwing, get outside and help Leafpaw check for injuries," Brambleclaw hissed. "We'll search the camp for stragglers."

Mothwing headed for the tunnel. "Hurry!" she called over her shoulder.

Trees were tipping and falling all around the camp, their leafless branches rattling together like dried bones. But Squirrelpaw had not heard her father's signal yet, so she had to assume it was safe to stay.

"Is everyone out?" Brambleclaw demanded.

"We need to check the dens again to make sure," Tawny-pelt panted.

"I've checked the nursery," Squirrelpaw meowed. "It's empty."

"Did Tallpoppy and her kits get out?"

"I helped a queen and her kits to the tunnel," Squirrelpaw told her.

Brambleclaw flicked his tail. "I'll check the warriors' den." He glanced at Tawnypelt. "You check the apprentices'."

"What about the medicine clearing?" Squirrelpaw called to Tawnypelt.

"Littlecloud's gone already."

"But are any sick cats there?" Squirrelpaw demanded.

Tawnypelt blinked. "I don't know," she admitted.

"I'll check," Squirrelpaw promised. "Where's the entrance?"

"Over there!" Tawnypelt pointed with a flick of her tail to a tangle of thorns beside the warriors' den.

Squirrelpaw squeezed her way through the narrow tunnel. It opened into a large den, sheltered from the camp and the forest by a thick covering of hawthorn branches. The den was empty, and she was about to push her way back out when she heard her father's yowl.

"Get out! The monsters have reached the camp!"

She began to struggle through the tunnel, but the brambles clung to her pelt. She thrashed wildly and felt the thorns dig deeper. A tree groaned overhead, its timber cracking as it began to fall. With a deafening crash it smashed into the ground so close to the camp wall that Squirrelpaw felt the ground shudder.

Wild with fear, she writhed harder, trying to pull herself free. "Brambleclaw!" she shrieked. "Help!" She expected a tree to crash down on top of her at any moment. Would she be killed trying to help ShadowClan, with no chance to see their new home?

Suddenly Squirrelpaw felt strong teeth sink into the scruff of her neck and haul her forward. The thorns raked her flanks like claws, but she did not care. She leaped to her paws. Brambleclaw was staring at her, his sides heaving.

"Thank you!" she breathed. She pressed her muzzle against his, but they weren't safe yet. Another tree groaned overhead, and Squirrelpaw looked up to see a shadow loom slowly over the camp. A huge sycamore was tipping toward them, its branches spreading across the sky as it began to topple.

"Where's Tawnypelt?" she cried.

"I told her to go," Brambleclaw meowed. "Everyone has left but us. Let's get out of here!"

The two cats pelted toward the camp entrance and shot through, almost crashing into Dustpelt, who was waiting outside.

"You're the last," he yowled. "Come on!"

Looking over her shoulder, Squirrelpaw saw the sycamore crash down onto the camp, crushing everything beneath its heavy branches. Another of the Clans' camps had been destroyed. The home that ShadowClan had lived in for uncountable moons was gone.

Dustpelt led them away through the forest. Tallstar and Onewhisker were waiting on the path, staring with wide, horrified eyes as the forest fell about them. Firestar, Leafpaw, and Tawnypelt were with them.

"Hurry!" Onewhisker urged. "The others are already heading for the Thunderpath!"

"I thought you hadn't heard my warning!" Firestar gasped.

"I got stuck," Squirrelpaw explained breathlessly.

"Where's Crowpaw?" Brambleclaw asked, looking around.

"Heading for the tunnel." Firestar flinched as another oak smashed into the ground nearby.

"Did all the queens and kits get out?" Tawnypelt demanded.

"Blackstar had a kit," Onewhisker answered. "And there was a tortoiseshell with two kits. . . ."

"What about Tallpoppy?"

"I thought Tallpoppy was the tortoiseshell!" Squirrelpaw gasped.

"Tallpoppy's a tabby!" Tawnypelt's voice rose in panic. "She's got three kits, not two!"

The cats gazed at one another in dismay.

"I thought everyone was out," spat Dustpelt.

"The camp was definitely empty," Squirrelpaw panted. "They must have run off into the forest!"

Squirrelpaw pricked her ears, listening for the mewling of kits.

"Over there!" Onewhisker cried. He pointed with his nose to a clearing surrounded by fragile, pale-barked saplings. They raced over, Squirrelpaw scrabbling to get a grip on the slippery leaves.

"Hurry!" Tallstar hissed behind her. She felt Brambleclaw nudging her flank. As she struggled to find her footing, a crack sounded above them and a tree smashed down onto the forest floor only tail-lengths ahead, separating them from the others. Squirrelpaw gasped and shut her eyes.

"Are you okay?" Brambleclaw demanded.

Blinking, she opened her eyes and saw the tree lying in front of them. Had Leafpaw and the others escaped? She darted forward away from Tallstar and scrambled onto the newly fallen trunk with Brambleclaw beside her.

"They're okay!" she yowled in relief. Tawnypelt and Leafpaw were standing in the clearing with Tallpoppy. Onewhisker was trying to round up her three kits, who were darting about in terror, their little tails stuck straight out behind them. Firestar was at the edge of the clearing, scanning the forest for the best escape route. Looking down, Squirrelpaw saw Tallstar squeezing through the branches of the fallen tree and limping quickly over to join the ThunderClan leader.

Through the trees, Squirrelpaw could see monsters on all sides, munching steadily closer. Suddenly she heard a terrifyingly familiar creaking sound. "Look out!" she shrieked.

An ancient birch tree was toppling toward the clearing.

"Save the kits!" Squirrelpaw yowled to Firestar as the tree

cast a shadow across his orange pelt. Tallpoppy heard her and grabbed a kit; Tawnypelt picked up another, and, with Leaf-paw and Tallstar fast behind, they pelted out of the way. But Onewhisker was still diving for the final kit, and Squirrelpaw stared in horror as the tree hurtled toward him.

Her heart seemed to stop as the moment stretched into a lifetime. Firestar leaped forward and hurled himself against Onewhisker's flank. Squirrelpaw just had time to see the WindClan warrior flung clear, the kit grasped safely between his jaws, before the tree hit the ground with a deaf-ening crash.

"Firestar! No!" Squirrelpaw bounded down from the trunk and pelted over to the fallen tree. Brambleclaw kept pace with her, swerving away toward a brown tabby shape staggering at the edge of the branches.

"Got you!" he cried as he dragged the WindClan warrior and the kit out from where they were tangled in the branch tips.

Leafpaw was stumbling, dazed, from underneath a buckled sapling that had protected her when the tree fell. But there was no sign of Firestar. A Twoleg howled, and another splin-tering groan made the air tremble.

"Get out of here!" Brambleclaw screeched.

"I'm not leaving without Firestar," Squirrelpaw cried.

"We'll find him!" Brambleclaw promised. He looked at Onewhisker. "Get the others to the Thunderpath!"

The earth shuddered as another tree crashed down behind them.

"We'll wait for you at the tunnel," Onewhisker promised.

As the WindClan and ShadowClan cats fled, Squirrel-paw ran over to where Leafpaw was scrabbling beneath the branches.

"I can see him!" she cried, clawing desperately at the earth.

Brambleclaw pushed past her, using his head to thrust aside the tangled splinters of wood. Squirrelpaw could see her father's orange pelt, slumped beneath a heavy branch. Brambleclaw stretched forward and grasped Firestar in his jaws. Trembling with effort, he dragged him out and laid him on the leaf-strewn earth.

A shaft of pale sunlight sliced into the clearing and lit up the ThunderClan leader's orange pelt. He lay very still with his eyes closed.

"He's losing a life," Leafpaw whispered.

"Firestar . . ." Squirrelpaw's tail began to tremble. "Father!" she yowled. Around them, monsters shook the ground, their yellow eyes blazing between the trees.

"We've got to get him out of here!" Brambleclaw hissed.

"We can't risk moving him," Leafpaw warned.

Squirrelpaw pressed her belly against the earth. "I'm not leaving without him."

An earsplitting crack exploded above them, and she screwed up her eyes as the forest suddenly went dark. Images flashed through her mind—Sandstorm, the old camp, the Tribe of Rushing Water, Feathertail. . . . *StarClan! Don't let me die yet. After everything we've been through, I need to know that the Clan survives!*

"Squirrelpaw!" Brambleclaw's call sounded muffled under the fallen branches that covered them. "Where are you?"

Squirrelpaw opened her eyes and took a long, shaky breath. The fallen tree was lodged on the trunk of the other, forming a tiny cavern. Brambleclaw's dark brown pelt was just visible through the twigs. She twitched her tail and flexed her paws one after the other. "I'm okay," she called. Nothing was broken, but her pelt stung where branches had scraped against it. "Brambleclaw, are you hurt?" With a grunt, she hauled herself toward him and stretched out her head to lick his flank.

"It's all right; I'm fine," Brambleclaw muttered, struggling to sit up. "Can you see your sister anywhere?"

Squirrelpaw strained her eyes in the gloom. "Leafpaw?"

"I'm over here," came a voice. Squirrelpaw could make out her shape now. She was crouching over Firestar, protecting his body with her own.

"The kit . . . is it safe?"

When Squirrelpaw heard her father's rasping mew, she wriggled upright, ducking her head under the branches until she could straighten her legs. She felt the blood pulsing though her paws, cold as ice. She forced her way through the twigs until her father's breath wafted against her cheek. His eyes were glazed, but open.

"Did you speak with StarClan?" Leafpaw whispered to him.

"I could hardly see them," Firestar croaked. "But I know they were there." He lifted his head. "Did Onewhisker rescue the kit?"

"Yes, they're both safe." Brambleclaw squeezed through the branches to Squirrelpaw's side.

Squirrelpaw searched Leafpaw's gaze. "Will Firestar be okay?"

"He'll be fine," Leafpaw replied. She pressed her nose against Squirrelpaw's cheek. "Don't be scared. This was meant to happen."

Squirrelpaw felt her heart beating in her throat. "How can we get him out of here?"

"I can walk," Firestar mewed, hauling himself unsteadily to his paws.

Suddenly a Twoleg howled above them. It sounded so close that Squirrelpaw spun around with a snarl. She looked up. A shadow loomed over the branches that covered them.

"We must go now!" Brambleclaw hissed.

The Twoleg was peering down through the tangle of twigs. Leafpaw flattened her belly against the ground, her eyes stretched wide in terror.

"I won't let them catch you again!" Squirrelpaw promised. She glanced at Brambleclaw. "Can you get them out if I distract the Twoleg?"

Brambleclaw blinked. "I'm not sure that's safe . . ." he began.

"I'll be okay," Squirrelpaw insisted. "Come on; we don't have much time."

Without waiting, she struggled out from the branches. She could see the Twoleg's hind legs in front of her. Giving a loud screech of fury she shot between them, raking the Twoleg's pelt with her claws as she rushed past. She heard it howl and glanced back to see it lumbering after her, away from her Clanmates.

Squirrelpaw pelted over the splinter-strewn forest floor. Ahead a monster lifted its claws into the air to bring down another tree. Squirrelpaw dodged into a swath of brambles and looked back for her Clanmates. *StarClan, help them!* Then she glimpsed her father's orange pelt weaving through the branches of the fallen tree, heading for the far side of the clearing. Brambleclaw ran beside him, and Leafpaw's brown tabby fur flashed behind. As they reached the open ground, where they could be seen more easily, Squirrelpaw tipped back her head and yowled. She heard the Twoleg run over and start kicking at the brambles, trying to flush her out. Squirrelpaw crawled backward, ducking her head, and yowled again. She had to keep the Twoleg focused on her while the others escaped.

Peering out through the thorns, she saw Brambleclaw glance in her direction, but he kept going until they reached the safety of the standing trees. Squirrelpaw straightened up with relief. Wriggling around, she forced her way through the brambles and skirted the edge of the clearing until she reached the path that led to the tunnel. Firestar, Brambleclaw, and Leafpaw were hurrying toward her.

"You made it!" Leafpaw gasped.

"Keep going!" Brambleclaw hissed.

Squirrelpaw fell in beside them. Firestar staggered, his paws stumbling on the packed earth.

"Don't stop now!" she urged, pressing against him.

Brambleclaw flanked his other side, and between them they kept their leader on his paws as they hurried to the safety of the tunnel that led to ThunderClan territory. They had escaped the Twolegs this time—but how much longer would it be before the whole forest was lost to them forever?

CHAPTER 15

♣

Leafpaw burst out of the tunnel that led under the Thunderpath. Brambleclaw and Squirrelpaw followed, with Firestar stumbling between them. For a moment, the light was blinding, and Leafpaw screwed up her eyes. Then they adjusted to the cold daylight after the shadows in the tunnel, and she looked around at the ShadowClan cats lying exhausted on the narrow strip of grass beside the deserted Thunderpath.

Tallpoppy's kits mewled as they huddled close to their mother. Littlecloud hurried from one cat to another, helpless without any of his supplies, and Blackstar stood staring at his Clan as if he couldn't believe what was happening to them. His white pelt was stained with blood, and his black paws were pricked with bark and splinters.

Firestar's voice croaked behind her. "Is everyone okay?"

"You should lie down," Leafpaw urged him. "There are no monsters here."

"We can't stay in the open!" Brambleclaw objected.

"We have to rest before we go on," Leafpaw insisted.

Tallstar limped toward her. "Is Firestar all right?" he asked hoarsely.

"Yes, but he lost a life when the tree fell," Leafpaw explained.

Tallstar closed his eyes and shuddered all the way to the tip of his long tail.

"I'm taking my warriors home," Mistyfoot called from where the RiverClan cats had gathered at the edge of the grassy space.

"Will you help us get ShadowClan to Sunningrocks first?" Firestar asked.

"Sunningrocks?" Blackstar narrowed his eyes. "Why do you want to take us there?"

"It's where ThunderClan lives now, and you'll be safe from Twolegs there," Firestar meowed. "Cinderpelt has herbs for your injured cats, and there's room for you all to rest."

And where else can ShadowClan go? Leafpaw thought grimly. There was hardly a place left in the forest that hadn't been taken over by Twolegs.

"Okay," Mistyfoot nodded. "We'll go with you as far as Sunningrocks. But just because you've welcomed ShadowClan onto ThunderClan territory doesn't mean they're welcome in ours."

"We'll be patrolling the border!" Hawkfrost warned, his eyes cold as ice.

Squirrelpaw glared at him. "How can you worry about borders at a time like this? When will you realize what our journey meant, for *all* the Clans?"

Brambleclaw silenced her with a glance. "ShadowClan will not cross the border," he promised.

"Of course we won't," snapped Blackstar.

Brambleclaw turned to Leafpaw. "How long before we can leave?"

When Leafpaw hesitated, Firestar lifted his head. "I'm growing stronger," he insisted. "We can go soon."

"Littlecloud?" she called to the ShadowClan medicine cat. "Can everyone make it to Sunningrocks?"

"I think so, if we travel slowly," the small tabby tom replied.

Leafpaw looked up at the sky. The sun was a fiery ball, sinking toward the treetops. "We should try to get back before it's dark," she told Brambleclaw. "Before it's too cold."

"Okay," Brambleclaw mewed. "We'll rest long enough for everyone to catch their breath, then we'll move on."

Thin clouds drifted in front of the sinking sun as the cats trekked through the woods.

"Tallpoppy?" Leafpaw matched her pace to the limping ShadowClan queen's. "Are your kits all right?"

Tallpoppy gazed at her three kits, carried now by warriors, and nodded. "Just scratches," she murmured.

"We can clean them and treat them with marigold when we get to Sunningrocks," Leafpaw promised.

Mistyfoot padded close beside Tallstar, pressing against the WindClan leader's flank whenever he stumbled. Brackenfur carried one of Tallpoppy's kits, and Tornear followed the ShadowClan apprentices, nudging them gently forward whenever they slowed their step.

"It's as if we don't belong to different Clans anymore,"

Leafpaw whispered, catching up with Squirrelpaw.

Her sister nodded. "This is what it was like on the journey to the sun-drown-place."

But as the cats limped onto the sloping surface of Sunningrocks, the old rifts returned. ShadowClan climbed to the top of the rock, while RiverClan halted beside the trees. Brackenfur placed the kit beside Tallpoppy and rejoined the ThunderClan cats as they padded slowly up the slope. He pressed his golden-brown flank against Sorreltail's, supporting her as her exhausted paws swayed beneath her. Tallstar lay down close to the base of the rock, too tired to climb any farther. Onewhisker, Tornear, and Crowpaw gathered around him.

"How did it go?" Whitepaw rushed over to Brightheart and pressed her nose into her flank. She drew back quickly. "You're bleeding!"

"Just some scratches," Brightheart reassured her.

"You're alive!" Cody hurried down from the overhang, with Birchkit stumbling after her. She pressed her muzzle against Leafpaw's.

Ferncloud appeared at the lip of the nursery and stared in bewilderment at the cats crowding onto the rock. "What happened?"

"Everyone's safe." Brambleclaw shouldered his way to the front of the patrol. "That's the main thing."

"Thank StarClan." The ThunderClan queen sighed.

Cinderpelt clambered out of her hollow. "Where's Firestar?"

"I'm here," Firestar croaked, weaving his way to the front.

Leafpaw followed him closely, aware that he was still shaking.

"Firestar lost a life," she murmured before Cinderpelt could say anything.

"What about the ShadowClan camp?" Frostfur demanded. "Did you save it?"

"We cannot fight the monsters," Firestar meowed bleakly. "We could do nothing except help ShadowClan escape before their camp was destroyed."

"They destroyed the camp?" Frostfur gasped.

"There's nothing left but fallen trees," Blackstar growled. "We have no home."

"You'll be safe here for now," Firestar told the ShadowClan leader.

Blackstar's eyes glimmered with relief for a moment. Then he turned to his medicine cat. "Littlecloud," he meowed. "Do what you can to help your Clanmates."

The small tabby tom began to pace quickly around the ShadowClan cats. He leaned down and sniffed Tallpoppy, then began to lick her flank. "There are many splinters here," he mewed, lifting his head.

"Tallstar has a gash on his hind leg," Onewhisker added.

Cinderpelt looked at the bloodstained pelts around her. "Fetch everything we have," she told Leafpaw. "We just have to hope it will be enough."

Leafpaw heard pawsteps following her as she hurried to the crevice where they stored their medicine supplies. It was Cody.

"There are so many injuries!" The kittypet's eyes were wide and frightened.

"But we're all still alive," Leafpaw pointed out, reaching down into the gully with her paw. She pulled out the first bundle of herbs she touched. "Can you take out splinters?"

"I can do more than that," Cody answered. "Come on, Birchkit!" she called, and they padded toward a group of ShadowClan kits trembling with fear and cold.

"Is this kittypet a medicine cat?" Blackstar growled.

"It's okay," Leafpaw called out. "She knows what she's doing."

Cody soothed each kit with a reassuring lick, then encouraged Birchkit to distract them while she searched their fur for cuts and splinters.

Leafpaw pushed her paw back into the crevice. She hoped there were enough berries to make poultices for all the cats who needed one. To her surprise she found the hiding place was better stocked than she had expected. She pulled out as much marigold as she could find and reached back in for the berries.

Cinderpelt appeared behind her and nodded when she saw the pile of herbs growing on the rock. "I went back to the ravine while you were away and brought as much as I could carry," she explained. She paused and looked at the mass of ShadowClan cats milling fretfully at the top of the slope, their faces bewildered and frightened. "Help ShadowClan first," she ordered. "There are too many for Littlecloud to manage alone, and I can cope with Tallstar and our own wounded."

"Will Blackstar mind if I help?" Leafpaw asked. The ShadowClan leader sat with his elders, his eyes fixed on Cody as she tackled another kit.

"You persuaded him to let Cody help," Cinderpelt reminded her.

"But she's not a *ThunderClan* cat . . ." Leafpaw mewed.

Cinderpelt gazed at her through narrowed eyes. "Blackstar's no fool. He knows his cats need our help."

Leafpaw nodded. Summoning up her courage, she padded toward the ShadowClan cats and called to Littlecloud, "Can I help?"

The look in Littlecloud's eyes gave away his relief and gratitude. But before he could reply, Blackstar rounded on Leafpaw, his eyes as hard as the Moonstone. "We can take care of our own cats, thank you."

"But you've already allowed Cody to help, and I have herbs," she offered, forcing herself to sound calm.

"Littlecloud will manage," Blackstar insisted.

Leafpaw shuffled her paws, torn between her duties as a medicine cat and nervous respect for Blackstar's wishes. Then Littlecloud mewed loudly, "Blackstar, we need those herbs."

Blackstar flattened his ears, but Littlecloud held his gaze. "With Leafpaw I can help our Clanmates twice as fast."

Blackstar twitched his ears. "Very well," he growled.

"Can I help too?" Mothwing padded across the rock to join them. "Mistyfoot said it would be okay."

"You may as well," Blackstar grunted, turning away.

"Thanks, Mothwing," Leafpaw whispered. She left the bundle of herbs at Mothwing's paws and hurried back to the crevice to fetch more. Cinderpelt was still there and had begun mixing a salve on a dried oak leaf.

"This is ready to use," she muttered through a mouthful of half-crushed berries. "Come back when you need more."

Leafpaw went back and dropped the salve beside Littlecloud, who was examining Runningnose's pelt. "Rub this in after you've pulled out the splinters," she told him. "It'll stop any infection." She gazed around at the ShadowClan cats. "Where would you like me to start?"

"The elders heal slowly, so they should be treated as soon as possible," Littlecloud advised without looking up.

Leafpaw went over to Boulder, who was lying beside Runningnose, his eyes glazed with shock. She nodded politely at him, and when he did not respond, she leaned down and began to lick his flank. The old cat sighed quietly as she pulled out a splinter with her teeth and rubbed in a tiny drop of salve.

Leafpaw worked on one cat after another till her paws ached with tiredness. As the moon began to brighten in the sky, she glanced up the slope toward her father. "Cody, can you take over here?" she asked. "There are only one or two apprentices left, and I want to see how Firestar is."

"Of course. You go right ahead."

Firestar was lying beside Sandstorm, washing dried blood from between his claws. "How are you?" Leafpaw whispered, touching her muzzle to his.

"I'm fine," he purred, his eyes soft and clear.

"Are you sure?" She searched his face. For all her connection with StarClan, she would never know what it felt like to lose a life. "D-did StarClan tell you we should leave the forest now?"

"They told me only to go back and do what I must to protect my Clan," Firestar told her. "And that's what I'm going to do."

Leafpaw heard the RiverClan cats gathering on the slope behind her. "We're returning to our camp," Mistyfoot announced to Firestar. "But we know that the time has come to make a decision about leaving the forest."

Leafpaw held her breath. The fate of all four Clans hung like a cobweb, fragile to the gentlest breath of wind.

"I'm sure many of you have noticed that the river is drying up," Mistyfoot went on.

Onewhisker padded forward. "The Twolegs have changed the course of the water," he meowed. "Our warriors have seen them digging great holes around the gorge to channel the river away."

Mistyfoot just blinked at him as if the reason for the disappearance of the river no longer mattered. "Leopardstar told me that if the ShadowClan camp was destroyed, then we must accept that the Twolegs are coming." She held Firestar's gaze steadily. "RiverClan will leave the forest with the other Clans."

Leafpaw felt her shoulders sag with relief. At last Firestar would have his wish, and all four Clans would leave together.

Firestar hauled himself to his paws, his eyes brightening.

"Onewhisker, tell your Clanmates that ThunderClan and RiverClan will travel with them." He turned his face toward Blackstar. "Will ShadowClan join us?"

Blackstar hesitated, but Firestar was in no mood to wait for an answer.

"You can't still plan to live among the Twolegs after you have seen what they are capable of?" he hissed.

Blackstar nodded slowly. "ShadowClan will travel with you," he meowed. "After all, we have no home and no territory now."

Firestar lifted his head to address all the cats on the rock. "We will leave at dawn!"

Mews of approval echoed through the air, and Leafpaw felt a tingle of excitement. Whatever the journey held—wherever they were going—nothing could be worse than to stay in this place with Twolegs and their monsters closing in on all sides. She glanced at Cody, still busy among the ShadowClan cats. Would there be time to escort her home first? Or had she become such a part of the Clan that she'd go with them?

"Where will we go?" Tornear was the first to ask, but his question echoed around the gathering.

Firestar looked expectantly at Brambleclaw. The tabby warrior looked down at his paws. Squirrelpaw, standing beside him, pressed her flank against his. Leafpaw tipped her head to one side, puzzled. They looked like a pair of unprepared apprentices who had just been asked the best way to catch water voles.

"As you know, Midnight's sign never came," Brambleclaw

began, dragging the words out as if they stuck in his throat like thorns. "So we don't know exactly where we should go. But we could head toward the sun-drown-place."

"If there's been no sign before we get there, we could find Midnight again and ask her," Squirrelpaw put in.

"How do we get to this sun-drown-place?" Blackstar called.

"We traveled two different routes—" Brambleclaw broke off and looked uncertainly at Squirrelpaw.

"And you don't know which one to take?" Firestar suggested.

"We . . ." Brambleclaw faltered. "We should head for High-stones first," he meowed at last. "Away from the Twolegs."

"Very well," Firestar agreed. "We shall meet at the edge of WindClan's territory at dawn."

Mistyfoot and Tallstar nodded.

"Then it's decided." Firestar turned to Blackstar. "It would be easier for us all if ShadowClan would sleep at Sunningrocks tonight," he meowed, choosing his words carefully. "We could make an earlier start if you were to rest here."

Blackstar seemed to appreciate Firestar's diplomacy. "Then we will stay," he meowed.

"As if they've got any other place to go!" Sorreltail muttered in Leafpaw's ear.

"But we will sleep apart from ThunderClan, and a guard will be posted," Blackstar warned.

"These cats have just saved your Clan!" Mistyfoot exclaimed. "Do you think ThunderClan brought you here only to attack you?"

"Let's hear whether Leopardstar agrees with your plan to leave the forest before you start making judgments on my decisions," Blackstar retorted.

Leafpaw winced. She glanced at her sister, but Squirrelpaw was no longer listening. She was staring into the forest, her face filled with anxiety.

Leafpaw padded quietly to her side. "Are you okay?"

"I just hope StarClan sends us a sign soon," Squirrelpaw mewed.

"I'm sure they will do what they can."

Squirrelpaw stared earnestly into her eyes. "You're right. Even without a sign, I know StarClan will be protecting us and guiding us wherever we go."

Leafpaw blinked. She wished she were that certain. There had been no sign of StarClan when ShadowClan had needed them most. It was only luck—and the other Clans' courage—that had gotten those cats out alive. More and more, it looked as if StarClan was powerless to help, and the cats would have to rely on one another, nothing else, to survive.

CHAPTER 16

♣

Clouds obscured the night sky as Leafpaw padded down the hard stone slope. A mild breeze promised that there would be no frost tonight, and she could smell rain. Most of the Clan was sleeping; ShadowClan was huddled near the edge of Sunning-rocks, as far from the ThunderClan cats as they could be.

Exhaustion dragged at Leafpaw's limbs, but her mind teemed with thoughts, memories of the day's horrors mingled with uncertainties about the journey to come. Knowing she would not be able to sleep, she headed for the forest. Even in leaf-bare, its musty odor and the feeling of the earth beneath her paws soothed her.

As she neared the trees she heard Cody's voice calling to her. "Leafpaw!" The kittypet was sheltering among some brittle fronds of bracken.

"Cody? What are you doing out here?"

"There's something I need to tell you." Cody scraped at the ground with her paw.

Leafpaw stared at her. "What?"

"I'm leaving," Cody mewed simply. "I'm going home."

Leafpaw fought back the urge to cry, *No! Please stay!* She

stepped forward and touched her nose to Cody's ear-tip.

"This is no life for me, all this death and blood and uncertainty," Cody went on. "I am happy with my housefolk, and they'll be missing me. I never meant to stay this long, but Birchkit needed me and I began to—"

"You began to enjoy the *freedom*," Leafpaw interrupted, suddenly desperate to remind her new friend what she would be giving up if she went back to her Twolegs.

"I guess I did," Cody admitted. "But today I saw just how fragile your freedom is. You have to fight for *everything*—for your food, even somewhere to shelter." She shook her head apologetically. "I like to know where I will be sleeping every night, and that there will always be food when my belly grows empty. And I like my housefolk. Not all Twolegs are as bad as the ones destroying your home."

"Would you like me to show you the way through the forest?" Leafpaw offered. "Firestar promised you an escort."

Cody shook her head. "The woods seem quiet enough," she mewed. "There won't be any monsters about at night. Anyway, you'll need to rest for your journey." She glanced back toward Sunningrocks. "Thank Firestar for me."

Leafpaw pressed her nose sadly against her new friend's cheek. Cody closed her eyes and sighed. Then she straightened up. "I've said good-bye to Birchkit. Ferncloud is eating properly again, and he'll be fine with her now."

"Thanks for taking care of me when we were in the Twoleg nest," Leafpaw whispered. "I'll miss you."

"I'll miss you, too. And I'll keep an eye out for Graystripe,"

Cody promised. "If I see him, I'll tell him where you've gone and that his Clan is waiting for him."

Leafpaw felt a warm tongue rasp her ear. "Bye, Leafpaw," Cody murmured. "Good luck."

"Good-bye, Cody." With an aching heart, and half wishing she could have convinced Cody to stay, Leafpaw watched her friend vanish into the shadows of the forest.

A rustle in the bracken made her jump, and Sorreltail slipped out from the trees. "Has Cody gone home?"

"She said her Twolegs would be missing her," Leafpaw explained.

"I heard." Sorreltail nodded. "Are you okay?"

"Of course." She braced herself for Sorreltail to make a sharp comment about how kittypets didn't belong in the wild, but instead Sorreltail just blinked sympathetically.

"Let's sleep out here tonight," she suggested. "It is our last night in the forest, after all."

The thought of never spending another night under these trees took Leafpaw's breath away, and for a moment she wanted to lie down and bury her face in the leaf-mold and forget that all this was happening. How could they leave if they didn't know where they were going? But she followed Sorreltail into the bracken, and together they flattened a patch into a nest big enough for the two of them. As she settled down, Leafpaw felt Sorreltail's soft tail brush her nose.

"Your Clan is still here," Sorreltail murmured.

"I know." Leafpaw tried not to think of Cody hurrying home through the forest alone.

Before she closed her eyes, she looked up at the branches and gave thanks to StarClan for the shelter they had given ThunderClan in past moons. If only she could be sure there was a home as safe as this had once been waiting for them at the end of their journey.

Cold rain woke Leafpaw, spattering on her fur, and she opened her eyes to a watery, gray dawn. She stretched and shook the raindrops from her pelt. Her movement awoke Sorreltail.

"Brrr," the tortoiseshell complained, hauling herself to her paws. "What a day for a journey!" She didn't suggest that Firestar might delay leaving until the rain stopped. Leafpaw realized bleakly that all of the cats knew they could not stay in the forest a moment longer.

They left their sodden nest and padded to the bottom of Sunningrocks, where the two Clans were beginning to gather. Tawnypelt was sharing tongues with a ShadowClan apprentice, stopping now and then to shake the rain from her ears.

"I wonder what it's like for Tawnypelt, being back with ThunderClan?" Sorreltail whispered, following Leafpaw's gaze.

"Strange, I guess," she murmured.

"It's going to be very wet underpaw." Ashfur's worried mew rose from the ThunderClan warriors and apprentices. The other cats looked anxiously at Brambleclaw, and Leafpaw knew it was not just the rain that was making their pelts bristle. The whole Clan was nervous about the journey ahead.

"Mud or no mud, we will leave as soon as RiverClan comes," Firestar insisted. "Can't you hear the Twoleg monsters?"

Leafpaw listened, and sure enough, through the drumming of the rain, she heard monsters rumbling behind the trees. She had never heard them this close to Sunningrocks before, and the thought of them bearing down on their final refuge filled her with alarm.

"I want all warriors and apprentices to catch whatever they can before the journey," Firestar meowed. "We'll share whatever we find with ShadowClan."

"ShadowClan will organize its own hunting patrols!" Blackstar called across the rock.

Leafpaw saw her father's face darken for a moment. "Very well. Our warriors will show you the best places to hunt."

"We can find our own prey," Blackstar growled.

Firestar curled his lip but said nothing. Instead he turned to Brambleclaw. The young warrior's tail was twitching, and he kneaded the ground impatiently. "I want you to organize two hunting patrols, Brambleclaw, but don't let any cat go near the Twolegs."

"It sounds as if he's talking to Graystripe!" Mousefur hissed in Leafpaw's ear. "Why doesn't he just name Brambleclaw deputy and be done with it?"

"Because that would be like admitting Graystripe is dead," Dustpelt growled back, overhearing.

Firestar flicked the rain from his whiskers and turned to Cinderpelt. "Prepare traveling herbs for everyone," he ordered. "Will you have enough?"

"Oh, yes," Cinderpelt answered. "I just hope that wherever we're going has the plants I need to replenish my stocks."

Leafpaw blinked. She hadn't thought about that before. Would their new home have marigold, yarrow, comfrey, and all the other precious plants she had learned to cure with? Her paws trembled at the thought of having to look after the Clan without them, and she took a steadying breath before hurrying over to help mix the herbs they would need for the journey.

Brambleclaw led a hunting patrol into the dripping woods, and Mousefur followed with another. Blackstar watched them disappear into the forest before muttering something to his deputy, Russetfur; a moment later the dark ginger she-cat, her pelt plastered against her thin body, headed down the slope with several ShadowClan warriors.

Cinderpelt shook her head. "ShadowClan should have joined the ThunderClan patrols," she murmured. "They'll have no idea of the best places to hunt, and with prey so scarce they'll need all the help they can get."

"Why is Blackstar being so stubborn?" Leafpaw mewed.

"ShadowClan has always been proud." Cinderpelt started to take supplies out of the cleft in the rock. "Now that they've been driven out of their home, pride is all they have left."

"But surely it would be wiser to combine our strengths?" Leafpaw protested. "We have a long, difficult journey ahead."

"The boundaries between the Clans run deep," Cinderpelt reminded her. "Traditions are all we have to cling to."

"Then you agree with Blackstar?" Leafpaw asked in disbelief.

"Of course not, but I understand him," Cinderpelt replied. "Although it is frustrating," she added. "I offered to check on their injured cats when I awoke, but Blackstar sent me away. He told me that ThunderClan had done enough for Shadow-Clan yesterday, and he didn't intend to make his Clan's debt any greater than it was."

"How can he talk about debts?" Leafpaw exclaimed. "Yesterday the four Clans faced the Twolegs together, and we were all as powerless as StarClan to stop them."

"I know," the medicine cat mewed. "But we're not powerless to find a new future for ourselves, so let's get on with mixing the traveling herbs. Every journey begins with a single pawstep, and this one is up to us."

As the rain fell steadily, they began to combine the bitter herbs that would give the cats strength for the journey. Half-starved for so long, they needed this ancient mixture, handed down from medicine cat to apprentice for countless moons, more than ever before.

When the pile of herbs was complete, Leafpaw remembered she had not told her father about Cody. "Can you spare me for a while?" she asked.

"There's nothing more we can do here," Cinderpelt assured her. "I'll check on Ferncloud." She glanced at the nursery hollow.

Ferncloud was sitting on the edge of the hollow, washing Birchkit. The kit struggled resentfully—looking as normal as any kit ever had—as his mother rasped his ears with her rough tongue. The sight gave Leafpaw a rush of hope. She imagined

Birchkit growing up and training to become a warrior in their new home, and a profound belief that ThunderClan would survive washed over her like sunshine. She quickly covered the traveling herbs with leaves to protect them from the rain and hurried up the slope toward her father.

He was staring across the treetops that stretched beyond Sunningrocks. He sat up straight, despite the pounding rain, with his tail curled over his paws and his ears pricked, scenting the air almost as though he welcomed the prospect of the journey ahead. It was hard to believe he had lost a life only yesterday.

When he heard Leafpaw calling him he turned his head. "Yes?"

"I thought I should let you know Cody went back to her Twolegs last night."

Firestar nodded.

"I had begun to hope she'd stay," Leafpaw confessed.

"Now is no time for a stranger to join the Clan," Firestar pointed out gently.

"But she was great with Birchkit!"

"That doesn't make her a Clan cat," he argued. "All the time she was with us, the scents of the forest never drew her from the safety of the camp. She fled here from the wooden nest because that danger was greater than the thought of living with us. I know what kittypets think of the cats who live in the forest. She'll be happier with her housefolk."

Leafpaw was surprised to hear her father use a kittypet word, and wondered if he was thinking of his early days with the Twolegs. Cody had not had time to talk with him about Smudge. Was he thinking of that kittypet friend now?

"You'll miss her, won't you?" he meowed unexpectedly.

"Yes, I will," Leafpaw admitted. "She was a good friend. But she knows we have to go away." She stared down into the forest. "We're leaving so many familiar things behind," she murmured.

Her father's eyes clouded with sorrow. "Yes. Like Graystripe."

Leafpaw couldn't think of anything to say that would comfort him. However much he wanted to believe that his deputy was still alive, it was still almost impossible that Graystripe could find his way back to them.

"I know we must go," Firestar went on. "I want to leave as much as any cat, but I can't bear the thought that I might never see him again."

"You don't know that for sure," Leafpaw mewed hopefully. "Cody told me she'd look out for him and tell him where we've gone."

A glimmer of hope sparked in Firestar's eye, then disappeared. "How will he escape the Twolegs?" he asked bleakly. "And then find our new home . . . ?"

"Are you going to name a new deputy?" she ventured.

"No!" Her father leaped up, and Leafpaw shrank back. "There's no need," he went on quietly. "If there is even the smallest chance he's alive, then Graystripe is still Thunder-Clan's deputy."

Before Leafpaw could say anything, mews sounded from

behind them. The ThunderClan hunting patrols had returned and were carrying fresh-kill up the rock—birds and mice, not many, but enough to allow each cat a small meal. Shadow-Clan's hunting patrol returned shortly after. They had found only one thrush between them.

"Will you share our catch with them?" Leafpaw mewed to her father.

"Blackstar would be insulted by the offer," Firestar replied.

"I suppose they can hunt while we travel," Leafpaw suggested.

"Hopefully we all can. There must be more prey out there than here." Firestar shook himself. "Go and get something to eat," he ordered. "RiverClan will be here soon."

"Okay." Leafpaw hurried down to where Brambleclaw and Squirrelpaw were sharing a chaffinch. They looked drenched, their pelts dark and sodden.

"Want some?" Squirrelpaw offered.

"Yes, please." Leafpaw's belly felt hollow, and the scent of fresh-kill made her mouth water. Squirrelpaw and Bramble-claw sat back and let her take a bite.

"Do you want to give some to your sister?" Leafpaw asked Brambleclaw. The ShadowClan cats were laboriously passing their meager catch around; each cat took only a small mouthful before pushing it on to the next.

Brambleclaw shook his head. "I wouldn't waste my time."

Leafpaw was startled by the bitterness in his voice.

"We met Tawnypelt while we were out hunting, and Brambleclaw asked if she wanted to hunt with us," Squirrelpaw explained. "She told us she was a ShadowClan warrior and would never hunt for another Clan."

"I don't know why she was so superior about it," Brambleclaw growled. "It's as if she's forgotten that she was born a ThunderClan cat, or that we journeyed to the sun-drown-place together."

"It must be difficult for her, being among ThunderClan again," Leafpaw ventured. "She probably feels she has to prove her loyalty to ShadowClan more than ever."

"Leafpaw's right," Squirrelpaw meowed. "Don't take it personally, Brambleclaw. It wasn't long ago that you were telling me that your first loyalty is to ThunderClan, not your kin. Allow Tawnypelt to have the same feelings for ShadowClan."

"I suppose so," Brambleclaw agreed grudgingly. "I just wanted to hunt with my sister again." Leafpaw heard the sadness in his voice and thought how hard it must be having a littermate in another Clan. She glanced at Squirrelpaw, grateful that she and her sister shared the same home wherever it was.

"Leafpaw!" Cinderpelt was calling from the den. "Come and help me!"

Leafpaw bounded up the slope.

"Will you take these herbs to the queen and the elders?"

"What about Birchkit?"

"Just give him half a dose."

Leafpaw glanced warily at Blackstar. "Are we sharing with ShadowClan?"

"We'll have some left over," Cinderpelt mewed, her eyes

glittering. "I'll offer them to Littlecloud and tell him we have no need for them. Blackstar can take them or leave them as he wants."

Leafpaw admired her mentor's kindheartedness as well as her craftiness; this was an offer Blackstar could accept without losing face. She picked up a bundle of herbs and carried it to Ferncloud. The she-cat accepted the bitter herbs gratefully, though Birchkit was not so thankful.

"It tastes like crow-food!" he complained.

"You've never eaten crow-food," Ferncloud pointed out. "Now just swallow it."

Leafpaw purred with amusement and carried her bundle to where Frostfur, Longtail, and Speckletail lay, sheltered by the overhang.

As she put the herbs down, Frostfur shook her head. "Don't waste those on us," she murmured. "We're not going with the Clan."

Leafpaw blinked. "Not going! Why?"

Firestar trotted over. "What's the matter?"

"Frostfur says they aren't coming with us!"

"We're too old to make such a journey," Speckletail rasped. "We'd only hold you back."

Longtail flicked his tail. "And what use would I be? I can't even see where I'm putting my paws!"

"The Clan would help you," Firestar assured him gently. He looked up at the elderly she-cats. "Just as they would help all of you."

"We know they would," Frostfur mewed. "But Speckletail

and I are too old for so much change. We'd rather die here beneath Silverpelt, knowing StarClan waits for us."

Leafpaw flinched. Surely StarClan would go wherever they did?

Firestar nodded gravely. "I cannot force you to come with us, Frostfur," he murmured. "I know your paws are weary, Speckletail's too, and you already hear StarClan whispering to you. But Longtail, I won't leave you behind." When the tabby warrior opened his mouth to argue, Firestar went on, "Yesterday you heard the WindClan cats coming before any other cat. You may have lost your eyes, but your ears and your sense of smell are as good as any warrior's. Please come with us."

Longtail closed his sightless eyes and took a deep, shuddering breath. Then he opened them again, and turned his face toward Firestar as if he were looking straight at him. "Thank you," he meowed. "I will come."

Stormfur bounded up the rocks. "Firestar! There is a problem. RiverClan cannot leave today."

Firestar's ears twitched with alarm. "Why not?"

"Mudfur is dying. We can't leave him alone."

Frostfur stepped forward. "We'll stay with him."

"We can look after him until StarClan is ready to take him," Speckletail agreed.

Stormfur looked them in surprise. "But he is not one of your Clan."

"It doesn't matter," Frostfur told him. "We are staying behind anyway. We might as well do what we can for Mudfur."

"The RiverClan camp is a lot more sheltered than this place," Leafpaw mewed. "You will be safe from Twolegs if you keep within the reeds."

"That's true," meowed Firestar. "We'll bring Frostfur and Speckletail to the RiverClan camp, and if Leopardstar agrees, we'll leave them with Mudfur while RiverClan joins us on our journey."

"What's happening?" Blackstar had approached the group.

"Mudfur is dying," Firestar explained. "We must go to the RiverClan camp before we travel to WindClan's territory."

Blackstar curled his lip. "We'll go ahead and wait for you at the edge of the forest."

A croaking voice sounded behind him, and Leafpaw recognized Runningnose's gray pelt. "I would like to say good-bye to Mudfur," mewed the elderly cat. "I've known him since I was an apprentice."

Blackstar looked at the old tom, and for the first time Leafpaw saw respect in his eyes. "Of course, Runningnose," he meowed. "You go with ThunderClan. We'll see you again at the edge of the forest."

Firestar scanned the rock. "Has everyone had traveling herbs?"

"Yes," Cinderpelt replied. "In fact, there are some left. ShadowClan may as well have them. It's not worth carrying them with us." Her casual tone gave nothing away.

Leafpaw glanced at Littlecloud, whose tail twitched with excitement. "May we use them, Blackstar?" pleaded the young medicine cat.

"No point letting them go to waste," Blackstar growled, and Littlecloud began handing out the bundles at once. The ShadowClan leader looked at Longtail, narrowing his eyes. Leafpaw braced herself, expecting him to say that they couldn't take a blind cat on such a long and dangerous journey.

But Blackstar only meowed, "The blind warrior can travel with us while you go to RiverClan. There's no point taking him across the river and back again. I have warriors who can lead him through the forest."

Firestar blinked gratefully at the ShadowClan leader. "Thank you." He touched Longtail with the tip of his tail. "Is that all right with you?"

Longtail nodded, and followed Blackstar down the slope to the waiting ShadowClan cats.

"Is every cat ready?" Firestar called to his own Clan.

Mews of assent sounded from across the rock, and the cats fell in behind Firestar as he led them down to the shore. The river was hardly more than a trickle, in spite of the ceaseless rain.

"Cinderpelt, Leafpaw, come with me," Firestar ordered, halting beside the river. Runningnose, Frostfur, and Speckle-tail were already clambering after Stormfur, over the stepping-stones. "The rest of the Clan should wait here until we return." He nodded at Brambleclaw, putting him in charge, and followed the elders across the river.

The reeds around the RiverClan camp were brown and brittle, their roots exposed. Leafpaw followed her father into the clearing and flinched as several cats spun around to look at the visitors with hostile surprise.

Leopardstar stood in the entrance to the medicine cats' den, her eyes blazing. "What are you doing here? Didn't Stormfur give you my message?"

"I did," Stormfur meowed, hurrying to the center of the clearing. "But Firestar has come to suggest something."

"Frostfur and Speckletail are staying behind," Firestar explained. "They have offered to care for Mudfur."

Leopardstar dipped her head. "That's kind of them," she meowed. "But it won't be necessary. Mudfur is nearly with StarClan."

Leafpaw jumped out of the way as Runningnose wheezed in shock and staggered toward the medicine clearing. Cinderpelt followed, and Leafpaw padded quickly after them, glancing at the RiverClan leader as she went past. But Leopardstar let them go without a word.

Mothwing looked up as they entered the clearing. Her eyes were clouded with grief. "There's nothing more any cat can do," she told Cinderpelt. "He's not in pain. I've made sure of that."

Mudfur lay in the middle of the clearing. Rain dripped through the branches onto his matted flank, but he made no attempt to move into a more sheltered spot. Shadepelt, an elderly RiverClan she-cat, sat beside Mothwing, sadly watching the dying cat.

Runningnose padded forward and touched his nose to Mudfur's shoulder. "Go swiftly to StarClan, my friend. We will look after your Clanmates."

Cinderpelt leaned down and rested her muzzle on Mudfur's pelt. As Leafpaw crouched to bury her nose in his fur, her throat filled with the unmistakable scent of death. Forcing herself not to draw away, she closed her eyes. *At least you can be sure StarClan is waiting for you*, she thought.

With a shuddering gasp, Mudfur drew his last desperate breath; his flank heaved once, then fell still forever as his spirit joined his warrior ancestors.

"He is with StarClan now," Mothwing murmured.

Leafpaw blinked sadly at the unmoving heap of fur. This was one cat who would never see their new home, wherever it lay. How many more cats would not make it to the end of their journey?

CHAPTER 17

❧

"How will I manage without him?" gasped Mothwing, her eyes huge and scared.

"You'll be fine," Cinderpelt assured her. "And there will be time to grieve, but not now."

Mothwing looked at her for a moment, then nodded and left the medicine clearing to tell her Clan that Mudfur was dead. Leafpaw waited until the RiverClan cats began to pad through the tunnel to pay their final respects, then hurried out into the main clearing.

Mothwing was sitting in the rain with her head bowed, water streaming from her whiskers. "I can't believe he's gone," she mewed.

"He hasn't gone far," Leafpaw comforted her. "He's with StarClan."

"I hope so," Mothwing murmured.

Leopardstar emerged from the medicine clearing and padded over to Firestar. "Shadepelt and Loudbelly will remain here with your elders," she meowed. "They are too old to travel and wish to sit in vigil for Mudfur."

Firestar nodded. "We will wait until RiverClan is ready to travel," he murmured.

Hawkfrost and Stormfur padded toward Leafpaw and Mothwing. For once, Hawkfrost's gaze was gentle as he rested his muzzle against his sister's cheek.

"I never thought we'd be leaving anyone behind." Stormfur sighed.

"Neither did I," Leafpaw agreed, gazing at Frostfur and Speckletail. The image of Graystripe staring out from the monster's belly flashed through her mind.

Leopardstar padded to the center of the clearing and looked around. "Is everyone ready?"

"We haven't hunted today," a RiverClan queen protested, wrapping her tail protectively around her kit.

"We can hunt on the way," Leopardstar told her.

The moment had arrived. Silently, the cats began to head for the camp entrance. Frostfur and Speckletail sat in the clearing watching their Clanmates leave.

"Good-bye, Frostfur," Leafpaw whispered. "Good-bye, Speckletail. Good hunting."

"Good hunting," Frostfur replied.

Leafpaw looked up at the gray sky crisscrossed by leaf-bare branches. The rain spattered on her face, and she blinked away the drops that clung to her eyelashes. It was as if StarClan wept to see their Clans leave the forest. Bleakly, Leafpaw wondered if their ancestors would travel with them, or whether this was a final farewell.

"Come on." Firestar's voice sounded softly in her ear. "The Clan will be waiting for us."

The trek through the forest was hard going, the rain making the leaves slippery underpaw. The RiverClan cats stayed together, keeping up with ThunderClan but traveling separately. Sorreltail fell into step beside Leafpaw and nudged her up each time she stumbled. As they neared the edge of the forest, where there was a narrow strip of RiverClan territory before the moorland began, Leafpaw scented ShadowClan cats. She lifted her head and saw them huddled under the trees, wet and shivering.

"We thought you'd never get here," Blackstar complained, shaking the water from his coat.

The ShadowClan cats paced impatiently around him. They were not comfortable under the trees that had once belonged to ThunderClan; even Tawnypelt looked eager to leave. But Leafpaw longed to linger here, suddenly unable to bear the thought of saying good-bye to the forest for the last time.

Firestar gazed at his Clan. "We must say good-bye to all we have known," he meowed.

Leafpaw felt Sorreltail's pelt pressing against hers, and she noticed Squirrelpaw draw closer to Brambleclaw.

"I want to go home!" one of Tallpoppy's kits mewled up at her mother with her eyes stretched wide.

"We are going home," Tallpoppy promised, her ears twitching. "Our new home."

As she spoke, a tawny-colored cat emerged from the trees a little way off. Even though the rain masked her scent, Leafpaw recognized the stranger at once. It was Sasha.

Mothwing recognized her too, because she bounded over and rolled on her belly like a kit. Hawkfrost padded after his sister more slowly, the tip of his tail flicking from side to side. The RiverClan cats watched them go with patient acceptance, but Leafpaw saw bewilderment in the eyes of the Thunder-Clan cats who did not know who Sasha was, and open hostility from the ShadowClan cats.

"What's she doing here?" Squirrelpaw whispered.

"Perhaps she knows we're leaving," Leafpaw guessed.

"But why did she come?"

Sasha finished greeting her kits and padded toward the watching cats. Ashfur hissed threateningly, but Firestar silenced him with a look.

"I didn't think we'd see you again," Leopardstar meowed, dipping her head to Sasha.

"Nor I you," Sasha admitted. "I have come to ask Hawk-frost and Mothwing to leave RiverClan and come with me. I've seen what the Twolegs are doing to your homes. It is no longer safe for them to stay with you."

Mothwing looked down at her paws and Leafpaw's heart skipped a beat. *Could she really be thinking about leaving?* She brushed past Sasha and faced the RiverClan medicine cat. "I know things have been tough lately, but you wouldn't really go, would you?"

Mothwing blinked. "I-I don't know. . . ."

"Your Clan needs you," Leafpaw protested. She rounded on Hawkfrost. "You wouldn't abandon your Clanmates, would you?"

"The decision is theirs." Firestar's voice rose above the sound of the falling rain. "But I agree they should remain with their Clan."

Sasha narrowed her eyes. "You want them to stay?" Suddenly the wind dropped, and every cat seemed to hold their breath as she went on, "In spite of the fact that Tigerstar was their father?"

Leafpaw scanned the shocked faces of the RiverClan cats. They obviously didn't know that Tigerstar was Hawkfrost and Mothwing's father, even though his kits had been raised in their Clan.

There was a long pause while Firestar held Sasha's gaze. "I want them to stay *because* Tigerstar was their father," he meowed. Brambleclaw sank his claws into the mud, and Squirrelpaw's eyes stretched even wider. "Tigerstar was a great warrior, and these cats have proved they have inherited his courage," Firestar went on. "Their Clan needs them now more than ever." He turned his gaze on Brambleclaw and Tawnypelt. "Tigerstar's children have earned their place in their Clans many times over."

There were no secrets now. Every cat knew that Tigerstar lived on in four cats, and that three Clans nurtured part of his legacy. Mothwing lifted her gaze, searching the faces of her Clanmates. Hawkfrost raised his chin as if he didn't care what they thought.

Leopardstar nodded. "Firestar is right. RiverClan needs all our warriors, and we certainly need our medicine cat."

"But they're Tigerstar's kits!" Dawnflower's hiss startled Leafpaw. The RiverClan queen was staring at Leopardstar as if she'd just invited a fox to join them.

Squirrelpaw's eyes blazed. "So what? That doesn't mean they can't be loyal!"

"Hawkfrost is one of our best warriors," Stormfur added. He looked around at his Clanmates. "Have any of you ever doubted his loyalty?"

"Never," Mistyfoot murmured.

Leopardstar looked at Hawkfrost and Mothwing. "Will you stay?"

"Of course," Hawkfrost answered at once. "I would never desert my Clan." He was staring at his Clanmates, his eyes glittering defiantly.

Leafpaw felt her tail quiver. Was it ambition or loyalty that fueled his decision? She glanced at Brambleclaw. How could two warriors with the same father be so different?

Mothwing glanced at her mother, her ears twitching. "I have to stay with my Clan too," she mewed. "I'm their medicine cat now. They need me."

Sasha nodded. "Very well." She swept her gaze over them. "Firestar is right," she murmured. "I see your father in both of you."

Leafpaw heard a low growl come from Dawnflower.

Sasha turned to the RiverClan queen. "Tigerstar never knew about these kits, but he would have been proud of them."

She glanced around the RiverClan cats. "You're lucky to have them."

She padded back to Hawkfrost and Mothwing, brushing her pelt against theirs. "I wish you well on your journey," she meowed. Then she turned and padded into the forest. The ferns quivered where she had disappeared, and the Clan cats stared after her in silence.

CHAPTER 18

"Look!" Rainwhisker yowled, making the cats jump. At the top of the rise that marked the beginning of WindClan territory, silhouetted against the gray sky, stood WindClan. They lined the crest of the hill like stones, waiting.

"Let's go," Blackstar ordered.

He plunged out of the shelter of the trees and hurried up the muddy slope, followed by his Clanmates. Squirrelpaw stared sadly at the forest, sinking her claws into the familiar rain-softened earth. All the RiverClan and ThunderClan cats lingered at the edge of the trees, as though leaving was harder than they had ever imagined.

"This is no longer our home," Firestar reminded them gently. "Home is waiting for us at the end of our journey." He began to pad away, lowering his head against the driving rain.

Squirrelpaw joined the other cats as they poured slowly out of the forest after him. Beside her, Brackenfur arched his back against the bracken fronds, brushing his scent on their dripping tips one last time.

"We thought you'd changed your mind," Mudclaw growled

as the three Clans neared the top of the slope.

"Mudfur was dying," Leopardstar explained. "We waited until he had gone to join StarClan."

Tallstar sat shivering beside his warriors. His ribs stuck out like gnarled twigs. As the Clans reached the top of the rise, he stood up, wincing at the stiffness in his limbs. "I'm sorry to hear about Mudfur," he meowed.

"At least he died beneath Silverpelt, which is more than we will," muttered Blackstar.

His words sent a shiver of unease down Squirrelpaw's spine. "We saw Silverpelt at the sun-drown-place," she objected. "StarClan will be waiting for us when we arrive."

Mudclaw's tail twitched. "You saw stars, but were they our warrior ancestors or someone else's?"

Squirrelpaw blinked, thinking of the Tribe of Endless Hunting who watched over the mountains. What if Mudclaw was right, and they were leaving StarClan behind as well as their homes?

Blackstar clawed the muddy ground. "Are we going or not?"

"We're ready," Tallstar replied.

The moorland that stretched ahead of them was unrecognizable, all the grass swept away to reveal bare, rutted earth.

Leopardstar stared across the broken ground. "Are there many monsters?"

"Too many," Tallstar growled.

As the cats scrambled over the first stretch of exposed ground, Squirrelpaw soon began to struggle. The mud sucked at her paws, and her legs felt stone-heavy with exhaustion.

Brambleclaw clawed his way back to join her. "Come on; you can make it."

"It's okay," she snapped. "I can manage."

He blinked. "I know you can," he meowed, and Squirrelpaw wished she hadn't been so harsh.

Dustpelt was behind them, carrying Birchkit in his jaws. Cloudtail struggled to his side. His pelt was streaked with mud, only his back kept white by the relentless rain. "I'll take the kit," he offered. He took Birchkit from Dustpelt's jaws, trying not to let the swaying bundle drag in the mud. Dustpelt nodded his thanks and plunged down a muddy ridge to help Ferncloud, who was fighting to stay on her paws.

Crowpaw was carrying a kit too. He looked on the verge of collapse, but his paws kept moving, his eyes fixed on the ground in front of him.

Squirrelpaw heard the rumble of Twoleg monsters ahead, and their stench reached her even through the rain. She lifted her face, raindrops stinging her eyes, and saw Twolegs cluttering the horizon. "How will we get past?" she gasped.

"Can we go around?" Firestar yowled to Mudclaw.

"They're everywhere on the moor," Onewhisker called back. "This is the quietest place to cross, I promise."

A monster with huge round paws and gleaming teeth roared across the landscape, while another churned up earth in its wake. Just beyond them, a small rocky outcrop rose from the mud.

"If we can make it that far, we'll be safe for a while," Mud-claw advised. "The Twoleg monsters can't climb those."

But they can crush them if they want, Squirrelpaw thought, remembering the Great Rock.

"You're right; it could be our only chance. Let's wait for these two monsters to pass and make a run for it." Firestar glanced at the other leaders, who each nodded their approval.

Squirrelpaw pressed her belly deeper into the mud, feeling the cold earth seep through her fur and drench her skin. Cinderpelt crouched beside Tallstar, pushing a pawful of herbs toward him. *The last of the traveling herbs, to give him strength*, Squirrelpaw guessed.

As soon as the monsters rumbled past, Firestar gave the command to run.

The ThunderClan cats rushed forward. Squirrelpaw staggered blindly through the mud, keeping her eyes fixed on Brambleclaw's tabby pelt. As long as he was in sight, she felt she would be safe. By the time she reached the rocks, she was panting with fear and exhaustion. Brambleclaw reached down and hauled her onto the ledge, where the others had already gathered. Firestar wove among them, his orange fur turned brown by the mud. His eyes were fixed on the cats still struggling toward the outcrop.

Crowpaw reached the rock and held up the kit for One-whisker to take before scrambling after it. Squirrelpaw heard a Twoleg shouting and turned to see it running unsteadily across the mud, waving its arms. It had seen the cats still heading for the rocks. Tawnypelt was among them, trying to drag a RiverClan apprentice out of the mud.

"Blackstar and Leopardstar must have hesitated before giving the order to run!" Squirrelpaw hissed.

The monsters were turning now, steering their paws toward the straggling cats.

"They'll never make it to the rocks in time!" Brambleclaw gasped.

"We must go back and help them!" Firestar yowled.

Desperation drove every scrap of tiredness from Squirrelpaw's body, and she leaped back down into the mud. Firestar flashed ahead of her. She felt Brambleclaw's pelt brush hers and then she spotted Crowpaw, pelting toward the RiverClan cats.

The monster's roar made Squirrelpaw's ears ring. She hurled herself among the RiverClan cats, reaching for an apprentice who was desperately trying to free himself from the mud. She plunged her teeth into his scruff to haul him out, and he raced away toward the rock.

"Thanks!"

Squirrelpaw looked up to see Stormfur watching her. He blinked gratefully and turned to yank another apprentice to its paws.

"My kit!" Dawnflower's screech made Squirrelpaw spin around. One kit lay at the RiverClan queen's paws. Another was racing panic-stricken straight toward a monster, too scared to see where he was going.

"I'll get him!" Crowpaw lunged forward and grasped the kit in his jaws. Mud sprayed from his paws as he skidded back toward the outcrop.

Squirrelpaw scooped up the other kit and gave Dawnflower a fierce nudge. "Quick!" she hissed.

She reached the rock and bounded up, finding a shadowy crevice out of sight of the Twolegs. She fled along the gully with the kit swinging in her jaws until she emerged on the other side. Dawnflower shot out behind her, followed by Firestar and a stream of RiverClan cats, and finally Crowpaw emerged with the other kit. Dawnflower raced over and gratefully took the kit from him.

Squirrelpaw placed the other kit at her paws and looked around for her sister. "Leafpaw!" she called.

She was crouching beside Tallstar. The WindClan leader's flanks heaved and his eyes looked wild with fear. "Hunted in my own territory!" he wheezed.

Leafpaw looked up when she heard Squirrelpaw's call.

"Can you look at these kits?" Squirrelpaw asked. Leafpaw glanced uncertainly at Tallstar, but Cinderpelt appeared beside her.

"I'll look after him," she murmured.

Leafpaw hurried over and sniffed each kit. She pressed her ear against the chest of one and then the other. "They're just scared and tired," she concluded. "They'll be fine."

"Of course I'm fine," squeaked one of the kits, a dark gray female. "That monster was never going to catch *us*."

"Hush, Willowkit," soothed Dawnflower. As she bent to wash the mud from her kits' faces, the ShadowClan cats emerged from the gully.

"Is every cat with you?" Firestar called to Blackstar.

Blackstar nodded, too breathless to speak.

The Clans rested on the rocks for a moment, but another swath of churned-up moorland still lay between them and the grassy slope that led down to the meadows, and the Twolegs would be looking out for them by now. It wasn't safe to linger too long near the monsters.

"We should stay closer together," Firestar suggested. "Travel like a single Clan."

"And who will give the orders?" Leopardstar demanded. "You?"

Firestar shook his head. "That's not important. I only meant it would be less dangerous if we were to stick together."

"You have no idea where we're going," Blackstar argued. "We have to trust the cats who've made this journey already, and each Clan has one of those. We can travel separately."

"But you fell behind just now," Firestar pointed out. "River-Clan, too. We must stick closer together, at least while we're near the Twolegs."

Blackstar narrowed his eyes. "Closer together, yes," he conceded. "But each Clan should follow its own leader's orders."

Squirrelpaw's paws pricked with frustration. Fighting a bone-weariness that made her head spin, she gazed across the stretch of land between the rocky outcrop and the edge of the moor. There were yet more monsters in the distance, lumbering up and down like terrifying border patrols.

Brambleclaw padded up to her. "I've spoken to the others." His voice was low, and Squirrelpaw understood that by "others," he meant Tawnypelt, Crowpaw, and Stormfur. "We've agreed to keep to the outside," he explained. "That way we can look out for trouble and help any cat who falls behind. Crowpaw and I will stay at the back. Stormfur will lead. You take one side, and Tawnypelt will take the other." Squirrelpaw nodded. "We've brought them this far—we have a responsibility to protect them," he added, his eyes darkening with worry.

Squirrelpaw twined her tail with his. "We've done the right thing," she whispered. "I'm still sure of that."

"Are we ready?" Firestar yowled.

Slowly the cats gathered on the brink of the rocks, huddling close to their Clanmates. Only Brambleclaw, Crowpaw, Squirrelpaw, Stormfur, and Tawnypelt slipped away from their Clans to take up positions at the edge of the group. Blackstar gave the order to move first, but Leopardstar, Firestar, and Mudclaw quickly followed, and the cats began to leap down from the reassuringly hard surface of the outcrop and back into the slippery mud.

They crept toward the monsters that guarded the edge of WindClan's territory, keeping low and quiet. Squirrelpaw skirted one edge of the group, keeping her ears pricked for any unexpected Twoleg activity, as well as looking out for any cats falling behind.

Leafpaw fell in beside her. "Is everything okay?"

"I think so," Squirrelpaw murmured.

"I meant are *you* okay?" Leafpaw persisted. "You don't have to protect all of us, you know. We made our own decisions to come on this journey."

Squirrelpaw blinked gratefully at her. "I know."

As the Clans neared the monsters they slowed down, crouching so low that Squirrelpaw felt she had almost turned into a lump of mud. At least with the cats this filthy, they blended into the earth around them. The monsters were far away to one side and showed no sign of straying back here yet.

"There's mud in my eye!" Birchkit squealed.

"Hush!" snapped Ferncloud, and Birchkit fell silent.

Squirrelpaw's heart pounded. Only a few more fox-lengths and they would reach the crest of the slope that would take them away from this mud and the monsters. Suddenly she heard a sound that turned her blood to ice. A dog howled from somewhere near the monsters, and when she lifted her head to look, she saw it pelting toward them, its ears flapping and its giant paws leaping over the mud.

"Dog!" yowled Leopardstar.

"Run!" Blackstar commanded.

Squirrelpaw stared around in panic. There was no way the kits and elders could outrun a dog! As the other cats pelted forward, Firestar and the other leaders raced among their Clans yowling orders.

"Pick up the kits!" Firestar commanded.

"Help the elders!" hissed Leopardstar.

Squirrelpaw looked for Birchkit, but Rainwhisker had already scooped him up and was racing for the top of the slope. Ferncloud hurtled after him, but Squirrelpaw could hear the terrifying howls of the dog getting closer. The huge creature bounded easily over the rutted ground, bearing down on the cats even faster than the monsters had done. Already the elders were falling behind, even though the other cats urged them forward with desperate yowls and nudges.

Squirrelpaw glanced back to find out where Brambleclaw was, and with a jolt of horror she watched him spin around and head straight toward the dog. Crowpaw and Tawnypelt raced beside him, hardly recognizable under the slick of mud that clung to their pelts. What were they doing?

Stunned, Squirrelpaw watched them charge toward the vicious snarling dog, and only when they got near did she understand what they were doing. Spreading out on Brambleclaw's hissed command, they surrounded the great black hound; at once the creature slowed down, swinging its massive head from side to side as it figured out which cat to chase. Then it fixed its eyes on Crowpaw and headed straight for the scrawny black warrior. Instantly Crowpaw swerved toward Tawnypelt, his paws sliding in the mud. Tawnypelt shot past him in the other direction, yowling abuse at the dog as she dodged its snapping jaws. The dog hesitated, snarling, then set off after the ShadowClan warrior. Squirrelpaw's heart pounded with terror as she saw it gaining on her, but

Brambleclaw was already racing up behind the dog. He raked its hind legs and swerved nimbly away as the dog spun around and gave chase.

The Twolegs had heard the commotion and one ran toward the dog, howling as Brambleclaw fled a fox-length ahead of the creature's glistening fangs. Crowpaw had turned and was running for the dog again, hurtling past its nose and bringing it to a bewildered halt. The dog gazed around, its eyes gleaming with fury. Crowpaw spun on his hind legs and raced back again. The dog lashed out, its jaws snapping close to Crowpaw's flank. The Twoleg howled again and leaned forward, reaching out with its paw.

Squirrelpaw's breath stopped in her throat. *Don't let the Twoleg catch you!* she silently begged Crowpaw. They couldn't lose another cat this way! Then the Twoleg's paw closed around the dog's collar and dragged it away. Squirrelpaw felt dizzy with relief.

Crowpaw tore away from the Twoleg with Tawnypelt and Brambleclaw on his tail. "Run!" he screeched as he streaked toward Squirrelpaw. She spun around and raced after her Clanmates. Most of them had reached the top of the rise and were pelting down the other side. Squirrelpaw checked to see if any cat needed help, but the last elders, two ShadowClan cats weak with fear, were being half dragged, half pushed to safety by Russetfur and Stormfur. Squirrelpaw followed them as they stumbled over the crest of the hill and fled down the slope.

Not until she was halfway down did she realize that she

had crossed the WindClan border and left Clan territory for the very last time. The scent markers had been washed away by the mud and the rain and the stench of the monsters.

Squirrelpaw forced herself not to look back. They had left their homes. The journey had truly begun.

CHAPTER 19

Like cloud shadows drifting over the ground, the Clans trekked in silence across a meadow. Squirrelpaw was grateful that Brambleclaw walked close beside her, shielding her from the icy wind. The rain was easing now, but the clouds had been raked into tatters by a thorn-sharp breeze that promised colder weather. Shivering, she looked up and saw a Twoleg nest looming ahead, even bigger than the Great Rock.

Her paws were sore from the prickly stubble that seemed to cover all the fields they had passed through, and she longed for the softness of leaves underpaw. The air was filled with unfamiliar scents—Twolegs, the monsters that prowled the crisscrossing Thunderpaths, the fresh scent of dog drifting from a Twoleg nest, and the recent scent of rogues. Squirrelpaw felt the instinctive tension of any cat that strayed from its territory, even though she was surrounded by more Clan cats than she had seen before in her life. She scanned the hedgerow, and her heart seemed to stop beating altogether when she saw the brown beech leaves rustle madly, shaken by more than just the wind.

Ravenpaw stepped out from his hiding place like a shadow coming to life, and stared at the Clans in surprise. A second cat slipped out of the hedge behind him. Squirrelpaw recognized the black-and-white pelt of Barley, the cat who had allowed Ravenpaw to share his home in a Twoleg barn for many moons.

"Firestar! Is that you?" Ravenpaw's ears twitched as he called out for his old friend. The Clan cats halted and stared at him. Every cat knew about the black-pelted ThunderClan apprentice who had been driven out by his mentor, Tigerstar. Even if they hadn't known him during his short time in the forest, many had met him on the journey to Highstones.

"Hello, Ravenpaw." Tallstar dipped his head in greeting.

"Ravenpaw!" Firestar pushed through the other cats to greet his old friend.

"Firestar!" Ravenpaw touched noses with the ThunderClan leader. He looked around. "Where's Graystripe?"

Firestar blinked. "Graystripe's not with us."

"Is he dead?" Ravenpaw's pelt bristled in shock.

Firestar shook his head. "Twolegs captured him."

"Twolegs?" Ravenpaw echoed. "Why?"

"They started trapping us." Firestar's mew was raw with grief. "We've been forced to leave the forest."

"*What?*" Ravenpaw lifted his nose to scent the air. "Is that WindClan and RiverClan with you? And ShadowClan?"

"The Twolegs are destroying all our homes," Firestar explained. "We would have been crushed by their monsters if we'd stayed, if we didn't starve first."

"You look half-starved already," Barley remarked, coming forward.

"Hello, Barley," Firestar greeted him. "How's the hunting?"

"Better for me than for you, by the looks of it," came the blunt reply.

"Where are you heading?" Ravenpaw asked.

"Highstones first, and then . . ." Firestar turned to look questioningly at Brambleclaw, but Brambleclaw just gazed back in silence.

"You'll stay with us tonight, won't you?" Ravenpaw asked. "The hunting is good this moon. The barn is full of rats sheltering from the cold."

"Wait, Ravenpaw," warned Barley. "This many cats will never fit into the barn. The Twolegs would have a fit when they came to get straw for the cows."

"That's true," Ravenpaw said. "But there must be a way to help."

"I suppose they could stay at the broken nest," Barley suggested.

"Of course!" Ravenpaw turned to Firestar. "You know the place—where you sheltered with Bluestar after the rat attack?"

Firestar glanced up at the reddening clouds. "I was hoping we'd make it to Highstones by tonight."

"We can't turn down the offer of food," Blackstar argued.

Firestar dipped his head. "You're right." He turned back to Ravenpaw. "Thank you."

"Let's get you settled; then we can show the warriors the

best places to hunt," Ravenpaw mewed. "There'll be plenty for every cat."

Squirrelpaw heard murmurs of excitement ripple through the Clans, and the kits began to mewl their hunger out loud now that it seemed there was a chance they would be fed.

"We need a rest and a meal more than you can imagine," Firestar meowed.

Ravenpaw gazed at his friend's mud-stained pelt. "Oh, Firestar," he murmured, "I think I can imagine."

The broken Twoleg place had no roof, but now the rain had stopped, its stone walls were enough to shelter the cats from the wind.

"I recognize this," whispered Ashfoot, a WindClan queen. "We slept here when Firestar led us back home, after Broken-star drove us out."

"I didn't think we'd ever see this place again," Webfoot growled.

The kits and elders streamed gratefully into the nest, glad of the chance to lie down. Ravenpaw and Barley led the warriors away to hunt, while the apprentices, Squirrelpaw and Crowpaw among them, stayed to guard the others. Cinderpelt and Leafpaw padded among the cats to check that none had been hurt in the desperate scramble across the moor.

"Squirrelpaw?" Leafpaw called. "Can you fetch some of that rain-soaked moss from outside? Some of the queens and elders are too tired to walk that far."

Squirrelpaw nodded and hurried away to pull pawfuls of

sodden moss from the ancient stones that formed the walls of the shelter.

The cats took it from her eagerly, lapping at the water that they squeezed out with their forepaws. When the last Wind-Clan elder had drunk her fill, Squirrelpaw decided she could settle down and rest her aching paws. As she made herself comfortable in a corner, the warriors returned, carrying fresh-kill. Warm, delicious scents filled the shelter, and Squirrelpaw felt a quiver of joy as Brambleclaw dropped a plump rat in front of her.

"Do you want to share?" she offered.

"No," Brambleclaw mewed. "It's all yours."

Squirrelpaw's belly ached by the time she had finished because she was unused to such a huge meal, but this sort of discomfort was far less frightening than hunger, and for the first time since returning to the forest, she felt warm and well fed.

"This is a good place to rest," Tallpoppy purred. "I don't think my kits could take another night in the open. They nearly froze in last night's rain."

"They'll be warm enough tonight," Ferncloud agreed.

It was dark when Brambleclaw returned. He settled down beside Squirrelpaw with a piece of fresh-kill as big as the one he'd given her.

Firestar was lying next to Sandstorm, their tails, pale ginger and dark red, curled together. "Will you rest with us tonight?" he mewed to Ravenpaw, who was watching the cats eat from the entrance to the nest.

"Yes, I'd like that." He padded over to the corner where ThunderClan had gathered. ShadowClan huddled opposite, while RiverClan and WindClan settled in separate corners.

"I never thought I'd sleep among the Clan again," Raven-paw murmured.

"I just wish it weren't under these circumstances." Firestar sighed.

Ravenpaw's eyes darkened. "How will you find a new home?"

"StarClan will tell us," Squirrelpaw mewed. She glanced at Brambleclaw, but he didn't look up. "Won't they?" She looked at Leafpaw, uncertainty pricking at her paws. Leafpaw dipped her head, but said nothing.

When Squirrelpaw woke, cold sunlight streamed into the nest. She flexed her claws, wondering how late it was. She had slept soundly. Looking up, she saw her father standing on a fallen stone that made a natural platform in the center of the broken nest. All around him, cats were drowsily lifting their heads and blinking in the daylight.

"We've slept too long," Firestar mewed. "It's sunhigh. We must push on to Highstones. Wherever we're going, we have a long journey ahead of us."

Mudclaw got to his paws, a stubborn expression on his face. "Why must we leave a place that has such good hunting?"

"My kits have fed well for the first time in moons!" Tall-poppy put in.

"This is a prey-rich place," Tallstar agreed. The WindClan

leader looked tired and drawn despite their long sleep.

"Ravenpaw only invited us to stay the night," Firestar argued.

"So? What could he do if we decided to stay longer?" Blackstar stared defiantly at Ravenpaw. "My Clan needs food and shelter, and they will take it by force if necessary."

Brambleclaw stood up. "This is not the place for us," he meowed. "I don't know exactly where we're going, but I know it's not here."

Squirrelpaw nodded. "Why would StarClan have made us journey all the way to the sun-drown-place if they only meant for us to make our homes here? We wouldn't need a sign for that."

Crowpaw twitched his ears. "We must finish the journey we've started," he growled.

"I agree," meowed Stormfur from the RiverClan corner.

"Me too." Tawnypelt stretched, arching her back. "We must carry on."

"I think they're right," Leopardstar meowed unexpectedly. "There are too many Twolegs around here. What if one of their dogs got loose? We'd be trapped in a place like this."

Blackstar narrowed his eyes. "Very well," he muttered.

Tallpoppy reluctantly got to her paws, nudging her kits awake. "Come on, my dears," she whispered. "We're leaving."

"But it's warm here," mewled one.

"And there's fresh-kill," squeaked another.

"We must go anyway," Tallpoppy told them. Her voice

was dull with tiredness, and Squirrelpaw felt a jolt of sympathy for the brave ShadowClan queen. She padded toward the entrance, and her kits followed, their fur sticking up in clumps where they had slept on it.

"I'll come with you to Highstones," Ravenpaw offered, brushing his tail against Firestar's flank.

The cats filed silently away from the shelter, heading for the crags of Highstones that towered in the distance, dark against the clearing sky. Squirrelpaw shivered as the wind ruffled her fur. Sunhigh was already past. If they slowed their pace to match the elders and kits, they would not reach Highstones until the sun had dipped below the horizon.

"So who is ThunderClan's deputy now?" she heard Ravenpaw ask Firestar.

Squirrelpaw glanced at Brambleclaw, but he kept his eyes fixed straight ahead.

"Graystripe is," Firestar growled.

Ravenpaw stared at his friend in surprise. "But he's gone."

Firestar rounded on him, his eyes glittering with pain. "Isn't it enough that we've had to leave our home? Don't ask me to give up on my friend as well. I know he would never give up on me." He started to trudge on again. "ThunderClan has a deputy, and there is no need to choose a new one."

Highstones was cast in blue-black shade as the sun sank low in the sky. The cats had seemed to take forever struggling up the steep, stony slope on paws already raw from the day's traveling. Now they lay exhausted outside Mothermouth. Squirrelpaw stared into the great black tunnel that led to the Moonstone. The Clan leaders and their medicine cats had disappeared into it as soon as they had arrived.

"I wish you'd gone with them," Squirrelpaw muttered to her sister. "You could have told me what StarClan said."

"Leopardstar said this wasn't a time for apprentices, and Firestar agreed with her," Leafpaw mewed.

"Do you think StarClan will tell them anything?"

"Who knows?" murmured Leafpaw.

There was the sound of loose stones crunching beneath paws, and Firestar padded out of the tunnel, followed by Tallstar, Leopardstar, and Blackstar. Their faces gave nothing away as they separated to join their Clans.

"I want to know what happened!" Squirrelpaw fretted.

"They can't tell us anything about the ceremony," Leafpaw reminded her.

Squirrelpaw felt a prickle of frustration. It was all right for Leafpaw; she had her own special connection with StarClan. Couldn't she help out the cats who didn't?

"Squirrelpaw!' Brambleclaw called. The tabby warrior was weaving his way toward her. "We're meeting up there!" he whispered. He nodded to the crest of the ridge. "We have to decide where we're going next."

Squirrelpaw put her head on one side. "I thought we were going to the sun-drown-place to find Midnight."

"This is our last chance to be sure it's the right thing to do," Brambleclaw replied. "After this, we'll be taking our

Clanmates into territory where they've never been before. Come on."

Squirrelpaw followed him up the steep slope, away from the rest of the Clans. She could see Stormfur hurrying to the top of the ridge from the RiverClan cats, his gray pelt glowing in the moonlight. Tawnypelt and Crowpaw already sat on top of the jagged spine of rocks, silhouetted against the star-clad indigo sky.

The shadowy world stretched away on the other side of Highstones, a huge black expanse that made Squirrelpaw's breath catch in her throat. Out there were snowcapped mountains, strange cats, dangerous creatures, and the sun-drown-place, that endless stretch of water where Midnight lived. Squirrelpaw shivered. *Oh, StarClan, what are we doing?*

"Does everyone agree we should head for the sun-drown-place and find Midnight?" Brambleclaw asked.

Tawnypelt's eyes were round with worry. "I can't think of what else we should do, but what if she's not there anymore?"

"It's a long and dangerous journey," Stormfur agreed.

"I was so sure we were going to lead them to a safe new home," Squirrelpaw meowed, remembering her excitement as she carried Midnight's message back from the sun-drown-place. "We were going to save them."

"And instead we might be leading them into unnecessary danger," Brambleclaw murmured.

"Why couldn't StarClan have chosen different cats to carry this message?" Stormfur sighed.

Squirrelpaw's heart ached for him. He had lost so much.

His sister had died on the first journey, and now Twolegs had taken his father. She moved closer to him, pressing her flank against his.

"Do you think our ancestors have abandoned us?" Tawnypelt mewed, voicing the fear that nagged at them all.

"Well, they haven't sent the sign Midnight promised," Brambleclaw admitted. "Have any of you seen a dying warrior?"

"Perhaps it was Mudfur?" Stormfur suggested.

"He was a medicine cat," Squirrelpaw pointed out.

"Would Midnight know the difference?" murmured Tawnypelt.

The cats looked at one another in silence.

"But Mudfur died on RiverClan territory!" A sickening pang of doubt suddenly twisted Squirrelpaw's belly. "If Mudfur's death was the sign, then we've come the wrong way!"

The five cats stared at one another, their eyes filled with dread as they imagined telling their leaders that they had to take the Clans all the way back into the heart of the forest to face the monsters once more.

Oh, StarClan, have we gotten it all wrong? Squirrelpaw lifted her face to the sky and closed her eyes. When she opened them again, a flash of movement caught her attention. She gasped, and the other cats followed her gaze. Above them, a falling star blazed a silvery trail before disappearing in a flash of light.

"The dying warrior!" Squirrelpaw breathed. It was the sign they had been waiting for, one of StarClan's own warriors scorching into nothingness to show them the way to go. Faint as cobweb, the star's fiery trail hung in the sky, stretching toward the horizon where the jagged peaks of the mountains jutted into the sky.

"Now we know which way to go," Brambleclaw murmured.

"Over the mountains," meowed Squirrelpaw.

CHAPTER 20

❧

Leafpaw pushed closer against Cinderpelt as the chill of dawn dragged her awake. The stone beneath her seemed to have soaked all the warmth from her body, and the air was so cold that when she opened her eyes she could see her breath billowing in small clouds. She stood up and stretched. The rocks glittered with frost in the pale dawn light, and a scent drifted up toward her so delicious it made her mouth water. Ravenpaw was padding up the slope with a freshly killed rabbit dangling from his jaws.

The other ThunderClan cats were still sleeping, clustered in a dip in the rock several fox-lengths away from where each of the other Clans had settled for the night. But the scent of the rabbit woke them, and they began to raise their heads as Ravenpaw wove among them. Firestar was already stretching, Sandstorm at his side, when Ravenpaw dropped the fresh-kill at the ThunderClan leader's paws.

"A parting gift," he mewed.

Firestar stared at him. "I wish you'd come with us," he meowed. "I've lost Graystripe; I don't want to leave another friend behind."

Ravenpaw shook his head. "My home is here, but I'll never forget you, I promise. I'll be waiting for you always."

Leafpaw wondered with a pang if they would ever come back. She knew they were going to be traveling a long way, but she had no idea how far.

"We have been through so much together," Firestar murmured, his eyes gleaming as he remembered. "We've seen the death of Bluestar, the defeat of Tigerstar. . . ." He sighed. "So much has happened, like water flowing past in a river."

"More water will flow before we join StarClan," Ravenpaw assured him. "This is not an end. It is a beginning. You will need the courage of a lion to face this journey."

"It's hard to find courage when so much is lost." Firestar's eyes clouded. "I never thought I'd leave the forest! Even when BloodClan came, I would have died to save my home."

Ravenpaw drew his tail gently along Firestar's flank. "If I see Graystripe, I'll tell him which way you've gone," he promised. He dipped his head formally. "Good-bye, Firestar, and good luck."

"Good-bye, Ravenpaw."

As the black loner bounded away down the slope, Leafpaw's heart ached for her father. He was leaving behind his two oldest and closest friends—without even knowing if one of them was still alive. She watched Sandstorm press her cheek against his as if to remind him he was not alone.

Cinderpelt stretched her forelegs one after the other. "We should check the cats and make sure they are all ready for the journey ahead," she meowed to Leafpaw.

Leafpaw nodded. She thought back to the night before, when Squirrelpaw had returned with the others from the top of the ridge. Their eyes had been shining.

"We've seen the dying warrior!" Brambleclaw's mew had been breathless with excitement.

"You've had the sign?" Firestar leaped to his paws from where he had been dozing beside Sandstorm.

"How can you be sure?" Cinderpelt asked.

"A star blazed through the sky, then vanished," Squirrelpaw explained. "It fell behind the mountains."

Blackstar ran over from where ShadowClan huddled on the rock. He looked puzzled. "Is this the sign we waited for at the Great Rock?"

Tawnypelt stared at him as if something had only just dawned on her. "Of course! This must be the great rock Midnight meant! Highstones, not the rock at Fourtrees!"

Stormfur nodded. "She's never been to the forest. What she saw obviously looked like a great rock, even though to us it meant something completely different."

Leopardstar shouldered her way to the front. "So what lies behind the mountains?"

"Mountains?" Ferncloud drew Birchkit closer to her.

"Last time we crossed them we found the sun-drown-place," Brambleclaw explained. "But this time the star seemed to fall farther along."

Hawkfrost narrowed his eyes. "So we'll have to find a new route?"

"Not exactly," Brambleclaw told him.

"It'll be safer if we cross the mountains the same way as we did last time," Tawnypelt mewed. "Otherwise we risk getting lost—and the snows might come at any time."

"We can head toward where the star fell once we're over them," Squirrelpaw put in.

Leafpaw saw her sister's whiskers twitch, and Brambleclaw flexed his claws on the rock as if he were bracing himself for the journey. But there was a hunted look in their eyes as well. They were frightened of what lay ahead, because they knew what the journey might hold. With a twinge of alarm, Leafpaw wondered why StarClan had chosen a *dying* warrior to show them the way. It seemed a dark omen on which to fix the hopes of the Clans.

"Come on, Leafpaw!" Cinderpelt's voice jolted her back to the frosty morning.

"Cinderpelt," Leafpaw meowed hesitantly. "Do you think the sign from StarClan means they're coming with us?"

The gray medicine cat gave her a long, thoughtful look. "I hope so."

"But you're not sure?" Leafpaw guessed.

Cinderpelt glanced around. No cat was near. "When we went to the Moonstone yesterday, I could hardly hear StarClan," she admitted.

"But did they say anything?" Leafpaw asked, alarmed.

Cinderpelt narrowed her eyes. "I know that they spoke to me, but I couldn't tell what they were saying. It was as if their voices were drowned by the roaring of a great wind."

"You couldn't make out anything?"

"Nothing." Cinderpelt closed her eyes for a moment. "But they were there."

"They must be suffering as much as we are," Leafpaw murmured. "It must be terrible to watch the forest being destroyed, and to be powerless to stop it. After all, it was once their home too."

Cinderpelt nodded. "You're right. But like us, they will recover, as long as all five Clans remain."

"But will they find us in our new home?" Leafpaw fretted. "Will they know where to look for us?"

"These are questions we cannot answer." Cinderpelt straightened up, and her voice became brisk. "Come on. Our Clanmates need us."

Leafpaw padded to where Ravenpaw had left the rabbit. It lay untouched beside her father. A patrol of warriors had already left to find more.

"May I take this to Ferncloud and Birchkit?" she asked, but Firestar seemed lost in thought.

"Of course," meowed Sandstorm.

Leafpaw glanced anxiously up at her mother. "Will he be okay?"

Firestar turned to face her. "Of course I will," he meowed. "Go ahead and take that to Ferncloud."

Leafpaw picked up the rabbit and hurried to where Ferncloud was curled around Birchkit. The tabby kit was shivering with cold, and Ferncloud was licking him fiercely to warm him up.

"It's too cold to be sleeping outside!" Ferncloud complained when Leafpaw appeared. "I hardly got a moment's rest." She gazed at Birchkit, her eyes glittering with fear, and Leafpaw guessed she had dreaded closing her eyes in case she woke to find the last of her kits dead.

"Here." She dropped the rabbit on the ground. "This should help."

Ferncloud's eyes lit up. Flashing a grateful glance at Leafpaw, she tore off a hind leg and placed it in front of Birchkit. "Try this," she urged him. "We used to eat rabbit all the time, but we haven't tasted it in moons."

"Make sure you have some too," Leafpaw advised Ferncloud.

"I will," Ferncloud promised.

Leafpaw's belly growled, and she hoped the hunting patrol would return soon. She looked around to see if any of the other cats looked as though they needed help, but most of them were moving about quite cheerfully, shaking the stiffness from their limbs and padding to the rocks to lap water from the tiny hollows. Several cats, Brambleclaw and Squirrelpaw among them, were sitting near the top of the ridge, the gray stone turned rosy by the sunrise.

Leafpaw heard Whitepaw pestering Brambleclaw. "Tell us what it was like. Please!"

Brambleclaw glanced over his shoulder at the far side of the ridge. "You'll find out for yourself soon enough."

"But if you told us, we'd be ready for anything!" Spiderpaw pointed out.

"He's right," Whitepaw mewed. "You've got to prepare us."

Brambleclaw drew his tail over his paws with a resigned sigh. "Well, there are lots of sheep, which are fluffy white woolly things that look a bit like clouds on legs. They're harmless, but you'll need to watch out for dogs when you see them, because the Twolegs use them to control the sheep. And Thunderpaths, of course—they're mostly small, but there are many to cross. And then there are the mountains. . . ."

His voice trailed away, and Leafpaw felt the cold wind pierce her fur. What was it about the mountains that frightened these cats so much? How would they get kits and elders through such a place? *Oh, StarClan, where are you?* If only she could believe StarClan was traveling with them, perhaps she wouldn't feel so afraid.

Leafpaw had never guessed such a vast world existed beyond Highstones. Field after field stretched before them, dotted with sheep, looking exactly like clouds, as Brambleclaw had described. Squirrelpaw padded beside her, her breath billowing into the frosty air.

"Do you remember this?" Leafpaw asked.

"A bit," Squirrelpaw mewed.

"So we're going the right way?"

"Yes."

Leafpaw wondered why her sister seemed so reluctant to talk. She watched her exchange an anxious glance with Brambleclaw. He had been weaving among the cats all morning, flanking first one side, then the other, as if he was afraid of losing one.

Leafpaw felt the air tremble, and a rumbling in the distance made her pause. It sounded as if a storm was coming, but the clear sky told her there couldn't be. She lifted her nose and sniffed the air. A Thunderpath.

"It's a big one," Squirrelpaw warned.

As they drew nearer, the rumbling grew to a roar, and the stench began to burn Leafpaw's throat. The cats in front slowed down, jostling together but still keeping closer to their Clanmates than the other cats. Squirrelpaw pushed forward, and Leafpaw followed until they reached a ditch with steeply sloping sides. Beyond it lay the Thunderpath.

"We should get the kits across first." Firestar led the way into the narrow gully. Leafpaw jumped down beside Sorreltail, her paws slipping on the greasy grass. Monsters roared past in both directions, and she flinched as the earth shook beneath her paws.

"Each Clan should take its own chances," Mudclaw insisted.

"RiverClan will cross first," Hawkfrost declared.

"Not all the warriors are as strong as RiverClan's," Leopardstar pointed out. "Firestar is right; we should help the weaker Clans."

"My Clan doesn't need your help!" hissed Mudclaw. "Besides, it would be chaos! No cat would know whose orders to follow!"

"Then why don't you command us all?" Firestar spat.

"No cat commands ShadowClan warriors except me!" Blackstar growled.

Brambleclaw pushed through the crowd to stand beside

Firestar. Leafpaw was close enough to scent the fear in him. "Cats will get killed while you're all bickering! Surely it doesn't matter who is in charge until every cat is safely on the other side?"

Blackstar flattened his ears and Hawkfrost lashed his tail.

"Let him continue," Firestar warned.

"I'll lead ThunderClan," Brambleclaw meowed. "Crowpaw can lead WindClan. Tawnypelt can take ShadowClan, and Stormfur, you guide RiverClan."

"Crowpaw can't lead WindClan," Mudclaw argued. "He's only an apprentice."

"Have you crossed this path before?" Brambleclaw demanded.

"No," Mudclaw spat. "But I have commanded my Clan before!"

"Crowpaw will lead!" Brambleclaw hissed.

Ignoring them both, Stormfur flicked his tail and led his Clanmates to the edge of the Thunderpath, where he crouched, waiting to give the signal. A monster roared past, its pelt glinting in the sunlight. As soon as it had gone, Stormfur yowled and the RiverClan cats surged up and over the Thunderpath. Leafpaw searched for Dawnflower, quickly spotting her pale gray coat and feeling a rush of relief when she saw that two RiverClan warriors were helping to carry her kits.

As the cats bundled onto the verge on the other side, Leafpaw heard the menacing rumble of another monster. Thanking StarClan that RiverClan had all made it safely, she looked up to see how far away it was. Her heart flipped over.

Mudclaw had told his Clan to start crossing without waiting for Crowpaw to give the command!

Crowpaw stared panic-stricken as the monster screamed toward them. "Hurry!" He bolted forward, scooped up a kit, and raced for the other side. Hurling the kit onto the verge, he raced back to grab another. "Carry the kits!" he ordered. Scrabbling to get a grip on the slippery surface, he grasped another kit by its scruff and raced for the far side once more. The warriors and apprentices seized the last of the kits and raced after him, with the queens at their heels. But Morning-flower, a WindClan elder, fell behind.

"Run!" Leafpaw yowled.

Above her, Firestar crouched at the edge of the Thunder-path. His gaze flicked at the oncoming monster, judging whether he could reach Morningflower in time.

"Stay where you are!" Brambleclaw screeched at him.

Firestar crouched lower and flattened his ears. "Keep going! You'll make it!" he called to the WindClan she-cat. The monster bore down like a whirlwind and suddenly veered across the Thunderpath, straight toward Firestar. Leafpaw felt a wave of terror and shut her eyes, waiting for the sicken-ing crunch of fur and bone.

It never came. She opened her eyes a tiny slit to see the monster sweep past Firestar so close that the wind tugged his fur. It roared away without slowing down. Leafpaw opened her eyes fully. Morningflower was limping determinedly across the Thunderpath, watched by her Clanmates from the other side. Firestar backed away from the edge, his flanks heaving.

"It's okay, he's safe." Sorreltail touched her nose to Leaf-paw's shoulder.

"I thought he was going to be killed," she whispered.

"Your father's brave," Sorreltail murmured, "but he's no fool."

Leafpaw turned back to watch ShadowClan waiting to cross. She hoped that Blackstar had learned caution from Mudclaw's recklessness. The ShadowClan leader was watching Tawnypelt.

An apprentice darted forward.

"Get back!" Tawnypelt hissed. Her tone stopped the apprentice in his tracks, and he darted back to join the other cats.

"We go together!" she insisted, glancing at Blackstar. He nodded.

There were no monsters in sight. Cautiously Blackstar padded forward, lifting his nose to scent the air. "Now!" he called, and the ShadowClan cats leaped up the side of the ditch and spilled onto the Thunderpath. Tallpoppy's kits were carried safely by warriors, and Tallpoppy herself was swept along by her Clan like a fish swimming downstream. Leafpaw sighed with relief as all the cats reached the other side just before a monster set the earth trembling once more.

"We'll go after this one," Brambleclaw called.

Suddenly a tiny cry came from the far side. Leafpaw stiffened. One of Tallpoppy's kits had wandered back onto the Thunderpath! Dazed, it wandered in a circle on the hard path, mewling for its mother.

Dustpelt and Mousefur flattened their bellies to the ground, ready to make a dash for the kit.

"Wait!" Brambleclaw ordered. "It's too dangerous."

The Clan held its position.

Tallpoppy began to struggle through the mass of Shadow-Clan cats to reach her kit, but one of the RiverClan queens was closer. Dawnflower leaped onto the Thunderpath and scooped the kit out of the way of the monster. She carried it back to the verge, dropped it on the grass, and began licking it roughly.

Suddenly she stopped and swiped her tongue around her lips in confusion as she realized the kit was not her own. She glanced self-consciously at her Clanmates as Tallpoppy bounded over and snatched up her kit. Leafpaw tensed, hoping Tallpoppy wasn't offended by the RiverClan queen's intervention. But her eyes were brimming with gratitude, and she dipped her head to Dawnflower before carrying her kit away.

"That's where Feathertail rescued me from the fence stuff." Squirrelpaw pointed with her nose to the shiny prickly thread that hung between the wooden posts. The Thunderpath was behind them now, and Leafpaw's paws had finally stopped shaking. She was grateful to her sister for distracting her with stories of her first journey here. "While the others were busy arguing about what to do," Squirrelpaw went on, "Feathertail rubbed my fur with some chewed-up dock leaves and I slipped out like a fish."

"You left half your pelt behind, though," Stormfur reminded her, and Squirrelpaw swatted him playfully with her forepaw in reply.

There seemed to be no danger here, no fresh scents of Twolegs or dogs; just lots of sheep that grazed noisily, paying little attention to the cats. The cats spread out across the meadow, each Clan keeping to itself. Only Crowpaw, Tawnypelt, Brambleclaw, Squirrelpaw, and Stormfur broke away from their Clanmates, taking turns hurrying up and down the line, watching for stragglers.

Tallstar trekked wearily along. Onewhisker had not left his side all day. The other leaders glanced at the elderly WindClan cat from time to time, clearly worried.

"We should find a place to rest," Barkface advised as the sky darkened and a chill breeze ruffled the cats' fur.

"There's a copse up ahead," Firestar meowed. "We could find shelter there."

The other leaders nodded, and the cats climbed to the top of the sloping field and padded into the wood. Leafpaw sank gratefully onto a pile of moss.

"I smell fox," Blackstar warned.

"The scent is stale," Leopardstar observed, scenting the air.

"But it might come back while we're sleeping," Mudclaw meowed.

"The Clans should all sleep together," called Dawnflower, reaching out with her tail to stop her tom kit, a plump, round-faced tabby, from wandering after a wood louse. "Lie down, Tumblekit," she scolded.

"The kits and queen, should sleep in the center," One-whisker suggested. "They'll be safest there." He glanced at Tallstar. "The oldest cats should join them."

"Very well," Blackstar agreed. "Each Clan will post two guards to keep watch."

Leafpaw padded over to Sorreltail, grateful for the shelter of the bracken. Ferncloud should sleep soundly tonight, she decided, with four Clans and thick undergrowth to keep Birchkit warm. The woods were very quiet, the frosty silence broken only by the hooting of an owl. It wasn't home, and the jumbled scents of four different Clans made Leafpaw's nose twitch, but she felt safe enough to curl up next to Cinderpelt and go to sleep.

Leafpaw slowly grew used to dealing with Thunderpaths as they trekked toward the setting sun. The Clans still crossed separately, but the queens watched out for each other's kits now, having seen how easily the youngest cats were confused by the noise and the stench of the monsters. Like cobwebs in the rain, the Clan boundaries were beginning to dissolve.

"We should reach the mountains this evening," Bramble-claw announced as Leafpaw did her morning rounds of the Clan, checking for injuries or signs of infection.

"Are we that close?" She stared up at the peaks, which had grown from a tiny line on the horizon into a forbidding mass of stone. She shivered at the sight of the snow that capped the highest crags. Some of the cats had already begun coughing, awakening Leafpaw's fear of greencough, the illness that could wipe out an entire Clan in leaf-bare.

"Leafpaw!" Firestar called. "Are you up for a little hunting?"

"Yes, please," she replied eagerly. She had been so busy tending to the Clan, padding cuts with cobweb, soothing scratches with dock, trying to make the best of what herbs she and Cinderpelt had found along the way, that she had not hunted in days.

"Go with Brambleclaw and Squirrelpaw, then," Firestar ordered. "See if you can bring back a mouse or two."

Squirrelpaw bounded to her side. "Which way shall we go?"

"There should be plenty of mice in that field over there." Brambleclaw pointed with his tail to an open meadow beyond the hedgerow.

"Come on then," Squirrelpaw urged.

Brambleclaw charged after her, and Leafpaw followed, wriggling through the hedge to find herself in a broad, grassy space.

While Brambleclaw and Squirrelpaw ranged around the edge of the field, she headed into the long grass battered down by the leaf-bare winds and rain. Almost at once she smelled mouse. After the long, hungry moons in the prey-scarce forest they had left behind, Leafpaw could not believe her luck. Crouching down, she prowled through the grass until she found the freshest trail. A moment later she spotted a twitch of brown scrabbling deep in the grass, and pounced.

The mouse darted away before her paws hit the ground,

and she only flattened the tussock where it had been sitting a heartbeat before.

"I see you're more accustomed to forest hunting." Hawkfrost's condescending mew made Leafpaw jump. She spun around to find the RiverClan warrior calmly watching her, his tail curled over his paws.

"Haven't you got anything better to do?" she challenged him. "Like hunt for your own Clan?"

"I've already caught three mice and a thrush," he meowed. "I think I have earned a rest."

As Leafpaw searched for a sharp reply, Hawkfrost lifted his nose and scented the air. "Dog!" he hissed. "Heading this way."

Leafpaw could hear the heavy pawsteps now, pounding through the grass. She stared around in terror, wondering which way to run.

"Get back to the hedge!" Hawkfrost commanded.

Leafpaw began to run, but an angry snarl made her freeze. Glancing over her shoulder, she saw Hawkfrost arching his back at a snarling black-and-white dog. The RiverClan warrior let out a hiss and leaped back, lashing out to rake his claws across the dog's snout.

"Brambleclaw! Squirrelpaw! Help!" Leafpaw yowled.

The dog lunged again; Hawkfrost sprang out of the way, but the dog turned in an instant and snapped at the air where Hawkfrost had been.

"Look out!" Brambleclaw burst out of the grass beside

Leafpaw and leaped onto the back of the dog. He clung on with piercing claws as it bucked and howled and struggled to shake him off. Brambleclaw hung on, but the dog twisted its head back and clamped its jaws shut only a mouse-length from Brambleclaw's face. Hissing in terror, Brambleclaw let go and was hurled to the ground. In the heartbeat it took him to recover, the dog had rounded on him, slavering with rage.

Just in time, Hawkfrost threw himself in front of Brambleclaw, aiming a flurry of thorn-sharp swipes at the dog's muzzle. Brambleclaw scrambled to his paws and joined the attack. Leafpaw stood stiff-legged with horror, watching the two warriors turn and move and hunch their massive shoulders as though one were a reflection of the other.

The dog began to back away with its tail clamped between its legs. Hawkfrost reared up on his hind legs and hissed so menacingly that the dog yelped and ran for the hedge.

"Brambleclaw, are you all right?" Leafpaw gasped.

"Yes, I'm fine."

"Good job I was here to save you," Hawkfrost sneered.

"I saved *you*, in case you've forgotten," Brambleclaw retorted.

Hawkfrost shrugged. "I suppose you did," he admitted ungraciously.

"Well, I guess you scared that mutt off pretty well," Brambleclaw conceded.

"What's going on?" Squirrelpaw hurried out of the long grass. "I smell dog."

"It attacked us. Brambleclaw and Hawkfrost scared it away," Leafpaw reported.

"You're kidding!" gasped Squirrelpaw.

"I'm going back now," Hawkfrost announced abruptly. Their narrow escape didn't seem to have made him any friendlier, and Leafpaw was quite happy to see the RiverClan warrior stalk away.

"Come on; let's keep hunting," meowed Brambleclaw. He bounded off through the grass.

"Come on, Leafpaw!" Squirrelpaw called over her shoulder. "You'll need to eat well before we head into the mountains."

Leafpaw looked up at the snow-dappled peaks. She wished she shared her sister's courage. The Clans had struggled enough getting this far—how would the kits and elders cope with rocks and ice, and sheer, dizzying cliffs? How would the warriors and apprentices cope, for that matter? She shut her eyes and uttered a silent prayer to StarClan, but she felt hollow with dread as her words came echoing emptily back, as if there were no one there to listen.

CHAPTER 21
❧

A bitter wind blew down from the mountains as the Clans joined the trail that led into the towering peaks. Heavy clouds blanketed the sky, and Leafpaw could tell by their yellow tinge that it would soon start snowing.

Brambleclaw and Stormfur were leading them along the side of a steep valley. It was as different from the forest as Leafpaw could possibly imagine. There were only a few trees, gnarled and stunted, clinging to the smooth gray stone, with nowhere that prey might live. Moons of desperate hunger had left the WindClan cats' fur thin and useless against the chill, but they plodded grimly on with their heads down. Tallstar looked as brittle as a leaf, often leaning on Onewhisker, who rarely strayed from his side. ShadowClan looked little better, their eyes weary and their pace slow, and RiverClan appeared shabby, their gleaming coats nothing but a memory, half-forgotten, like the days when every cat had enough to eat.

One of Tallpoppy's kits gazed up at the crags with eyes as wide as an owl's. "Are we really going up there?"

"Yes," Tallpoppy answered bleakly.

Morningflower paused, then stiffly lifted one paw and

grazed her tongue across its pad.

"Are you all right?" Leafpaw asked the elderly she-cat. Blood welled between Morningflower's claws. Leafpaw looked farther up the line, where Squirrelpaw and Brambleclaw padded side by side. "Squirrelpaw!"

Squirrelpaw turned at once.

"Can we stop? I need to dress Morningflower's paw."

"I'll tell Firestar," came the reply.

"Is there anything you need?" Brambleclaw meowed.

"Cobweb and comfrey, if possible." Leafpaw gazed at the barren landscape with little hope of finding anything that would help.

Brackenfur, in the middle of the stream of cats, lifted his head. "We'll find some," he promised. He murmured to the cats around him. Mews rippled through the throng, and warriors of all Clans began to range out and search among the rocks.

Leafpaw examined Morningflower's paw. "You've kept it clean," she mewed. "But if you go on softening it with your tongue, it'll never toughen."

Barkface pushed his way forward to join them. "What's wrong?"

"It's just raw from walking," Morningflower muttered.

"Will this do?" Russetfur came over and spat a mouthful of leaves onto the ground.

Leafpaw sniffed them cautiously. They didn't smell like anything she was used to. She lapped up a leaf, letting its flavor seep into her tongue before she dared bite it. The taste was bitter, but it had an astringent flavor that reminded her of marigold. "It might do." She glanced at Barkface. "Should we try it?"

Barkface sniffed a leaf. "It looks a little like something we used on the moors."

"You may as well try," Morningflower offered. "If it works, you can use it on others. I'll let you know soon enough if it hurts too much."

Leafpaw chewed the leaf and washed its green juice into Morningflower's paw.

The old cat winced and Leafpaw drew back. "It's okay," Morningflower grunted. "Just a sting. Carry on."

Mothwing bounded up, one forepaw swathed in sticky, white web.

"Great, thanks!" Carefully, Leafpaw teased the web from her outstretched paw and wrapped as much as she could around Morningflower's swollen pad. "Let me know if it starts to throb."

"I will." Morningflower pressed her paw gingerly to the ground. "Not bad," she mewed.

Brambleclaw hurried back to the head of the line, and the cats set off again. Squirrelpaw walked quietly beside Leafpaw, her head down.

"Is this the way you came home?" Leafpaw mewed after a while.

"I . . . I think so," Squirrelpaw mumbled.

Leafpaw glanced at her in surprise. They had come this way because Tawnypelt said it would be easier to follow the route they'd used before. She had assumed Squirrelpaw knew the way. She peered ahead to where the valley narrowed until it was little more than a cleft between the rocks. "Doesn't anything look familiar?"

Squirrelpaw blinked. "It looks different coming in this direction. The Tribe led us most of the way last time."

Leafpaw gulped. She wondered if they would meet any of the Tribe cats on their journey, these mud-streaked cats who worshiped strange ancestors and survived in a world of rock and ice.

As the Clans trekked on, higher and higher, only Stormfur looked comfortable. He leaped from rock to rock so easily he seemed quite unlike a RiverClan cat, and even his fur blended smoothly into the bare gray world.

There seemed to be no end to the climbing, neither that day nor the next. The terrain grew steeper and rockier, but still the peaks towered above them. Morningflower's paw had improved, and Leafpaw kept an eye out for more stocks of the herb she'd used to heal it.

"Are you sure we're going the right way?" Sorreltail whispered. "This path is getting really narrow."

She was right. The trail was leading them onto a ledge that spiraled around a dizzying gorge. The mountain fell away at one side of the path and rose up vertically on the other. The wind funneled through the gap like water through a ditch, tugging at Leafpaw's fur. She narrowed her eyes against the icy blast and kept her gaze fixed firmly ahead.

The cats fell into single file to pick their way along the ledge.

"Carry the kits!" Blackstar called down the line, and his yowl echoed eerily off the walls of the gorge.

The ledge followed the curve of the mountain, sloping up toward a narrow pass between two peaks. The mountainside echoed with the rattle of stones as the edge of the path crumbled beneath the cats' paws and sent grit showering down into the shadows below. Leafpaw walked as close as she could to the rock face, her heart hammering. She could feel Sorreltail's warm breath behind her.

Suddenly a wail rang out from up ahead, and a large chunk of rock clattered endlessly down into the abyss. A hole yawned in the narrow path, sending Smokepaw, a ShadowClan apprentice, plummeting into nothingness. For a moment he clutched desperately at the ledge, his claws scratching against the stone. Russetfur, the ShadowClan deputy, lunged to grab him, but her extra weight only dislodged more stones, and the edge where Smokepaw clung suddenly dropped away. Russetfur leaped backward, only just managing to save herself. The apprentice fell, twisting violently in the air, and disappeared into the darkness.

A ShadowClan queen leaned over the precipice. "Smokepaw!"

"Get back!" Stormfur yowled. He wove like a fish back along the ledge and dragged her back.

As the cats stared in frozen horror, Leafpaw willed StarClan to take the apprentice quickly. Blackstar peered over the edge.

"There's nothing we can do," he meowed, straightening up. "We have to keep going."

"You're going to leave him?" wailed the queen.

"He won't have survived that fall," Blackstar told her. "And we can't reach his body." He touched the queen's flank with his muzzle. "I'm sorry, Nightwing. ShadowClan won't forget Smokepaw; I promise."

Hollow-eyed with shock and grief, the cats set off once more, pressing so close to the cliff face that it scraped their fur. But Smokepaw's fall had left a gap in the ledge. Fortunately Longtail was among the cats that had been ahead of the RiverClan apprentice—Leafpaw gulped at the thought of helping the sightless tom across a gap he had no way of measuring—but there were still several cats on the wrong side of the terrifying hole.

Stormfur crouched on the far side, bracing his claws against the rock. "Come on," he called to Weaselpaw, a WindClan apprentice. "It's safe on this side. You can jump it easily."

Weaselpaw stared down at the shadows, his eyes stretched wide.

"The others will freeze waiting for you," Stormfur growled, losing his patience. "Just jump!"

Weaselpaw looked up and blinked. He crouched, keeping his weight well back on his haunches, then leaped across with his front legs outstretched. Stormfur caught him by the scruff as he landed, grunting with the effort. He gave him a nudge up the path and turned to the next cat.

"My kits can't jump that!" Tallpoppy shrank back.

"Can you pass them over?" Stormfur meowed.

Tallpoppy flattened her ears. "It's too far!"

"I'll take them." Crowpaw squeezed carefully past Stormfur and jumped the gap to land in front of Tallpoppy. She stared at him, her eyes filled with fear. "I won't drop them," he promised. He picked up the smallest and padded to the edge of the hole. The kit struggled beneath his chin, its terrified mewls echoing around the chasm. Tallpoppy watched, huge-eyed, as Crowpaw jumped. Pebbles showered from the ledge as he landed beside Stormfur, but he kept his footing. Leafpaw was amazed by his agility.

"Make sure he stays put," he meowed, placing the kit gently on the ledge. Then he turned and leaped back for the next.

When all three were safely over, Tallpoppy followed, clearing the gap easily with her long legs. "Thank you," she breathed. She pressed her muzzle against each of her kits before nudging them gently onward, up the slope.

"Let's get the others across," Crowpaw mewed to Stormfur. "You stay on this side; I'll go to the other."

When it was Leafpaw's turn, her paws trembled so hard that she was afraid they would shake her right over the edge.

"It's okay," Crowpaw murmured. "It's not as hard as it looks."

Leafpaw felt his warm breath on her fur and tried to concentrate on that instead of the gaping hole before her. She knew that back home, with nothing but the soft forest floor beneath her, she would leap this far without thinking. But here, the gap seemed to drag at her like a black river, pulling her down, down, down. . . .

"Don't think about it!" Stormfur called.

Leafpaw screwed up her eyes, feeling the lip of stone under her paws. *StarClan, help me!* She crouched down and sprang, landing in a skid that made her paws sting.

"Well done!" Stormfur yowled.

Leafpaw shuffled around and saw Sorreltail waiting to jump. She shrank back as Sorreltail hurtled toward her and skittered dangerously near the edge. Leafpaw lunged and grabbed her scruff.

"Thanks," Sorreltail breathed shakily.

"That's okay," Leafpaw muttered through a mouthful of tortoiseshell fur.

"Hurry and catch up with the others," Stormfur mewed. "We'll make sure the rest get over in one piece."

They padded gingerly up the slope. Tallpoppy had already disappeared through a narrow ravine, and Leafpaw followed her, eager to be away from the ledge. The ravine opened into a sloping valley that fell away toward another ridge. On one side, a great rock cliff soared toward the sky. On the other, a slope swept more gently upward to where heather and grass fought for space among the jutting stones. The other cats hovered like shadows among the rocks. Cinderpelt was already weaving among them, checking that everyone was all right.

Leafpaw's stomach growled. She hoped the hollows and crevices would conceal some small prey. The cats had hardly eaten since they had entered the mountains. The prey-rich fields of Twolegplace seemed a distant memory, and there didn't seem to be enough food here to feed one Clan, let alone four.

"It looks like some of the cats are already hunting," Sorreltail meowed. Tawnypelt was leading a small patrol up one side of the valley. Blackstar was heading for a rocky outcrop a little farther down, flanked by a pair of ShadowClan warriors.

"Leafpaw! Sorreltail!"

Leafpaw heard her father calling and bounded down to him.

"Brambleclaw's organizing hunting patrols," he meowed. "You two can join him."

"Shouldn't I help Cinderpelt?" Leafpaw asked.

Firestar glanced over to the gray medicine cat. "No cat is hurt, though a few are in shock. Cinderpelt told me she could manage."

"Okay," Leafpaw mewed. She hurried to join Brambleclaw, with Sorreltail beside her.

"Is Birchkit okay?" Leafpaw paused as they passed Ferncloud.

"He's fine," Ferncloud assured her. She looked at the clouds. "But once the snow starts . . ."

Birchkit narrowed his eyes when he saw Leafpaw. "Why couldn't Cody come with us?" he whined. "Did you tell her to go away?"

Leafpaw shook her head. "She has a home of her own," she told him gently.

"But she was fun!"

"There'll be plenty of time for fun when we get to our new home," Ferncloud promised.

"If we ever get there," Sorreltail muttered as they padded away.

"Of course we'll get there," Leafpaw told her, hoping she sounded as if she believed it.

Squirrelpaw looked up as they approached. "Brambleclaw's explaining how the Tribe hunts," she whispered. "We thought it might help."

"Up here, you need to rely on stillness rather than stealth when you're hunting," Brambleclaw was meowing.

"But we're not Tribe cats; we're Clan cats!" argued Rainwhisker. "Why should we be expected to hunt like them?"

"This isn't the forest," Brambleclaw snapped. "Without the cover of undergrowth, prey will spot you in an instant. Here, you have to wait, and keep so still that you blend into the mountain. Then the prey will come to you."

"What prey is going to be that stupid?" snorted Weaselpaw.

"That's what the Tribe taught me!" Brambleclaw's eyes flashed. "If you don't want to starve, you're going to have to learn to hunt like them!" He flicked his tail. "Spiderpaw, come with me. Squirrelpaw, you go with Rainwhisker, and you two"—he looked at Leafpaw and Sorreltail—"you two stick together."

"Where shall we hunt?" Leafpaw looked around the valley, at its perilous ledges and shadowy crevices, and thought with a shudder of the giant cat that had killed Feathertail. "Will we be safe?"

"If you're sensible, yes." Brambleclaw pointed with his tail to a ledge jutting out above them. "Try up there first," he suggested.

Sorreltail nodded and scrambled up the slope, sending a shower of dust and stones down onto the cats below. Leafpaw shook the grit from her fur and followed. Her tired legs ached, but she kept going till she reached the ledge. Sorreltail flicked her tail, signaling to her to be quiet, and Leafpaw smelled at once the familiar scent of mouse. She crouched beside Sorreltail to stare at a patch of coarse grass that sprang from a crack in the ledge. *Stay still*. She recalled Brambleclaw's advice, but it was hard to wait patiently when she was this hungry.

When the grass began to tremble, Sorreltail pulled herself slowly forward. Suddenly the grass shivered and the mouse darted out, heading for a crack in the rock. With a jolt of horror, Leafpaw watched Sorreltail leap after it and tumble straight over the edge.

Leafpaw's mind filled with the memory of Smokepaw vanishing into the gorge, and she had to force herself to look down the side of the valley. To her relief, Sorreltail was very much alive, wailing in terror as she half fell, half skidded down the steep slope. She came to a bone-jarring halt against a stunted hawthorn bush that buckled and quivered under her weight, but stopped her from sliding any farther.

"Sorreltail," she called. "Are you okay?"

The ThunderClan warrior looked up at her, eyes huge with shock. "I'm okay," she mewed. "Just grazed my paws." She began to claw her way back up the slope.

Brambleclaw came dashing across the slope, alarmed by the shower of stones Sorreltail had dislodged. "What happened?"

"I slipped, that's all," Sorreltail told him, though her eyes still glittered with fear.

"You have to be careful!" Brambleclaw hissed. He stopped abruptly and stared past them.

"What is it?" Leafpaw spun around, her heart thudding. With a flood of relief she realized he had just spotted the mouse creeping out of the crack in the rock.

"Stay still," Brambleclaw ordered in a whisper.

"But I could get it in one pounce," Sorreltail breathed back.

"Wait," Brambleclaw growled.

Leafpaw heard the faint beat of wings above her head. Looking up, she saw a huge bracken-colored bird circling overhead. She gulped, wondering exactly what it had spotted as prey—the mouse, or them?

"If we're lucky," Brambleclaw murmured as the eagle folded its wings and swooped down toward them as swift and silent as a StarClan warrior, "it'll go for that mouse and we'll be able to take the Clan something big enough to share."

"And if we're not lucky?" muttered Sorreltail. Brambleclaw didn't answer.

Above them, the eagle's wings seemed to stretch wider than the river that had separated ThunderClan from RiverClan. Leafpaw fought against the urge to turn tail and run. Closer and closer the bird came, until she could see each feather on its massive wings, and its eyes gleaming like tiny black pebbles.

"Wait, wait," Brambleclaw breathed through clenched teeth.

Just when Leafpaw could see the sinews on the bird's yellow talons, it plummeted past them, ignoring the mouse and the three cats on the ledge. It was heading straight for the Clans in the valley below!

Brambleclaw sprang to the edge and peered over. "Look out!" he yowled.

The mass of golden-brown feathers seemed to explode among the cats, who screeched in terror as they raced in all directions. Only the warriors held their ground, leaping up on their hind legs and thrashing the air with unsheathed claws as the eagle climbed up once more, beating its powerful wings. As it began to rise into the sky, Leafpaw saw a small, struggling creature grasped in its long talons, and heard the pitiful mewls of a terrified kit. *No!*

"Marshkit!" Tallpoppy shrieked.

Suddenly Brackenfur sprang into the air as though lifted by the wind. With his outstretched claws he grasped the eagle's talons a heartbeat before they rose out of reach. Yowling with rage, he clung on. The eagle screeched and shook the golden brown warrior off. Brackenfur collapsed onto the ground, but his attack had been enough to loosen the eagle's grasp, and the kit plummeted down beside him.

Leafpaw hurled herself off the ledge, landed clumsily,

and skidded down the valley. Stones tore at her claws as she slithered down. Brambleclaw and Sorreltail were scrambling behind her, zigzagging across the steep slope to stop themselves from falling headlong. But Leafpaw kept tumbling over and over. A bush broke her fall before she reached the bottom, its thin branches whipping her fur. It was enough to slow her down, and she managed to scrabble to her paws and dash across the valley floor.

"Check that Brackenfur's okay!" Leafpaw ordered Sorreltail. "I'll see to Marshkit."

Tallpoppy was crouching over the scrap of fur that lay on the stony ground. Ferncloud pressed her flank against the ShadowClan queen, trying to soothe her but understanding her terror.

Leafpaw leaned over the kit and licked his chest. She could feel his flanks heaving and his tiny heart hammering in his chest. Blood welled on his shoulder, but the cut was not deep.

"He'll be all right," Leafpaw promised. "As long as we keep him warm, he'll survive the shock." She looked up and was relieved to see Cinderpelt limping toward her.

"Lick the wound as clean as you can," Cinderpelt ordered. "We have precious few herbs to cure him if it gets infected."

Leafpaw obeyed immediately, tasting the salty tang of the kit's blood on her tongue.

Tallpoppy pulled her remaining kits close to her, shaking with fear. "Where have you brought us?" she yowled, looking around to find the cats who had led them into the mountain.

"I didn't think an eagle would attack so many!" Squirrel-paw gasped as she bounded across the valley floor.

"Did you know this might happen?" Blackstar demanded furiously.

"We knew eagles preyed upon the Tribe, but they always fought them off," Squirrelpaw mewed wretchedly.

"We are not the Tribe," Blackstar hissed. "You should have warned us so that we could have found shelter."

"What shelter?" Tallpoppy cried. "There's nowhere to hide. There's nowhere to hunt. *We're* the prey here!"

"It's true," Dawnflower mewed, her voice rising in panic. "We'll be picked off one by one."

"Not if we stick together," Dustpelt argued.

"Yes," Russetfur agreed. "Next time, we'll be more pre-pared."

"If another bird attacks, we'll drive it off before if gets close to the kits," Hawkfrost promised.

"Ten Clans couldn't drive off a bird like that!" Tallpoppy yowled.

"Maybe not," Leopardstar meowed. "But any cat here would die trying, for the sake of our kits." Her gaze flicked around the Clans, and mews of agreement rose from every warrior and apprentice.

Leafpaw blinked. There were no longer four Clans making this perilous journey. There was just one Clan, bound by fear and helplessness. She left Marshkit with Tallpoppy. Little-cloud was with them now.

"Is Brackenfur okay?" she called, padding to where

Sorreltail was sitting beside the golden warrior.

"I'm fine," Brackenfur meowed, pushing himself to his paws.

"I'll keep an eye on him," Sorreltail promised.

Leafpaw padded over and touched her sister's flank with her nose. "Surely it can't get any worse?" she murmured.

Squirrelpaw stared back wordlessly, her eyes clouded with doubt. In desperation Leafpaw turned her gaze toward the sky, praying for the protection of StarClan, wondering if her prayer would reach their ancestors through the snow-laden clouds.

As if in reply, the first freezing flakes began to fall.

CHAPTER 22

♣

Squirrelpaw glimpsed movement on the ledge above. She stopped, her paws sinking into the banked snow, and glanced up. A falcon was feasting on a shrew a few tail-lengths up the rocky outcrop. Squirrelpaw knew her ginger pelt must stand out like a sunset in a pale sky, and she stood motionless, hoping that the falcon hadn't noticed her.

The snow felt soothing against her raw pads. She wondered if she had the power to leap up the short distance and catch the falcon. Probably not. The past few days had sapped her strength until she almost couldn't be bothered to hunt at all.

The falcon flattened the shrew against the rock and stooped to pull the flesh from it. Squirrelpaw felt a wrench of envy as hunger clawed at her belly. Slow as melting ice, she prowled forward, praying the thickly falling snow would camouflage her pelt.

She had to catch some prey. The cold would start killing cats faster than any eagle if the Clans grew any hungrier. Despite their bold promises to Tallpoppy, the shock of losing Smokepaw and then nearly losing Marshkit had shaken the confidence of even the strongest warriors. Squirrelpaw felt a flood of regret so strong it stopped her in her tracks. She had helped to lead the Clans to their death. She was not even sure she would be able to find her way back to them if she caught the falcon. She knew only that they were somewhere near, huddled in the snow, praying to StarClan for deliverance.

If only she could be sure they had reached the place where the Tribe hunted, then at least they might get help from the cats they had met before. Stormfur had taken to ranging out at night, among the snowy crags. He alone seemed comfortable in this barren territory. She knew he was searching for Brook, or any sign of the Tribe, but he had found nothing so far. The Tribe had no need for borders or scent markers. No other cat wanted their unforgiving hunting grounds.

The falcon ruffled its feathers, shaking off some snow, and brought Squirrelpaw's wandering thoughts back to the hunt. She tensed her tired muscles and prepared to leap.

Suddenly a flash of fur above her made her draw back. Three lean, mud-streaked cats hurled themselves from the rocks above the falcon. One snared the falcon in its long claws, while the other two bundled Squirrelpaw backward, knocking the breath from her. She felt strong paws pinning her under the snow and struggled, but they were too strong for her, and after a few terrified moments she lay still, her breath hoarse and ragged.

"Squirrelpaw?"

She heard a familiar voice growl her name and felt paws

tug her out of the snow. She blinked cold flakes of ice from her eyes and saw Talon staring at her in undisguised surprise. Two more cave-guards stood behind him, wide-eyed with astonishment.

"What are you doing here?" he demanded.

As Squirrelpaw tried to gather her confused thoughts, she recognized one of the cave-guards. It was Jag, one of the outcasts who had returned to save their Tribemates from Sharptooth. Knowing two of the cats who stood in front of her made her feel a little better. "We've left the forest," she explained. "We're traveling over the mountains."

Talon narrowed his eyes. "Again?"

"We're all going this time."

"All?"

"The four Clans," Squirrelpaw mewed. "We couldn't stay in the forest any longer. There was too much destruction. But we never thought the journey would be this hard! Smokepaw fell into a ravine, and then an eagle tried to carry off Marsh-kit. . . ." She trailed off breathlessly.

"Kits?" Talon demanded. "Out here? Are you mad? You must bring all of these cats to the Cave of Rushing Water and rest. Where did you leave them?"

"We sheltered under some rocks. There was a tree jutting out above them like a giant claw."

Talon glanced at the cave-guards. "Tree-rock," he meowed. "Go there."

The cave-guards bounded away across the snowdrift, their

ears flattened against the falling snow.

"Let's find these Clans of yours before they freeze to death," Talon meowed, picking up the still-warm falcon in his jaws.

Squirrelpaw struggled to keep up with the tom as he raced after the guards.

"They'll be safe once we get them to the Cave of Rushing Water," Talon called over his shoulder. Hope gave Squirrelpaw new strength, and she scrambled on until she was clear of the drift and pounding after him along a rock ledge that had been shielded from the snow by a sharp overhang. Her paws sent stones showering down the steep slope, but she kept running.

"Eagle!" The cave-guards skidded to a halt where the ledge came to an abrupt end. Looking along the side of the valley, Squirrelpaw saw the rocky outcrop where she had left the Clans. Their pelts looked like dark smudges through the driving snow. Above them, Squirrelpaw recognized the predatory circling motion of the eagle and felt her belly twist in dread.

The cave-guards sank back onto their haunches, then sprang over the deep cleft that lay between them and the Clan cats. Talon followed, leaping easily over the gap even though he was carrying the dead falcon.

Squirrelpaw looked across the divide, then down at the long drop beneath her. Rocks sharp as teeth pierced the snow that pooled in the chasm beneath. Summoning up every last bit of her strength, she leaped toward the rocky ledge where Talon waited. Reaching out desperately with her forepaws, she grasped the ledge, her hind legs churning empty air. Talon lunged forward, and she felt his teeth sink into her scruff as he pulled her up to safety.

The moment she felt solid ground beneath her paws, Squirrelpaw raced after the Tribe cats. Above them, the eagle folded its wings and started to drop toward the ground.

"Birchkit!" Ferncloud's shriek tore through the air. Russet-fur leaped forward to scoop up the kit and thrust him and his mother into the shadows of the rock. Brambleclaw herded Dawnflower and her kits after them. Hawkfrost leaped to Onewhisker's side, and together they shielded Tallstar from the attack.

As the eagle swooped down, its talons raking the air, the cave-guards plunged among the Clans. Jag swiped at the bird's wing, and another cave-guard lunged at it, clawing a feather from its tail. The air thrummed with the beating of the great bird's wings as it swooped upward, screeching, into the blizzard.

The Clan cats crept out from the shelter of the rock and stared in amazement at their rescuers. They looked scrawny and miserable and bedraggled, and Squirrelpaw was suddenly afraid that the Tribe cats would tell them to give up trying to cross the mountains and go back to wait for warmer weather before restarting their journey.

Brambleclaw bounded over, flicking lumps of snow up from his paws. "Talon! Jag!" He touched noses happily with each cave-guard.

Crowpaw padded up and flicked his tail against Talon's flank. "Great timing," he mewed.

"This is Talon," Squirrelpaw announced to the Clans. "And Jag and . . ."

"I'm Night of No Stars," the third cave-guard meowed. Her voice carried the strange accent Squirrelpaw had forgotten; it was good to hear it again.

Talon looked around. "Where is Stormfur?"

"He went hunting," Tawnypelt explained.

Firestar shouldered his way to the front. "Are you able to help us? The kits are freezing," he meowed. "One is close to death."

"Let me see," ordered Talon.

"Here!" Leafpaw called from beneath the overhang where Tallpoppy was licking her limp kit. Instantly Night picked the kit up in her jaws and placed it on Tallpoppy's flank.

"Keep it off the ground," the Tribe she-cat growled. "The rock will suck the warmth from him. And don't lick. The wet will make him colder." She began to rub the kit roughly with her forepaws, ruffling its damp fur until the kit began to stir. "Keep rubbing," she told Leafpaw. "Remember, don't lick."

The ShadowClan queen stared at Night with eyes brimming with emotion, but the Tribe cat only nodded curtly and directed a question at Firestar.

"How long have you been here?" she asked.

"Too long," Squirrelpaw murmured. She felt the weakness

of hunger returning now the danger had passed. The cold was making her sleepy.

"We'll take you all back to the cave," Talon offered. "You can get warm and eat there."

"We have to keep going." Blackstar's eyes glittered. "We should leave the mountains before the snow gets any worse."

"You will die if you do not come with us," Talon meowed.

Blackstar flattened his ears.

Firestar turned his gaze on the ShadowClan leader. "The kits and elders will never make it," he mewed quietly.

"And Tallstar needs to rest," Onewhisker called out. The WindClan leader looked as tired and worn as any of the elders.

"We *all* need to rest," Leopardstar put in.

"But Crowpaw has told us there's moorland just beyond the mountains," Mudclaw argued. "We should head for that."

Blackstar turned to Littlecloud. "What do you think?"

"The elders don't have the strength to go on," the medicine cat mewed. "And the kits will freeze without food."

"This one will be dead by sundown if she doesn't get some shelter," Leafpaw called. She was rubbing Marshkit, watched closely by his mother, Tallpoppy.

"Very well." Blackstar stared at Talon. "We'll come with you."

Talon glanced at Mudclaw. Squirrelpaw wondered if he thought Mudclaw was one of the Clan leaders, since Tallstar was too frail to speak on behalf of the WindClan cats.

"We'll come too," Mudclaw muttered.

Talon dipped his head respectfully. "Good."

Tallpoppy picked up her kit by the scruff of her neck. Marshkit squirmed and gave a squeak of protest. "It's all right, little one," his mother murmured. "You'll be safe soon."

The others began to stir, hauling themselves to their paws as they prepared to follow the Tribe cats to the cave.

Suddenly a dark shape raced from a shadowy gully near the overhang.

"Brambleclaw! I've scented the Tribe!" It was Stormfur. He paused, staring around the surprised faces. Then he recognized Talon. "You're here!"

"We found Squirrelpaw," Talon explained.

Stormfur padded forward and touched the cave-guard's flank with his nose. "How's Brook?" he asked.

"She's fine," Talon replied. "We'd better get on." He glanced at Jag and Night. "I'll lead the way; you two bring up the rear."

Squirrelpaw felt exhaustion dragging at her paws as she helped to guide the Clans along the unseen paths that led toward the waterfall. She paused only when they reached the cleft in the mountain where the water thundered over the rocks and pounded, frothing, into the deep pool below. Brambleclaw, Crowpaw, Stormfur, and Tawnypelt stopped beside her.

"We're back," Squirrelpaw breathed.

Stormfur glanced at the mound of earth that marked his sister's resting place. "I wasn't sure we'd ever see this place again," he murmured.

The Clans padded past them, following Talon onto the narrow ledge that led behind the wall of water.

"Come on," Stormfur mewed. "The Clans will need us. They've never met the Tribe before." He hurried forward, Brambleclaw, Squirrelpaw, and Tawnypelt following. Crowpaw stayed behind, staring at Feathertail's grave.

The cats filed slowly behind the waterfall, their fur darkening as the spray soaked their pelts. Stormfur, Brambleclaw, and Tawnypelt wove among them. Squirrelpaw saw Ashfur stop at the edge of the thundering sheet of water. "We have to go behind *there*?"

Behind the waterfall, the light wavered on the rock, which glittered and dripped with moisture. "Go on," Squirrelpaw urged Ashfur. "It's warm inside; I promise."

The ThunderClan warrior stepped inside, and Squirrelpaw followed him. Half-forgotten scents washed over her, and, as her eyes adjusted to the gloom, she saw the Tribe staring at the visitors in astonishment.

One young she-cat, her brown tabby fur just visible beneath the streaks of mud that all Tribe cats wore, was looking around with something close to excitement, and even joy. It was Brook Where Small Fish Swim, the prey-hunter who had befriended the Clan cats on their last visit to the cave. Squirrelpaw saw her desperately searching the sea of faces, and knew she was looking for only one cat.

Squirrelpaw felt fur brush against hers as Stormfur bounded past. He headed straight for Brook, and the two cats touched noses with such tenderness that Squirrelpaw felt a rush of pity. It was all too clear that Stormfur had more heartbreak ahead of him, when the time came to leave the Tribe she-cat for a second time.

CHAPTER 23

♣

Leafpaw padded into the cave, blinking at the gloom. The roar of the waterfall made the air tremble, and the light filtering through the sheet of tumbling water quivered on the rocky walls. A stream sparkled like frost as it trickled down the mossy rocks and ran into a pool in the cave floor. Two tunnels led away into darkness, one at each end of the back wall, and narrow claws of stone hung down from the shadowy roof far above.

Leafpaw felt the Tribe cats staring at her, their eyes gleaming in the darkness. She padded over to Squirrelpaw. "They don't seem frightened of us."

Squirrelpaw blinked. "Why should they be? We hardly look threatening, as thin as we are. And besides, there are no other cats around here. Now that Sharptooth is dead, the only enemies the Tribe knows are eagles."

"I'd forgotten about Sharptooth," Leafpaw mewed. "All this would have been so much worse if he were still prowling the mountains."

"Yes," Squirrelpaw agreed, her gaze softening. "When Feathertail died, she did more than save the Tribe. She helped to protect us, too."

As her eyes adjusted, Leafpaw began to pick out individual shapes, some lithe and sleek, others well muscled and broad shouldered. Yet they were all smaller than the Clan cats—even WindClan—leaner, with broad heads and slender necks.

The kits playing outside the entrance to one of the tunnels stopped and gazed at the Clan cats as they filed into the cave, their eyes wide and curious. A gray-and-white queen padded over to Leafpaw and sniffed her pelt.

"This is Wing," Squirrelpaw explained. "She looked after Tawnypelt last time we were here, when she was sick from a rat bite."

The Tribe queen dipped her head. "Stoneteller said you were coming," she meowed. "The Tribe of Endless Hunting told him that old friends would return and bring new friends with them."

Despite her tiredness and hunger, Leafpaw's fur prickled with curiosity. "How did he know?" she whispered to Squirrelpaw.

"Stoneteller shares with the Tribe's ancestors like you do with StarClan," Squirrelpaw replied quietly.

Talon padded over. "There's caught-prey here," he offered, flicking his tail toward a pile of fresh-kill.

Leafpaw blinked. "Surely there can't be enough to share with us all?"

"Eat." Talon flicked his tail once more to the pile of fresh-kill. "Crag is organizing a hunt. There will soon be enough."

The smell of rabbit rising from the fresh-kill pile made Leafpaw's stomach growl, but she couldn't eat until she knew

the rest of the Clan was all right. Dipping her head respectfully, she left Squirrelpaw with her mountain friends and
found Cinderpelt among the other medicine cats gathered
near the entrance.

"A cat called Crag said we can use the nests over there."
Cinderpelt gestured to a cluster of shallow scoops in the earth
floor, lined with moss and feathers.

"Will there be enough room?" Littlecloud wondered.

"The coldest and weakest can use the nests," Barkface suggested. "The rest must sleep where they can find space. At
least we're safe from the snow and wind in here."

"And there's food." Leafpaw nodded toward the pile of
fresh-kill. Some of the Tribe cats were already taking pieces
of prey and bringing them over to the Clans. Talon dropped a
rabbit at Mudclaw's paws. The WindClan deputy looked at it
with hungry eyes and nodded a curt thanks to the cave-guard
before taking the rabbit to his queens and apprentices.

"We should get the kits into nests to warm up," Mothwing
mewed.

Leafpaw joined the other medicine cats as they began to
usher the youngest cats and their mothers toward the soft hollows in the cave floor. As she helped to settle Tallpoppy and
her kits into a nest, a long-bodied Tribe tom padded toward
her. His fur was so streaked with mud she could not make
out the color of his pelt. Only the white whiskers around his
muzzle betrayed his age.

"Who among you is healer?" he asked.

Startled, Leafpaw looked back at him. Squirrelpaw had

told her that the same cat was both healer and leader among the Tribe. Which did he wish to meet? She glanced toward Cinderpelt, but she was busy examining Dawnflower's kits.

"I'll take you to meet Firestar," she decided. She led him to where her father stood in quiet discussion with the other Clan leaders.

"We must not stay long," Blackstar was muttering. "The snows will only get worse." He looked around as Leafpaw approached.

"This is Stoneteller." Leafpaw dipped her head and backed away.

"You are healer?" Stoneteller asked Firestar.

"I'm leader of ThunderClan," he replied. "Cinderpelt is our Clan healer." He flicked his tail toward Cinderpelt, who was watching them with interest from the other side of the cave. "This is Blackstar, Leopardstar, and Tallstar." Firestar nodded to the three leaders in turn.

"You are all leaders?"

"Yes, we are," Leopardstar meowed.

Stoneteller's gaze rested on Tallstar, whose eyes were half-closed with exhaustion. "You are not well," he meowed. "We give you herbs." He glanced over his shoulder, catching the eye of a gray tabby she-cat. "Bird, bring strengthening herbs."

The tabby slipped away down one of the tunnels.

"The Tribe is grateful to your friends for killing Sharptooth. To Feathertail most of all. Her spirit will always be remembered by us."

"She had her father's courage," Firestar agreed, and Leafpaw winced to hear the grief still raw in his voice when he thought of Graystripe.

"You must eat and rest," Stoneteller went on.

"But after that we must continue our journey," Blackstar meowed.

Stoneteller dipped his head. "We would not delay you."

Bird returned with a mouthful of herbs and laid them in front of Tallstar.

Leafpaw felt her whiskers twitch with curiosity. "What herbs are those?"

Stoneteller's amber eyes gleamed in the half-light.

"I am learning to be a healer," Leafpaw explained quickly. "I know the herbs of the forest, but in the mountains . . ." She paused. "Everything is so different here."

"I hope she isn't bothering you." Cinderpelt's soft mew sounded beside them. "She's very inquisitive."

"Inquisitive is good in a healer," Stoneteller rasped. "She will learn much." He blinked kindly at Leafpaw. "The herbs are ragwort and lamb's ears. Good for strength."

"May I see some later, so I can recognize them if I find them again?"

"Of course." Leafpaw felt warmth in this wise old cat's voice, and she longed to learn from him, to understand the differences between Tribe and Clan. "Wing said you knew we were coming," she meowed. "Is that true?"

Stoneteller nodded. "The Tribe of Endless Hunting showed me."

"Do you share dreams with your ancestors?" Cinderpelt asked.

"Share dreams?" he echoed. "No, I interpret the signs of rock and leaf and water, and know that this is the voice of the Tribe of Endless Hunting."

"Cinderpelt interprets signs for our Clan," Leafpaw mewed eagerly. "Signs sent by StarClan. She's teaching me how to read them too."

"She has a natural talent for it," Cinderpelt added.

"Then perhaps she would like to see the Cave of Pointed Stones," Stoneteller suggested.

"Cave of Pointed Stones?" Leafpaw echoed. "Is that like our Moonstone?"

"I do not know your Moonstone," murmured Stoneteller as he turned toward one of the dark tunnels that led from the cave. "If it is the place where the voices of your ancestors speak loudest, then yes, it is like your Moonstone."

Her tail twitching with excitement, Leafpaw padded after Cinderpelt and Stoneteller down the narrow passage. She wondered if they would have to travel as far down into the darkness of the earth as they did to reach the Moonstone; but within a few tail-lengths the passage opened out into another cave, sealed by walls of slippery rock.

Blinking as her eyes adjusted to the gloom, Leafpaw peered around. It was much smaller than the main cave, but many more stone claws reached down from the roof, and some stretched up from the ground. A few had joined together, like paws meeting, and in the pale light that seeped from a gap in the roof, Leafpaw saw that they glistened with water, which trickled down into pools on the hard stone floor.

Stoneteller touched one of the pools with his paw and sent ripples flashing across it. "The snow will melt, and these pools will grow, and when starlight shines I will see in them what the Tribe of Endless Hunting wishes me to know."

"How often do you share with the Tribe of Endless Hunting?" Cinderpelt asked.

"When the pools form," Stoneteller replied.

"We meet at half-moon to share with StarClan. . . ."

Leafpaw found her gaze drifting around the cave. She padded away from where Cinderpelt and Stoneteller were exchanging experiences and wove among the stone claws until they were hidden from sight. Her paws felt heavy, and tiredness weighed on her pelt like water. She lay down on the damp stone floor and rested her nose upon her paws, mesmerized by the glitter of water dripping from stone. She closed her eyes. *StarClan? Are you here?*

Her mind swirled with the sound of rushing water. At the very edge of her thoughts, she heard the roaring of a lion and saw the rippling of shadowy pelts—pelts she did not recognize. *Who are you?* she asked desperately. Voices breathed back to her, speaking words she did not understand. Panic flooded Leafpaw, and she blinked open her eyes.

StarClan was not here. She could hear only the voices of the Tribe's ancestors. Leafpaw had never felt so alone in her life.

* * *

Though Leafpaw begged her father to let another cat take her place, Firestar insisted she sleep beside Cinderpelt in one of the feather-lined nests on the cave floor.

"The Clan needs its medicine cats now more than ever," he told her. "You must rest well."

How could she rest? It was all she could do to lick her ruffled, dirty fur. She just hoped Cinderpelt had not noticed the alarm in her eyes after visiting the Pointed Stones. *What will we do without StarClan?* The thought raced around her mind like a mouse trapped in its hole.

Squirrelpaw and Brambleclaw were already asleep, curled up together near the back of the cave. As Leafpaw kneaded the soft feathers beside Cinderpelt, she saw Brook slip out of the cave, followed by Crowpaw and Stormfur. "Where are they going?" she whispered to Cinderpelt.

"They're going to sit vigil for Feathertail," Cinderpelt murmured, closing her eyes.

Leafpaw settled down beside her mentor and tucked her tail over her nose. She wondered which ancestors Feathertail hunted with now. She pressed close to Cinderpelt, seeking comfort from her warm gray fur. How could she sleep knowing that StarClan had not come with them on this journey? But she was exhausted, and as soon as she closed her eyes, she felt sleep draw her in.

A shining expanse of water spread before her, its indigo surface glittering with stars. Nothing stirred. Even the wind was still. Leafpaw watched the water, too scared to look up in case the stars she saw reflected on the water were just an illusion. What if the sky was empty? It would be yet another sign that StarClan wasn't here.

Suddenly a breath of wind ruffled her fur. Leafpaw stared into the darkness, her fur quivering. A cat was speaking to her, so softly she could barely hear. She lifted her nose. The wind carried a familiar scent, too faint for her to be sure which cat it belonged to.

"Who's there?" she cried.

The wind blew harder, swelling the sound of the whispering voice until Leafpaw could just make out what it was saying: "Wherever you go, we will search for you."

Leafpaw turned to see the gentle face of Spottedleaf beside her. The tortoiseshell medicine cat's eyes glimmered, reflecting the starry waters, but her body shivered like a heat haze, no more solid than the stars in the water.

"You haven't left us!" Leafpaw breathed.

But Spottedleaf did not answer. The wind dropped and she faded into shadow.

"You're cheerful today," Cinderpelt mewed. She looked up at Leafpaw, who was sitting beside her, washing in the early morning light that shone through the waterfall.

Leafpaw stopped washing. "I had a dream," she confessed.

Cinderpelt sat up. "Did StarClan speak to you?"

Leafpaw blinked. Would Cinderpelt be offended that StarClan had chosen an apprentice for their message, and not ThunderClan's medicine cat? "I'm sorry," she began. "Perhaps they came when I was sleeping and you were awake, and that's why they chose me—"

Cinderpelt cut her off with the gentlest touch of her tail on Leafpaw's shoulder. "It's okay, Leafpaw," she mewed. "I've always known that you have a bond with StarClan that is stronger than anything I've seen before. It's a great responsibility, and I'm very proud of how you cope with it."

Leafpaw gazed at her, searching for words to express her relief and gratitude.

"What was the dream?" Cinderpelt prompted.

"It was very faint," Leafpaw warned her. "But I know for certain that StarClan is still watching us, and I believe they will be with us wherever we are going."

Firestar padded over, his fiery coat glowing almost white in the watery light.

"Are we leaving?" Cinderpelt asked.

Firestar shook his head. "It snowed all night, and Stoneteller says there's more on the way. The Tribe is organizing a hunt so we'll have enough fresh-kill to last out the bad weather."

"Does that mean we're stuck here?" Leafpaw mewed in alarm.

"For now." Firestar watched Blackstar pacing back and forth in front of the cave entrance. "We'll leave as soon as we can."

"Leafpaw!" Sorreltail bounded over. "Do you want to come hunting with some of the Tribe?" She glanced at Firestar. "If that's okay?"

Firestar turned to Cinderpelt. "Can you spare her?"

"Yes, of course," Cinderpelt answered.

"Thanks," Leafpaw mewed. After living in the forest it felt strange to be cooped up in the gloomy cave, and despite the cold she welcomed the feeling of fresh air in her fur.

She followed Sorreltail over to Talon and Crag. Brook was with them, with Stormfur at her side. Leafpaw was startled to see how different Stormfur looked. His fur was streaked with mud, just like the Tribe cats', and there was a toughness in his muscles that made him look more like a member of the Tribe than the skinny Clan cats.

"I hope they're not going to slow us down," Crag muttered to Brook and Talon. "We've got too many mouths to feed."

"Of course they won't slow us down," Brook mewed. "Stormfur was becoming a good prey-hunter by the time he left."

"I suppose he wasn't bad," Crag conceded. He glanced at Leafpaw. "You're an apprentice, right? What are you hoping to be? A prey-hunter or a cave-guard?"

Leafpaw stared at him, not understanding.

"The Tribe divides its duties," Stormfur explained. "The cave-guards protect the Tribe; the prey-hunters feed them. Brook is a prey-hunter and Crag is a cave-guard."

"Then why are you coming hunting?" Leafpaw asked Crag hesitantly.

Crag let out an unexpected purr of amusement. "Who's going to watch the skies while you've got your eye on the prey?" he asked, and Leafpaw remembered with a shudder the eagle that had attacked the Clan. She felt a prickle of resentment at Crag's superior attitude, but resisted the urge to tell him she was an apprentice medicine cat; to a Tribe cat, that might sound as if she were claiming to be a leader.

"In the forest we could scent for danger and hunt at the same time," Sorreltail mewed.

"Really? Well, how do you scent an eagle flying a mountain's height above your head?" Crag retorted.

"Come on," Brook meowed impatiently. "We're wasting time."

She led the way out from behind the waterfall and along a ledge that led them up among the peaks. The blizzard had died away, but the thick snow soon froze Leafpaw's feet. The air was so cold, it almost hurt to breathe, and her eyes started to stream as soon as they left the warmth of the cave. But there was no way she was going to complain; she wanted to prove to Crag that forest cats could handle anything the mountain cats could. She stifled a shiver and glanced up. Heavy yellow clouds nested on the mountaintops, promising more snow.

As they neared a stunted thornbush, its branches weighed down with fresh snow, Brook stopped and crouched low. Crag and Stormfur flanked her, ducking down as well. Leafpaw copied them, pressing her belly flat against the snow beside Sorreltail. Brook stared at the bush, her nose twitching as though she scented prey.

Leafpaw sniffed. The smell of rabbit wafted past her on the breeze. Instinctively she started to creep forward.

"Stop!" Stormfur warned her with a hiss. "Wait and watch how Brook does it."

Brook was as still as ice, only the faintest lift of her mud-streaked flank showing that she wasn't a rock embedded in the snow. Just when Leafpaw began to think she would turn into an icicle if she stayed still any longer, a young rabbit hopped from under the bush, testing the air with its quivering nose.

It hopped closer, not seeing the cats flat against the snow. Leafpaw opened her mouth. The prey-scent was still strong near the bush, which was odd if the rabbit had come out into the open. Perhaps the rabbit had been sheltering there for a long time. Suddenly Brook shot forward and lunged at the rabbit. She caught it in her jaws and killed it with merciful speed.

Out of the corner of her eye, Leafpaw noticed the bush tremble. She darted forward just as a second rabbit fled across the snow. It raced toward a rocky outcrop, but Leafpaw was fast—and hungry—and caught it before it could escape.

"Well spotted!" Brook congratulated her with a warm purr.

"I could smell two scents," Leafpaw panted.

Crag stared at her in surprise. "You smelled both rabbits at the same time?"

"We're used to the forest with all its plants and prey," she mewed, trying to explain. "The air up here is clearer; the scents are not so cluttered. It's easy to spot different smells."

Sorreltail blinked proudly at her, and Stormfur gave a small nod. Crag dipped his head in respect and, picking up one of the rabbits, led the way back to the waterfall.

* * *

Leafpaw sat near the entrance of the cave, warmed by the soft breathing of the cats around her. Dustpelt lay beside Onewhisker and Tallstar. Spiderpaw stretched out beside Crowpaw. Tallpoppy and Ferncloud shared tongues while their kits played together. Even Hawkfrost looked relaxed as he watched Mothwing grooming Morningflower's pelt for fleas. In spite of the peaceful scene, Leafpaw felt a tremor of concern. She had never seen the Clans so comfortable around each other before, not even at Gatherings. StarClan may be waiting for them, but would there still be four Clans by the time they reached their new home?

She stared through the sheet of thundering water and saw the full moon trembling above the peaks. None of the Clan cats had mentioned that it was a full moon, and time for a Gathering. There was no need. Suddenly she heard rasping breath by her ear, and she turned to see Stoneteller looking down at her.

"You are watching the moon for signs?" he meowed.

"I was thinking of the Gatherings," Leafpaw mewed.

"Gatherings?" Stoneteller looked puzzled.

"In the time before we left, the four Clans would meet in peace only at full moon."

"Clans did not live in harmony?"

"Not always," Leafpaw admitted. "Unlike you, we had clear boundaries between our hunting territories."

Stoneteller glanced around. "Trouble has brought you together," he observed.

"But there will always be boundaries between us," Leafpaw insisted.

"Why? Together you find food easier."

"There have always been four Clans. Loyalty to our own Clan makes us strong."

"But you all share a belief in your StarClan?"

"We will all become warriors in StarClan eventually," Leafpaw murmured. She gazed at the moon, a blurred white disk behind the falling water.

Stoneteller's eyes glowed. "You are still a to-be, yet you are wise."

Feeling her ears grow hot with embarrassment, Leafpaw looked away.

"We will have a gathering of our own tonight," Stoneteller went on. He raised his voice. "Cats of the Clans and of the Tribe, we have not celebrated our deliverance from Sharptooth," he meowed. "Instead we grieved for Feathertail, who died saving us. But tonight we shall honor the cats who came from far away and killed the terrible creature."

Mews of agreement rose among the Tribe cats. The kits mewed with excitement, and the boldest of them padded over to where Tallpoppy's kits played with Birchkit.

"Come and share with us," the Tribe kit offered.

Birchkit glanced at his mother, who nodded, her eyes shining with warmth. Tallpoppy and Dawnflower quickly gave their approval, and the Clan kits wasted no time in following the Tribe kit across the cave.

One by one, the Tribe cats got to their paws and took a piece of fresh-kill from the pile. They placed each piece solemnly at the paws of a Clan cat until every cat had been served. The Clan cats watched and waited, unsure what to do.

Leafpaw's eyes widened in surprise as Crag dropped a rabbit at her paws.

"May I share with you?" he asked.

She nodded shyly.

Stoneteller padded to the center of the cave. "We feast in honor of Feathertail," he declared. "Her spirit will live forever in the Tribe of Endless Hunting. We honor too the cats who refused to desert us and returned to fulfill the prophecy of our ancestors." He dipped his head in turn to Brambleclaw, Squirrelpaw, Tawnypelt, Crowpaw, and Stormfur, who each straightened proudly.

"Now let us eat!" Stoneteller called, his mew echoing around the cave.

Crag took a bite from the rabbit he had laid on the ground and then pushed it over to Leafpaw. Guessing this was a custom of the Tribe, she took a bite and passed it back to him. Back in the forest, the cats had shared food too, but there was usually enough fresh-kill for each cat to have a whole piece each. She wondered if the Tribe's formal sharing ritual arose from the scarcity of prey in the mountains.

After the meal, the cats lay, full-bellied, and quietly shared tongues. Tallstar limped to the center of the cave and gazed around at the cats until they fell silent. Onewhisker crept to his side, supporting the WindClan leader's frail body with his own.

"Who's that skinny old raven?" mewed a Tribe kit.

"Hush!" His mother cuffed him sharply. "That's a very noble Clan leader!"

But though he had to lean on the young warrior, Tallstar's eyes shone with as much strength and determination as a leader on his first life, rather than his last. "Crowpaw?"

The WindClan apprentice looked up, bewildered.

"Crowpaw has served his Clan with bravery and loyalty." Tallstar's voice cracked as he stifled a cough. "He should have received his warrior name long ago," he rasped. "But the tragedies of the past moons have prevented this. Tonight, if Stoneteller will do me the kindness of letting a Clan ceremony into his Tribe's home, I wish to honor Crowpaw's great skill and courage by giving him his warrior name."

Murmurs of agreement rose from the WindClan cats, but they turned to mews of surprise as Crowpaw stepped forward. This wasn't part of the warrior naming ceremony.

"May I ask something, Tallstar?" he mewed.

Tallstar narrowed his eyes and nodded for him to go on.

"I would like to choose my own warrior name. If it is all right, I wish to be known as Crowfeather." Crowpaw spoke so quietly, his voice was almost lost in the pounding water. "I wish to keep alive the memory of . . . of the cat who did not return from the first journey."

Stormfur's ears flicked, and he stared down at his paws.

There was a long pause; then Tallstar announced, "A noble request. Very well. I name you Crowfeather. May StarClan protect you and accept you as a WindClan warrior in life as well as after."

The WindClan cats jumped up and went over to congratulate their Clanmate.

"That was a brilliant idea!" Squirrelpaw bounded over to Crowfeather's side. Brambleclaw, Tawnypelt, and Stormfur joined her.

"It's a great name," Tawnypelt agreed as Brambleclaw wound his lean body around Crowfeather, purring. Stormfur touched his muzzle to Crowfeather's flank as if he were too moved to speak.

"Thank you," Crowfeather murmured. He gazed past them at the waterfall, turned silver by the light of the moon. "I will sit my vigil tonight beside Feathertail's grave."

Leafpaw watched as he slipped away from his friends and Clanmates and padded out of the cave.

"So he's a warrior now, yes?" Crag asked her, his eyes shining with curiosity.

"Yes." Leafpaw got to her paws. "Thank you for sharing with me," she murmured. The lonely moon called her from the crowded den, and she longed to search the clear sky for Silverpelt.

Padding out from behind the waterfall, she scrambled up the rocks and sat high above the pool where the tumbling water foamed and surged. The stars glittered overhead as Leafpaw gazed down to where Crowfeather sat vigil. He was sitting with his head bowed beside the low mound of rocks that marked Feathertail's grave. Was she really with the Tribe of Endless Hunting rather than StarClan? *Make her welcome, whoever you are,* Leafpaw begged silently.

She watched Crowfeather for a moment, her heart aching for his loss. Then she lifted her head and stared around the peaks, wondering if StarClan watched him too. There was a tranquillity in this high place she had not felt since she lay beneath the trees in the forest. In the bright moonlight, something caught her eye on a small ledge opposite the cave entrance, and Leafpaw thought she saw two silver pelts glowing beneath the stars. She was almost certain that two cats stood there, looking down at Crowfeather; one was slightly taller than the other, but their pelts were marked by the same mottled shadows, as though they were kin.

Feathertail and Silverstream?

Leafpaw blinked, and when she opened her eyes, the silver cats had vanished.

CHAPTER 24

Squirrelpaw hurried after Stormfur along a rocky trail that only days ago had been buried beneath a tail-length of snow. He seemed determined to cross most of the mountains in search of prey. The rocks echoed with the drip, drip, drip of melting ice. Even the deepest snowdrifts were thawing. Dark gray rainclouds rolled toward the mountains, carried on a milder wind that was releasing the peaks from the grip of the snow and ice.

Not for the first time, Squirrelpaw wondered why the RiverClan warrior had asked her to go hunting when back in the cave the Clans were getting ready to leave. They wouldn't be able to carry any fresh-kill with them; perhaps Stormfur wanted to catch some prey to say thank you to the Tribe for their hospitality.

"Why isn't Brook coming hunting with us?" she panted. The prey-hunter had seemed like Stormfur's shadow in the past few days.

Stormfur concentrated on jumping onto a boulder, and didn't reply.

"Have you had an argument with her?" The RiverClan warrior was clearly troubled by something. His shoulders were hunched, and he had hardly spoken since they left the cave. She scrabbled awkwardly onto the boulder next to him, her mind racing. Had Stormfur asked Brook to join the Clans, and travel with them to their new home? The thought made Squirrelpaw's tail quiver. It wouldn't be the first time an outsider had joined the Clans. Her own father had been raised as a kittypet. But at least Firestar had been born near the forest. Brook was a mountain cat, and Squirrelpaw knew that wherever the Clans settled, it would be nothing like this barren place.

She spotted a mouse on the ridge ahead, tiptoeing out from a crevice to find food. She hissed a warning to Stormfur, who stopped and crouched down, waiting until the mouse had wandered farther onto the trail. Though she longed to make the catch, Squirrelpaw knew Stormfur's coat would be more easily camouflaged here, and she pressed her orange belly as close to the ground as she could, hoping that stillness would keep her hidden.

Stormfur held still for another moment, then pounced. He snapped the mouse's spine and turned back to face Squirrelpaw, the fresh-kill hanging in his jaws.

"Is that a parting gift for Brook?" Squirrelpaw prompted gently.

Stormfur blinked.

"Look, what's wrong?" Squirrelpaw asked, unable to bear seeing her friend so troubled.

Stormfur dropped the mouse, suddenly looking exhausted.

When he lifted his head, his eyes were shadowed with uncertainty. "I've decided to stay with the Tribe."

"*What?*"

"I've lost Feathertail and Graystripe, and I never knew Silverstream. I have no kin left in the Clans. Even my mentor, Stonefur, is dead. Apart from Feathertail, he was the closest thing to kin that I had in RiverClan. I don't even have a home anymore. It feels as though everything has been stolen from me, one thing after another."

"But what about your Clan?" Squirrelpaw protested. "RiverClan needs you."

"RiverClan has good, strong warriors." He looked into Squirrelpaw's eyes and must have seen the wary look there. "Even Hawkfrost," he meowed as if he could read her mind. "RiverClan will be safe without me."

"But this is such a different place," Squirrelpaw argued. "Once we've found our new home, you can start again. . . ."

"Oh, Squirrelpaw, can't you understand? I love Brook, and I want to stay with her."

"I thought you might ask her to join the Clans!" Squirrelpaw blurted out.

Stormfur shook his head. "She would be lost without the mountains. But I know that I can live here. There's water here—noisier than the river—but it's still water. There's plenty of fresh-kill, now that I know how to hunt like the Tribe. And my sister's spirit is here. . . ." He let out a long sigh. "All the Clans have lost their homes, but I feel like I have lost more than any cat. This is the first time in many moons that I feel as if I have actually found something."

"There's no need to say any more," Squirrelpaw whispered sadly. "I understand."

As they walked back to the cave, her mind whirled. Once again, everything had changed, just when she thought there was nothing left to lose. They slipped behind the waterfall, and Stormfur carried the mouse to the fresh-kill pile, while Squirrelpaw stood at the cave entrance feeling dazed.

"Squirrelpaw!" Leafpaw rushed up to her. "Stoneteller has given us strengthening herbs to share with the Clans."

Squirrelpaw stared at her. "Th-that's great," she mewed.

"Are you okay?"

"Leafpaw!" Cinderpelt was calling to her across the cave.

"I have to go," Leafpaw breathed, turning away. "WindClan is waiting for the herbs."

Squirrelpaw watched her go, her eyes slowly adjusting to the gloom. Another shape loomed toward her from the shadows, and her heart sank as she recognized the massive tabby shoulders. What did Hawkfrost want with her?

"Squirrelpaw?"

She blinked. It was Brambleclaw. He was looking at her quizzically. "Are you coming in?" he meowed. "We have to make sure everyone's eaten."

Squirrelpaw felt dizzy.

"Is something wrong?" Brambleclaw stared at her.

Squirrelpaw shook her head helplessly. Across the cave, she

could see Stormfur murmuring something to Brook.

Brambleclaw followed her gaze. "Stormfur's staying, isn't he?"

"He wants to stay with Brook," Squirrelpaw whispered.

There was a long pause. "You'll miss him, won't you?"

"Of course I will!" Squirrelpaw replied, surprised. She turned to look up at Brambleclaw and saw a flicker of something in his amber eyes. Was he feeling *jealous*? "Oh, Brambleclaw," she breathed. "My heart is with ThunderClan; don't you know that?" She lightly brushed her tail along his flank. "My heart is with *you*."

His eyes closed, and Squirrelpaw suddenly hoped she hadn't said the wrong thing. Then he blinked them open again and looked at her so gently that she felt as if she could have stood there forever.

"We must all follow our hearts," he murmured. Squirrelpaw's fears about what lay ahead seemed to dissolve in an instant, like mist in greenleaf. She would lose a friend when Stormfur stayed behind, but she would never be alone.

A movement caught her eye. Stoneteller was padding to the center of the cave.

"The Clans are leaving," he announced to his Tribe. "I want some of you to go with them to show them the path out of the mountains. They head for hillplace, not sunset, so take them along the path that leads toward the Great Star."

Squirrelpaw felt a rush of excitement. Were the Tribe cats going to take them straight to where the dying warrior had disappeared behind the mountain range?

Stoneteller dipped his head to each of the Clan leaders in turn. "I wish the cats of StarClan good hunting."

"Thank you, Stoneteller." Firestar dipped his head. "Your Tribe has shown us more kindness than we could have dreamed of, and we are sad to leave. But we are expected at another place promised to us by our warrior ancestors." He turned to the other Clan leaders. "Tallstar, is WindClan ready?"

The WindClan leader stared at him, his eyes clouded with confusion, then glanced at Onewhisker, who was standing next to him. Onewhisker nodded back at him encouragingly, but before Tallstar could say anything, Mudclaw raised his head. "We're ready," he meowed.

"ShadowClan is ready too," Blackstar called.

Leopardstar raised her tail. "All my cats are ready."

"Not all of them." Stormfur stepped forward. "I'm staying here."

There was a stunned silence from all the cats. Then Dustpelt spoke. "You can't leave your Clan now!"

"He is free to choose," murmured Tallpoppy. Her eyes rested on Brook, her gaze gentle and understanding.

"Graystripe's kit would not make such a decision lightly," Sandstorm put in.

Firestar looked thoughtfully at Stormfur. "I remember how hard it was for Graystripe to choose Silverstream over his Clan," he mewed. "But from that difficult choice, you and Feathertail were born. Without you both, everything would have been different for the Tribe and for the Clans.

Feathertail killed Sharptooth, and you finished a difficult journey to bring StarClan's message back to us. No cat can question your loyalty and courage, nor criticize your choice, for as your father proved, great things come from listening to your heart."

Approving murmurs echoed around the cave until Leopardstar silenced the cats with a sharp yowl.

Squirrelpaw's pelt prickled. Would Leopardstar let her warrior go?

The RiverClan leader stared at Stormfur, her eyes narrowed. "Stormfur," she meowed at last, "RiverClan will miss your courage and skill, but so much has changed in our lives that it is not impossible we will meet again, in this life or the next." She dipped her head, accepting Stormfur's decision without anger. "I wish you well."

Brook brushed her tail against Stormfur's flank as the Clans filed slowly out of the cave. Squirrelpaw looked sadly back at her friend, wishing he could at least be part of the patrol that would accompany them to the edge of the Tribe's territory. But Stormfur stayed where he was, his gray pelt glowing in the shimmering light of the waterfall, his eyes betraying the depths of his grief. However much he wanted to live with the Tribe, Squirrelpaw knew that watching the Clans leave without him must be like losing Silverstream, Feathertail, and Graystripe all over again.

"Do you think he'll be all right?" she asked Brambleclaw.

He gave her ear a swift lick. "I do."

They followed the other cats out of the gorge and up into the peaks, the sun to one side of them as they headed along the mountain range.

"Do you think they're taking us the right way?" she whispered to Brambleclaw.

Brambleclaw blinked. "I hope so." He craned his neck. "It does seem to be the same direction we saw the star fall. I just hope they don't lead us too far and we miss it."

As he spoke, the Tribe cats veered their path and headed down through a winding pass. The ground suddenly fell away and the land rolled ahead of them, hill after hill, grassy here, shadowed with woodland there. From where the Clans stood, on the edge of the mountains, the greenness seemed strange after the endless gray and white of the crags. In the sunshine Squirrelpaw could see streams glimmering among the bare trees like silver birch bark in an oak forest.

"Is that it?" Brambleclaw breathed.

"'Hills, oak woods for shelter, running streams.'" Squirrelpaw found herself quoting Midnight's prophecy.

"But there's so much of it!" Tawnypelt had slipped beside them. "How will we know where to stop?"

Brambleclaw shook his head, and they stared in silence until a flicker above their heads caught Squirrelpaw's eye. Something was moving on the crest of the rocks that lined the mountain pass. Her pelt prickled with fear. Was it an eagle? She forced herself to look up and saw that it was not a bird. It was Stormfur and Brook, racing along the ridge, calling their good-byes to the departing Clans.

As Stormfur bounded nimbly from rock to rock, Brook matched him step for step, so that their pelts brushed each other's with every leap. Stormfur's mud-slicked fur was visible only when he crossed a patch of snow, and Squirrelpaw could not help thinking that the RiverClan cat looked almost Tribe-born.

CHAPTER 25

❧

Leafpaw shook the drizzle from her whiskers and padded after the others up the heather-covered slope. They had trekked all morning, leaving the snow and mountains behind, chased by the rain that rolled down from the mountains after them.

"Have you noticed Tallstar?" Sorreltail whispered, padding beside her.

The WindClan leader was walking beside Onewhisker through the banks of heather. Despite the rain, he no longer leaned against Onewhisker's flank, but padded confidently, as if he finally believed he was within reach of his Clan's new home. He pricked his ears as a rabbit darted from a boulder farther ahead. Onewhisker glanced at his leader, and, when Tallstar nodded, he darted after the rabbit. Tornear and Webfoot raced up the slope after him.

"I think the smell of the heather has given WindClan some of their old spirit back," Leafpaw purred.

All the cats seemed more relaxed than they had been in the mountains, not just WindClan. Blackstar padded next to Firestar. Dustpelt walked alongside Russetfur, the heather brushing his striped flank as he talked comfortably to the ShadowClan deputy.

"I never thought I'd see Dustpelt so comfortable around the other Clans," Leafpaw commented.

"He'll soon be back to his old self," Sorreltail replied matter-of-factly, "once we're settled in our new home and things are back to normal."

"There will always be four Clans," Leafpaw murmured, half to herself. But would there really? Looking around, she realized with a shock that it was impossible to tell from the throng of cats where one Clan ended and another began.

"I'm just glad to be out of the mountains," Sorreltail mewed. "Stormfur was brave to stay."

"He had so little left in the Clans," Leafpaw murmured.

"Well, I'd rather be here," Sorreltail decided.

"Even though we don't know where we're heading?" Leafpaw asked her, surprised.

"Look at this place!" Sorreltail flicked her tail at the land around them. "No sign of monsters or churned earth. And it's good to smell prey again." She swiped her tongue around her lips.

As she spoke Onewhisker came trotting back toward the Clans, a rabbit dangling from his jaws. Leafpaw knew she was right—this place felt safer than anywhere they had been for many days and nights—but with no sign from StarClan, was it really their new home?

* * *

"Leafpaw!"

Cinderpelt's voice shocked her into wakefulness. She blinked open her eyes. It was still dark.

"Is everything okay?" she asked, struggling to her paws and staring around the shadowy copse where the Clans had sheltered for the night. A chilly wind whipped between the trees.

"Firestar wants to set off as early as possible," Cinderpelt told her.

"Why can't we stay here?" Leafpaw heard Birchkit's fretful mew and, as her eyes became accustomed to the predawn light, she saw him staring up at his mother, crouched between the roots of a tree.

"We can't stop yet." Brambleclaw's deep mew rang out before Ferncloud could reply. "StarClan will tell us when we have found our new home."

"But the sign might come if we wait here," Dustpelt meowed.

"Wait here?" Mudclaw glared at the ThunderClan cats. "These trees may feel like home to you, but not to us."

"The streams here aren't wide enough for fish," Leopardstar pointed out.

Squirrelpaw nodded. "We must keep going."

"Going where, exactly?" Hawkfrost growled.

Squirrelpaw narrowed her eyes. "Do we have to know everything?"

Brambleclaw flicked his tail to silence her, then glanced at Cinderpelt. "Have you had any sign from StarClan?"

Cinderpelt shook her head. "Not me. But Leafpaw had a dream," she meowed.

Leafpaw's heart lurched as the eyes of all the Clans turned to her, gleaming in the half-light. "I-I don't know if it was a sign," she mewed quickly. "I dreamed I sat before a great stretch of shining water. . . ."

"Shining water?" Leopardstar interrupted. "You mean a river?"

Leafpaw shook her head. "No, not a river. These waters were smooth, not churning. I could see Silverpelt reflected, all the stars shining as clearly as if they were swimming in the sky."

"Is that all?" Blackstar demanded.

"Spottedleaf was there too, and she told me StarClan would find us," Leafpaw forced herself to meet the Shadow-Clan leader's gaze even though her legs were shaking.

"So we should head for water?" Tallstar mewed hopefully.

Leafpaw's ears twitched. "I think it was just a dream," she whispered. "I've had no sign from StarClan since." She looked unhappily at her paws. "I'm beginning to think I just dreamed what I wanted to."

"Then we have nothing," Blackstar muttered, turning away.

"Are you sure it was just a dream?" Brambleclaw asked Leafpaw.

She searched her heart for the truth. "I don't know."

She had never been wrong about her dreams before, but if the dream had really carried a message from their warrior ancestors, wouldn't some sign—a falling star, another dream—have told them by now that StarClan was with them in this strange place?

"Well, we'll just have to keep going." Brambleclaw padded out from the trees. A grassy bank sloped down in front of him to a narrow valley. Beyond, a ridge rose into the indigo sky, its curving side shadowed by forest.

As the cats began to pad out of the copse, still blinking and stretching, Leafpaw glanced up at the sky. Clouds obscured the stars.

"Don't worry about the sign." Her father's voice surprised her, and she turned to find him standing beside her. "You are still an apprentice medicine cat," he murmured. "You shouldn't feel responsible if StarClan wishes to remain silent."

She gazed gratefully into his emerald eyes as he went on. "I'm proud of you. And Squirrelpaw too—even though Cinderpelt's prophecy frightened me for a while."

"Cinderpelt's prophecy?" Leafpaw echoed.

"StarClan's sign that fire and tiger would destroy the Clan."

Leafpaw blinked. Cinderpelt's ominous warning seemed a lifetime away now.

"Now I think I understand what it meant." Firestar gazed after Squirrelpaw and Brambleclaw as they led the cats down into the valley. Their fur glowed like the moon and its shadow in the gloom. "The daughter of Firestar and the son of Tigerstar did destroy the Clan," he meowed. "But not as I feared they would. They led us from our old home, away from danger and into the unknown. Many would have been put off by the difficulties that faced them, but they held on to their faith and brought us all to safety." He glanced at Tawnypelt and Crow-feather prowling protectively on either side of the Clans. "The cats who first crossed the mountains—whether they are still with us or live among other warriors—will always be honored by every Clan for their courage."

He flicked his tail, then bounded away to catch up with Sandstorm. Leafpaw felt a surge of pride in her sister, and gratitude to her father for being willing to trust Brambleclaw and Squirrelpaw to lead them to a place of safety.

She wove her way to Sorreltail's side as they reached the foot of the slope and began to climb upward again on the other side of the valley.

"I'm hungry," Sorreltail complained.

"It's nearly dawn," Leafpaw answered her. "I'm sure we can hunt then."

"At least it looks like good hunting territory here," Sorreltail commented, looking around at the young beech trees that crowded the slope.

Leafpaw recognized her sister's voice drifting from up ahead. "I can smell prey and leaves and ferns like we had back in the forest!" Squirrelpaw bounded back to them. "I hope we get some sort of sign here." She peered through the trees to where Brambleclaw's pelt flitted through the shadows like a fish. "I hope he's all right. He's hardly spoken today."

"He's just worried," Leafpaw reassured her.

"What do you think the sign will be?" Sorreltail fretted.

Leafpaw shook her head. "I don't know," she admitted. Beneath the trees, she could hardly see a pawstep in front of her, but she followed the scents of her Clanmates as they climbed steadily upward.

As if every cat were waiting for something, tension rippled through the Clans, stiffening muscles and making pelts bristle. No cat spoke as they reached the top of the ridge. They filed along its treeless crest in a single line, silhouetted against the murky sky. A cool wind breathed over them, and Leafpaw felt it ruffle her fur. She closed her eyes for a moment and sent a desperate prayer to StarClan.

Let Spottedleaf's words be true. Show me you are waiting for us, she begged.

The breeze grew stronger, tugging at her fur, and far above them the clouds shifted to reveal the moon, shining round and bright onto the cats below.

Leafpaw opened her eyes, and her breath caught in her throat. On the far side of the ridge, the ground sloped steeply away to a vast, smooth expanse of water. All the stars of Silverpelt were reflected in the lake, glittering silver against indigo-black, as if they were swimming in the night sky.

Leafpaw's heart flooded with joy. She knew with all her heart that they had reached the end of their journey. Her faith had been enough, and their warrior ancestors had been waiting for them all along.

She lifted her gaze. The distant horizon was reddening as dawn began to push away the night, gradually revealing more of the Clans' new home.

This is the place we were meant to find, and StarClan is here.

ERIN HUNTER

is inspired by a love of cats and a fascination with the ferocity of the natural world. As well as having great respect for nature in all its forms, Erin enjoys creating rich mythical explanations for animal behavior. She is also the author of the bestselling Seekers and Survivors series.

Download the free Warriors app and chat on Warriors message boards at www.warriorcats.com.

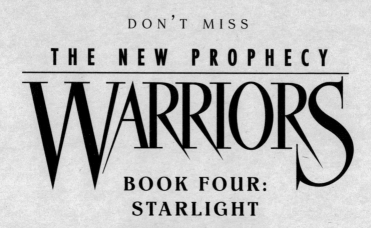
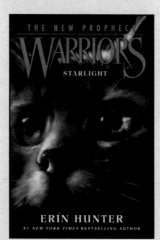

CHAPTER 1

❧

Brambleclaw stood at the top of the slope, gazing at the claw-pricks of silver fire reflected in the lake below. The Clans had finally found their new home, just as Midnight had promised. StarClan was waiting for them, and they were safe from the Twoleg monsters at last.

Around him warriors from all four Clans murmured to each other, staring uneasily at the dark, unfamiliar space at the foot of the hill.

"It's impossible to tell what's down there in this light." Brightheart, a ginger-and-white ThunderClan warrior, swung around so that her one good eye could take in the whole of the landscape.

Her mate, Cloudtail, twitched his tail. "How bad can it be? Think what we've come through to get here. We can fight off anything on four legs."

"And what about Twolegs?" demanded Russetfur, the ShadowClan deputy.

"The journey has left us all tired and weak," Blackclaw of RiverClan added. "Foxes and badgers could track us down easily when we're all out in the open like this."

For a moment Brambleclaw felt a tremor of fear. Then he braced his shoulders. StarClan would not have brought them here if they did not believe the Clans could survive in their new territories.

"What are we waiting for?" a new voice spoke up. "Are we going to stand here all night?"

Stifling a *mrrow* of laughter, Brambleclaw turned to see his Clanmate Squirrelpaw standing behind him. The ginger apprentice was tearing the tough, springy grass with her front paws, her green eyes glowing with anticipation.

"Brambleclaw, look!" she purred. "We did it! We found our new home!"

She tucked her hind legs under her, ready to dash down the hill, but before she could take off, Firestar pushed through the cats and stood in her way.

"Wait." The ThunderClan leader touched his daughter's shoulder affectionately with the tip of his tail. "We'll go together, and keep a sharp lookout for trouble. This may be the place that StarClan wished us to find, but they would not expect us to leave our wits in the forest."

Squirrelpaw dipped her head respectfully and stepped back, but when she shot a sideways glance at Brambleclaw, he saw that her eyes still gleamed with excitement. For Squirrelpaw, their journey's end could not possibly be scary.

Firestar padded over to join Blackstar and Leopardstar, the leaders of ShadowClan and RiverClan. "I suggest we send a patrol ahead," he meowed. "Just a couple of cats, to find out what it's like down there."

"Good idea—but we can't just stand here and wait for them to return," Leopardstar objected. "It's much too exposed."

Blackstar grunted in agreement. "If a fox came along now, it could pick off the weaker cats with no trouble at all."

"But we need to rest." Mudclaw of WindClan came up to join the discussion. His leader, Tallstar, lay on the ground a little way off, with the medicine cat Barkface crouching over him. "Tallstar can't go much farther."

"Then let's send the patrol right away," Firestar suggested, "and the rest of us will follow more slowly until we find somewhere more sheltered. Yes, Mudclaw," he added, as the WindClan deputy opened his mouth to argue, "we're all tired, but we'll sleep more easily if we're not stuck out on the open hillside like this."

Blackstar called Russetfur over to him, while Leopardstar signaled with her tail for her deputy, Mistyfoot.

"I want you to go as far as the lake, then come straight back," Leopardstar ordered. "Find out what you can, but be quick, and stay out of sight."

The two cats flicked their ears, then whirled and raced away, loping along with their bellies close to the ground; within a couple of heartbeats they had vanished into the darkness.

Firestar watched them go before letting out a yowl to call the rest of the cats around him. Mudclaw went back to Tallstar and nudged the old leader to his paws. Their Clans clustered together behind the leaders of ThunderClan, RiverClan, and ShadowClan and began to follow them down the slope toward the lake.

"What's the matter?" Squirrelpaw demanded, noticing that Brambleclaw wasn't moving. "Why are you standing there like a frozen rabbit?"

"I want . . ." Brambleclaw glanced around and spotted his sister Tawnypelt padding past a little way off; he summoned her with a jerk of his head. "I want all of us to go down together," he explained when the tortoiseshell she-cat joined them. "All the cats who made the first journey."

Four cats remained from the six who had left the forest in search of a new home many moons ago. They had gained something very precious on that journey, as well as a safe place for their Clans to live: a strong bond of friendship had been forged between them, stronger than rock and deeper than the endless water that washed against the cliffs where Midnight the badger lived.

Now Brambleclaw wanted to travel with his friends one more time before their duties to their separate Clans forced them apart.

Tawnypelt let out a purr of approval. Meeting her green gaze, Brambleclaw knew that, like him, she understood they would soon be rivals again; that the next time they met could be in battle. The pain of parting swelled in his heart, and he pressed his muzzle to his sister's, feeling her breath warm against his whiskers.

"Where's Crowfeather?" she asked.

Brambleclaw looked up and spotted the young Wind-Clan warrior a few tail-lengths away, anxiously pacing beside

Tallstar. The WindClan leader looked so exhausted he could hardly put one paw in front of the other; his long tail dragged on the ground and he was leaning heavily on the brown tabby warrior Onewhisker. The WindClan medicine cat, Barkface, walked close behind, a worried look on his face.

"Hey, Crowfeather!" Squirrelpaw called.

The WindClan cat bounded across. "What do you want?"

Brambleclaw ignored his unwelcoming tone. Crowfeather's tongue was sharp enough to slice your ears off, but if danger threatened he would fight to his last breath to defend his friends.

"Travel down to the lake with us," he urged. "I want us to finish the journey how we started—together."

Crowfeather bowed his head. "There's no point," he murmured. "We'll never be together again. Stormfur lives in the mountains now, and Feathertail is dead."

Brambleclaw ran his tail lightly over the young warrior's shoulder. He shared his grief for the beautiful RiverClan cat who had sacrificed her life to save Crowfeather and the Tribe cats from the terrible lion-cat known as Sharptooth. Then Feathertail's brother Stormfur had stayed with the Tribe of Rushing Water because of his love for the prey-hunter Brook. Brambleclaw missed him bitterly, but knew that pain was nothing compared to the agony Crowfeather felt over Feathertail's death.

"Feathertail is with us now," Squirrelpaw insisted, coming to join them. Her eyes shone with the strength of her belief. "If you don't know that, Crowfeather, you're even more mouse-brained than I thought. And we'll see Stormfur again, I'm sure. We're closer to the mountains here than we were in the forest."

Crowfeather let out a long sigh. "Okay," he meowed. "Let's go."

Most of the cats had gone past them already, moving cautiously across the unfamiliar territory, keeping close to each other as they had done throughout the long and dangerous journey to get here. A little way ahead, Brambleclaw saw Mothwing, the RiverClan medicine cat, walking beside a group of apprentices from all four Clans. On the far side of a patch of gorse, the ground fell away into a grassy hollow. Tallpoppy, a ShadowClan queen, was struggling to guide her kits down the steep slope; Cloudtail and Brightheart from ThunderClan darted over to help, each picking up a kit in their jaws. Farther down the slope, Cedarheart, a gray ShadowClan tom, prowled along the edge of a thorn thicket, his gaze flicking back and forth as he kept watch for foxes and badgers that might be looking for easy prey.

If he had not known these cats all his life, Brambleclaw would not have been able to distinguish one Clan from another; they walked side by side, helping one another. He wondered grimly how long it would be before they were divided again, and how painful that separation would be.

At an impatient exclamation from Squirrelpaw—"Come *on*, Brambleclaw, or we'll leave you to make a den for yourself here!"—he headed down the slope, pausing every so often to draw in the night air. The scent of cat was strongest, but beneath it he could detect the scents of mouse and vole and rabbit. He couldn't remember when he had last eaten; surely the leaders would allow them to hunt soon?

He was imagining the delicious taste of fresh-kill when he was startled by a hiss from Tawnypelt, who was a couple of tail-lengths ahead of him. "Look at that," spat the Shadow-Clan warrior, pointing with her tail.

Brambleclaw's ears pricked when he saw the thin mesh of a Twoleg fence shining like a huge cobweb in the pale dawn light. Two or three of the other cats had paused to stare apprehensively at it as well.

"I knew we'd come across Twolegs sooner or later!" Squirrelpaw meowed with a disgusted twitch of her tail.

Brambleclaw tasted the air again. He could pick up the scent of Twolegs, but it was faint and stale. There was another, less familiar scent too, and he had to think hard before he remembered what it was.

"Horses." Crowfeather confirmed his guess. "There's one over there."

He gestured with his tail, and Brambleclaw noticed a large, dark shape standing under a clump of trees some way inside the fence. He thought there was another one beside it, though it was hard to tell in the shadows cast by the branches.

"What are horses?" Whitepaw mewed worriedly as she peered through the fence.

"Nothing to worry about," Tornear from WindClan reassured her, touching the apprentice's shoulder with the tip of his tail. "They used to run across our territory sometimes, with Twolegs on their backs."

Whitepaw blinked as if she couldn't quite believe him.

"We saw some of them on our journey to the sun-drown-place," Brambleclaw added. "They didn't take any notice of us when we crossed their field. It's the Twolegs looking after them that we need to watch out for."

"I can't see any Twoleg nests," Tawnypelt pointed out. "Maybe these horse things look after themselves."

"Let's hope so," meowed Brambleclaw. "Horses alone shouldn't bother us."

"Provided we stay away from their clumsy feet," added Squirrelpaw.

The cats followed the Twoleg fence until they came to a thicket of trees where the other cats were gathering. Glancing around, Brambleclaw spotted Cinderpelt, the ThunderClan medicine cat, and her apprentice, Leafpaw, Squirrelpaw's sister.

"What's going on?" Squirrelpaw demanded. "Why are we stopping?"

"The patrol the leaders sent has just come back," Cinderpelt explained.

Following her gaze, Brambleclaw saw the leaders of the four Clans and the WindClan deputy, Mudclaw, standing close together beside a tree stump. Mistyfoot and Russetfur, who had been sent on the patrol, faced them. The other cats had sunk down on the short, springy grass around the tree stump, glad of the chance to rest.

With the others behind him, Brambleclaw wove through

the cats until he was close enough to hear what the Clan leaders were saying.

Mistyfoot was just giving her report: "The ground's very boggy by the lake. There's no point going any farther until daylight. We don't want to lose any cats in the mud."

"ShadowClan is used to wet ground underpaw," Blackstar reminded her, before any of the other leaders could comment. "But we'll stay with the rest of you if that's what you want." There was an edge to his tone, as if ShadowClan were granting them a huge favor by not going ahead to explore on their own.

Brambleclaw narrowed his eyes. It seemed too soon for the Clans to begin competing with one another over who claimed which part of the new territory. He had grown used to having all four Clans around him, ignoring the differences that had kept them apart for more seasons than any cat could remember. He was also afraid that some cats were weaker and more exhausted than others, which might make any clashes more damaging than they needed to be.

He hoped the leaders would decide to stay where they were for the rest of the night. The hills were still close enough to cut down the force of the wind, and the trees provided even more welcome shelter. A strong scent of prey drifted from the shadows, and his paws itched to hunt.

"I think we should stay here," Firestar meowed, to Brambleclaw's relief. "We all need to rest, and it sounds pretty uncomfortable by the lake."

Leopardstar murmured agreement. Before Firestar had

finished speaking, Tallstar collapsed onto his side and lay there panting, as if he couldn't manage a single pawstep more. Mudclaw stalked up to him, sniffed him briefly, and spoke a word or two in his ear.

"Tallstar looks exhausted," Brambleclaw murmured to Crowfeather. "This is his last life, isn't it?"

Crowfeather nodded, his face somber. "He'll be fine now that we're here," he meowed, though Brambleclaw suspected that he was trying to convince himself as much as any other cat.

Blackstar leaped up to the top of the tree stump. The powerful white tom stood with tail held high, his huge black paws planted on the rough wood. He let out a commanding yowl, and the faces of all the cats turned toward him to listen.

"Cats of all Clans!" he called as the last stragglers came up. "We have reached the place StarClan meant us to find, but we are all tired and hungry. We will make camp here until we have rested."

"Who asked him to speak for the leaders?" Squirrelpaw muttered. Her green eyes flashed indignantly as Brambleclaw, spotting a couple of ShadowClan warriors within earshot, silenced her with a flick of his tail across her mouth.

"What about fresh-kill?" a cat called from the back.

"We will wait until sunrise," Blackstar replied. "Then the prey will be running and there'll be enough for us all."

"Meanwhile we ought to keep watch," Firestar added, leaping up beside Blackstar so that the ShadowClan leader had to step back a pace. "Deputies, find two or three warriors who can stay awake for a while longer. We don't want foxes sneaking up on us while we're asleep."

Mudclaw, who seemed to be speaking for WindClan since Tallstar was so weak, meowed his agreement, followed by the RiverClan leader, Leopardstar. The brief meeting broke up and the cats began looking for places to sleep. Barkface nudged Tallstar to his feet and helped him to a clump of long grass, where the frail WindClan leader lay down again, trembling from nose to tail. Onewhisker sat close to him and began to lick his fur gently.

"I guess I'll be needed," Crowfeather mewed, and he loped away to join the other WindClan cats.

Tawnypelt touched noses with her brother. "I'd better check in with Russetfur," she meowed. "See you later, Brambleclaw." Whisking around, she headed for a group of her Clanmates who were clustered around the ShadowClan deputy.

Brambleclaw wondered if he ought to volunteer to keep watch. Even though he had been a warrior for fewer than four seasons, ThunderClan needed every cat to help feed and protect their Clanmates—especially since they had lost their deputy just before leaving the forest. Shivering, Brambleclaw remembered how Graystripe had been trapped by Twolegs and carried away inside a Twoleg monster. He glanced at Firestar to see his leader giving orders to Sorreltail and Brackenfur. He guessed he wouldn't be needed right away, so he looked around to see if any of the other ThunderClan cats could use his help.

Dustpelt stood in the shadows beneath the trees with

his mate, Ferncloud, and their son Birchkit, the only one of their latest litter to survive the lack of prey back in the forest. Ferncloud was crouched over Longtail, nosing him anxiously as he lay in the grass. Longtail was not many seasons older than Dustpelt, but he had been forced to join the elders when his eyesight failed; the journey from the forest had been particularly hard for him. Goldenflower, Brambleclaw's mother, lay close to his flank on the other side. She was the oldest ThunderClan queen, and Brambleclaw realized with a pang of sympathy that she looked too weary to do anything more than press her warm fur against Longtail.

Dustpelt nudged the pale tabby tom's shoulder. "Come on, Longtail," he meowed. "Not far now."

As Squirrelpaw bounded over to help, Brambleclaw spotted a sheltered place where the ground fell away a couple of tail-lengths beyond the clump of trees; grass grew thickly there, and a few bushes with low-growing branches.

"What about making a den over there?" he suggested, pointing with his tail.

"Good idea," meowed Dustpelt. He nosed Longtail again. "It's all right, Longtail; you can sleep as long as you want once we get you to a more sheltered place."

Longtail heaved himself to his paws; Squirrelpaw padded beside him with her tail curled around his neck to guide him. Brambleclaw let Goldenflower lean on his shoulder, while Ferncloud encouraged Birchkit to follow.

"This had better be the place we're looking for," Dustpelt remarked, looking around at the exhausted cats. "None of us have the strength to travel any farther."

Brambleclaw didn't reply. He knew Dustpelt was right—but he couldn't tell him for sure that this was the place StarClan had meant them to find. He watched the others slide between the branches and settle into the piles of dry leaves under the bushes. Catching a glimpse of Leafpaw padding past with a mouthful of moss for bedding, he recalled the medicine cat apprentice's unquestioning faith that their warrior ancestors had made the journey with them. He wished he could feel the same certainty. All along he had clung to the belief that their troubles would be over when they reached their new territory. Now, daunted by the strangeness of everything around him, he could see they were only just beginning.

Squirrelpaw's voice broke into his thoughts. "Dustpelt, do you want us to hunt for you?"

Her mentor flicked her ear with his tail. "No, we'll all hunt later. Look at you; you're asleep on your paws. Go with Brambleclaw and get some rest."

"Okay." Squirrelpaw's jaws split into an enormous yawn.

"What about under that gorse bush?" Brambleclaw led the way to the spot he had pointed out a few tail-lengths up the slope, and crawled under the lowest boughs.

Squirrelpaw followed him and curled into a tight ball with her tail over her nose. "Good night," she murmured indistinctly.

Brambleclaw scrabbled in the debris underneath the bush until he had made a comfortable nest. Curling up close to Squirrelpaw, he breathed in her warm, familiar scent. He was glad that they had not made a proper camp yet, where warriors and apprentices would have their separate dens. He would miss sleeping next to Squirrelpaw, he realized with the last flicker of conscious thought. Then sleep covered him like the lapping of a soft black wave.

Brambleclaw's dreams were dark and confused. He was searching for something in the middle of a thick forest, but he could not remember what he was looking for, and every path he took ended abruptly in tangles of briar or impassable walls of thorn. In desperation, he tried to force his way through, but a branch poked him painfully in the side.

"Wake up, Brambleclaw! You've been asleep forever—what do you think you are, a hedgehog?"

Brambleclaw's eyes flew open to see Squirrelpaw prodding him with her forepaw. Watery yellow daylight was seeping through the branches of the gorse bush.

"It's morning," Squirrelpaw went on. "Let's go and see if we can hunt. If you can stop hibernating, that is."

Blinking sleep from his eyes, Brambleclaw staggered to his paws, shook scraps of dead leaves from his pelt, and followed Squirrelpaw into the open.

The confusion of his dream slipped away when he remembered where he was. But it was replaced with a renewed feeling of anxiety as he looked at the landscape in daylight for the first time. He wondered if this vast, unfamiliar place would ever seem like home.

A cold breeze blew, ridging the surface of the lake and

rattling through the reeds that edged the shore. The shining gray water stretched in front of Brambleclaw for almost as far as he could see; above the hills that rose on one side, a glow in the sky showed where the sun would shortly rise. Back the way they had come, the land sloped up more gently to bare moorland. The Twoleg fence stretched across it, and in the growing light Brambleclaw could just make out a couple of Twoleg nests in the distance. He let out a faint sound of approval; such small nests couldn't hold many Twolegs, and being so far away they were unlikely to interfere with the Clans.

Farther around the lake, below the hills, was a smudge that looked like gray-green mist; Brambleclaw realized it was a mass of leafless branches, stretching along the shore and up to the crest of the ridge. His heart lifted to think that soon he could be underneath trees again, however strange they might be.

At the far end of the lake the gray smudge of trees darkened, and Brambleclaw guessed that they were pines, still green in the depths of leaf-bare. They covered the ground like a gently rippling pelt as the wind stirred them.

The glow on the horizon grew too bright to look at as the sun edged up; the last stars were fading, and the sky was a clear, pale blue.

"Time to hunt," Brambleclaw meowed to Squirrelpaw, who was standing beside him.

He looked around for Firestar or one of the senior warriors, to find out if any patrols were being sent out. His leader was emerging from a nearby gorse thicket with Leopardstar,

Blackstar, and Mudclaw. The leaders must have been holding a meeting, Brambleclaw guessed, and he felt a twinge of
apprehension to see Mudclaw in Tallstar's place, representing
WindClan.

"I wonder if Tallstar went to join StarClan during the
night," he muttered, his belly clenching with grief at the
thought.

Squirrelpaw shook her head. "I don't think so," she mewed.
"Or they would have brought his body out so his Clan could
pay their respects."

Brambleclaw hoped she was right. Before he could say
anything else, Firestar leaped onto the tree stump where the
leaders had addressed the Clans yesterday. Blackstar jumped
up beside him, and Mudclaw scrambled up on the other side.
There was barely room for all three cats to stand together on
the flat top of the stump, so Leopardstar did not try to join
them, but sat on a twisted root at the base.

"We'll need a new place to hold Gatherings," Squirrelpaw
remarked.

Firestar's yowl, calling the Clans together, interrupted her.
Stems of grass and fern parted, and the branches of bushes
shook as the cats emerged from their sleeping places. They all
looked thin and worn, easy prey for any hostile creatures the
territory might conceal, and they glanced around nervously,
as if they could feel hungry eyes burning into their pelts on
every side.

Brambleclaw bounded down the slope toward the stump,
with Squirrelpaw close behind. Halfway down he spotted

Tallstar's black-and-white shape curled in the grass where he had gone to sleep the night before. The WindClan medicine cat, Barkface, was sitting beside him, sniffing anxiously at his fur. Neither cat made any attempt to join the others gathered around the tree stump; it was obvious Tallstar wasn't well enough to take part in the meeting.

"Cats of all Clans," Firestar was announcing as Brambleclaw reached his Clanmates. "Today there are decisions to be made and tasks to be carried out—"

"Hunting patrols will go out right away," Mudclaw interrupted, shouldering Firestar aside. "WindClan will take the hills and RiverClan can fish in the lake. ThunderClan—"

His Clanmate Onewhisker sprang to his paws with a hiss of anger. "Mudclaw, what are you doing, giving orders like this?" he growled. "The last time I looked, Tallstar was still leader of WindClan."

"Not for much longer."

Brambleclaw blinked in surprise at the deputy's cold voice. He hoped Tallstar hadn't heard, and, craning his neck, he was relieved to see that the old cat was still asleep in his grassy nest with Barkface beside him.

"Some cat has to take charge," Mudclaw went on. "Or do you want the other Clans to divide the territory among themselves and leave WindClan out?"

"As if we would!" Squirrelpaw mewed indignantly.

Onewhisker glared at Mudclaw, his fur bristling and his eyes blazing with fury. "Show a bit of respect!" he spat. "Tallstar was the leader of our Clan when you were a kit mewling in the nursery."

"I'm not a kit now," Mudclaw retorted. "I'm the deputy. And Tallstar hasn't done much to lead us since we left the forest."

"That's enough." Firestar silenced the WindClan deputy with a wave of his tail. "Onewhisker, I know you're worried about Tallstar. Mudclaw is only doing his duty."

"He needn't act like he's leader already," Onewhisker growled. He sat down with a sharp glance from side to side, as if he were challenging any other cat to make a comment.

"Onewhisker has a fair point," Firestar went on to Mudclaw. "It's difficult for a deputy to stand in for their leader—difficult for the rest of the Clan as well as for the deputy."

Mudclaw, who had raised his head arrogantly when Firestar seemed to be backing him up, looked furious. His jaws parted, but before he could speak he was forestalled by Blackstar.

"If WindClan has a problem over their leadership, let them discuss it in private. We're wasting time."

Mudclaw let out an angry hiss and pointedly turned his back. Brambleclaw flexed his claws, ready to spring if the WindClan deputy caused more trouble. Mudclaw was one of the most aggressive cats in all four Clans, and he had never liked Firestar or ThunderClan. Brambleclaw could foresee trouble when he became WindClan's leader, especially now, when new Clan boundaries had to be established.

Firestar's voice interrupted his troubled thoughts. "I would like to start ThunderClan's life here by honoring a new war-rior. Squirrelpaw, where are you?"

"What? Me!" In her astonishment, Squirrelpaw squeaked like a kit. She sprang to her paws, her ears pricked and her tail standing straight up.

"Yes, you." Brambleclaw saw a gleam of amusement in Firestar's eyes as he beckoned to his daughter. "ThunderClan owes you more than I can say for making the journey to the sundrown-place, and helping lead the Clans to this new home. Dustpelt and I agree that if ever an apprentice deserved her warrior name, you do."

Brambleclaw stretched out and gently touched his muzzle against the tip of Squirrelpaw's ear. "Go on," he murmured. "Firestar is right. You deserve to become a warrior after everything you've done for the Clan."

She blinked at him, too shocked to speak, then turned and picked her way to the tree stump where Firestar was waiting. Before she reached it, her mother, Sandstorm, stepped forward. Squirrelpaw stopped in front of her. Sandstorm's eyes glowed with pride as she gave her daughter a few swift licks to smooth her fur. Brambleclaw watched Leafpaw come over as well to press her muzzle against her sister's side.

Squirrelpaw's mentor, Dustpelt, padded up to lead her the rest of the way to the stump, and he stood beside her as they waited for Firestar to speak.

Firestar leaped down and blinked encouragingly at Squirrelpaw before lifting his head to address the gathered cats. "This is the first time any cat has spoken these words in our new home," he began. "I, Firestar, leader of Thunder-Clan, call upon my warrior ancestors to look down on this apprentice. She has trained hard to understand the ways of your noble code, and I commend her to you as a warrior in her turn."

There was a burning intensity in his eyes, and Brambleclaw understood how much this moment meant to Firestar, not just for ThunderClan but for all four Clans that had journeyed here from their home far away. By calling upon StarClan to make a new warrior, they were claiming this unfamiliar place as their own. There had been many, many times on the journey when they had feared they had left their warrior ancestors behind, but Firestar addressed them now as confidently as if their starry spirits glowed overhead. Brambleclaw felt his fur prickle with guilt, wishing he could be so certain that StarClan had made the journey with them. Still, he told himself, they had reached somewhere that looked as if it would make a safe home for the Clans; perhaps his leader was right to feel confident. He shook his head, forcing his concerns away, and listened to the warrior ceremony.

"Squirrelpaw," the ThunderClan leader was saying, "do you promise to uphold the warrior code and to protect and defend your Clan, even at the cost of your life?"

Squirrelpaw's reply rang out clearly. "I do."

"Then by the powers of StarClan I give you your warrior name. Squirrelpaw, from this moment you will be known as Squirrelflight. StarClan honors your courage and your determination, and we welcome you as a full warrior of ThunderClan."

Firestar rested his muzzle on Squirrelflight's head, and

she gave his shoulder a respectful lick. Determination was an unusual virtue to mention in the warrior ceremony; in Squirrelflight, it sometimes showed as stubbornness, and had led her close to trouble more than once. Brambleclaw wondered if father and daughter were remembering all the times they had clashed, when Squirrelflight's fierce independence had brought her into conflict with her leader and the warrior code. But then, Brambleclaw reflected, there had been times on their journey when her determination and will to succeed had put fresh heart into all her companions. Pride flooded him as he remembered her tireless courage, her refusal to think they would ever fail to reach their journey's end.

When she stepped away from Firestar, Leafpaw bounded up to her, greeting her by her new name. "Squirrelflight! Squirrelflight!"

Her call was taken up by the cats around them. Squirrelflight looked around, her green eyes shining with pride. All four Clans seemed pleased that she had been given her warrior name—but then, all four Clans had had plenty of opportunity to see how much she deserved it. As Brambleclaw thrust his way to her side he saw Tawnypelt and Crowfeather heading toward her, too. Those who had made the journey to Midnight's cave would always have the most special bond with Squirrelflight.

"Congratulations," Tawnypelt meowed, while Crowfeather nodded and rested his tail-tip on her shoulder for a moment.

Brambleclaw pressed his muzzle to hers. "Well done, Squirrelflight," he murmured. "Mind you," he added teasingly, "you'll still have to pay attention to senior warriors."

Squirrelflight's eyes gleamed with wicked amusement. "You can't order me around now—I'm not an apprentice anymore!"

"I can't see that it will make much difference," Dustpelt put in, overhearing her. "You never did as you were told anyway."

Squirrelflight let out a *mrrow* of laughter and affectionately butted her former mentor on his shoulder. "I must have listened to something," she meowed. She blinked, and added, "Really, thanks for everything, Dustpelt."

The meows of welcome died down as Blackstar stepped forward and signaled with his tail for silence. "This is all very touching, but now we must find out about this new place so that we can start establishing our new territories. We're going to send a patrol with one cat from each Clan to explore the lakeshore and the land around it."

Brambleclaw's ears pricked, and he felt Squirrelflight tense beside him, her pelt just brushing his. He caught Tawnypelt's eye, and saw an answering gleam of anticipation.

"We decided to send three of the cats who made the first journey together," Firestar went on. "Brambleclaw from ThunderClan, Crowfeather from WindClan, and Tawnypelt from ShadowClan."

Excitement thrilled through Brambleclaw from ears to tail-tip. It felt right that the cats who had made the first journey should be chosen.

Blackstar curled his lip as Firestar named each cat, but didn't argue.

"Huh!" Tawnypelt muttered. "It's the first time he's ever let me represent ShadowClan."

Brambleclaw swept his tail soothingly over her shoulder. He knew that Blackstar was unlikely to forget that Tawnypelt had been born in ThunderClan, however hard she tried to prove she was a loyal warrior of ShadowClan.

"Mistyfoot will go for RiverClan," meowed Leopardstar, speaking for the first time, and reminding Brambleclaw painfully that neither of the RiverClan cats who had made the journey was still with their Clan. A hollow place yawned inside him as he thought of Feathertail and Stormfur.

"But what about *me*?" Squirrelflight protested. "I went on the journey too. Why can't I go on the patrol?"

"Because that would make two cats from ThunderClan," Blackstar replied crushingly. Brambleclaw knew the Shadow-Clan leader was wrong if he thought that would silence Squirrelflight.

"A patrol of four cats isn't enough to go into unknown territory," she objected.

Blackstar opened his mouth to disagree, but Firestar spoke first. "She could be right," he pointed out. "I think we should let her go. It could be her first warrior task. She can't sit vigil tonight like other new warriors, as we have no proper camp."

Blackstar glanced at Leopardstar, who twitched her tail, giving nothing away, and then at Mudclaw, who dipped his head. "WindClan has no objection," he meowed.

"Very well," Blackstar growled. "But don't think for one moment that will give ThunderClan any extra rights over the territory."

Brambleclaw exchanged an exasperated glance with Crow-feather. Trust Blackstar to think that other Clans were trying to steal an advantage before the new territories had been divided up!

"Of course not," Firestar replied evenly. "Squirrelflight, you may go with the patrol."

Squirrelflight's tail curled up in delight.

"Go all the way around the lake, and explore as much of the surrounding land as you can," Firestar instructed. "We need to know what kind of territory it is, and where the best hunting places will be. Think about the different sorts of hunting each Clan will require, because it might help with setting boundaries later on. It would be good to get an idea of how the territory could be split up, and where might be good places for camps. And keep a close watch for Twolegs, or anything else that might be dangerous."

"Is that all?" Crowfeather muttered.

"I reckon you'll need two days to travel all the way around the lake," Firestar went on. He lifted his head and narrowed his eyes as he peered across the water, trying to judge the distance. "Try not to spend too much time exploring. We're exposed to danger while we stay here, so we need to get all the Clans settled as soon as we can."

"We'll do our best, Firestar," a new voice called out. Brambleclaw glanced over his shoulder to see Mistyfoot, the RiverClan deputy, padding over to join them.

"Hi, there," he mewed, moving up to make room for her.

Mistyfoot looked wary about joining the close band of cats that had made the first journey.

"Good luck," called Leopardstar, and Firestar added, "May StarClan go with you all."

By now the sun had risen well above the hills. His paws itching to be off, Brambleclaw dipped his head toward Firestar and the other leaders, and raised his tail to signal the others to follow him. Out of the corner of his eye he saw Tawnypelt wince, and he heard a hissing intake of breath from Crow-feather. His fur prickled with embarrassment as he realized that Mistyfoot ought to be in charge of the patrol, since she was the deputy of her Clan. He stopped and took a pace back; Mistyfoot gave him a long, cool look, then nodded briefly to him as she took the lead.

"Mouse-brain!" Squirrelflight whispered.

They headed for the edge of the lake, with Blackstar's voice drifting behind them on the breeze as he began to arrange the hunting patrols.

"Squirrelflight! Wait!" Brambleclaw looked back to see Leafpaw bounding after her sister. "Be careful, won't you?" she begged.

Squirrelflight touched noses with the young medicine cat. "Don't worry about us," she meowed. "We can look after ourselves."

"But you're as tired as the rest of us from the journey," Leafpaw warned. "Hunt as soon as you can, and don't stray too far from the lake or you might get lost."

Squirrelflight brushed her tail across Leafpaw's mouth to

stop her. "We'll be fine," she insisted. She lifted her head and pointed with her nose to the gleaming stretch of water below them. "Look, you can see exactly where we're going. We'll be back before you know it." She paused for a moment, then added quietly, "Have you had a sign from StarClan? Is that why you're so worried?"

Leafpaw shook her head. "No, nothing like that, I promise. It's just hard to let you go again. It feels too much like the first time you left, when you went to the sun-drown-place."

Brambleclaw went over and rested his muzzle against Leafpaw's shoulder to comfort her. "And we came safely home, didn't we? Trust me, Leafpaw, I'll look after her."

Squirrelflight jerked away in mock indignation. "I don't need looking after! It's more likely to be me watching out for your battered old fur!"

Leafpaw gave a purr of amusement, letting them lighten the mood. "Well, just take care, all of you. And if you have a chance to look out for any herbs, that would be great. Our medicine supplies will need refilling very soon."

Squirrelflight licked her ear. "Sure. I'll keep my eyes open—when I'm not looking for foxes, badgers, Twolegs, Thunderpaths. . . ."

"Are we going or not?" growled Crowfeather. "We don't have much daylight, and we need to get at least halfway around the lake before nightfall."

Leafpaw ignored him. "StarClan go with you," she murmured to Squirrelflight, before whisking around and bounding back up the slope.

Brambleclaw tasted the air and listened to the lapping of waves on the shore. The gray water was flooded with color as the sun rose higher over the hills. It stretched ahead so far that the trees on the distant shore were nothing more than a greenish blur, and curved hungrily around the marshy land in front of them. Something about the stillness of the water, the silence that hung over it like mist, told Brambleclaw that it was much, much deeper than the river in the forest, even when it flooded. He gave Mistyfoot a swift sidelong glance. She looked daunted too, though like all RiverClan cats she was an excellent swimmer.

As if aware that his eyes were on her, the RiverClan deputy gave herself a shake. "Right," she meowed, gazing around at the patrol. "This is it. Let's see where StarClan has brought us."

THE TIME HAS COME
FOR DOGS TO RULE THE WILD

SURVIVORS

BOOK ONE:
THE EMPTY CITY

Lucky is a golden-haired mutt with a nose for survival. Other dogs have Packs, but Lucky stands on his own . . . until the Big Growl strikes. Suddenly the ground splits wide open. The longpaws disappear. And enemies threaten Lucky at every turn. For the first time in his life, Lucky needs to rely on other dogs to survive. But can he ever be a true Pack dog?

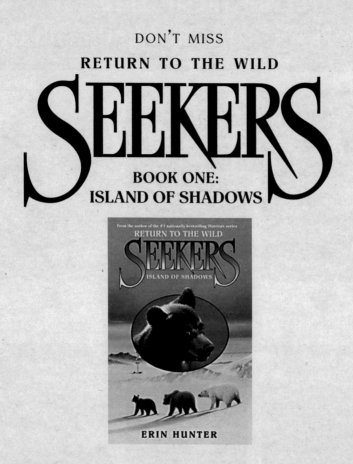

WARRIORS: THE NEW PROPHECY

1. THE NEW PROPHECY — WARRIORS — MIDNIGHT — ERIN HUNTER — #1 *NEW YORK TIMES* BESTSELLING AUTHOR
2. THE NEW PROPHECY — WARRIORS — MOONRISE — ERIN HUNTER — #1 *NEW YORK TIMES* BESTSELLING AUTHOR
3. THE NEW PROPHECY — WARRIORS — DAWN — ERIN HUNTER — #1 *NEW YORK TIMES* BESTSELLING AUTHOR
4. THE NEW PROPHECY — WARRIORS — STARLIGHT — ERIN HUNTER — #1 *NEW YORK TIMES* BESTSELLING AUTHOR
5. THE NEW PROPHECY — WARRIORS — TWILIGHT — ERIN HUNTER — #1 *NEW YORK TIMES* BESTSELLING AUTHOR
6. THE NEW PROPHECY — WARRIORS — SUNSET — ERIN HUNTER — #1 *NEW YORK TIMES* BESTSELLING AUTHOR

In the second series, follow the next generation of heroic cats as they set off on a quest to save the Clans from destruction.

HARPER
An Imprint of HarperCollinsPublishers

www.warriorcats.com

WARRIORS: POWER OF THREE

In the third series, Firestar's grandchildren begin their training as warrior cats. Prophecy foretells that they will hold more power than any cats before them.

HARPER
An Imprint of HarperCollinsPublishers

www.warriorcats.com

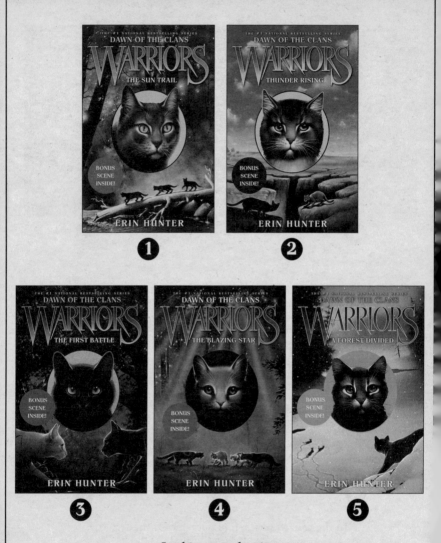

WARRIORS: DAWN OF THE CLANS

In this prequel series,
discover how the warrior Clans came to be.

HARPER
An Imprint of HarperCollinsPublishers

www.warriorcats.com

WARRIORS: SUPER EDITIONS

These extra-long, stand-alone adventures will take you deep inside each of the Clans with thrilling adventures featuring the most legendary warrior cats.

WARRIORS: BONUS STORIES

Discover the untold stories of the warrior cats and Clans when you download the separate ebook novellas—or read them in two paperback bind-ups!

WARRIORS: FIELD GUIDES

Delve deeper into the Clans with these Warriors field guides.

ALSO BY ERIN HUNTER:
SEEKERS

SEEKERS: THE ORIGINAL SERIES

Three young bears . . . one destiny.
Discover the fate that awaits them on their adventure.

SEEKERS: RETURN TO THE WILD

The stakes are higher than ever as the bears search for a way home.

SEEKERS: MANGA

The bears come to life in manga!

HARPER
An Imprint of HarperCollinsPublishers

www.seekerbears.com